CORNELL WOOLRICH

REAR WINDOW

Cornell Woolrich was born in 1903. He began writing fiction while at Columbia University in the 1920s, and went on in the '30s and '40s to become, along with Raymond Chandler and James M. Cain, one of the creators of the *noir* genre, producing such classics as *Rear Window* (the basis for the 1954 Alfred Hitchcock film starring James Stewart and Grace Kelly), *The Bride Wore Black*, *Phantom Lady*, *I Married a Dead Man*, and the so-called "Black Series" of suspense novels. Under the pseudonyms William Irish and George Hopley, Woolrich made the elements of tension, tragedy, and terror the trademarks of his timeless thrillers. More of his work has been adapted to film, TV, and radio than any mystery author since Edgar Allan Poe; among these adaptations are *The Night Has a Thousand Eyes*, *Obsession*, *Deadline at Dawn*, *The Leopard Man*, *Nightmare*, and *The Black Angel*. Woolrich died an alcoholic recluse in 1968.

"No one has ever surpassed Cornell Woolrich for sheer suspense, or equaled him for exciting entertainment."

—*Robert Bloch*

"Woolrich can distill more terror, more excitement, more downright nail-biting suspense out of even the most commonplace happenings than nearly all his competitors."

—*Ellery Queen*

AVAILABLE NOW

ALFRED HITCHCOCK MYSTERIES
The Vertigo Murders by J. Madison Davis

ALO NUDGER MYSTERIES
by John Lutz
Nightlines • *The Right to Sing the Blues*
Ride the Lightning

AMOS WALKER MYSTERIES
by Loren D. Estleman
Motor City Blue • *Angel Eyes*
The Midnight Man • *The Glass Highway*
Sugartown • *Every Brilliant Eye*

CHARLOTTE MacLEOD CLASSIC MYSTERIES
The Resurrection Man

CORNELL WOOLRICH CLASSIC MYSTERIES
The Bride Wore Black • *Phantom Lady*

MASAO MASUTO MYSTERIES
by Howard Fast
Masuto Investigates
Masuto: The Hollywood Murders

MOSES WINE MYSTERIES
by Roger L. Simon
The Big Fix • *Wild Turkey*
Peking Duck • *California Roll*
The Straight Man • *The Lost Coast*

OTTO PENZLER HOLLYWOOD MYSTERIES
Laura by Vera Caspary
The Lady Vanishes by Ethel Lina White

PHILIP MARLOWE MYSTERIES
Raymond Chandler's Philip Marlowe
Anthology; Byron Preiss, Editor

SHERLOCK HOLMES MYSTERIES
Revenge of the Hound
by Michael Hardwick
Sherlock Holmes vs. Dracula
by Loren D. Estleman

TOBY PETERS MYSTERIES
by Stuart M. Kaminsky
Murder on the Yellow Brick Road
He Done Her Wrong • *Never Cross a Vampire*
The Devil Met a Lady

REAR WINDOW

Cornell Woolrich

Selected by Maxim Jakubowski

Introduction by Richard Rayner

books

new york

www.ibooksinc.com

An Original Publication of ibooks, inc.

An ibooks, inc. Book

Distributed by Simon & Schuster, Inc.
1230 Avenue of the Americas, New York, NY 10020

ibooks, inc.
24 West 25th Street
New York, NY 10010

The ibooks World Wide Web Site Address is:
http://www.ibooksinc.com

ISBN 0-7434-2371-2
First ibooks, inc. printing September 2001
10 9 8 7 6 5 4 3 2 1

Cover illustration and design by Steranko

Printed in the U.S.A.

CONTENTS

Introduction

Richard Rayner

The life of Cornell George Hopley-Woolrich is a pulp legend, but one might as well start with the facts. He was born on December 4 1903, his parents separated when he was young, and he spent much of his childhood in South America with his father. The young Woolrich was in Mexico in 1913, and witnessed the activities of the guerrilla Pancho Villa and his band. Various skirmishes took place in the town where Woolrich lived, and afterwards he would collect the spent cartridges which littered the streets. Aged eight, he saw a French repertory company perform Puccini's *Madame Butterfly* in Mexico City and was heartbroken when he was told that, like Cio-Cio San, he would one day die. He later described the experience in his autobiography: "I had that trapped feeling, like some sort of poor insect you've put inside a downturned glass, and it tries to climb up the glass, and it can't, and it can't, and it can't." The sentence is typical of Woolrich's developed style. No-one ever accused him of over-subtlety of effect, but he could make an emotion (particularly fear) come off the page with the intensity of the big theme emerging in opera.

Woolrich was sent back to New York, to live with his mother. Claire Attalie Woolrich was rich and domineering, and he never escaped her influence. She did, however, let him out on a leash that went as far as Columbia University. It was here that he began to write, when his foot became infected after the heel was rubbed raw by a loose-fitting gym shoe, and he was confined to bed for six weeks. The result was a novel, *Cover Charge*, a Jazz-Age chronicle which was published in 1926 and began like this: "Luminaires lit up the walls and from an orange dish a pencil-line of azure hung breathlessly above an expiring cigarette." His prose, happily, was to become more economical. Consider the virtuoso opening of *Rear Window*: "I didn't know their names. I'd never heard their voices. I didn't even know them by sight, strictly speaking, for their faces were too small to fill in with identifiable features at that distance. Yet I could have constructed a timetable of their comings and goings, their daily habits and activities. They were the rear-window dwellers . . ."

Rear Window was some years in the future, however, when Woolrich's second book, *Children of the Ritz*, appeared in 1927. This was another trip through Manhattan with the Bright Young Things, titled with a nod in the direction of Scott Fitzgerald, Woolrich's favourite author of the period. *Children of the Ritz* won a $10,000 prize from *College Humor* magazine, and prompted First National Pictures to invite Woolrich to Hollywood. So Woolrich went west, put in his years as a scriptwriter (no credits) and in 1929 met and married a producer's daughter. It would be charitable to describe the marriage as a disaster. First, it was never consummated. Second, it caused Woolrich to discover his homosexuality (at night he would don the sailor's uniform he kept beneath the marital bed and cruise Los Angeles looking for partners) and helped him feel guilty about the fact. Third, it sent him scuttling back to New York, and mother.

For the rest of his life, nearly forty years, he lived in hotel rooms, overcome by melancholy and paranoia, thinking *where did I go wrong?*, drinking and working, sometimes apart from his mother, but usually with her right there at his elbow, saying "Pull yourself together, George."

In the early 1930s Woolrich lived in cheap dives, trying unsuccessfully to establish an independent life. He witnessed the Depression at first hand, and his fictional concerns began to change. In August 1934 he published a story titled "Death Sits in the Dentist's Chair" in *Detective Fiction Weekly*. It was second-rate, but it indicated that Cornell Woolrich had discovered suspense and that, in turn, the crime genre had acquired a writer who would become one of its finest exponents, a writer who could not only layer pain, anxiety and horror over even the most clichéd plot but was also obsessed by the notion of ordinary people struggling under the triple burden of sex, fate and money, and by the frightening impact of the everyday gone wrong. Woolrich was set to become, in the words of critic Francis M. Nevins, "the Poe of the twentieth century".

Over the next six years Woolrich concentrated on writing suspense stories, and he became more and more skilled at his craft. There were hundreds, published in magazines such as *Story*, *Dime Mystery*, *Detective Fiction Weekly*, *Argosy* and the legendary *Black Mask*, as well as low-grade pulpsters such as *Thrilling Mystery*. Some are collected here, and they are among the best ever written in the horror and suspense genres.

In the early 1940s Woolrich's prolific production of short stories began to fall off, and he concentrated more and more on the novel, publishing his classic "Black" series, and a clutch of other novels besides. His publishers Simon & Schuster pleaded that he was writing too fast, and Woolrich invented the pseudonyms George Hopley and William Irish so that he could by-pass his obligation to Simon & Schuster and get all his work into print.

It was Woolrich's best time. His writing found a large audience, gained a good response from the critics (the reviews of *Rendezvous in*

Black and the splendidly titled *I Married a Dead Man*, for instance, were appreciative to the point of ecstasy), and earned a lot of money. There were frequent sales to Hollywood. In 1948 he won the prestigious US Mystery Writers' Edgar Award. Then: mother became ill.

The illness was protracted and, with Woolrich spending more and more time looking after her, his output slowed. Frederic Dannay and Manfred B. Lee, the partners who wrote as Ellery Queen, championed his cause throughout the 1950s, reprinting many old stories as well as some slightly revised ones in *Ellery Queen's Mystery Magazine*. But by the time his mother died in 1957 Woolrich had little desire to live, let alone write. Yet he survived for another ten years. Bitter, frustrated, diabetic and alcoholic, Woolrich at this time was as lonely and despairing as any character in his fiction. The novelist and screenwriter Steve Fisher used Woolrich as a model for a character in his story "I Wake Up Screaming". The description goes like this: "He had red hair and thin, white skin and red eyebrows and blue eyes. He looked sick. He looked like a corpse." Woolrich developed gangrene, didn't go to a doctor until too late, and a leg had to be amputated. A stroke finally killed him on September 25 1968.

Woolrich's funeral was unattended, and his *New York Times* obituary was an inaccurate mess. His estate was worth $1m and the money was endowed to Columbia to set up a creative writing course. The course is named, inevitably, not after Woolrich himself but after his mother. So ended a life which had been as bizarre, as filled with success and failure and humiliation, as tortured as anything Hollywood has dreamed up before or since. Citizen Kane himself, having been a newspaperman, would have recognised Woolrich's life for the extraordinary drama it was.

An autobiography was left behind, unfinished, and notebooks which contained possible story titles. One such as "First You Dream, Then You Die." Woolrich didn't even dream. He had *nightmares*, then he died. Those nightmares are his legacy.

The Woolrich nightmare features characters who are solitary and fearful. An innocent man accused of murder fights against time to explain the million-to-one chance (vanished wife, vanished witness, vanished alibi) which seems to condemn him. A woman seizes an opportunity for happiness, only to see the situation evolve into something which might have been invented by Kafka on a bad day. The Woolrich nightmare takes place in bars and hotel rooms and lonely city streets. Woolrich was a chronicler and poet of the terror of urban life: "It's the city itself. You think of it as just a place on a map, don't you? I think of it as a personal enemy, and I know I'm right." ("Deadline at Dawn".)

Woolrich's fictional world is more discordant and threatening, and therefore, perhaps, more contemporary than that of either Hammett or

Chandler. It is also more imaginative. Chandler himself admitted that Woolrich was "the best ideas man". The truth is that Woolrich's plots are often very bizarre indeed. A leopard terrorises a town. After a murder at a marathon dance contest the investigating detective forces a suspect to dance with the corpse until he confesses. A woman becomes a time bomb. A home-loving American man marries a Hindu snake priestess. And so on. Woolrich uses these devices for just one purpose: to build suspense.

Suspense is not mystery. Mystery does not engage the reader with the emotion of a threatened protagonist. Nor is it surprise. Surprise is the narrative coup which reveals the identity of the murderer in Ira Levin's "A Kiss Before Dying", or the brutally unexpected murder of Janet Leigh in "Psycho". Suspense is telling the reader that a major character is about to die *forty pages before it happens*, as Woolrich does in "Speak to Me of Death". The story was a trial run for *Night has a Thousand Eyes*, one of his best novels, and it features one of Woolrich's weirdest plots: a recluse predicts the death of a millionaire at the jaws of a lion. That Woolrich has you avidly following this stuff is testament to his skill. The story is superb exercise in control, and also neatly debunks the tidy rationalism of most mysteries.

The stories in this collection are varied in both plot and tone, ranging from the terror of "The Light in the Window" to the more light-hearted "The Book That Squealed". "I Won't Take a Minute" and "You'll Never See Me Again" are brilliant variations on the-lady-vanishes storyline, while one of the best is "For the Rest of Her Life", a late story in which Woolrich returned to a favourite theme: love turned sour.

The stories differ, but suspense is the link. Woolrich understood better than any other writer in the crime genre that the creation of suspense is a playful, even sadistic process. The point is not to have a bomb explode under a bed, but to tell everyone that there is a bomb and pose some questions. Will it go off? When? And will it hurt the small child asleep in the next room?

Woolrich was expert in this kind of manipulation, but his writing was never cold-blooded. When he plunged a character into situations where everything was off-key, unexpected, dangerous, it was not simply to create atmosphere and tension. For Woolrich, paranoia was not just a way of teasing the audience, but a way of perceiving the world. He found life to be terrible and terrifying, and he believed he could do nothing about it.

That paranoia is reflected always in the relationships he allowed his male and female characters. In Woolrich sex is at best an ambivalent experience. More often it involves death, or fear, or (at least) humiliation. Small wonder that when Alfred Hitchcock read "Rear Window" he recognised the current of male sexual terror which runs through

Woolrich's work, and gave the disabled voyeuristic photographer a fear of marriage to contend with as well as a fear of being hunted by the man who he believes to have committed a murder. For Hitchcock, like Woolrich, was another superb craftsman who made a career by fashioning entertainment from a deep-rooted sexual anxiety.

Perhaps that's why the stories of Cornell Woolrich, like the films of Hitchcock, have aged well. They touch a contemporary nerve. They are also written in a style that is easy and colloquial, with characters who are always believable and plots that hurtle forward like a runaway lorry. And *then* there's the suspense. Pulp writer Frank Gruber recalls that Woolrich once tried to write an entire novella in a single evening. This was in the 1930s when *Black Mask* paid Woolrich one and a half cents a word. He always delivered more than anyone bargained for.

Rear Window

I didn't know their names. I'd never heard their voices. I didn't even know them by sight, strictly speaking, for their faces were too small to fill in with identifiable features at that distance. Yet I could have constructed a timetable of their comings and goings, their daily habits and activities. They were the rear-window dwellers around me.

Sure, I suppose it *was* a little bit like prying, could even have been mistaken for the fevered concentration of a Peeping Tom. That wasn't my fault, that wasn't the idea. The idea was, my movements were strictly limited just around this time. I could get from the window to the bed, and from the bed to the window, and that was all. The bay window was about the best feature my rear bedroom had in the warm weather. It was unscreened, so I had to sit with the light out or I would have had every insect in the vicinity in on me. I couldn't sleep, because I was used to getting plenty of exercise. I'd never acquired the habit of reading books to ward off boredom, so I hadn't that to turn to. Well, what should I do, sit there with my eyes tightly shuttered?

Just to pick a few at random: Straight over, and the windows square, there was a young jitter-couple, kids in their teens, only just married. It would have killed them to stay home one night. They were always in such a hurry to go, wherever it was they went, they never remembered to turn out the lights. I don't think it missed once in all the time I was watching. But they never forgot altogether, either. I was to learn to call this delayed action, as you will see. He'd always come skittering madly back in about five minutes, probably from all the way down in the street, and rush around killing the switches. Then fall over something in the dark on his way out. They gave me an inward chuckle, those two.

The next house down, the windows already narrowed a little with perspective. There was a certain light in that one that always went out each night too. Something about it, it used to make me a little sad. There was a woman living there with her child, a young widow I suppose. I'd see her put the child to bed, and then bend over and kiss her in a wistful sort of way. She'd shade the light off her and sit there painting her eyes and mouth. Then she'd go out. She'd never come back till the night was nearly spent. Once I was still up, and I looked out and she was sitting there motionless with her head buried in her arms. Something about it, it used to make me a little sad.

The third one down no longer offered any insight, the windows were just slits like in a medieval battlement, due to foreshortening. That brings us around to the one on the end. In that one, frontal vision came back full-depth again, since it stood at right angles to the rest, my own included, sealing up the inner hollows all these houses backed on. I could see into it, from the rounded projection of my bay window, as freely as into a doll house with its rear wall sliced away. And scaled down to about the same size.

It was a flat building. Unlike the rest it had been constructed originally as such, not just cut into furnished rooms. It topped them by two stories and had rear fire escapes, to show for this distinction. But it was old, evidently hadn't shown a profit. It was in the process of being modernized. Instead of clearing the entire building while the work was going on, they were doing it a flat at a time, in order to lose as little rental income as possible. Of the six rearward flats it offered to view, the topmost one had already been completed, but not yet rented. They were working on the fifth-floor one now, disturbing the peace of everyone all up and down the "inside" of the block with their hammering and sawing.

I felt sorry for the couple in the flat below. I used to wonder how they stood it with that bedlam going on above their heads. To make it worse the wife was in chronic poor health too; I could tell that even at a distance by the listless way she moved about over there, and remained in her bathrobe without dressing. Sometimes I'd see her sitting by the window, holding her head. I used to wonder why he didn't have a doctor in to look her over, but maybe they couldn't afford it. He seemed to be out of work. Often their bedroom light was on late at night behind the drawn shade, as though she were unwell and he was sitting up with her. And one night in particular he must have had to sit up with her all night, it remained on until nearly daybreak. Not that I sat watching all that time. But the light was still burning at three in the morning, when I finally transferred from chair to bed to see if I could get a little sleep myself. And when I failed to, and hopscotched back again around dawn, it was still peering wanly out behind the tan shade.

Moment later, with the first brightening of day, it suddenly dimmed around the edges of the shade, and then shortly afterward, not that one, but a shade in one of the other rooms – for all of them alike had been down – went up, and I saw him standing there looking out.

He was holding a cigarette in his hand. I couldn't see it, but I could tell it was that by the quick, nervous little jerks with which he kept putting his hand to his mouth, and the haze I saw rising around his head. Worried about her, I guess. I didn't blame him for that. Any husband would have been. She must have only just dropped off to sleep, after night-long suffering. And then in another hour or so, at the most, that sawing of wood and clattering of buckets was going to start in over them again. Well, it wasn't any of my business, I said to myself, but he really ought to get her out of there. If I had an ill wife on my hands. . . .

He was leaning slightly out, maybe an inch past the window frame, carefully scanning the back faces of all the houses abutting on the hollow square that lay before him. You can tell, even at a distance, when a person is looking fixedly. There's something about the way the head is held. And yet his scrutiny wasn't held fixedly to any one point, it was a slow, sweeping one, moving along the houses on the opposite side from me first. When it got to the end of them, I knew it would cross over to my side and come back along there. Before it did, I withdrew several yards inside my room, to let it go safely by. I didn't want him to think I was sitting there prying into his affairs. There was still enough blue nightshade in my room to keep my slight withdrawal from catching his eye.

When I returned to my original position a moment or two later, he was gone. He had raised two more of the shades. The bedroom one was still down. I wondered vaguely why he had given that peculiar, comprehensive, semicircular stare at all the rear windows around him. There wasn't anyone at any of them, at such an hour. It wasn't important, of course. It was just a little oddity, it failed to blend in with his being worried or disturbed about his wife. When you're worried or disturbed, that's an internal preoccupation, you stare vacantly at nothing at all. When you stare around you in a great sweeping arc at windows, that betrays external preoccupation, outward interest. One doesn't quite jibe with the other. To call such a discrepancy trifling is to add to its importance. Only someone like me, stewing in a vacuum of total idleness, would have noticed at all.

The flat remained lifeless after that, as far as he could be judged by its windows. He must have either gone out or gone to bed himself. Three of the shades remained at normal height, the one masking the bedroom remained down. Sam, my day houseman, came in not long after with my eggs and morning paper, and I had that to kill time with for awhile. I stopped thinking about other people's windows and staring at them.

The sun slanted down on one side of the hollow oblong all morning long, then it shifted over to the other side for the afternoon. Then it started to slip off both alike and it was evening again – another day gone.

The lights started to come on around the quadrangle. Here and there a wall played back, like a sounding board, a snatch of radio program that was coming in too loud. If you listened carefully you could hear an occasional clink of dishes mixed in, faint, far off. The chain of little habits that were their lives unreeled themselves. They were all bound in them tighter than the tightest straitjacket any jailer ever devised, though they all thought themselves free. The jitterbugs made their nightly dash for great open spaces, forgot their lights, he came careening back, thumbed them out, and their place was dark, until the early morning hours. The woman put her child to bed, leaned mournfully over its cot, then sat down with heavy despair to redden her mouth.

In the fourth-floor flat at right angles to the long interior "street" the three shades had remained up, and the fourth shade had remained at full length, all day long. I hadn't been conscious of that because I hadn't particularly been looking at it, or thinking of it, until now. My eyes may have rested on those windows at times, during the day, but my thoughts had been elsewhere. It was only when a light suddenly went up in the end room behind one of the raised shades, which was their kitchen, that I realized that the shades had been untouched like that all day. That also brought something else to my mind that hadn't been in it until now: I hadn't seen the woman all day. I hadn't seen any sign of life within those windows until now.

He'd come in from outside. The entrance was at the opposite side of their kitchen, away from the window. He'd left his hat on, so I knew he'd just come in from the outside.

He didn't remove his hat. As though there was no one there to remove it for any more. Instead, he pushed it farther to the back of his head by pronging a hand to the roots of his hair. That gesture didn't denote removal of perspiration, I knew. To do that a person makes a sidewise sweep – this was up over his forehead. It indicated some sort of harassment of uncertainty. Besides, if he'd been suffering from excess warmth, the first thing he would have done would be to take off his hat altogether.

She didn't come out to greet him. The first link, of the so-strong chain of habit, of custom, that binds us all, had snapped wide open.

She must be so ill she had remained in bed, in the room behind the lowered shade, all day. I watched. He remained where he was, two rooms away from there. Expectancy became surprise, surprise incomprehension. Funny, I thought, that he doesn't go in to her. Or at least go as far as the doorway, look in to see how she is.

Maybe she was asleep, and he didn't want to disturb her. Then immediately; but how can he know for sure that she's asleep, without at least looking in at her? He just came in himself.

He came forward and stood there by the window, as he had at dawn. Sam had carried out my tray quite some time before, and my lights were out. I held my ground, I knew he couldn't see me within the darkness of the bay window. He stood there motionless for several minutes. And now his attitude was the proper one for inner preoccupation. He stood there looking downward at nothing, lost in thought.

He's worried about her, I said to myself, as any man would be. It's the most natural thing in the world. Funny, though, he should leave her in the dark like that, without going near her. If he's worried, then why didn't he at least look in on her on returning? Here was another of those trivial discrepancies, between inward motivation and outward incidication. And just as I was thinking that, the original one, that I had noted at daybreak, repeated itself. His head went up with renewed alertness, and I could see it start to give that slow circular sweep of interrogation around the panorama of rearward windows again. True, the light was behind him this time, but there was enough of it falling on him to show me the microscopic but continuous shift of direction his head made in the process. I remained carefully immobile until the distance glance had passed me safely by. Motion attracts.

Why is he so interested in other people's windows. I wondered detachedly. And of course an effective brake to dwelling on that thought too lingeringly clamped down almost at once: Look who's talking. What about you yourself?

An important difference escaped me. I wasn't worried about anything. He, presumably was.

Down came the shades again. The lights stayed on behind their beige opaqueness. But behind the one that had remained down all along, the room remained dark.

Time went by. Hard to say how much – a quarter of an hour, twenty minutes. A cricket chirped in one of the back yards. Sam came in to see if I wanted anything before he went home for the night. I told him no, I didn't – it was all right, run along. He stood there for a minute, head down. Then I saw him shake it slightly, as if at something he didn't like. "What's the matter?" I asked.

"You know what that means? My old mammy told it to me, and she never told me a lie in her life. I never once seen it to miss, either."

"What, the cricket?"

"Any time you hear one of them things, that's a sign of death – someplace close around."

I swept the back of my hand at him. "Well, it isn't in here, so don't let it worry you."

He went out, muttering stubbornly. "It's somewhere close by, though. Somewhere not very far off. Got to be."

The door closed after him, and I stayed there alone in the dark.

It was a stifling night, much closer than the one before. I could hardly get a breath of air even by the window at which I sat. I wondered how he – that unknown over there – could stand it behind those drawn shades.

Then suddenly, just as idle speculation about this whole matter was about to alight on some fixed point in my mind, crystallize into something like suspicion, up came the shades again, and off it flitted, as formless as ever and without having had a chance to come to rest on anything.

He was in the middle windows, the living room. He'd taken off his coat and shirt, was bare-armed in his undershirt. He hadn't been able to stand it himself. I guess – the sultriness.

I couldn't make out what he was doing at first. He seemed to be busy in a perpendicular, up-and-down way rather than lengthwise. He remained in one place, but he kept dipping down out of sight and then straightening up into view again, at irregular intervals. It was almost like some sort of calisthenic exercise, except that the dips and rises weren't evenly timed enough for that. Sometimes he'd stay down a long time, sometimes he'd bob right up again, sometimes he'd go down two or three times in rapid succession. There was some sort of widespread black V railing him off from the window. Whatever it was, there was just a sliver of it showing above the upward inclination to which the window sill defected my line of vision. All it did was strike off the bottom of his undershirt, to the extent of a sixteenth of an inch maybe. But I hadn't seen it there at other times, and I couldn't tell what it was.

Suddenly he left it for the first time since the shades had gone up, came out around it to the outside, stooped down into another part of the room, and straightened again with an armful of what looked like varicolored pennants at the distance at which I was. He went back behind the V and allowed them to fall across the top of it for a moment, and stay that way. He made one of his dips down out of sight and stayed that way a good while.

The "pennants" slung across the V kept changing color right in front of my eyes. I have very good sight. One moment they were white, the next red, the next blue.

Then I got it. They were a woman's dresses, and he was pulling them down to him one by one, taking the topmost one each time. Suddenly they were all gone, the V was black and bare again and his torso had reappeared. I knew what it was now, and what he was doing. The dresses had told me. He confirmed it for me. He spread his arms to the ends of the V, I could see him heave and hitch, as if exerting pressure, and suddenly the V had folded up, become a cubed wedge. Then he made rolling motions with his whole upper body, and the wedge disappeared off to one side.

He'd been packing a trunk, packing his wife's things into a large upright trunk.

He reappeared at the kitchen window presently, stood still for a moment. I saw him draw his arms across his forehead, not once but several times, and then whip the end of it off into space. Sure, it was hot work for such a night. Then he reached up along the wall and took something down. Since it was the kitchen he was in, my imagination had to supply a cabinet and a bottle.

I could see the two or three quick passes his hand made to his mouth after that. I said to myself tolerantly: That's what nine men out of ten would do after packing a trunk – take a good stiff drink. And if the tenth didn't, it would only be because he didn't have any liquor at hand.

Then he came closer to the window again, and standing edgewise to the side of it, so that only a thin paring of his head and shoulder showed, peered watchfully out into the dark quadrilateral, along the line of windows, most of them unlighted by now, once more. He always started on the left-hand side, the side opposite mine, and made his circuit of inspection from there on around.

That was the second time in one evening I'd seen him do that. And once at daybreak, made three times altogether. I smiled mentally. You'd almost think he felt guilty about something. It was probably nothing, just an odd little habit, a quirk, that he didn't know he had himself. I had them myself, everyone does.

He withdrew into the room again, and it blacked out. His figure passed into the one that was still lighted next to it, the living room. That blacked next. It didn't surprise me that the third room, the bedroom with the drawn shade, didn't light up on his entering there. He wouldn't want to disturb her, of course – particularly if she was going away tomorrow for her health, as his packing of her trunk showed. She needed all the rest she could get, before making the trip. Simple enough for him to slip into bed in the dark.

It did surprise me, though, when a match-flare winked some time later, to have it still come from the darkened living room. He must be lying down in there, trying to sleep on the sofa or something for the night. He hadn't gone near the bedroom at all, was staying out of it altogether. That puzzled me, frankly. That was carrying solicitude almost too far.

Ten minutes or so later, there was another match-wink, still from that same living room. He couldn't sleep.

The night brooded down on both of us alike, the curiosity-monger in the bay window, the chain-smoker in the fourth-floor flat, without giving any answer. The only sound was that interminable cricket.

I was back at the window again with the first sun of morning. Not because of him. My mattress was like a bed of hot coals. Sam found me there when he came in to get things ready for me. "You're going to be a wreck, Mr Jeff," was all he said.

First, for awhile, there was no sign of life over there. Then suddenly I saw his head bob up from somewhere down out of sight in the living room, so I knew I'd been right, he'd spent the night on a sofa or easy chair in there. Now, of course, he'd look in at her, to see how she was, find out if she felt any better. That was only common ordinary humanity. He hadn't been near her, so far as I could make out, since two nights before.

He didn't. He dressed, and he went in the opposite direction, into the kitchen, and wolfed something in there, standing up and using both hands. Then he suddenly turned and moved off side, in the direction in which I knew the flat-entrance to be, as if he had just heard some summons, like the doorbell.

Sure enough, in a moment he came back, and there were two men with him in leather aprons. Expressmen. I saw him standing by while they laboriously maneuvered that cubed black wedge out between them, in the direction they'd just come from. He did more than just stand by. He practically hovered over them, kept shifting from side to side, he was so anxious to see that it was done right.

Then he came back alone, and I saw him swipe his arm across his head, as though it was he, not they, who was all heated up from the effort.

So he was forwarding her trunk, to wherever it was she was going. That was all.

He reached up along the wall again and took something down. He was taking another drink. Two. Three. I said to myself, a little at a loss: Yes, but he hasn't just packed a trunk this time. That trunk has been standing packed and ready since last night. Where does the hard work come in? The sweat and the need for a bracer?

Now, at last, after all those hours, he finally did go in to her. I saw his form pass through the living room and go beyond, into the bedroom. Up went the shade, that had been down all this time. Then he turned his head and looked around behind him, in a certain way, a way that was unmistakable, even from where I was. Not in one certain direction, as one looks at a person. But from side to side, and up and down, and all around, as one looks at – *an empty room.*

He stepped back, bent a little, gave a fling of his arms, and an unoccupied mattress and bedding upended over the foot of a bed, stayed that way, emptily curved. A second one followed a moment later.

She wasn't in there.

They use the expression "delayed action." I found out then what it meant. For two days a sort of formless uneasiness, a disembodied suspicion. I don't know what to call it, had been flitting and volplaning around in my mind, like an insect looking for a landing place. More than once, just as it had been ready to settle, some slight thing, some slight reassuring thing, such as the raising of the shades after they had been down unnaturally long, had been enough to keep it winging aimlessly, prevent it from staying still long enough for me to recognize it. The point of contact had been there all along, waiting to receive it. Now, for some reason, within a split second after he tossed over the empty mattresses, it landed – *zoom*! And the point of contact expanded – or exploded, whatever you care to call it – into a certainty of murder.

In other words, the rational part of my mind was far behind the instinctive, subconscious part. Delayed action. Now the one had caught up to the other. The thought-message that sparked from the synchronization was: He's done something to her!

I looked down and my hand was bunching the goods over my kneecap, it was knotted so tight. I forced it to open. I said to myself, steadyingly: now wait a minute, be careful, go slow. You've seen nothing. You know nothing. You only have the negative proof that you don't see her any more.

Sam was standing there looking over at me from the pantry way. He said accusingly: "You ain't touched a thing. And your face looks like a sheet."

It felt like one. It had that needling feeling, when the blood has left it involuntarily. It was more to get him out of the way and give myself some elbow room for undisturbed thinking, than anything else, that I said: "Sam, what's the street address of that building down there? Don't stick your head too far out and gape at it."

"Somep'n or other Benedict Avenue." He scratched his neck helpfully.

"I know that. Chase around the corner a minute and get me the exact number on it, will you?"

"Why you want to know that for?" he asked as he turned to go.

"None of your business," I said with the good-natured firmness that was all that was necessary to take care of that once and for all. I called after him just as he was closing the door. "And while you're about it, step into the entrance and see if you can tell from the mailboxes who has the fourth-floor rear. Don't get me the wrong one now. And try not to let anyone catch you at it."

He went out mumbling something that sounded like, "When a man ain't got nothing to do but just sit all day, he sure can think up the blamest things – " The door closed and I settled down to some good constructive thinking.

I said to myself: What are you really building up this monstrous supposition on? Let's see what you've got. Only that there were several little things wrong with the mechanism, the chain-belt, of their recurrent daily habits over there. 1. The lights were on all night and the first night. 2. He came in later than usual the second night. 3. He left his hat on. 4. She didn't come out to greet him – she hasn't appeared since the evening before the lights were on all night. 5. He took a drink after he finished packing her trunk. But he took three stiff drinks the next morning, immediately after her trunk went out. 6. He was inwardly disturbed and worried, yet superimposed upon this was an unnatural external concern about the surrounding rear windows that was off-key. 7. He slept in the living room, didn't go near the bedroom, during the night before the departure of the trunk.

Very well. If she had been ill that first night, and he had sent her away for her health, that automatically canceled out points 1, 2, 3, 4. It left points 5 and 6 totally unimportant and unincriminating. But when it came up against 7, it hit a stumbling block.

If she went away immediately after being ill that first night, why didn't he want to sleep in their bedroom *last night*? Sentiment? Hardly. Two perfectly good beds in one room, only a sofa or uncomfortable easy chair in the other. Why should he stay out of there if she was already gone? Just because he missed her, was lonely? A grown man doesn't act that way. All right, then she was still in there.

Sam came back parenthetically at this point and said: "That house is number 525 Benedict Avenue. The fourth-floor rear, it got the name of Mr and Mrs Lars Thorwald up."

"Sh-h," I silenced, and motioned him backhand out of my ken.

"First he want it, then he don't," he grumbled philsophically, and retired to his duties.

I went ahead digging at it. But if she was still there, in that bedroom last night, then she couldn't have gone away to the country, because I never saw her leave today. She could have left without my seeing her in the early hours of yesterday morning. I'd missed a few hours, been asleep. But this morning I had been up before he was himself, I only saw his head rear up from that sofa after I'd been at the window for some time.

To go at all she would have had to go yesterday. Then why had he left the bedroom shade down, left the mattresses undisturbed, until today? Above all, why had he stayed out of that room last night? That was evidence that she hadn't gone, was still in there. Then today, immediately after the trunk had been dispatched, he went in, pulled up the shade, tossed over the mattresses, and showed that she hadn't been in there. The thing was like a crazy spiral.

No, it wasn't either. *Immediately after the trunk had been dispatched* –

The trunk.

That did it.

I looked around to make sure the door was safely closed between Sam and me. My hand hovered uncertainly over the telephone dial a minute. Boyne, he'd be the one to tell about it. He was on Homicide. He had been, anyway, when I'd last seen him. I didn't want to get a flock of strange dicks and cops into my hair. I didn't want to be involved any more than I had to. Or at all, if possible.

They switched my call to the right place after a couple of wrong tries, and I got him finally.

"Look, Boyne? This is Hal Jeffries – "

"Well, where've you been the last sixty-two years?" he started to enthuse.

"We can take that up later. What I want you to do now is take down a name and address. Ready? Lars Thorwald. Five twenty-five Benedict Avenue. Fourth-floor rear. Got it?"

"Fourth-floor rear. Got it. What's it for?"

"Investigation. I've got a firm belief you'll uncover a murder there if you start digging at it. Don't call on me for anything more than that – just a conviction. There's been a man and wife living there until now. Now there's just the man. Her trunk went out early this morning. If you can find someone who saw *her* leave herself – "

Marshaled aloud like that and conveyed to somebody else, a lieutenant of detectives above all, it did sound flimsy, even to me. He said hesitantly, "Well, but – " Then he accepted it as was. Because I was the source, I even left my window out of it completely. I could do that with him and get away with it because he'd known me years, he didn't question my reliability. I didn't want my room all cluttered up with dicks and cops taking turns nosing out of the window in this hot weather. Let them tackle it from the front.

"Well, we'll see what we see," he said. "I'll keep you posted."

I hung up and sat back to watch and wait events. I had a grandstand seat. Or rather a grandstand seat in reverse. I could only see from behind the scenes, but not from the front. I couldn't watch Boyne go to work. I could only see the results, when and if there were any.

Nothing happened for the next few hours. The police work that I knew must be going on was as invisible as police work should be. The figure in the fourth-floor windows over there remained in sight, alone and undistured. He didn't go out. He was restless, roamed from room to room without staying in one place very long, but he stayed in. Once I saw him eating again – sitting down this time – and once he shaved, and once he even tried to read the paper, but he didn't stay with it long.

Little unseen wheels were in motion around him. Small and harmless as yet, preliminaries. If he knew, I wondered to myself, would he remain there quiescent like that, or would he try to bolt out and flee? That mightn't depend so much upon his guilt as upon his sense of immunity, his feeling that he could outwit them. Of his guilt I myself was already convinced, or I wouldn't have taken the step I had.

At three my phone rang. Boyne calling back. "Jeffries? Well, I don't know. Can't you give me a little more than just a bald statement like that?"

"Why?" I fenced. "Why do I have to?"

"I've had a man over there making inquiries. I've just had his report. The building superintendent and several of the neighbours all agree she left for the country, to try and regain her health, early yesterday morning."

"Wait a minute. Did any of them see her leave, according to your man?"

"No."

"Then all you've gotten is a second-hand version of an unsupported statement by him. Not an eyewitness account."

"He was met returning from the depot, after he'd bought her ticket and seen her off on the train."

"That's still an unsupported statement, once removed."

"I've sent a man down there to the station to try and check with the ticket agent if possible. After all, he should have been fairly conspicuous at that early hour. And we're keeping him under observation, of course, in the meantime, watching all his movements. The first chance we get we're going to jump in and search the place."

I had a feeling that they wouldn't find anything, even if they did.

"Don't expect anything more from me. I've dropped it in your lap. I've given you all I have to give. A name, an address, and an opinion."

"Yes, and I've always valued your opinion highly before now, Jeff – "

"But now you don't, that it?"

"Not at all. The thing is, we haven't turned up anything that seems to bear out your impression so far."

"You haven't gotten very far along, so far."

He went back to his previous cliché. "Well, we'll see what we see. Let you know later."

Another hour or so went by, and sunset came on. I saw him start to get ready to go out, over there. He put on his hat, put his hand in his pocket and stood still looking at it for a minute. Counting change. I guess. It gave me a peculiar sense of suppressed excitement, knowing they were going to come in the minute he left. I thought grimly, as I saw him take a last look around. If you've got anything to hide, brother, now's the time to hide it.

He left. A breath-holding interval of misleading emptiness descended on the flat. A three-alarm fire couldn't have pulled my eyes off those windows. Suddenly the door by which he had just left parted slightly and two men insinuated themselves, one behind the other. There they were now. They closed it behind them, separated at once, and got busy. One took the bedroom, one the kitchen, and they started to work their way toward one another again from those extremes of the flat. They were thorough. I could see them going over everything from top to bottom. They took the living room together. One cased one side, the other man the other.

They'd already finished before the warning caught them. I could tell that by the way they straightened up and stood facing one another frustratedly for a minute. Then both their heads turned sharply, as at a tip-off by doorbell that he was coming back. They got out fast.

I wasn't unduly disheartened, I'd expected that. My own feeling all along had been that they wouldn't find anything incriminating around. The trunk had gone.

He came in with a mountainous brown-paper bag sitting in the curve of one arm. I watched him closely to see if he'd discover that someone had been there in his absence. Apparently he didn't. They'd been adroit about it.

He stayed in the rest of the night. Sat tight, safe and sound. He did some desultory drinking. I could see him sitting there by the window and his hand would hoist every once in a while, but not to excess. Apparently everything was under control, the tension had eased, now that – the trunk was out.

Watching him across the night, I speculated: Why doesn't he get out? If I'm right about him, and I am, why does he stick around – after it? That brought its own answer: Because he doesn't know anyone's on to him yet. He doesn't think there's any hurry. To go too soon, right after she has, would be more dangerous than to stay awhile.

The night wore on. I sat there waiting for Boyne's call. It came later than I thought it would. I picked the phone up in the desk. He was getting ready to go to bed, over there, now. He'd risen from where he'd been sitting drinking in the kitchen, and put the light out. He went into the living room, lit that. He started to pull his shirt-tail up out of his belt. Boyne's voice was in my ear as my eyes were on him, over there. Three-cornered arrangement.

"Hello, Jeff? Listen, absolutely nothing. We searched the place while he was out – "

I nearly said, "I know you did, I saw it," but checked myself in time.

" – and didn't turn up a thing. But – " He stopped as though this was going to be important. I waited impatiently for him to go ahead.

"Downstairs in his letter box we found a post card waiting for him. We fished it up out of the slot with bent pins – "

"And?"

"And it was from his wife, written only yesterday from some farm upcountry. Here's the message we copied: 'Arrived O.K. Already feeling a little better. Love, Anna.' "

I said, faintly but stubbornly: "You say, written only yesterday. Have you proof of that? What was the postmark-date on it?"

He made a disgusted sound down in his tonsils. At me, not it. "The postmark was blurred. A corner of it got wet, and the ink smudged."

"All of it blurred?"

"The year-date," he admitted. "The hour and the month came out O.K. August. And seven thirty p.m., it was mailed at."

This time I made the disgusted sound, in my larynx. "August, seven thirty p.m. – 1937 or 1939 or 1942. You have no proof how it got into the mail box, whether it came from a letter carrier's pouch or from the back of some bureau drawer!"

"Give up, Jeff," he said. "There's such a thing as going too far."

I don't know what I would have said. That is, if I hadn't happened to have my eyes on the Thorwald flat living room windows just then.

Probably very little. The post card *had* shaken me, whether I admitted it or not. But I was looking over there. The light had gone out as soon as he'd taken his shirt off. But the bedroom didn't light up. A match-flare winked from the living room, low down, as from an easy chair or sofa. With two unused beds in the bedroom, he was *still staying out of there.*

"Boyne," I said in a glassy voice. "I don't care what post cards from the other world you've turned up, I say that man has done away with his wife. Trace that trunk he shipped out. Open it up when you've located it – and I think you'll find her!"

And I hung up without waiting to hear what he was going to do about it. He didn't ring back, so I suspected he was going to give my suggestion a spin after all, in spite of his loudly proclaimed skepticism.

I stayed there by the window all night, keeping a sort of death-watch. There were two more match-flares after the first, at about half-hour intervals. Nothing more after that. So possibly he was asleep over there. Possibly not. I had to sleep some time myself, and I finally succumbed in the flaming light of the early sun. Anything that he was going to do, he would have done under cover of darkness and not waited for broad daylight. There wouldn't be anything much to watch, for a while now. And what was there that he needed to do any more, anyway? Nothing, just sit tight and let a little disarming time slip by.

It seemed like five minutes later that Sam came over and touched me, but it was already high noon. I said irritably: "Didn't you lamp that note I pinned up, for you to let me sleep?"

He said: "Yeah, but it's your old friend Inspector Boyne. I figured you'd sure want to —"

It was a personal visit this time. Boyne came into the room behind him without waiting, and without much cordiality.

I said to get rid of Sam: "Go inside and smack a couple of eggs together."

Boyne began in a galvanized-iron voice. "Jeff, what do you mean by doing anything like this to me? I've made a fool out of myself, thanks to you. Sending my men out right and left on wild-goose chases. Thank God, I didn't put my foot in it any worse than I did, and have this guy picked up and brought in for questioning."

"Oh, then you don't think that's necessary?" I suggested, drily.

The look he gave me took care of that. "I'm not alone in the department, you know. There are men over me I'm accountable to for my actions. That looks great, don't it, sending one of my fellows one-half-a-day's train ride up into the sticks to some God-forsaken whistle-stop or other at departmental expense —"

"Then you located the trunk?"

"We traced it through the express agency," he said flintily.

"And you opened it?"

"We did better than that. We got in touch with the various farmhouses in the immediate locality, and Mrs Thorwald came down to the junction in a produce-truck from one of them and opened it for him herself, with her own keys!"

Very few men have ever gotten a look from an old friend such as I got from him. At the door he said, stiff as a rifle barrel: "Just let's forget all about it, shall we? That's about the kindest thing either one of us can do for the other. You're not yourself, and I'm out a little of my own pocket money, time and temper. Let's let it go at that. If you want to telephone me in the future I'll be glad to give you my home number."

The door went *whopp*! behind him.

For about ten minutes after he stormed out my numbed mind was in a sort of straitjacket. Then it started to wriggle its way free. The hell with the police. I can't prove it to them, maybe, but I can prove it to myself, one way or the other, once and for all. Either I'm wrong or I'm right. He's got his armor on against them. But his back is naked and unprotected against me.

I called Sam in. "Whatever became of that spyglass we used to have, when we were bumming around on that cabin-cruiser that season?"

He found it some place downstairs and came in with it, blowing on it and rubbing it along his sleeve. I let it lie idle in my lap first. I took a piece of paper and a pencil and wrote six words on it: *What have you done with her?*

I sealed it in an envelope and left the envelope blank. I said to Sam: "Now here's what I want you to do, and I want you to be slick about it. You take this, go in that building 525, climb the stairs to the fourth-floor rear, and ease it under the door. You're fast, at least you used to be. Let's see if you're fast enough to keep from being caught at it. Then when you get safely down again, give the outside doorbell a little poke, to attract attention."

His mouth started to open.

"And don't ask me any questions, you understand? I'm not fooling."

He went, and I got the spyglass ready.

I got him in the right focus after a minute or two. A face leaped up, and I was really seeing him for the first time. Dark-haired, but unmistakable Scandinavian ancestry. Looked like a sinewy customer, although he didn't run to much bulk.

About five minutes went by. His head turned sharply, profile-wards. That was the bell-poke, right there. The note must be in already.

He gave me the back of his head as he went back toward the flat-door. The lens could follow him all the way to the rear, where my unaided eyes hadn't been able to before.

He opened the door first, missed seeing it, looked out on a level. He closed it. Then he dipped, straightened up. He had it. I could see him turning it this way and that.

He shifted in, away from the door, nearer the window. He thought danger lay near the door, safety away from it. He didn't know it was the other way around, the deeper into his own rooms he retreated the greater the danger.

He'd torn it open, he was reading it. God, how I watched his expression. My eyes clung to it like leeches. There was a sudden widening, a pulling – the whole skirt of his face seemed to stretch back behind the ears, narrowing his eyes to Mongoloids. Shock. Panic. His hand pushed out and found the wall, and he braced himself with it. Then he went back toward the door again slowly. I could see him creeping up on it, stalking it as though it were something alive. He opened it so slenderly you couldn't see it at all, peered fearfully through the crack. Then he closed it, and he came back, zigzag, off balance from sheer reflex dismay. He toppled into a chair and snatched up a drink. Out of the bottle neck itself this time. And even while he was holding it to his lips, his head was turned looking over his shoulders at the door that had suddenly thrown his secret in his face.

I put the glass down.

Guilty! Guilty as all hell, and the police be damned!

My hand started toward the phone, came back again. What was the use? They wouldn't listen now any more than they had before. "You should have seen his face, etc." And I could hear Boyne's answer. "Anyone gets a jolt from an anonymous letter, true or false. You would yourself." They have a real live Mrs Thorwald to show me – or thought they had. I'd have to show them the dead one, to prove that they both weren't one and the same. I, from my window, had to show them a body.

Well, he'd have to show me first.

It took hours before I got it. I kept pegging away at it, pegging away at it, while the afternoon wore away. Meanwhile he was pacing back and forth there like a caged panther. Two minds with but one thought, turned inside-out in my case. How to keep it hidden, how to see that it wasn't kept hidden.

I was afraid he might try to light out, but if he intended doing that he was going to wait until after dark, apparently, so I had a little time yet. Possibly he didn't want to himself, unless he was driven to it – still felt that it was more dangerous than to stay.

The customary sights and sounds around me went on unnoticed, while the main stream of my thoughts pounded like a torrent against that one obstacle stubbornly damming them up: how to get him to give the location away to me, so that I could give it away in turn to the police.

I was dimly conscious. I remember, of the landlord or somebody bringing in a prospective tenant to look at the sixth-floor apartment, the one that had already been finished. This was two over Thorwald's; they were still at work on the in-between one. At one point an odd little bit of synchronization, completely accidental of course, cropped up. Landlord and tenant both happened to be near the living room windows on the sixth at the same moment that Thorwald was near those on the fourth. Both parties moved onward simultaneously into the kitchen from there, and, passing the blind spot of the wall, appeared next at the kitchen windows. It was uncanny, they were almost like precision-strollers or puppets manipulated on one and the same string. It probably wouldn't have happened again just like that in another fifty years. Immediately afterwards they digressed, never to repeat themselves like that again.

The thing was, something about it had disturbed me. There had been some slight flaw or hitch to mar its smoothness. I tried for a moment or two to figure out what it had been, and couldn't. The landlord and tenant had gone now, and only Thorwald was in sight. My unaided memory wasn't enough to recapture it for me. My eyesight might have if it had been repeated, but it wasn't.

It sank into my subconscious, to ferment there like yeast, while I went back to the main problem at hand.

I got it finally, it was well after dark, but I finally hit on a way. It mightn't work, it was cumbersome and roundabout, but it was the only way I could think of. An alarmed turn of the head, a quick precautionary step in one certain direction, was all I needed. And to get this brief, flickering, transitory give-away, I needed two phone calls and an absence of about half an hour on his part between them.

I leafed a directory by matchlight until I'd found what I wanted: *Thorwald, Lars. 525 Bndct. . . . SWansea 5–2114.*

I blew out the match, picked up the phone in the dark. It was like television. I could see to the other end of my call, only not along the wire but by a direct channel of vision from window to window.

He said "Hullo?" gruffly.

I thought: How strange this is. I've been accusing him of murder for three days straight, and only now I'm hearing his voice for the first time.

I didn't try to disguise my own voice. After all, he'd never see me and I'd never see him. I said: "You got my note?"

He said guardedly: "Who is this?"

"Just somebody who happens to know."

He said craftily: "Know what?"

"Know what you know. You and I, we're the only ones."

He controlled himself well. I didn't hear a sound. But he didn't know he was open another way too. I had the glass balanced there at proper height on two large books on the sill. Through the window I saw him pull open the collar of his shirt as though its stricture was intolerable. Then he backed his hand over his eyes like you do when there's light blinding you.

His voice came back firmly. "I don't know what you're talking about."

"Business, that's what I'm talking about. It should be worth something to me, shouldn't it? To keep it from going any further." I wanted to keep him from catching on that it was the windows. I still needed them, I needed them now more than ever. "You weren't very careful about your door the other night. Or maybe the draft swung it open a little."

That hit him where he lived. Even the stomach-heave reached me over the wire. "You didn't see anything. There wasn't anything to see."

"That's up to you. Why should I go to the police?" I coughed a little. "If it would pay me not to."

"Oh," he said. And there was relief of a sort in it. "D'you want to – see me? Is that it?"

"That would be the best way, wouldn't it? How much can you bring with you for now?"

"I've only got about seventy dollars around here."

"All right, then we can arrange the rest for later. Do you know where Lakeside Park is? I'm near there now. Suppose we make it there." That was about thirty minutes away. Fifteen there and fifteen back. "There's a little pavilion as you go in."

"How many of you are there?" he asked cautiously.

"Just me. It pays to keep things to yourself. That way you don't have to divvy up."

He seemed to like that too. "I'll take a run out," he said, "just to see what it's all about."

I watched him more closely than ever, after he'd hung up. He flitted straight through to the end room, the bedroom, that he didn't go near any more. He disappeared into a clothes-closet in there, stayed a minute, came out again. He must have taken something out of a hidden cranny or niche in there that even the dicks had missed. I could tell by the piston-like motion of his hand, just before it disappeared inside his coat, what it was. A gun.

It's a good thing, I thought, I'm not out there in Lakeside Park waiting for my seventy dollars.

The place blacked and he was on his way.

I called Sam in. "I want you to do something for me that's a little risky. In fact, damn risky. You might break a leg, or might get shot, or you might even get pinched. We've been together ten years, and I wouldn't ask you anything like that if I could do it myself. But I can't, and it's got to be done." Then I told him. "Go out the back way, cross the back yard fences, and see if you can get into that fourth-floor flat up the fire escape. He's left one of the windows down a little from the top."

"What do you want me to look for?"

"Nothing." The police had been there already, so what was the good of that? "There are three rooms over there, I want you to disturb everything just a little bit, in all three, to show someone's been in there. Turn up the edge of each rug a little, shift every chair and table around a little, leave the closet doors standing out. Don't pass up a thing. Here, keep your eyes on this." I took off my own wrist watch, strapped it on him. "You've got twenty-five minutes, starting from now. If you stay within those twenty-five minutes, nothing will happen to you. When you see they're up, don't wait any longer, get out and get out fast."

"Climb back down?"

"No." He wouldn't remember, in his excitement, if he'd left the windows up or not. And I didn't want him to connect danger with the back of his place, but with the front. I wanted to keep my own window out of it. "Latch the window down tight, let yourself out the door, and beat it out of the building the front way, for your life!"

"I'm just an easy mark for you," he said ruefully, but he went.

He came out through our own basement door below me, and scrambled over the fences. If anyone had challenged him from one of the surrounding windows, I was going to backstop for him, explain I'd sent him down to look for something. But no one did. He made it pretty good for anyone his age. He isn't so young any more. Even the fire escape backing the flat, which was drawn up short, he managed to contact by standing up on something. He got in, lit the light, looked over at me. I motioned him to go ahead, not weaken.

I watched him at it. There wasn't any way I could protect him, now that he was in there. Even Thorwald would be within his rights in shooting him down – this was break and entry. I had to stay in back behind the scenes, like I had been all along. I couldn't get out in front of him as a lookout and shield him. Even the dicks had a lookout posted.

He must have been tense, doing it. I was twice as tense, watching him do it. The twenty-five minutes took fifty to go by. Finally he came over to the window, latched it fast. The lights went, and he was out. He'd made it. I blew out a bellyful of breath that was twenty-five minutes old.

I heard him keying the street door, and when he came up I said warningly: "Leave the light out in here. Go and build yourself a great big two-story whisky punch; you're as close to white as you'll ever be."

Thorwald came back twenty-nine minutes after he'd left for Lakeside Park. A pretty slim margin to hang a man's life on. So now for the finale of the long-winded business, and here was hoping. I got my second phone call in before he had time to notice anything amiss. It was tricky timing but I'd been sitting there with the receiver ready in my hand, dialing the number over and over, then killing it each time. He came in on the 2 of 5–2114, and I saved that much time. The ring started before his hand came away from the light switch.

This was the one that was going to tell the story.

"You were supposed to bring money, not a gun; that's why I didn't show up." I saw the jolt that threw into him. The window still had to stay out of it. "I saw you tap the inside of your coat, where you had it, as you came out on the street." Maybe he hadn't, but he wouldn't remember by now whether he had or not. You usually do when you're packing a gun and aren't an habitual carrier.

"Too bad you had your trip out and back for nothing. I didn't waste my time while you were gone, though. I know more now than I knew before." This was the important part. I had the glass up and I was practically fluoroscoping him. "I've found out where – it is. You know what I mean. I know now where you've got – it. I was there while you were out."

Not a word. Just quick breathing.

"Don't you believe me? Look around. Put the receiver down and take a look for yourself. I found it."

He put it down, moved as far as the living room entrance, and touched off the lights. He just looked around him once, in a sweeping, all-embracing stare, that didn't come to a head on any one fixed point, didn't center at all.

He was smiling grimly when he came back to the phone. All he said, softly and with malignant satisfaction, was. "You're a liar."

Then I saw him lay the receiver down and take his hand off it. I hung up at my end.

The test had failed. And yet it hadn't. He hadn't given the location away as I'd hoped he would. And yet that "You're a liar" was a tacit admission that it was there to be found, somewhere around him, somewhere on those premises. In such a good place that he didn't have to worry about it, didn't even have to look to make sure.

So there was a kind of sterile victory in my defeat. But it wasn't worth a damn to me.

He was standing there with his back to me, and I couldn't see what he was doing. I knew the phone was somewhere in front of him, but I thought he was just standing there pensive behind it. His head was slightly lowered, that was all. I'd hung up at my end. I didn't even see his elbow move. And if his index finger did. I couldn't see.

He stood like that a moment or two, then finally he moved aside. The lights went out over there; I lost him. He was careful not even to strike matches, like he sometimes did in the dark.

My mind no longer distracted by having him to look at, I turned to trying to recapture something else – that troublesome little hitch in synchronization that had occurred this afternoon, when the renting agent and he both moved simultaneously from one window to the next. The closest I could get was this: it was like when you're looking at someone through a panel of imperfect glass, and a flaw in the glass distorts the symmetry of the reflected image for a second, until it has gone on past that point. Yet that wouldn't do, that was not it. The windows had been open and there had been no glass between. And I hadn't been using the lens at the time.

My phone rang, Boyne, I supposed. It wouldn't be anyone else at this hour. Maybe after reflecting on the way he'd jumped all over me – I said "Hello" unguardedly, in my own normal voice.

There wasn't any answer.

I said, "Hello? Hello? Hello?" I kept giving away samples of my voice.

There wasn't a sound from first to last.

I hung up finally. It was still dark over there, I noticed.

Sam looked in to check out. He was a bit thick-tongued from his restorative drink. He said something about "Awri' if I go now?" I half heard him. I was trying to figure out another way of trapping *him* over there into giving away the right spot. I motioned my consent absently.

He went a little unsteadily down the stairs to the ground floor and after a delaying moment or two I heard the street door close after him. Poor Sam, he wasn't much used to liquor.

I was left alone in the house, one chair the limit of my freedom of movement.

Suddenly a light went on over there again, just momentarily, to go right out again afterwards. He must have needed it for something, to locate something that he had already been looking for and found he wasn't able to put his hands on readily without it. He found it, whatever it was, almost immediately, and moved back at once to put the lights out again. As he turned to do so, I saw him give a glance out the window. He didn't come to the window to do it, he just shot it out in passing.

Something about it struck me as different from any of the others I'd seen him give in all the time I'd been watching him. If you can qualify such an elusive thing as a glance. I would have termed it a glance with a purpose. It was certainly anything but vacant or random, it had a bright spark of fixity in it. It wasn't one of those precautionary sweeps I'd seen him give, either. It hadn't started over to the other side and worked its way around to my side, the right. It had hit dead-centre at my bay window, for just a split second while it lasted, and then was gone again. And the lights were gone, and he was gone.

Sometimes your senses take things in without your mind translating them into their proper meaning. My eyes saw that look. My mind refused to smelter it properly. "It was meaningless," I thought. "An unintentional bull's-eye, that just happened to hit square over here, as he went toward the lights on his way out."

Delayed action. A wordless ring of the phone. To test a voice? A period of bated darkness following that, in which two could have played at the same game – stalking one another's window-squares, unseen. A last-moment flicker of the lights, that was bad strategy but unavoidable.

A parting glance, radioactive with malignant intention. All these things sank in without fusing. My eyes did their job, it was my mind that didn't – or at least took its time about it.

Seconds went by in packages of sixty. It was very still around the familiar quadrangle formed by the back of the houses. Sort of a breathless stillness. And then a sound came into it, starting up from nowhere, nothing. The unmistakable, spaced clicking a cricket makes in the silence of the night. I thought of Sam's superstition about them, that he claimed had never failed to fulfil itself yet. If that was the case, it looked bad for somebody in one of these slumbering houses around here –

Sam had been gone only about ten minutes. And now he was back again, he must have forgotten something. That drink was responsible. Maybe his hat, or maybe even the key to his own quarters uptown. He knew I couldn't come down and let him in, and he was trying to be quiet about it, thinking perhaps I'd dozed off. All I could hear was this faint jiggling down at the lock of the front door. It was one of those old-fashioned stoop houses, with an outer pair of storm doors that were allowed to swing free all night, and then a small vestibule, and then the inner door, worked by a simple iron key. The liquor had made his hand a little unreliable, although he'd had this difficulty once or twice before, even without it. A match, would have helped him find the keyhole quicker, but then, Sam doesn't smoke. I knew he wasn't likely to have one on him.

The sound had stopped now. He must have given up, gone away again, decided to let whatever it was go until tomorrow. He hadn't gotten in, because I knew his noisy way of letting doors coast shut by themselves too well, and there hadn't been any sound of that sort, that loose slap he always made.

Then suddenly it exploded. Why at this particular moment, I don't know. That was some mystery of the inner workings of my own mind. It flashed like waiting gunpowder which a spark has finally reached along a slow train. Drove all thoughts of Sam, and the front door, and this and that completely out of my head. It had been waiting there since midafternoon today, and only now – More of that delayed action. Damn that delayed action.

The renting agent and Thorwald had both started even from the living room window. An intervening gap of blind wall, and both had reappeared at the kitchen window, still one above the other. But some sort of hitch or flaw or jump had taken place, right there, that bothered me. The eye is a reliable surveyor. There wasn't anything the matter with their timing, it was their parallel-ness, or whatever the word is. The hitch had been vertical, not horizontal. There had been an upward "jump."

Now I had it, now I knew. And it couldn't wait. It was too good. They wanted a body? Now I had one for them.

Sore or not, Boyne would *have* to listen to me now. I didn't waste any time, I dialed his precinct-house then and there in the dark, working the slots in my lap by memory alone. They didn't make much noise going around, just a light click. Not even as distinct as that cricket out there –

"He went home long ago," the desk sergeant said.

This couldn't wait. "All right, give me his home phone number."

He took a minute, came back again. "Trafalgar," he said. Then nothing more.

"Well? Trafalgar what?" Not a sound.

"Hello? Hello?" I tapped it. "Operator, I've been cut off. Give me that party again." I couldn't get her either.

I hadn't been cut off. My wire had been cut. That had been too sudden, right in the middle of – And to be cut like that it would have to be done somewhere right here inside the house with me. Outside it went underground.

Delayed action. This time final, fatal, altogether too late. A voiceless ring of the phone. A direction-finder of a look from over there. "Sam" seemingly trying to get back in a while ago.

Surely, death was somewhere inside the house here with me. And I couldn't move, I couldn't get up out of this chair. Even if I had gotten through to Boyne just now, that would have been too late. There wasn't time enough now for one of those camera-finishes in this. I could have shouted out the window to that gallery of sleeping rear-window neighbors around me. I supposed. It would have brought them to the windows. It couldn't have brought them over here in time. By the time they had even figured which particular house it was coming from, it would stop again, be over with. I didn't open my mouth. Not because I was brave, but because it was so obviously useless.

He'd be up in a minute. He must be on the stairs now, although I couldn't hear him. Not even a creak. A creak would have been a relief, would have placed him. This was like being shut up in the dark with the silence of a gliding, coiling cobra somewhere around you.

There wasn't a weapon in the place with me. There were books there on the wall, in the dark, within reach. Me, who never read. The former owner's books. There was a bust of Rousseau or Montesquieu, I'd never been able to decide which, one of those gents with flowing manes, topping them. It was a monstrosity, bisque clay, but it too dated from before my occupancy.

I arched my middle upward from the chair seat and clawed desperately up at it. Twice my fingertips slipped off it, then at the third raking I got it to teeter, and the fourth brought it down into my lap, pushing me down into the chair. There was a steamer rug under me. I didn't need it around me in this weather, I'd been using it to soften the seat of the chair. I tugged it out from under and mantled it around me like an Indian brave's blanket. Then I squirmed far down in the chair, let my head and one shoulder dangle out over the arm, on the side next to the wall. I hoisted the bust to my other, upward shoulder, balanced it there precariously for a second head, blanket tucked around its ears. From the back, in the dark, it would look – I hoped –

I proceeded to breathe adenoidally, like someone in heavy upright sleep. It wasn't hard. My own breath was coming nearly that labored anyway, from tension.

He was good with knobs and hinges and things. I never heard the door open, and this one, unlike the one downstairs, was right behind me. A little eddy of air puffed through the dark at me. I could feel it because my scalp, the real one, was all wet at the roots of the hair right then.

If I was going to be a knife or head-blow, the dodge might give me a second chance, that was the most I could hope for. I knew. My arms and shoulders are hefty. I'd bring him down on me in a bear-hug after the first slash or drive, and break his neck or collarbone against me. If it was going to be a gun, he'd get me anyway in the end. A difference of a few seconds. He had a gun, I knew, that he was going to use on me in the open, over at Lakeside Park. I was hoping that here, indoors, in order to make his own escape more practicable –

Time was up.

The flash of the shot lit up the room for a second, it was so dark. Or at least the corners of it, like flickering, weak lightning. The bust bounced on my shoulder and disintegrated into chunks.

I thought he was jumping up and down on the floor for a minute with frustrated rage. Then when I saw him dart by me and lean over the window sill to look for a way out, the sound transferred itself rearwards and downwards, became a pummelling with hoof and hip at the street door. The camera-finish after all. But he still could have killed me five times.

I flung my body down into the narrow crevice between chair arm and wall, but my legs were still up, and so, was my head and that one shoulder.

He whirled, fired at me so close that it was like looking a sunrise in the face. I didn't feel it, so – it hadn't hit.

"You – " I heard him grunt to himself. I think it was the last thing he said. The rest of his life was all action, not verbal.

He flung over the sill on one arm and dropped into the yard. Two-story drop. He made it because he missed the cement, landed on the sod-strip in the middle. I jacked myself up over the chair arm and flung myself bodily forward at the window, nearly hitting it chin first.

He went all right. When life depends on it, you go. He took the first fence, rolled over that bellywards. He went over the second like a cat, hands and feet pointed together in a spring. Then he was back in the rear yard of his own building. He got up on something, just about like Sam had – The rest was all footwork, with quick little corkscrew twists at each landing stage. Sam had latched his windows down when he was over there, but he'd reopened one of them for ventilation on his return. His whole life depended now on that casual, unthinking little act –

Second, third. He was up to his own windows. He'd made it. Something went wrong. He veered out away from them in another pretzel-twist, flashed up toward the fifth, the one above. Something sparked in the darkness of one of his own windows where he'd been just now, and a shot thudded heavily out around the quadrangle enclosure like a big bass drum.

He passed the fifth, the sixth, got up to the roof. He'd made it a second time. Gee, he loved life! The guys in his own windows couldn't get him, he was over them in a straight line and there was too much fire escape interlacing in the way.

I was too busy watching him to watch what was going on around me. Suddenly Boyne was next to me, sighting. I heard him mutter: "I almost hate to do this, he's got to fall so far."

He was balanced on the roof parapet up there, with a star right over his head. An unlucky star. He stayed a minute too long, trying to kill before he was killed. Or maybe he was killed, and knew it.

A shot cracked, high up against the sky, the window pane flew apart all over the two of us, and one of the books snapped right behind me.

Boyne didn't say anything more about hating to do it. My face was pressing outward against his arm. The recoil of his elbow jarred my teeth. I blew a clearing through the smoke to watch him go.

It was pretty horrible. He took a minute to show anything, standing up there on the parapet. Then he let his gun go, as if to say: "I won't need this any more." Then he went after it. He missed the fire escape entirely, came all the way down on the outside. He landed so far out he hit one of the projecting planks, down there out of sight. It bounced his body up, like a springboard. Then it landed again – for good. And that was all.

I said to Boyne. "I got it. I got it finally. The fifth-floor flat, the one over his, that they're still working on. The cement kitchen floor, raised above the level of the other rooms. They wanted to comply with the fire laws and also obtain a dropped living room effect, as cheaply as possible. Dig it up – "

He went right over then and there, down through the basement and over the fences, to save time. The electricity wasn't turned on yet in that one, they had to use their torches. It didn't take them long at that, once they'd got started. In about half an hour he came to the window and wigwagged over for my benefit. It meant yes.

He didn't come over until nearly eight in the morning; after they'd tidied up and taken them away. Both away, the hot dead and the cold dead. He said: "Jeff, I take it all back. That damn fool that I sent up there about the trunk – well, it wasn't his fault, in a way. I'm to blame. He didn't have orders to check on the woman's description, only on the contents of the trunk. He came back and touched on it in a general way. I go home and I'm in bed already, and suddenly pop! into my brain – one of the tenants I questioned two whole days ago had given us a few details and they didn't tally with his on several important points. Talk about being slow to catch on!"

"I've had that all the way through this damn thing," I admitted ruefully. "I call it delayed action. It nearly killed me."

"I'm a police officer and you're not."

"That how you happened to shine at the right time?"

"Sure. We came over to pick him up for questioning. I left them planted there when we saw he wasn't in, and came on over there by myself to square it up with you while we were waiting. How did you happen to hit on that cement floor?"

I told him about the freak synchronization. "The renting agent showed up taller at the kitchen window in proportion to Thorwald, than he had been a moment before when both were at the living room windows together. It was no secret that they were putting in cement floors, topped by a cork composition, and raising them considerable. But it took on new meaning. Since the top floor one has been finished for some time, it had to be the fifth. Here's the way I have it lined up, just in theory. She's been in ill health for years, and he's been out of work, and he got sick of that and of her both. Met this other – "

"She'll be here later today, they're bringing her down under arrest."

"He probably insured her for all he could get, and then started to poison her slowly, trying not to leave any trace. I imagine – and remember, this is pure conjecture – she caught him at it that night the light was on all night. Caught on in some way, or caught him in the act. He lost his head, and did the very thing he had wanted all along to avoid doing. Killed her by violence – strangulation or a blow. The rest had to be hastily improvised. He got a better break than he deserved at that. He thought of the apartment upstairs, went up and looked around. They'd just finished laying the floor, the cement hadn't hardened yet, and the materials were still around. He gouged a trough out of it just wide enough to take her body, put her in it, mixed fresh cement and recemented over her, possibly raising the general level of the flooring an inch or two so that she'd be safely covered. A permanent, odorless coffin. Next day the workmen came back, laid down the cork surfacing on top of it without noticing anything. I suppose he'd used one of their own trowels to smooth it. Then he sent his accessory upstate fast, near where his wife had been several summers before, but to a different farmhouse where she wouldn't be recognized, along with the trunk keys. Sent the trunk up after her, and dropped himself an already used post card into his mailbox, with the yeardate blurred. In a week or two she would have probably committed 'suicide' up there as Mrs Anna Thorwald. Despondency due to ill health. Written him a farewell note and left her clothes beside some body of deep water. It was risky, but they might have succeeded in collecting the insurance at that."

By nine Boyne and the rest had gone. I was still sitting there in the chair, too keyed up to sleep. Sam came in and said, "Here's Doc Preston."

He showed up rubbing his hands, in that way he has. "Guess we can take that cast off your leg now. You must be tired of sitting there all day doing nothing."

I Won't Take a Minute

She was always the last one out, even on the nights I came around to pick her up – that was another thing burned me up. Not with her of course, but with her job there. Well, she was on the last leg of it now, it would be over with pretty soon. We weren't going to be one of those couples where the wife kept on working after the marriage. She'd already told them she was leaving anyway, so it was all settled. I didn't blame her for hanging on up to the very end. The couple of extra weeks pay would come in handy for a lot of little this-ems and that-ems that a girl about to settle down always likes to buy herself (knowing she's going to have a tough time getting them afterwards). But what got me was, why did she always have to be the last one out?

I picketed the doorway, while the cave-dwellers streamed out all around me. Everyone but her. Back and forth and back and forth; all I needed was a "Don't Patronize" sign and a spiel. Finally I even saw the slave-driver she worked for come out, but still no her. He passed by without knowing me, but even if he had he wouldn't have given me any sunny smiles.

And then finally she came – and the whole world faded out around us and we were just alone on the crowded sidewalk. I've heard it called love.

She was very good to look at, which was why I'd waited until I was twenty-five and met her. Here's how she went: first a lot of gold all beaten up into a froth and poured over her head and allowed to set there in crinkly little curls. Then a pair of eyes that – I don't know how to say it. You were in danger of drowning if you looked into them too deep, but, boy, was drowning a pleasure. Yes, blue. And then a mouth with real lines. Not one of those things all smeared over with red jam.

She had about everything just right, and believe me I was going to throw away the sales-slip and not return the merchandise once it got up to my house.

For trimmings, a dark-blue skirt and a short little jacket that flared out from her shoulders, and a kind of cockeyed tam o'shanter. And a package. I didn't like the looks of that package.

I told her so the minute I stepped up and took off my hat, while she was still looking down the other way for me. "What's that?"

She said: "Oh, Kenny, been waiting long? I hurried up all I could. This? Oh, just a package. I promised His Nibs I'd leave it at a flat on

Martine Street on my way home."

"But you're not going home. I've got two ducats for 'Heavensabustin' and I was gonna take you to Rafft's for dinner first; I even brought a clean collar to work with me this morning. Now this is going to cut down our time for eating to a shadow—"

She tucked her free hand under my arm to pacify me. "It won't take any time at all, it's right on our way. And we can cut out the fruit-cup or something."

"Aw, but you always look so classy eating fruit-cup," I mourned.

But she went right ahead; evidently the matter had already been all settled between us without my knowing about it. "Wait a minute, let me see if I've got the address straight. Apartment 4F, 415 Martine Street. That's it."

I was still grouching about it, but she already had me under control. "What are you supposed to do, double as an errand-girl, too?" But by that time we were halfway there, so what was the use of kicking any more about it.

"Let's talk about us," she said. "Have you been counting the days?"

"All day. Thirteen left."

"And a half. Don't forget the half, if it's to be a noon-wedding." She tipped her shoulders together. "I don't like that thirteen by itself. I'll be glad when it's tomorrow, and only twelve left."

"Gee you're cute," I beamed admiringly. "The more I know you, the cuter you get."

"I bet you won't say that a year from now. I bet you'll be calling me your old lady then."

"This is it," I said.

"That's right, 415." She backed up, and me with her. "I was sailing right on past it. See what an effect you have on me?"

It was the kind of building that still was a notch above a tenement, but it had stopped being up-to-date about 1918. We went in the outer vestibule together, which had three steps going up and then a pair of inner glass doors, to hold you up until you said who you were.

"All right, turn it over to the hallman or whoever it is and let's be on our way."

She got on that conscientious look that anything connected with her job always seemed to bring on. "Oh no, I'm supposed to take it right up personally and get a receipt. Besides, there doesn't seem to be any hallman . . ."

She was going to do it her way anyway, I could see that, so there was no use arguing. She was bent over scanning the name-plates in the brass letter-boxes set into the marble trim. "What'd I say that name was again?"

"I dunno, Muller or something," I said sulkily.

"That's it. What would I do without you?" She flashed me a smile for a bribe to stay in good humor, then went ahead scanning. "Here it is. 4F. The name-card's fallen out of the slit and gotten lost, no wonder I couldn't find it." She poked the button next to it. "You wait downstairs here for me," she said. "I won't take a minute."

"Make it as fast as you can, will you? We're losing all this good time out of being together."

She took a quick step back toward me. "Here," she said, "let this hold you until I come down again." And that mouth I told you about, went right up smack against mine – where it belonged. "And if you're very good, you may get a chaser to that when I come down again."

Meanwhile the inner vestibule-door catch was being sprung for her with a sound like crickets with sore throats. She pushed it open, went inside. It swung shut again, cutting us off from one another. But I could still see her through it for a moment longer, standing in there by the elevator-bank waiting to go up. She looked good even from the back. When the car came down for her, she didn't forget to turn around and flash me another heartbreaker across her shoulder, before she stepped in and set the control-button for the floor she wanted. It was self-service, nobody else in it.

The door closed after her, and I couldn't see her any more. I could see the little red light that told the car was in use, gleaming for a few minutes after that, and then that went out too. And there wasn't anything left of her.

I lit a cigarette and leaned against the right-hand wall waiting. Then my shoulder got tired and I leaned against the left-hand wall. Then my both shoulders got tired and I just stood up by myself in the middle.

I've never timed a cigarette. I suppose they take around five minutes. This one seemed to take longer, but then look who I was waiting for. I punched it out with my foot without bothering to throw it out through the door; I didn't live there after all.

I thought: "Nice and fast. I mighta known it." I thought: "What's she doing, staying to tea up there?"

I counted my change, just to give myself something to do. I took off my hat and looked it over, like I'd never seen it before.

Things happened. Nothing much, little things that were to last so long. The postman came into the vestibule, shoved letters in here and there. 4F didn't get any. He shifted his girth straps and went out again. A stout lady in a not-very-genuine fur coat came in, one arm full of bundles, and hauling a yowling little kid by the other. She looked to see if there was any mail first. Then she looked for her key, and it took a lot of juggling. Then she looked at me, kind of supercilious. If a look can be translated into a single word, hers said: "Loafer!" Meanwhile the kid was beefing away. He had adenoids or something, and you couldn't tell if he was talking English or choking to death. She seemed to be able to tell the difference though. She said: "Now Dwight, I don't want to hear another word! If pot cheese is good enough for your father, pot cheese is good enough for you! If you don't hush up, I'll give you to this man here!"

I thought: "Oh no you won't, not with a set of dishes thrown in!"

After they'd gone in, more waiting started in. I started to trace patterns with my feet, circles, diagonals, Maltese crosses. After I'd covered about a block-and-a-half that way, I stopped to rest again. I started to talk to myself, under my breath. "Must be out of pencils up there, to sign the receipt with, and she's waiting while they whittle out a new one! We'll be in time for the intermission at the show—"

I lit another cigarette. That act, slight as it was, put the finishing-touch to my self-control. I no sooner finished doing it than I hit the opposite wall with it. "What the hell is this anyway?" It wasn't under my breath any more, it was a full-toned yap. I stepped over, picked out 4F, and nearly sent the button through to the other side of the wall.

I didn't want to go in, of course. I just wanted to tip her off I was still alive down here. Aging fast, but still in fairly usable shape. She'd know who it was when she heard that blast. So when they released the catch on the door, I intended staying right outside where I was.

But they didn't. They were either ignoring the ring or they hadn't heard it. I gave it a second flattening. Again the catch on the door remained undisturbed. I knew the bell wasn't out of order, because I'd seen her give just a peck at it and the door-catch had been released for her. This time I gave it a triple-header. Two short ones and a long one, that went on for weeks. So long that my thumb joint got all white down to my wrist before I let go.

No acknowledgment. Dead to the world up there.

I did the instinctive thing, even though it was quite useless in the present case. Backed out into the street, as far as the outer rim of the sidewalk, and scanned the face of the building. There was just a checkerboard pattern of lighted squares and black ones. I couldn't tell which windows belonged to 4F, and even if I could have it wouldn't have done me any good unless I intended yelling her name up from the open sidewalk – and I didn't yet.

But being all the way out there cost me a chance to get in free, and lost me some more valuable time in the bargain. A man came out, the first person who had emerged from inside since I'd been waiting around, but before I could get in there and push through in his wake, the door had clicked shut again.

He was a scrawny-looking little runt, reminded you of an old-clothes-man on his night off. He went on out without even looking at me, and I tackled the 4F bell some more, gave it practically the whole Morse Code.

I wasn't frightened yet, just sizzling and completely baffled. The only thing I could figure, far-fetched as it was, was that the bell-apparatus had been on its last gasp when she rang it, and had given up the ghost immediately afterwards. Otherwise why didn't they hear it, the kind of punishment I was giving it?

Then the first little trickle of fright did creep in, like a dribble of cold water down your back when you're perspiring. I thought: "Maybe there's some guy up there trying to get funny with her, that's why the bell isn't answered. After all, things like that do happen in a big city all the time. I better get up there fast and find out what this is!"

I punched a neighboring bell at random, just to get past the door, and when the catch had been released for me, I streaked into the elevator, which the last guy had left down, and gave it the 4-button.

It seemed to me to set a new record for slowness in getting up there, but maybe that was just the state of mind I was in. When it finally did and I barged out, I made a false turn down the hall first, then when I came up against 4B and C and so on, turned and went back the other way.

It was at the far end of the hall, at the back. The bell I'd rung was evidently on some other floor, for none of the doors on this one opened to see who it was. I went close against it and listened. There were no sounds of a scuffle and I couldn't hear her saying "Unhand me, you brute!" so I calmed down by that much. But not all the way.

I couldn't hear anything at all. It was stone-silent in there. And yet these flat-doors weren't soundproof, because I could hear somebody's radio filtering through one at the other end of the hall clear as day.

I rang the bell and waited. I could hear it ring inside, from where I was. I'd say: "Will you ask that young lady that brought a package up here whether she's coming down tonight or tomorrow?" No, that sounded too dictatorial. I'd say: "Is the young lady ready to leave now?" I knew I'd feel slightly foolish, like you always do when you make a mountain out of a molehill.

Meanwhile, it hadn't opened. I pushed the bell again, and again I could hear the battery sing out on the inside. I rapped with my knuckles. Then I rang a third time. Then I rattled the knob (as though that would attract their attention, if ringing the bell hadn't!) Then I pounded with the heel of my hand. Then I alternated all three, the whole thing became a maelstrom of frenzied action. I think I even kicked. Without getting the results I was after – admittance.

Other doors began to open cautiously down the line, attracted by the noise I was making. But by that time I had turned and bolted down the stairs, without waiting for the paralytic elevator, to find the janitor. Fright wasn't just a cold trickle any more, it was an icy torrent gushing through me full-force.

I got down into the basement and found him without too much

trouble. He was eating his meal or something on a red-checkered tablecloth, but I had no time to assimilate details. A glimpse of a napkin tucked in collarwise was about all that registered. "Come up with me quick, will you?" I panted, pulling him by the arm. "Bring your passkey, I want you to open one of those flats!"

"What's matter, something wrong?"

"I don't like the looks of it. My girl took a package up – I've been waiting for her over twenty minutes and she never came down again. They won't answer the bell—"

He seemed to take forever. First he stood up, then he finished swallowing, then he wiped his mouth, then he got a big ring of keys, then finally he followed me. As an afterthought he peeled off the napkin and threw it behind him at the table, but missed it. He even wanted to wait for the elevator. "No, no, no," I groaned, steering him to the stairs.

"Which one is it?"

"It's on the fourth floor, I'll show you!" Then when we got up there, "Here – right here."

When he saw which door I was pushing him to, he suddenly stopped. "That one? No, now wait a minute, young fellow, it couldn't be. Not that one."

"Don't try to tell me!" I heaved exasperatedly. "I say it is!"

"And don't you try to tell me! I say it couldn't be!"

"Why?"

"I'll show you why," he said heatedly. He went ahead up to it, put his passkey in, threw the door open, and flattened himself to let me get a good look past him.

I needed more than just one. It was one of those things that register on the eye but don't make sense to the brain. The light from the hall filtered in to make a threadbare half-moon, but to make sure I wasn't missing any of it, he snapped a switch inside the door and a dim, left-over bulb somewhere further back went on flickeringly. You could see why it had been left in – it wasn't worth taking out. It threw a watery light around, not much better than a candle. But enough to see by.

"Now! You see why?"

The place was empty as a barn. Unfurnished, uninhabited, whatever you want to call it. Just bare walls, ceiling, and floor-boards. You could see where the carpet used to go: they were lighter in a big square patch in the middle than around the outside. You could see where a picture used to go, many moons ago: there was a patch of gray wool-dust adhering like a fiber to the wall. You could even see where the telephone used to go; the wiring still led in along the baseboard, then reared up to waist-level like a pothook and ended in nothing.

The air alibied for its emptiness. It was stale, as though the windows hadn't been opened for months. Stale and dusty and sluggish.

"So you see? Mister, this place ain't been rented for six months." He was getting ready to close the door, as though that ended it; pulling it around behind his back, I could see it coming toward me, the "4F" stencilled on it in tarnished gold-paint seemed to swell up, got bigger and bigger until it loomed before me a yard high.

"No!" I croaked, and planted the flat of my hand against it and swept it back, out of his backhand grasp. "She came in here, I tell you!"

I went in a step or two, called her name into the emptiness. "Steffie! Steffie!"

He stayed pat on the rational, everyday plane of things as they ought to be, while I rapidly sank down below him onto a plane of shadows and terror. Like two loading platforms going in opposite directions, we were already miles apart, cut off from each other. "Now, what're you doing that for? Use your head. How can she be in here, when the place is empty?"

"I saw her ring the bell and I saw the door open for her."

"You saw *this* door?" He was obdurately incredulous.

"The downstairs door. I saw the catch released for her, after she rang this bell."

"Oh, that's different. You must have seen her ring some other bell, and you thought it was this one; then somebody else opened the building-door for her. How could anyone answer from here? Six months the people've been out of here."

I didn't hear a word. "Lemme look! Bring more lights!"

He shrugged, sighed, decided to humor me. "Wait, I get a bulb from the hall." He brought one in, screwed it into an empty socket in the room beyond the first. That did for practically the whole place. It was just two rooms, with the usual appendages: bath and kitchenette.

"How is it the current's still on, if it's vacant?"

"It's on the house-meter, included in the rent. It stays on when they leave."

There was a fire-escape outside one pair of windows, but they were latched on the inside and you couldn't see the seams of the two halves any more through the coating of dust that had formed over them. I looked for and located the battery that gave juice to the downstairs doorbell. It had a big pouch of cobweb hanging from it, like a thin-skinned hornet's nest. I opened a closet and peered into it. A wire coat-hanger that had been teetering off-balance for heaven knows how long swung off the rod and fell down with a clash.

He kept saying: "Now listen, be sensible. What are you a child?"

I didn't care how it looked, I only knew how it felt. "Steffie," I said. I didn't call it any more, just said it. I went up close to him. He was something human, at least. I said, "What'll I do?" I speared my fingers through my hair, and lost my new hat, and let it lie.

He wasn't much help. He was still on that other, logical plane, and I had left it long ago. He tried to suggest we'd had a quarrel and she'd given me the slip; he tried to suggest I go to her home, I might find her there waiting for me.

"She didn't come *out* again, damn you!" I flared tormentedly. "If I'd been down at the corner – But I was right at the front door! What about the back way – is there a back way out?"

"Not a back way, a delivery-entrance, but that goes through the basement, right past my quarters. No one came down there, I was sitting there eating my supper the whole time."

And another good reason was, the stairs from the upper floors came down on one side of the elevator, in the front hall. Then they continued on down to the basement on the *other* side of it. To get down to there anyone would have to pass in front of the elevator, for its entire width. I'd been right out there on the other side of the glass vestibule-door, and no one had. So I didn't have to take his word for it. I had my own senses.

"Is there a Muller in the house anywhere at all?"

"No, no one by that name. We never had anyone by that name in the whole twelve years I been working here."

"Someone may have gotten in here and been lurking in the place when she came up—"

"It was locked, how could anyone? You saw me open it with the passkey."

"Come on, we're going to ask the rest of the tenants on this floor if they heard anything, saw her at all."

We made the rounds of the entire five flats. 4E came to the door in the person of a hatchet-faced elderly woman, who looked like she had a good nose – or ear – for the neighbors' activities. It was the adjoining flat to 4F, and it was our best bet. I knew if this one failed us, there wasn't much to hope for from the others.

"Did you hear anything next-door to you within the past half hour?" I asked her.

"How could I, it's empty," she said tartly.

"I know, but *did you hear anything* – like anyone walking around in there, the door opening or closing, voices, or—" I couldn't finish it. I was afraid to say "a scream." Afraid she'd say yes.

"Didn't hear a pin drop," she said, and slammed the door. Then she opened it again. "Yes I did, too. Heard the doorbell, the downstairs one, ringing away in there like fifty. With the place empty like it is, it sounded worse than a fire-alarm."

"That was me," I said, turning away disheartenedly.

As I'd expected after that, none of the others were any good either. No one had seen her, no one had heard anything out of the way.

I felt like someone up to his neck in a quicksand, and going down deeper every minute. "The one underneath," I said, yanking him toward the stairs. "3F! If there was anything to be heard, they'd get it quicker through their ceiling than these others would through their walls. Ceilings are thinner than walls."

He went down to the floor below with me and we rang. They didn't open. "Must be out, I guess," he muttered. He took his passkey, opened the door, called their name. They were out all right, no one answered. We'd drawn another blank.

He decided he'd strung along with me just about far enough – on what after all must have seemed to him to be a wild goose chase. "Well," he said, slapping his sides and turning up his palms expressively. Meaning, "Now why don't you go home like a good guy and leave me alone?"

I wasn't having any. It was like asking you to leave your right arm behind you, chopped off at the shoulder. "You go up and stick there by that empty flat. I'm going out and get a cop." It sounds firm enough on paper, it came out plenty shaky and sick. I bounded down the stairs. In the vestibule I stopped short, punched that same 4F bell. His voice sounded hollowly through the interviewer after a minute. "Yuss?"

"It's me. The bell works all right up there, does it?"

"Sure."

"Okay, stay there. I'll be right back." I didn't know what good that had done. I went on out, bareheaded.

The one I brought back with me wasn't anything to rave about on the score of native intelligence. It was no time to be choosey. All he kept saying all the way back to the house was "All right, take it easy." He was on the janitor's plane, and immediately I had two of them against me instead of one.

"You saw her go in, did ye?"

I controlled myself with an effort. "Yes."

"But you don't know for sure which floor she got off at?"

"She rang 4F, so I know she got off at the fourth —"

"Wait a minute, you didn't *see* her, did ye?"

"No, I didn't see her."

"That's all I wanted to know. You can't say for sure she went into this flat, and the man here says it's been locked up for months."

He rang every bell in every flat of the building and questioned the occupants. No one had seen such a girl. The pot-cheese lady with the little boy remembered having seen me, that was the closest he got to anything. And one other flat, on the fifth, reported a ring at their bell with no follow-up.

I quickly explained I'd done that, to gain admittance to the building.

Three out of the twenty-four occupancies in the building were out; 1B, 3C and 3F. He didn't pass them by either. Had the janitor passkey their doors and examined the premises. Not a trace of her anywhere.

That about ended his contribution. According to his lights he'd done a thorough job, I suppose. "All right," he said, "I'll phone it in for you, that's the most I can do."

God knows how he expressed it over the wire. A single plainclothesman was dropped off at the door a few minutes later, came in to where the three of us were grouped waiting in the inner lobby. He looked me over like he was measuring me for a new suit of clothes. He didn't say anything.

"Hello, Gilman," the cop said. "This young fellow says he brought a girl here, and she disappeared in there." Putting the burden of the proof on me, I noticed. "I ain't been able to find anyone that saw her with him," he added helpfully.

"Let's see the place," the dick said.

We all went up there again. He looked around. Better than I had, maybe, but just as unproductively. He paid particular attention to the windows. Every one of the six, two regular-size apiece for the two main rooms, one small one each for the bath and kitchenette, was latched on the inside. There was a thick veneer of dust all around the frames and in the finger-grips. You couldn't have grabbed them any place to hoist them without it showing. And it didn't. He studied the keyhole.

He finally turned to me and gave me the axe. "There's nothing to show that she – or anyone else – ever came in here, bud."

"She rang the bell of this flat, and someone released the doorcatch for her from up here." I was about as steady as jello in a high wind about it. I was even beginning to think I could see a ghost in the corner.

"We're going to check on that right now," he said crisply. "There's already one false ring accounted for, attributable to you. What we want is to find out if there was a second one registered, anywhere in the building."

We made the rounds again, all twenty-four flats. Again the fifth-floor flat reported my spiked ring – and that was all. No one else had experienced any, for the past twenty-four hours or more. And the fifth-floor party had only gotten the one, not two.

That should have been a point in my favor: she hadn't rung any of the other flats and been admitted from them, therefore she must have rung 4F and been admitted from there – as I claimed. Instead he seemed to twist it around to my discredit: she hadn't rung any of the other flats and been admitted from them, and since there could have been no one in 4F to hear her ring and admit her from there, she hadn't rung any bell at all, she hadn't been admitted at all, she hadn't been with me at all. I was a wack. Which gave me a good push in the direction of being one, in itself.

I was in bad shape by now. I started to speak staccato. "Say listen, don't do this to me, will you? You all make it sound like she didn't come here with me at all."

He gave me more of the axe. "That's what it does sound like to us."

I turned northeast, east, east-by-south, like a compass on a binge. Then I turned back to him again. "Look." I took the show-tickets out of my pocket, held them toward him with a shaky wrist. "I was going to take her to a show tonight —"

He waved them aside. "We're going to build this thing from the ground up first and see what we've got. You say her name is Stephanie Riska." I didn't like that "you say." "Address?"

"120 Farragut."

"What'd she look like?"

I should have known better than to start in on that. It brought her before me too plainly. I got as far as "She comes up to here next to me —" Then I stopped again.

The cop and janitor looked at me curiously, like they'd never seen a guy cry before. I tried to turn my head the other way, but they'd already seen the leak.

The dick seemed to be jotting down notes, but he squeezed out a grudging "Don't let it get you," between his eye-tooth and second molar while he went ahead doing it.

I said: "I'm not scared because she's gone. I'm scared because she's gone in such a fairy-tale way. I can't get a grip on it. Like when they sprinkle a pinch of magic powder and make them disappear in thin air. It's got me all loose in the joints, and my guts are rattling against my backbone, and I believe in ghosts all over again."

My spiritual symptoms didn't cut any ice with him. He went right ahead with the business at hand. "And you met her at 6:15 outside the Bailey-Goodwin Building, you say, with a package to be delivered here. Who'd she work for?"

"A press-clipping service called the Green Star; it's a one-man organization, operated by a guy named Hessen. He just rented one dinky little rear room, on the ground floor of the Bailey-Goodwin Building."

"What's that?"

"I don't know myself. She tried to explain it to me once. They keep a list of clients' names, and then they sift through the papers, follow them up. Any time one of the names appears, in connection with any social activity or any kind of mention at all, they clip the item out, and when they've got enough of them to make a little batch, they send them to the client, ready for mounting in a scrap-book. The price for the service is about five bucks a hundred, or something like that."

"How is there any coin in that?" he wanted to know.

"I don't know myself, but she was getting twenty-two a week."

"All right. Now let's do a little checking." He took me back with him to where she worked, first of all. The building was dead, of course, except one or two offices, doing night-work on the upper floors. He got the night-watchman, showed his credentials, and had him open up the little one-room office and let us in.

I'd never been in the place myself until now. I'd always waited for her outside at the street-entrance at closing time. I don't think it was even intended for an office in the first place; it was more like a chunk of left-over storage-space. It didn't even have a window at all, just an elongated vent up near the ceiling, with a blank shaft-wall about two feet away from it.

There was a flat-topped desk taking up one side, his I guess, with a phone on it and a wire paper-basket and nothing else. And a smaller-size "desk," this time a real table and not a desk at all, with nothing on it at all. The rest was just filing cabinets. Oh yeah, and a coat-rack. He must have been getting it for a song.

"What a telephone-booth," remarked the dick.

He looked in the filing-cabinets; they were just alphabetized names, with a scattering of newspaper-clippings distributed among them. Some of the names they didn't have any clippings for, and some of the letters they didn't even have any clients for – and I don't mean only X.

"There's about a hundred bucks' worth of clippings in the whole kitty," Gilman said, "at your own estimate of what the charge was." He didn't follow up with what he meant by that, and I was too worried about her to pay any attention to his off-side remarks. The only thing that meant anything to me was, there was nothing around the place to show him that she had ever worked here or even been here in her life. Nothing personalized, I mean. The single drawer of the little table just had a pair of shears for clipping and a pot of paste for mounting, and a stack of little salmon-colored paper mounts.

The night-watchman couldn't corroborate me, because the place was always locked up by the time he came on-shift. And the elevator-runners that worked the building in the daytime wouldn't have been able to either, I knew, even if they'd been on hand, because this hole-in-the-wall was on a branch-off of the main entrance-corridor, she didn't have to pass the cars on her way in from or out to the street, so they'd probably never seen her the whole time she'd worked here.

The last thing he did, after he'd gotten Hessen's name and address, which was readily available in the place itself, was to open a penknife and cut a notch from the under-side of the small table. At least, it looked like he was doing that from what I could see, and he kept his back to me and didn't offer any explanation. He thumbed me at the door and said, "Now we'll go out there and hear what he has to say." His tone held more of an eventual threat in it toward me than toward her employer though, I couldn't help noticing.

It was a bungalow-type place on the outskirts, and without being exactly a mansion, it wasn't low-cost housing. You walked up flat stones to get to the door, and it had dwarf Japanese fir-trees dotted all around it.

"Know him?" he said while we were waiting.

"By sight," I swallowed. I had a feeling of that quicksand I'd been bogging into ever since she'd left me in the lobby at Martine Street, being up to my eyes now and getting ready to close over the top of my head. This dick mayn't have taken sides yet, but that was the most you could say; he certainly wasn't on my side.

A guy with a thin fuzz on his head, who looked like he belonged to some unhealthy nationality nobody ever heard of before, opened the door, stepped in to announce us, came back and showed us in, all in fast time.

A typewriter was clicking away busily somewhere near at hand, and I thought it was him first, her boss, but it wasn't. He was smoking a porcelain-bowled pipe and reading a book under a lamp. Instead of closing the book, he just put his finger down on the last word he'd read to keep his place, so he could go right ahead as soon as this was over with. He was tall and lean, with good features, and dark hair cut so short it just about came out of his scalp and then stopped.

Gilman said: "Did you ever see this young fellow before?"

He eyed me. He had a crease under one eye; it wasn't a scar so much as an indentation from digging in some kind of rimless glass. "No-o," he said with a slow benevolence. A ghost of a smile pulled at his mouth. "What's he done?"

"Know anyone named Muller, at 415 Martine Street?" There hadn't been any Muller in the filing-cabinets at the office.

"No-o, I don't know anyone by that name there or anywhere else. I think we have a Miller, a Mrs. Elsie Miller on our list, who all the time divorces and marries. Will that do?" He sighed tolerantly. "She owes us twenty-nine dollars."

"Then you didn't send a package over to Muller, Apartment 4F, 415 Martine Street, at 6:15 this evening?"

"No," he said again, as evenly as the other two times. I started forward spasmodically. Gilman braked me with a cut of his hand. "I'm sure I didn't. But wait, it is easy enough to confirm that." He raised his voice slightly, without being boorish about it. And right there in front of me, right there in the room with me, he called – "Stephanie. Stephanie Riska, would you mind coming in here a moment?"

The clicking of the typewriter broke off short and a chair scraped in the next room. "Steffie," I said huskily, and swallowed past agony, and the sun came up around me and it wasn't night any more, and the bad dream was over.

"My assistant happens to be right here at the house tonight; I had some dictation to give her and she is transcribing it. We usually mail out clippings however, only when there is an urgent request do I send them around by personal messen —"

"Yes sir?" a velvety contralto said from the doorway.

I missed some of the rest of it. The lights took a half-turn to the right, streaking tracks across the ceiling after them like comet-tails, before they came to a stop and stood still again. Gilman reached over and pulled me up short by the coatsleeve, as though I'd been flopping around loose in my shoes or something.

She was saying, "No, I don't believe I do," in answer to something he had asked her, and looking straight over at me. She was a brunette of an exotic foreign type, and she came up as high as me, and the sun had gone out again and it was night all over again.

"That isn't Steffie!" I bayed. "He's calling somebody else by her name!"

The pupils of Hessen's eyes never even deflected toward me. He arched his brows at Gilman. "That is the only young lady I have working for me."

Gilman was holding me back with sort of a half-nelson. Or half a half-nelson. The brunette appeared slightly agitated by my outburst, no more. She hovered there uncertainly in the doorway, as though not knowing whether to come in or go out.

"How long have you been working for Mr. Hessen?" Gilman asked her.

"Since October of last year. About eight months now."

"And your name is Stephanie Riska?"

She smiled rebukingly, as if at the gratuitousness of such a question. "Yes, of course." She decided to come a little further forward into the room. But she evidently felt she needed some moral support to do so. She'd brought a small black handbag with her, tucked under her arm, when she left the typewriter. She opened it, so that the flap stood up toward Gilman and me, and plumbed in it for something. The two big gold-metal initials were so easy to read, even upside-down; they were thick, bold Roman capitals, *S.R.* The bag looked worn, as though she'd had it a long time. I could sense, rather than see, Gilman's mind's eye turned accusingly toward me: "What about it now?" though his physical ones were fastened on the bag.

She got what she was looking for out of it, and she got more than she was looking for. She brought up a common ordinary stick of chewing-gum in tin-foil, but she also accidentally brought up an envelope with it, which slipped through her fingers to the floor. She was very adroitly awkward, to coin a phrase.

Gilman didn't exactly dive for it, but he managed to get his fingers on it a half-inch ahead of hers. "Mind?" he said. I read the address on it with glazed eyes, over his shoulder. It had been postmarked and sent through the mail. "Miss Stephanie Riska, 120 Farragut Street." He stripped the contents out of it and read the single sheet of notepaper. Then he gravely handed it back. Again I could feel his mind's eye on me.

She had broken the stick of chewing-gum in half, put part between her lips, and the rest she was preparing to wrap up in tin-foil again for some other time. She evidently didn't like to chew too much at a time.

Gilman absently thumbed a vest-pocket as though he would have liked some too. She noticed that. "May I offer you some?" she said gravely.

"I wish you would, my mouth's kind of dry." He put the second half-piece in his own trap. "And you didn't deliver a package for Mr. Hessen at 415 Martine Street this evening?" he said around it.

"No, sir, I did not. I'm afraid I don't even know where Martine Street is."

That about concluded the formalities. And we were suddenly outside again, him and me, alone. In the dark. It was dark for me, anyway. All he said when we got back in the car was:: "This 'girl' of yours, what kind of gum did she habitually chew, wintergreen or licorice or what have you?"

What could I tell him but the truth? "She didn't use gum, she detested the habit."

He just looked at me. Then he took the nugget he'd mooched from the brunette out of his mouth, and he took a little piece of paper out of his pocket that held another dab in it, and he compared them – by scent. "I scraped this off that desk in the office, and it's the same as what she gave me just now. Tutti-frutti. Not a very common flavor in chewing-gum. She belongs in that office, she parked her gum there. She had a letter addressed to herself in her handbag, and the initials on the outside checked. What's your racket, kid? Are you a pushover for mental observation? Or are you working off a grudge against this guy? Or did *you* do something to some little blonde blue-eyed number and are you trying to pass the buck in this way before we even found out about it?"

It was like a ton of bricks had landed all over my dome. I held my head with both hands to keep it in one piece and leaned way over toward the floor and said, "My God!"

He got me by the slack of the collar and snapped me back so viciously it's a wonder my neck didn't break.

"Things like this don't happen," I groaned. "They can't. One minute all mine, the next she isn't anywhere. And no one'll believe me."

"You haven't produced a single person all evening long that actually laid eyes on this 'blonde girl' of yours," he said hard as flint. "Nowhere, d'you understand?"

"Where'd I get the name from then, the address?"

He looked at me when I said that. "I'll give you one more spin for your money. You stand or fall by the place she lived." He leaned forward and he said "120 Farragut" to the driver. Then he kept eyeing me like he was waiting for me to break down and admit it was a hoax or I'd done something to her myself, whoever she was.

Once he said, "Remember, this girl at his place had a letter, three days old, addressed to *her*, giving this same address we're heading for now. If you still want to go through with it . . ."

"I took her home there," I said.

"Parents?"

"No, it's a rooming-house. She was from Harrisburg. But the landlady – He —" Then I went, "O-oh," and let my head loll limply back against the back of the seat. I'd just remembered he'd recommended the place to her.

He was merciless, noticed everything. "D'ye still want to make it there – or d'ye want to make it Headquarters? And the tougher you are with me, the tougher I'm going to be with you, buddy." And his fist knotted up and his eyes iced over.

It was a case of self-preservation now. We were only minutes away. "Listen. Y'gotta listen to me. She took me up one night, just for a minute, to lend me a magazine she had in the room. Y'gotta listen to this, for heaven's sake. Sticking in the mirror of the dresser she's got a litho of the Holy Mother. On the radiator she's got a rag doll that I won for her at Coney Island." I split open my collar in front trying to bring it all back. "On a little shelf against the wall she's got a gas-ring, with a tube rubbing up to the jet. From the light-fixture to that jet there runs a string, and she'll have stockings hanging from it to dry. Are you listening? Will you remember these things? Don't you see I *couldn't* make all these things up? Don't you see she's *real*?"

"You almost persuade me," he said half under his breath. Which was a funny thing coming from a detective. And then we got there.

We stepped down and went in. "Now if you open your mouth," he said to me, teeth interlocked, "and say one word the whole time we're in here, I'll split your lip so wide open you'll be able to spit without opening your mouth." He sent for the landlady. I'd never seen her before. "Y'got a girl named Stephanie Riska living in your house?"

"Yep. Fourth-floor front." That was right.

"How long?"

"Riska?" She took a tuck in her cheek. "She's been rooming with me now six months." That was right too.

"I want to know what she looks like." He took a wicked half-turn in my arm that dammed up the blood.

"Dark hair, sort of dark skin. About as tall as this young fellow you got with you. She talks kind of husky."

"I want to see her room. I'm the police." He had to practically support me all the way up the four flights of stairs.

She threw open a door, gave it the switch. I came back to life enough to open my eyes. On the mirror, no picture. On the radiator, no rag doll.

On the shelf no gas-ring, but a row of books. The jet had no tube plugged in, was soldered-over with lead. No string led from it to the light. No nothing.

"Has she always had it fixed this way?" Gilman asked.

"Always since the first day she's here. She' a real clean roomer, only one thing I got to complain about – There it is again." She went over to the washstand and removed a little nugget of grayish substance that had been plastered to the underside of it. But she smiled indulgently, as though one such peccadillo were permissible.

Gilman took it from her on a scrap of paper, shifted it from left to right across his face. "Tutti-frutti," he said.

"Look out, you better hold your friend!" she exclaimed in sharp alarm.

He swung me so that instead of going down flat, I landed against him and stayed up. "Let him fold," he said to her. "That isn't anything to the falls he's going to be taking five or ten minutes from now." And we started down the stairs again, with two pairs of workable feet between the three of us.

"What'd he do, *murder* her?" she breathed avidly on the way down.

"Not her, but I got a good hunch he murdered someone – and picked the wrong name out of a hat."

She went: "Tsk-tsk-tsk-tsk. He don't *look* like —"

I saw some rheumatic lodger's knotty walking-stick up-ended out of a brass umbrella-stand at the foot of the stairs. As he marched me by, I was on that side, luckily. I let my right arm fall behind us instead of in front of us where it had been – he didn't have me handcuffed yet, remember – and the curved handle of the stick caught in my hand, and it came up out of the holder after me.

Then I swung it and beaned him like no dick was ever beaned before. He didn't go down, he just staggered sidewise against the wall and went, "Uff!"

She was bringing up in the rear. She went, "Oh!" and jumped back. I cleared the front steps at a bound. I went "Steffie! Steffie!" and I beat it away in the dark. I didn't know where I was going and I didn't care, I only knew I had to find her. I came out so fast the driver of the headquarters-car we'd left at the door wasn't expecting me. I'd already flashed around the corner below before his belated "Hey, you!" came winging after me.

I made for the Martine Street flat. That was instinctive: the place I'd last seen her, calling me back. Either the car didn't start right up after me or I shook it off in my erratic zigzag course through the streets. Anyway I got there still unhindered.

I ganged up on the janitor's bell, my windpipe making noises like a stuffed drainpipe. I choked, "Steffie!" a couple of times to the mute well-remembered vestibule around me. I was more demented than sane by now. Gilman was slowly driving me into the condition he'd already picked for me ahead of time.

The janitor came up with a sweater over his nightshirt. He said, "You again? What is it – didn't you find her yet? What happened to the other fellow that was with you?"

"He sent me back to take another look," I said craftily. "You don't have to come up, just gimme the passkey."

He fell for it, but killed a couple of valuable minutes going down to get it again. But I figured I was safe for the night; that it was my own place, across town, Gilman would make a beeline for.

I let myself in and lit it up and started looking blindly all around – for what I didn't know, where a professional detective had been over this ground once already and gotten nothing. The story-book ending, I kept looking for the story-book ending, some magic clue that would pop up and give her back to me. I went around on my hands and knees, casing the cracks between the floorboards; I tested the walls for secret panels (in a $50-a-month flat!); I dug out plaster with my bare nails where there was a hole, thinking I'd find a bullet, but it was only a mouse-hole.

I'd been in there about ten minutes when I heard a subtle noise coming up the hall-stairs outside. I straightened to my feet, darted through the door, ran down the hall to the stairs. Gilman was coming up, like thunder 'cross the China Bay, with a cop and the janitor at his heels. It was the fool janitor's carpet-slippers, which had no heelgrip, that were making more noise than the other two's shoes put together. Gilman had tape on the back of his skull and a gun in his hand. "He's up there now," the janitor was whispering. "I let him in about ten minutes ago; he said you sent him."

I sped up the stairs for the roof, the only way that was open to me now. That gave me away to them, and Gilman spurted forward with a roar. "Come down here you, I'll break every bone in your body! You won't live to get to Headquarters!" The roof-stairs ended in a skylight-door that I just pushed through, although it should have been latched on the inside. There was about a yard-high partition-wall dividing the roof from the next one over. I tried to clear it too fast, miscalculated, and went down in a mess, tearing a hole in my trouser-knee and skinning my own knee beneath. That leg wouldn't work right for a minute or two after that, numb, and before I could get upright again on it and stumble away, they were out on me. A big splatter of white shot ahead of me on the gravelled roof from one of their torches, and Gilman gave what can only be described as an Iroquois war-whoop and launched himself through space in a flying tackle. He landed crushingly across my back, flattening me a second time.

And then suddenly the rain of blows that I'd expected was held in check, and he just lay inert on top of me, doing nothing. We both saw it at the same time, lying on the roof there a few yards ahead of us, momentarily played up by the cop's switching torch, then lost again. I could recognize it because I'd seen it before. *The package that she'd brought over here tonight.*

"Hold that light steady!" Gilman bellowed, and got off of me. We both got over to it at the same time, enmity forgotten. He picked it up, tore open the brown paper around it, and a sheaf of old newspapers slowly flattened themselves out. With squares and oblongs scissored out of them here and there. She hadn't been sent over with clippings, but with the valueless remnants of papers after the clippings had already been taken out. It was a dummy package, a decoy, used to send her to her – disappearance.

The rest of it went double-quick – or seemed to. It had built up slow; it unraveled fast.

"Someone did bring a package here tonight, kid," was the way he put it. "And if I give you that much, I'll give you the whole thing on credit alone, no matter what the odds still outstanding against it are. Blonde, really named Stephanie Riska, works for Hessen, lives at 120 Farragut, *never* chews gum, and all the rest of it. Come on. My theory in a pinch would be she was jumped from behind outside the door of that vacant flat before she had a chance to cry out, spirited up over this roof, down through the next house and into a waiting car – while you hugged the vestibule below. Calhoun, call in and have someone get out there fast to Hessen's house, Myrtle Drive, and keep it spotted until we can get out there. I want to take another crack at that office first."

On the way over I gasped, "D'you think they —?"

"Naw, not yet," he reassured me. "Or they would have done it right in the empty flat and let you take the rap." Whether he meant it or not I couldn't tell, so it didn't relieve me much."

The second knot came out in the office. I went over the little table she'd used, while he turned the filing-cabinets inside-out. Again our two discoveries came almost simultaneously. "Look!" I breathed. It was stuck in a crack in the floor, hidden by the shadow of the table. A gilt hairpin she must have dropped one time at her work. Such as no brunette like the one Hessen had showed us at his house would have ever used in her life. "Blonde, all right," he grunted, and tipped me to his own find. "I muffed this before, in my hurry: about every third name in this card-index of 'clients' has a foreign mailing-address. Neutral countries, like Switzerland and Holland. Why should they be interested in social items appearing in papers over here? The mere fact that they're not living here shows the items couldn't possibly refer to them personally. If you ask me, the guy's an espionage-agent of some kind, and these 'clippings' are some kind of a code. With a scattering of on-the-level ones interspersed, to cover up. But that's a job for the FBI. I'm only interested in this girl of yours. My lieutenant can notify their local office about the rest of it, if he sees fit.

"The second leg of my theory," he went on, as we beat it out of there fast, "is she found out something, and they figured she was too dangerous to them. Did she say anything to you like that?"

"Not a word. But she had told him she was quitting end of next week to get married."

"Well, then she *didn't* find out anything, but he thought she did, so it amounted to the same thing. He could not afford to let her quit. And did he cover up beautifully, erase her existence! They only slipped up on that package. Maybe some tenant came up on the roof to take down her wash, before they could come back and pick it up, so they had to leave it there, rather than risk being identified later. Come on, we'll stop off at that rooming-house on the way, I want that landlady picked up. She's obviously one of them, since he recommended the girl there as a lodger in the beginning. Changed the whole room around, even to sticking a wad of tutti-frutti gum on the washstand."

"Let's go," I cried.

A second knot came out at the rooming-house, but it was simply a duplicate of the one at her office: confirmation of the color of her hair. "A girl shampoos her hair once in a while," he said to me, and stuck a matchstick down the drain of the washbasin. He spread something on a piece of paper, showed it to me: two unmistakably blonde hairs. "Now why didn't I think of that the first time?" He turned the steel-plated landlady over to a cop to be sent in, and we were on our way again – this time out to the Myrtle Drive house, fast.

There was no sign of the guy he'd sent out ahead of us to keep it cased, and he swore under his breath, while my heart deflated. The place was dark and lifeless, but neither of us was foolish enough to believe they'd gone to bed yet. He took the front door and I took the back, with a gun he furnished me – he was on my side now, don't forget. We blew the locks simultaneously and met in the middle of the hall that ran through the place. In three minutes we were downstairs again. Nothing was disturbed, but the birds had flown; suave Hessen, and the butler, and the pinch-hitting brunette. No incriminating papers, but a very incriminating short-wave set. Incriminating because of the place it was located. It was built into the overhead water-tank of a dummy toilet, not meant to hold water or be used. Gilman made the discovery in the most natural way possible.

"Spy-ring, all right," he grunted, and phoned in then and there from the place itself.

That wasn't getting me back Steffie. I was in such a blue funk that I didn't notice it as soon as I should have; I mean, something had seemed to tickle my nostrils unpleasantly the whole time we were in there. It only registered *after* I came out into the open again with him, and we stood there crestfallen in front of it. Before I could call his attention to it, headlights slashed through the dark and a car drew up in front.

We crouched back, but it was only the spotter that was supposed to have been hung up there before. Gilman rushed him with a roar. "What the hell's the idea? You were supposed to —"

"I tailed 'em!" the guy insisted. "They piled into a car, locked up the house, and lit. I tailed 'em the whole way, those were the only orders I got!"

"Where'd they go?"

"Pier 07, North river. They boarded some kind of a fuzzy tramp-steamer, and it shoved off in less than a quarter of an hour later. I tried to reach you at Head —"

"Was there a blonde girl with them?" Gilman rapped out.

"No, just the three that were in the house here when I first made contact; the two men and a dark-haired girl. There was no one else smuggled aboard ahead of them either; I pumped one of the crew —"

Meanwhile, my heart's eight lives had died, and its ninth was wearing thin. "They're out of our reach now," I groaned, "we'll never —"

"Oh no they're not," Gilman promised viciously. "They may have cleared the pier; a police-launch can pull them off again at Quarantine." He spilled in the house again, to phone in the alarm.

I went after him; that was when I again noticed that unpleasant tickling. I called his attention to it when he got through on the wire. "Don't it smell as though they've had this place fumigated or some —"

He twitched the end of his nose. Then his face got drab. "That's gasoline!" he snapped. "And when you smell it that heavy – indoors like this – it's not a good sign!" I could tell he was plenty scared all at once – which made me twice as scared as he was. "Bill!" he hollered to the other guy. "Come in here fast and give us a hand! That girl they *didn't* take with them must be still around these premises someplace, and I only hope she isn't —"

He didn't finish it; he didn't have to. He only hoped she wasn't dead yet. I wasn't much good to them, in the sudden mad surge of ferreting they blew into. I saw them dimly, rustling around, through a sick haze.

He and I had been over the house once already – the upper part of it – so they found the right place almost at once. The basement. A hoarse cry from Gilman brought myself and the other guy down there after him. I couldn't go all the way, went into a paralysis half-way down the stairs. She was wedged down out of sight between two trunks, she'd been loosely covered over with sacking. I saw them lifting her up between them, and she carried awfully inert.

"Tell me now," I said, "don't wait until you get her —" I waited for the axe to fall.

"She's alive, kid," Gilman said. "Her chest's straining against the ropes they've got around —" Then he broke off, said to the other guy, "Don't stop to look at her now, hurry up out of here with her! Don't you hear that ticking down around here someplace, don't you know what that gasoline-reek means —?"

I was alive again; I jumped in to help them, and we got her up and out of the cursed place fast. So fast we were almost running with her.

We untied her out by the car. She was half-dead with fright, but they hadn't done anything to her, just muffled her up. The other guy wanted to go back in again and see if they could locate the bomb, but Gilman stopped him. "You'll never make it, it'll blow before you —"

He was right. In the middle of what he was saying, the whole house seemed to lift a half-foot above its foundations, it lit up all lurid inside, there was a roar, and in a matter of minutes flame was mushrooming out of all the lower-story windows.

"An incendiary-bomb," Gilman said. "Turn in a fire-alarm, Bill, that's about all we can do now." He went off someplace to use a phone, and when he came back some time later, he had a mean face. A face I wouldn't have wanted to run up against on a dark night. I thought he'd heard bad news. He had – but not for us. "They got 'em," he said. "Yanked 'em off it just as the tub was clearing the Narrows. They're earmarked for the FBI, but before we turn them over, I wouldn't be surprised if they show wear and tear – She *is* pretty at that, kid."

She was sitting there in the car by now, talking to me and crying a little. I was standing on the outside of it. I was standing up, that was my mistake.

"Well, I gotta go," I heard him say. And then something hit me. It felt like a cement-mixer.

Our roles changed. When my head cleared, she was the one bending over me, crooning sympathetically. "— and he said to tell you, No hard feelings, but when anyone socks Dick Gilman on the head with a walking-stick, they get socked back even if they're the best of friends. And he said he'd see us both down at Headquarters later in the night, to be sure and get there on time if we don't want to miss the fun."

I was still seeing stars, but I didn't care, I was seeing her too. And now it was only twelve days off, we'd licked the thirteenth.

Speak To Me of Death

A slick-looking roadster stopped in front of Headquarters at about nine that night, and its lone occupant sat there in it for a moment before cutting the ignition, as if trying to make up her mind what to do. The car had money written all over it, money without flash. The number was so low it was almost zero. The girl in it took a cigarette out of the box fitted to the door, pulled a patented lighter out of the dash, inhaled deeply as if to brace herself. Then she got out and went up the steps between the two dark-green lights.

She was tall and slim and young. She wore a little leopard-skin jacket that didn't come below her elbows. The price of it probably ran into three figures. Her face was pale, paler than powder could have made it. At the top of the steps she took a second and final drag. Then she dropped the cigarette, stepped on it, and went in. She asked to see the lieutenant in charge.

His name was McManus and he brought a chair forward with his own hands for her in the back room. She was that kind of a girl.

She said, "My name is Ann Bridges." Then she looked down at the floor. You could see her wrists were trembling, where she held them folded over one knee. Diamond-splinters flashed around her wrist-watch from the slight vibration.

"Any relative of John T. Bridges?" McManus said.

Ann Bridges looked up again. "I'm his niece," she said. "In fact his only relative." She took it in her stride, said it almost off-handedly. To McManus it was a stunning piece of information; it was like finding yourself in the same room with the heir-apparent to a throne. He never thought of doubting her. There was something 14-karat about her that couldn't have been faked.

She said, "It isn't the pleasantest thing in the world to come to the police like this —" she broke off abruptly. Then she went ahead: "I don't even know what there is you people can do about it. But something's got to be done —"

McManus' voice was kind. "You tell me what it is."

"That's the worse part of it. It doesn't sound like anything when you tell it. Anything at all. But it is something!" Her voice rose almost to the point of hysteria. "I can't just stand by and watch him – sink into the grave before my eyes! I *had* to tell somebody – *had* to get it off my chest! I've waited too long as it is!" Her eyes misted. "I've driven down here four nights in a row – and the first three times I lost my nerve, drove on around the block without stopping. I said to myself, 'Ann, they'll think you're crazy, Ann, they'll laugh at you —'"

McManus went over to her and rested a fatherly hand on her shoulder. "We don't laugh at people," he said gently. "We run across anything and everything, in our line – but we don't laugh at people who are in trouble." It wasn't because she was Ann Bridges; it was because she was so young and lovely and there was such distress written on her face.

"Something has hold of us," she said. "Something that started in by being nothing at all, by being just a joke over the luncheon table; something that's grown and grown, until now it's like an octopus throttling us. I can't name it to you, because I don't know what to call it, don't know what it is. It threatens him, not me, but you see I love him, and so the threat is to the two of us."

She gave a little sob deep in her throat.

"Call it a prophecy, call it a prediction, call it fate – call it what you will. I fought against it hard enough, God knows. But the evidence of my own eyes, my own ears, my own senses, is too much for me. And the time's too short now. I'm afraid to take a chance. I haven't got the nerve to bluff it out, to sit pat. You don't gamble with a human life. Today's the 13th, isn't it? It's too close to the 14th; there isn't time-margin enough left now to be skeptical, to keep it to myself any longer. Day by day I've watched him cross off the date on his desk-calendar, drawing nearer to death. There are only two leaves left now, and I want help! Because on the 14th – at the exact stroke of midnight, as the 15th is beginning —"

She covered her face with both arms and shook silently.

"Yes?" urged McManus. "Yes?"

"He's become convinced – oh, and almost I have too – that at exactly midnight on the 14th he's to die. Not just die but meet his death in full vigor and health, a death rushing down to him from the stars he was born under – rushing down even before he existed at all. A death inexorable, inescapable. A death horrid and violent, inconceivable here in this part of the world where we live."

She took a deep, shuddering breath, whispered the rest of it. "*Death at the jaws of a lion.*"

McManus didn't answer for an awfully long time. When he spoke, it wasn't to her at all. He opened the door, called to someone, said, "I'm not to be disturbed – until further orders, hear?"

When he came back to her she said limply, "Thanks – for not laughing, for not smelling my breath, for not hinting that I should see a doctor. Oh, thanks, anyway!"

He took a package of cigarettes out of the desk-drawer, passed them to her. "I know you modern kids," he said paternally. "Smoke up. Pull yourself together. Tell it in your own way. Begin at the beginning – and tell it right straight through —"

It all started (Ann Bridges said) about an airplane ride. My Uncle John was going to 'Frisco on business, and he'd bought his ticket. He showed it to me at lunch, and I saw that the take-off was dated Friday the 13th. Half-kiddingly I suggested he put off leaving until the day after. There'd been a bad crack-up a week before, but lord! we were both joking, not serious about it.

My maid must have overheard us. She came to me later and said, "Beg your pardon, miss, but if that were I, I'd never let him do a thing like that."

I said, "Be your age."

She said, "I know of someone who could warn you, if there is to be any trouble. A man who's gifted with second sight. Why don't you let me take you to him?"

I gave her a cold look and I said, "Just what do I look like to you? Are you seriously suggesting that I go to some flea-bitten fortune-teller with a dirty cloth wrapped around his head and —"

"He's not a fortune-teller," she defended. "He'd resent being called that. He doesn't make a profession of it, and he doesn't take money for it."

"I bet he doesn't refuse it, either," I said cynically.

"He's a good man," she said stoutly, "not a sharper of any kind. He happens to be born with this gift, he can't help that. He doesn't trade on it in any way, in fact he doesn't like to use it. My family and I have known him for years —"

I smiled to myself, as anyone would have. "He's certainly sold himself to you, Elaine," I remarked.

"We won't talk any more about it, miss," she said stiffly. "Only, you remember that time I was in trouble —" She'd got mixed up with some man, and I'd straightened it out for her; it wouldn't be fair for me to give you the details. "You were the only one who knew about that, Miss Bridges. I didn't say a word at home, I didn't dare. He took me aside one night and told me the whole thing. He told me how it was going to end up, too. He said the man was going to meet death, and I'd be rid of him once and for all. I fainted dead away on the floor. You remember how we heard two months later he'd been run over on the street?"

I did, but my skepticism wouldn't dent much. "You didn't say a word to me at the time, how was that?"

"He made me promise not to. I've broken my word to him today. He doesn't want it to become known. He hates his gift himself, says it causes him nothing but misery —"

All of which sounded reasonable enough, but I was definitely not impressed. I've had very good common sense all my life, and you have to watch your step – when you own twenty millions.

My uncle took off from Newark early the next morning, and when I got back to the house the maid blurted out: "There's nothing to worry about, Miss Bridges. I – I asked him about this trip, and he said it was safe to make it."

"Oh, you did, did you?" I said severely. "And who told you to?"

"I didn't tell him who it was or anything about it. Just asked him about this morning's plane," she defended. "But Mr. Bridges needn't have gone at all, could have saved himself the trouble. He told me that whoever this party is that's going out there, he or she is doomed to disappointment; nothing will come of it, he'll just have wasted his time."

My uncle's in the import and export business; he'd gone to see about an important consignment of silk from Japan, but the maid couldn't have known that, much less this seer of hers. I'm afraid I snickered rudely right in her face.

Nothing daunted, she rushed on: "But don't let Mr. John come back by air, Miss Bridges, whatever you do! Wire him to take the train instead. The eastbound plane *is* going to run into trouble – he saw it clearly. Not a crack-up, but it's going to be grounded somewhere in the Rockies and half of them are going to die of exposure before they're located. He saw snow piled all around it and people with frozen hands and feet having to have them amputated later —"

I blew up. I said, "One more word out of you, and I'll give you your week's notice!"

She didn't open her mouth from then on, just went around looking sorry for me.

Uncle John had told me he was starting back the following Saturday. Take-off was at seven Pacific Coast Time, ten back here. I'll admit I got a little worried Friday night, wondered whether or not I oughtn't to send that wire after all. I was afraid he'd laugh at me. More than that even, I hated to give in to her after the way I'd talked. I went to bed without sending the wire. It was too late when I woke up in the morning, he would have started already.

He should have got in about noon Sunday. I drove to the airport to meet him, and he wasn't on the plane. That gave me a nasty turn. I asked at the airport-office, and they told me he'd booked a seat from Chicago east, along with several other people, on this one, and none of them had shown up to make the connection; the 'Frisco plane had been overdue when they left Chicago.

I went home plenty worried. It was in the papers and on the radio already, reported missing somewhere over the Rockies with fourteen people in it!

The maid saw how I was taking it, so finally she came out with: "I suppose I'm discharged, but I knew better than you – I took the liberty of sending Mr. John a wire over your name last night, begging him to come by train instead —"

Discharged? I could have kissed her! But then anxiety raised its head again. "He's stubborn, he'd never listen to a message like that —"

"I – I told him that one of his associates wanted to consult him about a very important matter, and mentioned a place where the planes don't stop, so he'd have to take a train. *He* says," she went on, "that it won't be found for three days, the plane. It wouldn't have meant death, it isn't Mr. John's time yet, but he would have lost both feet and been a helpless cripple for the rest of his —"

All of which evoked a pretty creepy feeling in me. It wasn't helped any when my uncle got off the train three days later, safe and sound. The first words out of his mouth were that he'd made the trip for nothing: a maritime strike had broken out on the Coast and his silk-shipment was tied up indefinitely at Honolulu; he hadn't been able to accomplish a thing.

The snow-bound plane was sighted from the air later that same day, and when the rescue-parties got to it, seven of the fourteen were dead from exposure, and several of the survivors had to have their hands or feet amputated as soon as they got them to a hospital. Just as *he'd* foretold – rescue-date, circumstances, number of casualties, and all! It was uncanny. I didn't want to believe, I fought like anything against believing – and yet there it was.

I told my uncle the whole story of course – who wouldn't have? – and he was as impressed as I was. What we did next was what anyone else would have done after what had happened. We asked the maid to take the two of us to this man, we wanted to see him for ourselves. She wasn't to tell him who we were, just two friends of hers. I even put on an old coat and hat of hers, to look properly working-class, and we left the car home, went there on foot.

It was a big let-down, at first. This fortune-teller was merely a middle-aged man sitting in a furnished-room with his suspenders hanging down! His name was Jeremiah Tompkins, about as unimpressive a name as they come. And worst of all, he was just a bookkeeper. Had been, rather, for he wasn't working just then. If I remember correctly, he was reading the want ads in a newspaper when we came in.

I could see my uncle was more disappointed; he was almost resentful. After all, Uncle John is a levelheaded, intelligent businessman. That a figure like this should be able to spout prophecies, should know more than he did himself about what was going to happen to him, was too much for him to swallow.

"Watch," he said to me out of the corner of his mouth. "I'll show you.

I'll show you he's just a phony, that all this was just a coincidence. I've got something here that's the best little miracle-eraser in the world!"

And he took out five hundred dollars in cold cash and pressed it into Tompkins' hand. Tompkins had been reading the want ads, remember, and Elaine told me later her people were having him in for meals with them out of sheer pity.

"You've done something for me I can never repay you for," my uncle said as a come-on. "This is just a token of my gratitude. Call on me at any time and I'll be more than glad to —"

Tompkins didn't let him finish. He threw the money down at my uncle's feet. "I don't like being insulted," he said quietly. There was a sort of dignity about the way he said it, at that. "It's like being paid for – for showing a gruesome scar or some deformity. I don't do that for money, and I won't take money for it. This girl here —" he pointed to Elaine – "is a friend of mine. She asked me some questions about a plane and I answered them for her, that's all. Please go. I don't like being made a holy show of."

"But you don't know who I am," my uncle began protestingly.

Tompkins gave a bleak smile and put his hand up to his head, as though he had a headache. Not in that theatrical way clairvoyants do when they're about to "go into their trance," but as though something were hurting him, wouldn't let him alone.

He answered as though he were speaking against his will. "You're John Bridges," he said. "Your mother died when you were fourteen years old, and it was the sight of the beautiful silk kimonos and wrappers she wore that really made you go into the export and import business later on. . . ."

Elaine could have told him all that, was the unspoken thought in my mind.

He turned to me and answered it as though it had been said aloud. I went white and nearly fell through the floor! "But here's something she couldn't have," he said. "About you. You took off your dance-slippers under a restaurant-table one night last week and a waiter accidentally kicked one halfway across the room. Rather than admit it was yours, you left in your stocking-feet. And you've got a diamond and ruby necklace with twenty stones in it in Safety-Box No. 1805 at the National Security Bank. Also a bundle of letters you bought back from a gigolo in Paris for fifty thousand francs."

My own uncle didn't know about that!

"I don't ask you to believe in me, I don't care whether you do or not," this Tompkins went on somberly. "I didn't ask you to come here in the first place. You're going to the police about me some day, anyway, and get me in a lot of trouble."

My hands strayed up and down the blank wall trying to find the door where there wasn't any door. My eyes were blurred. I moaned, "Get me out of here!" The whole world was turning upside-down on its axis. I felt like a fly walking on the ceiling.

My uncle took me home. The five hundred stayed there on Tompkins' floor. Elaine brought it back with her when she returned, after we did.

"Wouldn't touch it," she murmured. "What do you think he did, though? Borrowed five dollars from me, to tide himself over."

That business of the $500 sold the fortune-teller to my uncle more than any number of bull's-eye predictions could have. He was convinced now that Jeremiah Tompkins wasn't a phony, a fake, a schemer of any kind. That he was a phenomenon: an ordinary, in fact subordinary, human being with this frightful gift – or blight – or prognostication. In other words, the groundwork of credulity had been laid. The rest followed in due course.

To begin with, Uncle John tried to make the man a gift of money again – no longer to show him up, but in all sincerity and respect now. He mailed him his personal check, for $1000 this time. It came back inside a readdressed envelope, almost by return mail, torn into eight neat pieces. That failing, my uncle got Tompkins a job – and made sure he'd accept it by keeping his own name out of it. He had a friend advertise for a bookkeeper. The friend, without knowing the details, agreed to bar all except one of the applicants who might answer it – Jeremiah Tompkins. In other words, it was a one-man ad. Elaine was posted to call the man's attention to it in the paper, in case it should escape his eye. It all worked out according to plan; he took the job.

"But," I insisted stubbornly to the two of them, "if he's the actual mindreader he showed himself to be, how is it he didn't know at once who was in back of this paid ad you showed him? Why couldn't he see that the job came through Uncle John?"

"He doesn't go around all day, reading what's in people's minds – he'd kill himself doing that," Elaine protested, as though I had disparaged the man. "It seems to come to him in flashes, only when he'll let it – and he doesn't like to. It's there in his unconscious self the whole time." She meant subconscious. "And he lets it flicker out once in awhile, or else it gets out in spite of him – I don't know."

Anyway, Tompkins took the job, and if he was a first-class mystic, he wasn't any great shakes as a bookkeeper. My uncle's friend had to let him go in about six weeks. The friend didn't, of course, know the inside story; he claimed the man was too moony and moody – in plain English, shiftless.

Meanwhile Tompkins kept getting under my uncle's skin deeper and deeper. The strike on the Pacific Coast gave signs of going on all the rest of the summer. The silk shipment, which was worth thousands, was stuck there in Honolulu, rotting away. My uncle got an offer from a Japanese dealer in the islands, considerably below its intrinsic value, let alone any profit. It looked like a case of take what he could get or lose the whole thing. It wasn't a question of the money so much, with him, but he hated to come out second best in any transaction, hated to admit himself licked.

He'd already drafted the cable accepting the Jap offer, then at the last minute held it without filing. He went and looked up Tompkins by himself, without confiding in anyone.

I don't know what passed between them. All I know is that Uncle John came home that night and told me he'd cabled the Japs to go to hell; the shipping strike was going to be over in forty-eight hours, right when the deadlock seemed at its worst.

I don't have to remind you what happened. You've read how the Chief Executive himself intervened unexpectedly two days later and the strike was arbitrated and called off between sun-up and sundown. The President's own advisers hadn't known he was going to do it, so it was said. My uncle's consignment beat every other cargo into 'Frisco; and by getting into port first – well, it was quite a windfall. Uncle John got exactly double the usual price for the shipment.

A man in a shabby furnished-room, without a job of his own, had saved his firm exactly $200,000 all told!

I kept out of it from then on. I wanted to hang onto my peace of mind; more than that even, my sanity. I didn't want to turn into a neurotic ghost-ridden candidate for a mental clinic. I wouldn't even discuss Tompkins with Uncle John, or let him mention the man to me. So I can't give you the intermediate steps.

But then the thing finally clamped down on my uncle, as anyone might have known it would eventually. Three months ago, I saw the change come over him and asked him what it was. He suddenly retired from business, sold out – or rather gave away his interest for next to nothing. He lost concern in everything and anything. He got haggard. I could see the mortal terror standing out in his eyes, day by day.

He'd gone to Tompkins again about some enormous venture he was contemplating. He was gambling more and more on these "inside tips", growing more reckless all the time. But this time there was a different answer, a catastrophic answer.

The thing under discussion was a long-term transaction, that would have taken about six months to pay off. "It doesn't matter one way or the other," Tompkins told him indifferently, "unless of course it's the firm itself you're thinking about, and not yourself personally." And then very indifferently, as though he'd known it all along: "Because you'll be dead by that time. Your life's coming to an end at midnight on the 14th-to-15th of next March."

I don't know whether Tompkins told it to him all at once, or doled it out piece-meal. I don't know how many times my uncle had to seek him out – plead with him maybe, or grovel on bended knees. I don't know anything at all. Uncle John wouldn't have been human if he hadn't asked the man how he would die, in what manner, and what could be done to prevent it.

"Nothing," was the merciless answer. "You can't stop it from happening, can't evade it. Though you fly to the far ends of the world, though you hide yourself in the depths of the earth, though you gather a thousand men about you to shield you, it will still find you out. It's there – written down for you – *Death by the jaws of a lion*."

And then Uncle John started going slowly to pieces. Oh, it's not the money, Lieutenant McManus! It's not that he's endowed Tompkins with hundreds of thousands of dollars at a time, that he's dissipating our fortune, my inheritance, trying to buy minutes and *seconds* of life back from a man who admits, himself, that he has no control over it, can do nothing about it. I don't mind that.

It's that he's dying by inches, before my very eyes, day by day. It's that the Spanish Inquisition, the Chinese, the Iroquois, never devised tortures to compare to what he's going through now. It's that it's become communicated to me; I'm terrified, and sick with horror, and beating my hands together in the dark. It's that the sun has gone out and we're two people trapped in a black pit. It's that there's only tomorrow left now. I want help! *I want help!*

She was so overwrought that she fell forward across his desk, burying her face against it, pounding it helplessly with her little clenched fist, again and again. McManus had to send out for a sedative. When she had drunk the spirits of ammonia, she lay down on a cot in another room and rested, dozed off for awhile. McManus covered her up to the chin with his own overcoat, with his own hands.

When he went back again alone to his office, he spat out: "Gad, what things you run into!" Twenty million dollars, eighteen years old, and her very soul taken from her. On the border-line of gibbering idiocy, almost. As for the uncle, McManus could imagine the shape *he* was in.

He sat down at his desk, stayed there staring blankly before him as though he'd forgotten the whole incident.

After about five minutes, he picked up the phone very slowly, and he said even more slowly: "Send Tom Shane in here to me. And Schafer. And Sokolsky. And Dominguez. Send out a short-wave if you have to, I want 'em here right away. Tell 'em to drop whatever they're on, no matter what it is. . . ."

Tom Shane was just a pleasant-looking fellow in a thirty-dollar herringbone suit. He didn't look dumb and he didn't look bright either.

Just a guy you wouldn't mind having a glass of beer with. He lined himself up to the left of the other three.

"Shane," said McManus, "are you afraid of lions?"

"I wouldn't go to bed with one," admitted Shane frankly.

"Shane," said McManus, "do you think you can keep a millionaire from being mangled by a lion at exactly twelve o'clock tomorrow midnight?"

It wasn't really a question. McManus seemed to be talking absent-mindedly while he did a lot of thinking behind the smoke-screen of words. "I may as well tell you now that the 'lion' might take almost any kind of a shape. It might be a bullet. It might be a poisoned cup of coffee. Then again it just might be an honest-to-goodness lion. I could fill that house with fellows like you, have 'em hanging from the chandeliers like mistletoe, but I don't want to do that. Then the 'lion' would only defer its visit, come around some other time, maybe six months from now, when it was least expected. I don't want that to happen; I want it to come when it's due to come, so I can make sure it'll never come again. So there's only one man going up there to that house with those two people, and I don't want him to fall down on the job. It's a double-header too. If this is what I think it is, that girl's as doomed as her uncle. That would mop up the twenty millions nicely, otherwise she could always bring suit to recover what's already been given away of it.

So, Tom Shane, you go in there in the next room and sit by Ann Bridges, and go home with her when she's feeling fit enough. You're not a detective – you're her boy-friend on a week-end visit as her house-guest, or her new butler, or a traveling-salesman trying to sell her vacuum-cleaners, I don't care. But keep those two people alive. Midnight tomorrow's the deadline."

Tom Shane wheeled around and went out without a word. He still didn't look bright, but he didn't look dumb either. Just a well-built guy in a herringbone suit.

McManus said, "Schafer, you're on a girl named Elaine O'Brien – and all her family too. I want to know more about 'em than they know about themselves. And be ready to pinch.

"Sokolsky, you're on a guy named Jeremiah Tompkins. And don't kid yourself by the way he looks that he's no great shakes of a guy. He's the kingpin in this, whatever it is. Don't let him out of your sight. Dictaphones and every trick of the trade. And try not to think while you're at it; the guy's supposed to be a mind-reader. Take somebody else on it with you, it's not going to be any pushover. And be even readier to pinch than Schafer. Tompkins has got to be in custody long before midnight – whether you get anything on him or not."

There was just a guy left that looked a little like Valentino, only better-looking.

"Dominguez," McManus said, "I've gotta lotta little odd-jobs for you. But they're just as important as the other guy's assignments, don't bluff yourself they're not. Find out what zoos there are within a 500-mile radius of here. Check with every one of them and find out if they keep lions. Find out if any have escaped or been swiped."

"Swipe a lion?" breathed the detective.

"Warn the keepers of all of 'em to keep extra watch over their lion cages tonight and all day tomorrow. Report to me. Got that? *Then*, find out at what night-club Miss Ann Bridges had a slipper kicked across the dance floor two years ago. And what became of it. Also, the mate to it. Use your Latin looks, apply for a job there or something. Find out what waiter picked 'em up after she'd gone, and what he did with them. If you can get hold of him, bring him in. Report to me. *Then*, buttonhole one of the big-shots at the National Security Bank, ask his cooperation, see if you can trace the leak by which the number of Miss Bridges' safe-deposit box – 1805 – and what it had in it, came into the possesh of a third party. There's nothing criminal in that, in itself, but it would give us a swell lead.

"Y'got less than twenty-four hours to do all this in! Y'ain't eating and y'ain't sleeping and y'ain't even taking time off to talk from now on! Get going!"

And when he was all by himself once more, McManus picked up the phone and asked for long distance. "Gimme Paris, France," he said matter-of-factly, "the Chief of the *Surêté*."

Many blackmailing gigolos have had telephone love-calls, but few have ever been the cause of a transatlantic long-distance from police official to police official!

The University Club Building has two entrances, one on the side street, the other on the avenue. An L-shaped lobby connects them. It's just for men, of course – college men – and women aren't allowed above the mezzanine floor, but the lobby's usually full of them, calling for pinch-hitters to fill in at dances, theatre-parties, house-parties, etc.

Ann Bridges and Tom Shane arrived there simultaneously, she in her car at the main entrance, he in a taxi at the side entrance. He had a cowhide overnight-bag with him, and had changed in the cab itself. He had Princeton written all over him and – no offense – was now veering dangerously toward the dumb side of the not-dumb, not-bright equation. He had a polo coat hanging down his back below the elbows, orange-and-black tie (very narrow diagonals, not loud), the usual thick brogues. If you'd have unbuttoned his jacket, you'd have seen a fraternity pin on the lower tab of his vest. He looked about twenty-three. He jelled perfectly.

The girl was just coming in one side of the lobby as Shane showed up from the other, bag in hand. They were collegiately informal – and loud. He didn't raise his hat; she punched him on the shoulder. "Hi, toots." " 'Lo ducky!" He grabbed her arm and they went sailing outside to her car, two young things without a care in the world.

Heads turned after them. Somebody mentioned her name. Everybody wondered who he was. All this to baffle watchful eyes that otherwise might have seen her drive away from Headquarters with Shane and would have known him to be a detective. A ticket for a traffic violation she had actually received two days previously was screen enough for her visit there tonight. McManus had had the desk-sergeant enter a dummy complaint against her in his records, and a Headquarters reporter had fallen for it, phoned in a couple of lines about it to his paper.

In the car she took the wheel. Shane pitched his bag into the back seat, lay back on the base of his skull. But as they shot off, he suddenly grew up again.

"Fell well enough to drive?" he asked.

"It'll keep my mind busy till we get there. College men usually let the other fellow do their driving for them anyway. If you're not one to the life —! How did you do it so quickly?"

"Borrowed the outfit from a friend who really went to one – changed in the cab. . . . Who's out there with him?" he asked abruptly.

"We have a cook, and a door-opener; then there's Elaine, and Uncle John's secretary. My uncle will be all right – I know what you're thinking – but he'll be all right until tomorrow night. He wants to live too badly to – to do anything to himself ahead of time. It's tomorrow night we've got to worry about." She few in her breath fearfully and repeated it a second time: "Tomorrow night."

"Step it up a little," Shane said quietly. "Ninety won't hurt it any." The clock on the dashboard said midnight. The midnight before *the* midnight.

It was a palatial place, lost in the midst of its own grounds. Couldn't see it from the main road, it was so far back, but a private driveway led to it. Lighted by their own private roadlights.

Two granite lions couchant, like a sort of omen, were the first things met Shane's eye as he got out in front of the entrance. A little like the lions in front of the Public Library in New York, but smaller. They went up the steps between them.

"I bet it hasn't helped any to have those things staring him in the face every time he went in or out the last few weeks," Shane muttered grimly.

"He's spoken several times of having them removed and replaced by something else," the girl said, "but this terrible lethargy, this fatalism, that's come over him, has prevented his doing even that."

The butler let them in. Shane, taking a snapshot of the man through his mask of collegiate vacuity, decided this wasn't one of those crime-story butlers who are to be suspected at sight. He was an old man – sixty or more – had loyalty written all over him, and looked pretty worried in the bargain.

"How is he, Weeks?" the girl asked in a whisper.

The butler shook his head. "I can't stand much more of it myself, Miss Ann. Just watching him. He's sat in one place ever since you left, staring at a clock on the wall." The old man looked sort of hopefully toward Shane; then, noting the get-up, his hopes seemed to fade a little.

"Yes, he knows about it, Weeks," the girl said; "that's why he's here. Take his bag up – put him in the room next to my uncle."

On each side of the long entrance hall a ceiling-high stained-glass panel was set into the blank wall, with electric lights hidden behind them to throw them into relief. They gleamed out in beautiful medieval tones of ruby, emerald, sapphire and mauve. Each leaded sub-division bore the head of some mythological or heraldic animal – a unicorn, a wild boar, a lion rampant, a phoenix. . . .

She saw Shane looking at the windows as they went by. "They came from England," she said dully. "Some royal abbey or other. Time of the Plantagenets."

Shane didn't know who the Plantagenets were. He wasn't supposed to, anyway. "Pretty old, I guess, eh?" he hazarded. It occurred to him that, judging by the number of decorative animals around, the prophecy might very well have originated right here in the house, in someone's evil, fertile mind.

"*He* ever been here, to your knowledge?" he asked.

"Who, Tompkins? Never."

She took the detective in to see the doomed John Bridges.

Bridges sat in the middle of a big room, and he had gathered three time-pieces around him. A big clock on the wall, a medium-sized one on the table before him, an expensive white-gold watch on his wrist. All three were ticking remorselessly away in the silence, like the mechanism of a time-bomb. There was a minute's difference, Shane noted, between the wall and table clocks. Bridges turned two feverish, burning eyes in hollow sockets toward his niece as she came in.

"Which is right?" he pleaded. "What does yours say?"

"It's twenty-nine past twelve, not half-past," the girl said.

His face lit up joyously. "Oh, Ann!" he cried. "Oh, Ann! That gives me a minute more! Just think, a minute more!"

Tom Shane thought, "For what he's done to this guy already, Tompkins deserves the chair, whether he intends doing anything more or not."

Aloud he said, cheerfully, "You and I, oldtimer, are going to have a good stiff highball together – then we're going up to bed!"

"Yes, yes," Bridges agreed pathetically. "My next-to-the-last night on earth! I must celebrate, I must —" His voice broke dismally. "Oh, help me to forget, fellow, for just five minutes! Just five minutes, that's all I ask!" He opened a drawer, pulled out a checkbook, scribbled hastily in it. "If you can take my mind off it for just five minutes, write your own figure in here over my name! Five thousand, ten thousand, I don't care!"

Shane thought: "I wonder how many times friend Tompkins has cashed in like this?" He went out to mix the highballs himself, and gave Bridges a shot of Scotch that would have lifted a horse off its shoes. McManus' words came back to him: "It may be a poisoned cup of coffee." He sampled the drink himself first, rinsing his mouth with it carefully. The taste was so good he hated to waste it, so he swallowed it. "Pleasant way of dying, anyway," he consoled himself.

He took the drinks inside. "You go to bed, kid," he told the girl. "Lock your door. It's my job from now on."

She said, "You're swell. Keep us alive," with a funny little catch in her voice as she sidled by him and went up the stairs.

The wall-clock chimed one, with a horrid, shuddery, brazen sound. "Twenty-three hours to go," John Bridges said.

Shane clicked their glasses together with almost enough force to shatter them. "Here's to crime!" he said huskily. He winked one eye deliberately at the doomed man.

3 A.M. – Schafer, lieutenant. Sorry to wake you up, but I've lost this Elaine O'Brien twist, Miss Bridges' maid —"

You've lost her? Well, find her again! Whaddye mean by —

It ain't that. I know where she is, but she's no good to us any more. She's dead.

Dead? What happened to her?

She did the Dutch. Took a run up to the bathroom just before I closed in on her, and swallowed something. I called an ambulance right away, but it was too late.

So then she *was* implicated! She knew something and was afraid we'd get it out of her!

She didn't know I was on her tail. I had just about located her house, when I heard the screaming start up inside. Time I busted in, it was all over. I'm holding the rest of them. They claim it was the prophecy preying on her mind. She came home tonight and told them she couldn't stand the gaff, waiting around there for it to happen. I checked on the drugstore where she got the stuff, and she bought it a full three days ago, long before Miss Bridges came to us. What'll I do with the rest of 'em?

Bring 'em in Shafer – and keep 'em from swallowing things.

10 A.M. – Dominguez, lieutenant. I took a dishwashing-job at the Club Cuckoo, where Miss Bridges lost her shoes. My hands are red as lobsters!

Never mind your hands, I'm no palm-reader. What'd you get?

They knew who she was, so they knew whose shoes they were. First the manager was going to send 'em out to her house next day – after all, they cost about fifty bucks a pair – but a Frenchman fella who was sitting there at one of the tables buttonholes him. This gee gives the manager a lotta malarkey about how he's an old friend of Miss Bridges, knew her in Paris, and he'll see she gets 'em back. I got all this from a waiter, who I gave a tip on the horses to while I was massaging the crockery —

Well, you got something, Don. I was just asking about that very guy at the rate of twenty bucks a syllable. The shake-down racket made Paris too hot for him, so he came over here about two years ago. You gotta descriptch, I suppose?

Yeah. Misplaced eyebrow on his lip. When he's doing the hot spots he wears one eyeglass in his right lamp. Very good-looking. A short little devil, about five —

That's enough. One of his names is Raoul Berger, but he's got twenty others. So he got the shoes?

No. The pay-off is the manager wanted all the credit for himself and hung onto them. But this Frog didn't seem to mind —

Sure he didn't. All he cared about was knowing what had taken place, so he could tip off Tompkins and get under her skin. I'm sending out a general alarm for Berger right away. They're probably working hand-in-glove together, and intend splitting the Bridges millions between 'em at the windup. Probably the idea was originally Berger's, since he'd already shaken her down once in Europe.

Now, about the safe-deposit box, chief. I been conferring with Cullinan – he's the manager of that branch of the National Security – and we questioned the vault-keeper. I think I've cleared up pretty definitely about how the number of Miss B's box, 1805, was known – but not its contents. The vault custodian seems straight enough; he's been with them for years. He recalls definitely that one day about a year and a half ago, Miss B. took her box into one of the little private cubbyholes that are provided for that purpose down in vault room. The custodian recalls it, because she came out and absent-mindedly left her key behind her in there. . . . Now, two of these keys are used at a time, see. The custodian has one, and the owner of the box has the other. The number of the box it opens is engraved on the shaft of each key. Well, Miss B. stepped right back inside, that day she mislaid her key, and the custodian went with her to help her look. The key wasn't in there. They came out again – she went through her purse and everything – no sign of it. He stepped in again a second time, and there it was, right on the slab! . . . The custodian's pretty certain that the adjoining booth was occupied at the time, but is hazy about just who was in there. That doesn't matter. The partitions don't run all the way up to the ceiling. Obviously it was our friend Berger, and obviously he'd been in there every time she was, waiting for just such a thing to happen. And when it did, he probably used a fish-hook or a magnet on the end of a string to draw the key up, memorize its number, then replace it again. All to add to Tompkin's buildup with her as a wizard. But about what the contents of the box were, I don't know, unless he used some kind of a mirror as a periscope —

More likely she bought that necklace in Paris. Berger'd seen it on her over there, and he figured it would be in the box. Also the letters she'd written to him. Took a guess at it and scored a bull's-eye. To get into the vaults all he'd have to do was rent a box under a phony name for five, six bucks, stuff it with old newspapers, and keep showing up each time she did. Still, it isn't as easy as it sounds. Berger had to stay out of sight – she knew what he looked like – and he had to get in right next door to her each time, not further down the line.

For twenty million bucks I'd go to that much trouble myself.

Get busy on them zoos, or you won't even be earning forty-eight-hundred.

Zoos! That's gratitude for ya!

5 P.M. – Sokolsky, lieutenant —

It's about time I was hearing from you! Where've you been all this time? What've you got?

A pretty bad case of the jitters, for one thing. And Dobbs – I took him on this detail with me – is about ready to crack wide open. I don't think he'll be any good for the rest of this case.

I ain't asking for a health report, I wanna know —

It's uncanny about that guy – Tompkins, I mean. He – he can see through walls and things —

Less words and more facts!

Yes, sir. We took a room in the same house he lives in. We got a lucky break and got the one right over his. Tompkins was out at the time, so we fixed up a dictaphone and led it up through the ceiling behind the steampipe. The landlady don't like him, on accounta he read what was in her mind when she insured her third husband so heavily, after losing two in a year, and also 'cause he's hep that the color of the hair she goes around wearing ain't her own. She didn't tell me this; I put two and two together from the remarks she let drop. Anyway, I got around her and found out some French cake-eater's been calling on Tompkins off and on for the past year or so.

Your voice makes sweet music! We're getting places fast, now!

The landlady thinks this Frenchy is the nuts, but that's neither here nor there. The point is, he's the only person at all – outside of the O'Brien girl and the old man Bridges himself – who has been near Tompkins since he's living in the house. . . .

Well, the O'Brien girl's out of it now. I don't think she was in on it, anyway. Just a stooge they used to pump facts out of about the Bridges family. I think maybe she found out there was something phony up, after it was too late, and realizing what she'd done to her benefactors, committed the old harry. Go ahead, Sock, what else?

I gave Tompkins' room a good going-over while I was in there, and came across any number of checks made out by Bridges. Way up in the high brackets too, telephone numbers! The only thing that don't jell right, was some of 'em were dated six months or more back. He hauls 'em in all right, but don't seem to bother cashing 'em! Maybe he's just cagey, afraid to go too heavy yet while Bridges is still alive. Maybe he's saving them all up until B. and the girl have been done away with!

Will those checks build us a case against him and his French shill! What'd you do with them?

I was afraid he'd miss them if I impounded them this soon. Dobbs and I rushed a few of the biggest ones out, had 'em photostated, and then replaced 'em again.

Good work!

Tompkins came in about midnight, just as we were getting through, so we beat it upstairs to listen in. About two in the morning this French pal of his pays him a visit. Dobbs took down everything in shorthand, until he went haywire, and I'll read it to you.

Tompkins says, "You again? What do you want now?"

"Endorse me another one of them checks – I'm running short."

T. refuses at first, says he don't want Bridges' money, and Frenchy has no right to it either. Frenchy pulls a gun on him or something, and makes him do it. Then Frenchy says, "Now you get hold of Bridges tomorrow and have him change his will, while there's still time. I'll supply the lawyer, a friend of mine. He's to turn over everything to you, see? Kid him that you'll call off the prophecy if he does it."

Tompkins says, "But I can't. It's not in my power. It's there. It's going to happen."

The French guy does a slow burn. "You think I believe that stuff? Save that for him! You do what I tell you, or —"

Tompkins answers quietly, "You're not going to get hold of his money, Berger. You're not going to live long enough to. Why, you're going to die even sooner than he is! His time is tomorrow night, but yours is right tonight! You're never even going to get out of this house alive. There are two dicks in the room over us right now, listening to every word we say – their names are Sokolsky and Dobbs —"

The notes break off there, loot, because Dobbs keeled over right at the mike and pulled a dead faint on the floor. Yeah, honest! It gave me a pretty stiff jolt myself. Just seeing the leadwire of the dictaphone, which I'm sure he didn't, wouldn't have given this Tompkins our names – nor how many of us there were.

I'll have to quote the rest from memory: "Death," says Tompkins, "is rushing at you right now, I hear the beat of his swift wings. I feel it, I see it, it's on its way. You have only minutes left. And for me there is imprisonment waiting, and lingering death in a little stone room —"

I heard the Frenchman yell out, "So you framed me, you dirty double-crossing lug! Well, see if you saw this in your crystal ball!"

And with that the gun goes off, and nearly busts my eardrum. The Frenchman has shot him.

I didn't wait to hear any more. I unlimbered my own gun and lit out and down the stairs hell-bent for leather. Berger had beaten me out to the stairs; he was already a flight below me.

I yelled, "Hold it! Stay where you are!" Instead he turned and fired at me, and I fired at the same time he did. He fell all the rest of the way down to the ground floor, and when I got to him he was dead.

Tompkins came out of his room unhurt, but with a powder burn across his forehead. Berger must have fired at point-blank range, and still didn't hit him! He started coming down slowly to where I was, with nothing in his hands. Dobbs had come to, and came down behind him, looking like he'd seen a ghost.

Well, this is the hardest part to believe; look, you can suspend me if you want to, but it's the God's honest truth. This man Tompkins came all the way down to where I was bending over the body at the foot of the stairs. I straightened up and covered him with my gun. It didn't faze him in the least, he kept moving right on past me toward the street-door. Not quickly, either; as slowly as if he was just going out for a walk. He said, "It isn't my time yet. You can't do anything to me with that."

I said, "I can't, eh? You take one step away from me, and it'll not only be your time, but you'll be a minute late!"

Dobbs was practically useless; he almost seemed to be afraid of the guy.

Tompkins turned his back on me and took that one step more. I fired a warning shot over his head. He put his hand on the doorknob. So I lowered the gun and fired at the back of his knee, to bring him down. The bullet must have gone right through between his legs. I heard it hit wood along the door-frame. Tompkins opened the door and stepped into the opening, and I got mad. I reared after him and fired point-blank at the back of his head. He wasn't five yards away from me. It was brutal – would have been murder and I'm willing to admit it myself, even though technically he was resisting arrest! I'm telling you he didn't even stagger; it never even got him. He went on through and the darkness swallowed him up.

I leaned there against that door for a minute seeing ghosts, then I ran out after him. He was clean gone, not a sign of him up or down the block.

Loot, I'm in a frame of mind where I don't care what you do to me. My job is to get flesh-and-blood guys that know a bullet when they feel one, not protoplasms that don't even know enough to lie down when they're hit. . . .

Awright, Sokolsky, pull yourself together. Bring in the stiff and rinse yourself out with a jolt of rye; maybe it'll help you carry out instructions better next time! All I know is you let Tompkins slip right through your fingers, and we're right back where we were. We got to start all over again. We've stopped the crook, but the maniac or screwball or whatever you want to call him, the more dangerous of the two, is at large. And every minute he stays that way, Bridges and his niece are in danger of their lives! Tompkins wasn't bluffing when he walked out that door. He believes in that hooey himself; and if the prophecy don't work, he'll help it work! We've got seven hours to pick him up again, out of seven million people!

"Don't!" Shane yelled at the man roughly. "Take your eyes off that clock! You're starting to get me myself, doing that! I'm only human!" He took a quick step over to the table and turned the instrument face down.

John Bridges gave a skull-like grin, all teeth and no mirth. "You're only human – that's right. That's the truest thing you ever said, son. You're a detective too, aren't you, son? That's why you've been hanging around here all day. Don't try to tell me, I know. This poor child here thinks you can save me. *You* think you can save me, too. You poor fools! Nothing can – nothing! *He* said I'm to die, and I've got to die."

"He's lying through his teeth!" Shane yelled hotly. "That Tompkins is a faker and a crook and a skunk. He'll fry in hell, before anything gets near you. I'll live to see it, and so will she – and so will you!"

Bridges' head fell forward, over his lap. "Will it hurt much?" he whined. "I guess it must. Those terrible fangs in their mouths! Those sharp, cruel claws, tearing your skin to ribbons! But it won't be the claws – it's the jaws that will mangle me, worry me like a cat worries a mouse! By the *jaws* of a lion, he said – by the *jaws* of a lion!"

Ann Bridges put her hands over her ears. "Don't," she murmured quietly. She gave Shane a look. "I'm trying so hard to – to stay all in one piece."

Shane poured a dynamic drink, all Scotch with just a needle of seltzer. He handed it to Bridges with a stony face. "Give yourself a little bravemaker," he suggested in an undertone.

The millionaire deliberately thrust the glass away from him. Liquor spilled all over the carpet; the glass bounced and rocked on its side without breaking. "Alcohol! Trying to ward off death with bottled slops!"

Shane took out his gun, pointed it butt-first at the old millionaire. "Don't this mean anything to you? Don't it mean anything to you that every window and door of this house is locked fast, that there's an electric alarm on them? That there's dozens of armed men within call hidden all around this estate, ready to jump in and grab anyone or anything the minute it shows? That we're sealed up tight, just the five of us?"

The secretary had lit out in panic sometime during the previous night. Just as Elaine O'Brien had fled. Shane had found a note from him that morning, saying he couldn't stand it, resigning the job.

Bridges cackled horribly, like a chicken about to have its neck wrung. "Five against Fate. Five against the stars. And what a five! A fat Finnish cook, an old-man butler, a slip of a girl, a loud-mouthed boy with a gun, and I —!"

"Fate, hell! Stars, hell!" Shane smashed the butt of his gun fiercely at the face of the clock on the wall. Thick glass dribbled off it. "That for Fate, and that for the stars!"

Something happened to the clock. The damaged mechanism started whirring violently, the hands began to fluctuate – the hour-hand slowly, the minute-hand more rapidly. They telescoped, jammed together in a straight line pointing at the top of the dial, stayed that way. The whirring sound stopped, the apparatus went dead.

Bridges pointed a bloodless finger at the omen; he didn't have to say anything.

In the silence the old butler came to the door, stood looking in at them a minute. "Dinner is served," he said hollowly.

"The Last Supper," Bridges shuddered. He got up, swayed, tottered toward the dining room. "Eat, drink, let us be merry, for – tonight we die!"

Ann Bridges ran to the detective, clung to him. What difference did it make, at a time like this, that Shane was still a stranger to her, that she hadn't even known him twenty-four hours before?

"And I still say it was just a coincidence," he muttered pugnaciously. "You say it too! Look at me and say it! It was just a coincidence. That happened to be the nearest place on the dial where they both met exactly, those two hands. My blows dented them. They got stuck there just as the works died, that was all. Stay sane whatever you do. Say it over and over. It was just a coincidence!"

Outside the tall French windows, in the velvety night-sky, the stars in all their glory twinkled derisively in at them.

10:45 P.M. – Dominguez, Mac. I've been trying to get through to you for fifteen minutes. Must be some trouble along the line somewhere. I'm way the hell out at a little crossroads called Sterling Junction – yeah, it's only about ten miles from the Bridges place, in the other direction. Very bad grief. Checking zoos like you told me, I dig up a traveling roadshow – a carnival or whatever you want to call it – making a one-night stand here.

Now they had two lions – yes, I said *had*, that's the grief. Two monsters, a male and a female, both in one cage. My check-up was a postmortem. They'd both busted out not twenty minutes before – don't know if the cage was left open through the keeper's carelessness, or deliberately tampered with. I beat it right up here to find out what I could. The female was shot dead just outside the carnival-grounds but the male got away clean. A posse is out after it with everything from shotguns to fire-extinguishers, hoping to rub it out before it gets anyone. They think it's heading toward the Bridges estate. Someone in a Ford reported sighting what he mistook to be an enormous tawny dog with iridescent green eyes in the underbrush as he went by.

Earlier in the evening, the keeper tells me, there was a peculiar-looking duck mooning around the lion cage. Kept staring at them like he was trying to hypnotize the two brutes. The keeper caught this guy teasing them with a bit of goods torn from a woman's dress, flitting it at them through the bars. He sent him about his business, without having sense enough to try and find out what the idea was. It may have been our friend Tompkins, then again it may not. Plenty of village half-wits can't resist riling caged animals like that.

D'you suppose brutes like that can be mesmerized or hypnotized in some way, loot? D'you suppose they can be given the scent of one particular person, through a bit of clothing, like bloodhounds? Yeah, I know, but then this whole affair is so screwy from first to last, nothing would surprise me any more. You better contact Shane right away and let him know he's up against the real thing, not a metaphor any more. There's a lot of difference between a man-eater like that and a little runt like Tompkins, when it comes to a showdown!

John Bridges was slumped in a big overstuffed chair by now, staring wild-eyed at nothing. Shane was perched on the chair arm, his gun resting on his thigh, finger around the trigger, safety off. Ann Bridges was standing behind the chair, leaning over it, pressing soothing hands to her uncle's forehead.

The portières were drawn across the French windows now, veiling the stars outside – that were there nevertheless. In addition, a ponderous bookcase blocked one window, a massive desk the other. The double-doors were locked on the inside, and the key to them was in Shane's vest pocket. The butler and the Finnish cook were, at their own request, locked in the scullery. If death must come to the head of the house, perhaps it would pass them by. They were not marked for it.

It was the awful silence that was so hard to bear. They couldn't get the old millionaire to say anything any more. Their own voices – Shane's and Ann's – were a mockery in their ears, so they quit trying to talk after a while. Bridges wouldn't drink either, and even if he had, he was past receptivity by now; it wouldn't have affected him.

The girl's face was the color of talcum. Her uncle's was a death mask, a bone structure overlaid by parchment. Shane's was granite, with a glistening line of sweat just below his hair line. He'd never forget this night, the detective knew, no matter what else happened for the rest of his life. They were all getting scars on their souls, the sort of scars people got in the Dark Ages, when they believed in devils and black magic.

The travesty of food and drink that Shane had swallowed at that shadowy supper-table a while before was sticking in his craw. How can wine warm you when the toast is death at midnight? He'd tried to urge the girl to leave while there was time, to get out and let the two of them face it alone. He hadn't been surprised at her staunch refusal; he admired her all the more for it. He would nevertheless have overriden her by physical force if necessary – the atmosphere had grown so macabre, so deadly – but for one fact, one all important fact that he hadn't mentioned.

When he'd tried to contact McManus, to have a special bodyguard sent out to take Ann away, he found out that the phone was dead. They were cut off here. She couldn't go alone, of course; that would have been worse than staying.

They had a clock with them in the room again. Bridges begged and pleaded so hard for one, that Shane had reversed his edict. The mental agony of Bridges, and the strain on Ann and himself, he noticed, were much worse without a clock than with one. It was far better to know just how much time there was left. Shane had brought in a large one with a pendulum, from the entrance hall. It was fourteen minutes to twelve, now.

Tick, tick, tick, tick, tick – and it was thirteen minutes to twelve. The pendulum, like a harried gold planet, kept flashing back and forth behind the glass pane that cased it. Ann kept manipulating her two solacing hands over the doomed man's temples, stroking gently.

"It goes so fast, so fast," John Bridges groaned, eyes on the clock. The minute-hand, shaped like a gold spearhead, had just notched forward again – eleven to twelve.

"Damn!" Shane said with a throaty growl, "Damn!" He began to switch the muzzle of his gun restlessly up and down on his thigh. Something to shoot at, he thought; gimme something to shoot at! A drop of sweat ran vertically down his forehead as far as the bridge of the nose, then off into one of the tear-ducts beside it.

Tick, tick, tick – whish, whish, whish – eleven to twelve.

Bridges said suddenly, without taking eyes off the clock: "Son –

Shane, or whatever your name is – call Warren 2424 in the city for me. Ask *him* once more – oh, I've asked him so many times, so many thousand times already – but ask him once more, for the last time, if there isn't any hope for me? Ask him if I've got to go, if he still sees it?"

Shane said, "Who?" But he knew who. Bridges wasn't aware yet that Tompkins was no doubt in custody long ago, that McManus had probably seen to that item right after Ann's visit, first thing.

"Tompkins," the dead man in the chair answered. "I haven't – haven't heard from him in two days now. And if – if there isn't any hope, then say goodbye for me."

Shane said curiously, sparring for time because he knew the phone was dead, "You want me to unlock those doors, go out there into the other room where the phone is?"

"Yes, yes," Bridges said. "It's still safe, we have – yes, there's ten minutes yet. You can be back in here inside of a minute. His landlady will answer. Tell her to hurry and bring him down to the phone —"

Shane snapped his fingers mentally, got off the arm of the chair. "Maybe I can bring this baby back to life," he thought. "Why didn't I think of this before?" He gave the girl a look. "Stay right by him, where you are, Miss Ann. I'll just be outside the door."

He took the doorkey out, opened the two tall halves, stepped quickly to the phone in the room beyond. The lights were on all over the house, everything was still.

The phone was still dead, of course. One of the lines must be down somewhere. He said loudly into the silent mouthpiece, "Give me Warren 2424, hurry it up!" He feigned a pause, then he said: "Bring Jeremiah Tompkins to the phone, quickly! This call is from John Bridges."

He faked another wait, slightly longer this time. He could hear the clock ticking remorselessly away in there where Ann Bridges and her uncle were, everything was so quiet. He kept his gun out in his right hand; the phone was a hand-set. A gust of wind or something scuffed and snuffed at one of the French windows over on the other side of the house; instantly his gun was pointing in that direction, like the magnetic needle of a compass. There was something almost animal about the sound – *Phoof!* like that. A snuffle.

It wasn't repeated, and the fact that he was staging an act out here, a lifesaving act, took Shane's mind off the interruption. He said aloud, into empty space: "Tompkins? I'm talking on behalf of Mr. Bridges. Does that still hold good, for tonight at twelve? It's nearly that now, you know."

There was a long mirror-panel in the wall over him. In it he could see the room he had left, see the two of them in there, the girl and her uncle, tense, bending forward, drinking in every word he uttered.

"Fight fire with fire," he thought. "I don't know why McManus didn't sweat Tompkins down to the bone, then make him eat his prophecy to Bridges's face. That would have undone the damage quicker than anything else!"

He raised his voice. "That's more like it!" he said. "When did you find this out? Re-checked, eh? You should have let him know first thing – he's been worried sick! I'll tell him right away!" He hung up, wondering just how good an actor he was going to be.

He went briskly in again, gave them the bridgework. He could tell by the girl's face that, woman-like, she saw through the bluff; maybe she had found out already that the phone was n.g. But if he could sell the death-candidate himself—

"It's all off!" he announced cheerfully. "Tompkins just told me so himself. There's been a change in – in, uh, the stars. He's not getting the death-vibrations any more. Can't possibly be midnight tonight. He'll tell you all about it himself when he —" Something in the old man's face stopped him. "What's the matter, what're you looking at me like that for? Didn't you hear what I just said?"

John Bridges' head was thrown wearily back, mouth open. He began to roll it slowly from side to side in negation. "Don't mock me," he said. "Death's too serious to be mocked like that. I just remembered – after I sent you out there – his landlady had that phone taken out a month ago. Too much trouble calling roomers to it all the time, she said. There is no phone at all now in the house where Tompkins lives."

Shane took it like a man. He turned away without a word, closed the doors behind him, leaned his back against them. Tossing the key up and down in the hollow of his hand, he smiled mirthlessly out of the corner of his mouth.

The figure in the chair was holding out a hand toward him, a trembling hand. "It's five-to," he quavered. "I'm going to say goodbye now. Thank you for sticking by me, anyway, son. Ann, my dear, come around in front of me. Kiss me goodbye."

Shane said in a hoarse, offensive voice: "What'll you have for breakfast?" He ignored the outstretched hand.

Bridges didn't answer. The girl crouched down before him and he kissed her on the forehead. "Goodbye, dear. Try to be happy. Try to forget – whatever horror you're about to witness in the next few minutes."

Shane said belligerently, trying to rally him: "Not to want to die is one thing. Not to lift a finger to keep from dying is another! Were you always like this, all your life?"

The doomed man said, "It's easy to be brave with forty years ahead of you. Not so easy with only four minutes —"

The tick of the clock, the hiss of its pendulum, seemed louder than all their voices. Three minutes to twelve . . . two minutes. John Bridges' eyes were like billiardballs in his head, so rounded, so hard, so white, straining toward those two hands closing in on one another. Shane's trigger-finger kept twitching nervously, aching to pull, to let go – but in which direction he didn't know, couldn't tell.

That was the worst part of it, there wasn't anything to shoot at!

One minute to go. The space between the two hands was a sliver of white, a paring, a thread. Three pairs of eyes were on it. Dying calf-eyes; frightened woman's eyes; hard, skeptical policeman's eyes that refused to believe.

Then suddenly the space was gone. The two hands had blended into one.

A bell, a pair of them, rang out jarringly. The phone that Shane had thought dead, that *had* been dead until now, was pealing on the other side of the door. The shock lifted him off his heels. The girl jolted too. Bridges alone gave no sign, seemed already half into the other world.

Bong! the clock went mellowly, majestically.

Before the vibration had died away Shane was already outside at the signaling instrument, gun-hand watchfully fanning the empty air around him. A trick? A trap to draw him away? He'd thought of that. But Bridges and the girl were in full sight of him; to get to them anything would have to pass him first. And he had to find out what this call was.

It must be vital, coming at just this precise —

It was vital, *Bong!* went the clock a second time, over McManus' distant voice in his ears: "Hello! Shane – Shane? Line was down, couldn't get through to you till now. Been trying for an hour. . . . Everything's under control, Shane. We've beaten the rap, the guy's saved! No time to tell you now. I'll be out there the quickest I can —"

Bong! cut across the voice, third stroke of the hour.

"Hurry, chief," said Shane. "The poor guy is sweating his very life away with terror. I want to tell him it's all O.K."

"General alarm was out for Tompkins. At half-past ten tonight he walks in here of his own accord, gives himself up! Yeah, Headquarters! Said he knew he'd be arrested anyway. Was he! He's still spouting Bridges has to die. Also that he's going to conk out himself, in jail waiting for his trial to come up. The latter he has my best wishes on. Here's something for you, kid, after what you must have gone through out there tonight – according to Tompkins, you're marrying twenty-million bucks inside a year. Ann Bridges, before the year is out!"

Bong!

"Oh, one other thing. I just got word they shot a lion that was heading your way, cornered it on the outskirts of the estate. A real one that broke out of its cage earlier tonight. We thought at first Tompkins had something to do with it, but he's been able to prove he wasn't anywhere near there when it happened. Just one of those spooky coincidences —"

The girl's frenzied scream seared through Shane like cauterization. He dropped the phone like a bar of red-hot iron, whirled. Bridges flashed by before he could stop him. The old man whisked out the other door, and turned down the entrance-hall like something bereft of its senses.

"Hold him! He's gone out of his mind!" Ann Bridges screamed.

Bong! sounded dismally.

Shane raced after him. Glass crashed far down the lighted hall. Bridges was standing there, stock still, when Shane turned into the hallway. The millionaire seemed to be leaning over against the wall, up where those two stained-glass panels were.

The detective didn't see what had happened until he got there. Then he stood frozen, unable to breath. For John Bridges was headless, or seemed to be; he ended at the neck. . . . Then Shane saw that was because he'd thrust his head through one of those leaded panes, clear to the other side.

Jagged teeth of thick, splintered glass held his neck in a vise, had pierced his jugular. You could see the dark shadow running down the inside of the lighted pane that was the millionaire's life-blood.

He was gone, gone. . . . And the square of glass he'd chosen, in his blind, headlong flight, out of all the squares, was that one of the lion rampant!

Bong!

The mane and rabid eyes and flat, feline nostrils of the beast still showed undestroyed above John Bridges' gashed neck, as though the painted image were swallowing the man bodily. And for fangs now, instead of painted ones there were jagged spears of glass, thrusting into Bridges' flesh from all sides of the orifice he himself had created.

Shane felt the cold horror which washed his spine and turned his blood into ice water.

Death by the jaws of a lion!

Bong! the clock went for the twelfth time, and then all was silence.

McManus raised worried eyes above the report he was making out. "What'll I put in here? Would you call it murder by mental suggestion?"

"I'm not so sure," Shane answered low.

"Are you starting to go superstitious on me too?" the lieutenant snapped. But his eyes went uneasily toward the window, beyond which the stars were paling into dawn.

They both kept looking troubledly out and up, at those distant inscrutable pin-points of brilliance, that no man can defy or alter.

The Dancing Detective

Patsy Marino was clocking us as usual when I barged in through the foyer. He had to look twice at his watch to make sure it was right when he saw who it was. Or pretended he had to, anyway. It was the first time in months I'd breezed in early enough to climb into my evening dress and powder up before we were due on the dance floor.

Marino said, "What's the matter, don't you feel well?"

I snapped, "D'ya have to pass a medical examination to get in here and earn a living?" and gave him a dirty look across the frayed alley-cat I wore on my shoulder.

"The reason I ask is you're on time. Are you sure you're feeling well?" he pleaded sarcastically.

"Keep it up and you won't be," I promised, but soft-pedalled it so he couldn't quite get it. He was my bread and butter after all.

The barn looked like a morgue. It always did before eight – or so I'd heard. They didn't have any of the 'pash' lights on yet, those smoky red things around the walls that gave it atmosphere. There wasn't a cat in the box, just five empty gilt chairs and the coffin. They had all the full-length windows overlooking the main drag open to get some ventilation in, too. It didn't seem like the same place at all; you could actually breathe fresh air in it!

My high heels going back to the dressing-room clicked hollowly in the emptiness, and my reflection followed me upside-down across the waxed floor, like a ghost. It gave me a spooky feeling, like tonight was going to be a bad night. And whenever I get a spooky feeling it turns out to be a bad night all right.

I shoved the dressing-room door in and started, "Hey, Julie, why didn't you wait for me, ya getting too high-hat?" Then I quit again.

She wasn't here either. If she wasn't at either end, where the hell was she?

Only Mom Henderson was there, reading one of tomorrow morning's tabs. "Is it that late?" she wanted to know when she saw me.

"Aw, lay off," I said. "It's bad enough I gotta go to work on a empty stomach." I slung my cat-pelt on a hook. Then I sat down and took off my pumps and dumped some foot powder in them, and put them back on again.

"I knocked on Julie's door on my way over," I said, "and didn't get any answer. We always have a cup of Java together before we come to work. I don't know how I'm going to last the full fifteen rounds. . . ."

An unworthy suspicion crossed my mind momentarily: Did Julie purposely dodge me to get out of sharing a cup of coffee with me like I always took with her other nights? They allowed her to make it in her rooming-house because it had a fire-escape; they wouldn't allow me to make it in mine. I put it aside as unfair. Julie wasn't that kind; you could have had the shirt off her back – only she didn't wear a shirt, just a brassière.

"Matter?" Mom sneered. "Didn't you have a nickel on you to buy your own?"

Sure I did. Habit's a funny thing, though. Got used to taking it with a side-kick and – I didn't bother going into it with the old slob.

"I got a feeling something's going to happen tonight," I said, hunching my shoulders.

"Sure," said Mom. "Maybe you'll get fired."

I thumbed my nose at her and turned the other way around on my chair. She went back to her paper. "There haven't been any good murders lately," she lamented. "Damn it, I like a good juicy murder wanst in a while!"

"You're building yourself up to one right in here." I scowled into the mirror at her.

She didn't take offence; she wasn't supposed to, anyway. "Was you here when that thing happened to that Southern girl – Sally, I think, was her name?"

"No!" I snapped. "Think I'm as old as you? Think I been dancing here all my life?"

"She never showed up to work one night, and they found her – That was only, let's see now . . ." She figured it out on her fingers. . . . "Three years ago."

"Cut it out!" I snarled. "I feel low enough as it is!"

Mom was warming up now. "Well, for that matter, how about the Fredericks kid? That was only a little while before you come here, wasn't it?"

"I know," I cut her short. "I remember hearing all about it. Do me a favour and let it lie."

She parked one finger up alongside her mouth. "You know," she breathed confidentially, "I've always had a funny feeling one and the same guy done away with both of them."

"If he did, I know who I wish was third on his list!" I was glowering at her when, thank God, the rest of the chain gang showed up and cut the death-watch short. The blonde came in, and then the Raymond tramp, and the Italian frail, and all the rest of them – all but Julie.

I said, "She was never as late as this before!" and they didn't even know who or what I was talking about. Or care. Great bunch.

A slush-pump started to tune up outside, so I knew the cats had come in too.

Mom Henderson got up, sighed, "Me for the white tiles and rippling waters," and waddled out to her beat.

I opened the door a crack and peeped out, watching for Julie. The pash lights were on now and there were customers already buying tickets over the bird-cage. All the other taxi-dancers were lining up – but not Julie.

Somebody behind me yelled: "Close that door! Think we're giving a free show in here?"

"You couldn't interest anyone in that second-hand hide of yours even with a set of dishes thrown in!" I squelched absent-mindedly, without even turning to find out who it was. But I closed it anyway.

Marino came along and banged on it and hollered, "Outside, you in there! What do I pay you for, anyway?" and somebody yelled back, "I often wonder!"

The cats exploded into a razz-matazz just then with enough oompah to be heard six blocks away, so it would pull them in off the sidewalk. Once they were in, it was up to us. We all came out single file, to a fate worse than death, me last. They were putting the ropes up, and the mirrored tops started to go around in the ceiling and scatter flashes of light all over everything, like silver rain.

Marino said, "Where you goin' Ginger?" and when he used your front name like that it meant he wasn't kidding.

I said, "I'm going to phone Julie a minute, find out what happened to her."

"You get out there and gonna-goo!" he said roughly. "She knows what time the sessions begins! How long's she been working here, anyway?"

"But she'll lose her job, you'll fire her," I wailed.

He hinged his watch. "She is fired already," he said flatly.

I knew how she needed that job, and when I want to do a thing I do it. A jive-artist was heading my way, one of those barnacles you can't shake off once they fasten on you. I knew he was a jive, because he'd bought enough tickets to last him all week; a really wise guy only buys them from stretch to stretch. The place might burn down for all he knew.

I grabbed his ticket and tore it quick, and Marino turned and walked away. So then I pleaded, "Gimme a break, will you? Lemme make a phone call first. It won't take a second."

The jive said, "I came in here to danst."

"It's only to a girl-friend," I assured him. "And I'll smile pretty at you the whole time." (*Clink! Volunteer* 8–IIII.) "And I'll make it up to you later, I promise I will." I grabbed him quick by the sleeve. "Don't go away, stand here!"

Julie's landlady answered. I said, "Did Julie Bennett come back yet?"

"I don't know," she said. "I ain't seen her since yesterday."

"Find out for me, will ya?" I begged. "She's late and she'll lose her job over here."

Marino spotted me, came back and thundered, "I thought I told you —"

I waved the half ticket in his face. "I'm working," I said. "I'm on this gentleman's time," and I gonna-gooed the jive with teeth and eyes, one hand on his arm.

He softened like ice cream in a furnace. He said, "It's all right, Mac," and felt big and chivalrous or something. About seven cents' worth of his dime was gone by now.

Marino went away again, and the landlady came down from the second floor and said, "She don't answer her door, so I guess she's out."

I hung up and I said: "Something's happened to my girl-friend. She ain't there and she ain't here. She wouldn'ta quit cold without telling me."

The gonna-goo was beginning to wear off the jive by this time. He fidgeted, said, "Are you gonna danst or are you gonna stand there looking blue?"

I stuck my elbows out. "Wrap yourself around this!" I barked impatiently. Just as he reached, the cats quit and the stretch was on.

He gave me a dirty look. "Ten cents shot to hell!" and he walked off to find somebody else.

I never worry about a thing after it's happened, not when I'm on the winning end, anyway. I'd put my call through, even if I hadn't found out anything. I got back under the ropes, and kept my fingers crossed to ward off garlic-eaters.

By the time the next stretch began I knew Julie wasn't coming any more that night. Marino wouldn't have let her stay even if she had, and I couldn't have helped her get around him any more, by then, myself. I kept worrying, wondering what had happened to her, and that creepy feeling about tonight being a bad night came over me stronger than ever, and I couldn't shake it off no matter how I gonna-gooed.

The cold orangeade they kept buying me during the stretches didn't brace me up any either. I wasn't allowed to turn it down, because Marino got a cut out of the concession profits.

The night was like most of the others, except I missed Julie. I'd been more friendly with her than the rest of the girls, because she was on the square. I had the usual run of freaks.

"With the feet, with the feet," I said wearily, "lay off the belt-buckle crowding."

"What am I supposed to do, build a retaining wall between us?"

"You're supposed to stay outside the three-mile limit," I flared, "and not try to go mountain climbing in the middle of the floor. Do I look like an Alp?" And I glanced around to see if I could catch Marino's eye.

The guy quit pawing. Most of them are yellow like that. But on the other hand, if a girl complains too often, the manager begins to figure her for a troublemaker. 'Wolf!' – you know – so it don't pay.

It was about twelve when they showed up, and I'd been on the floor three and a half hours straight, with only one more to go. There are worse ways of earning a living. You name them. I knew it was about twelve because Duke, the front man, had just wound up 'The Lady is a Tramp', and I knew the sequence of his numbers and could tell the time of night by them, like a sailor can by bells. Wacky, eh? Half past – 'Limehouse Blues'.

I stared at them when I saw them come into the foyer, because customers seldom come in that late. Not enough time left to make it worth the general admission fee. There were two of them: one was a fat, bloated little guy, the kind we call a 'belly-wopper', the other was a pip. He wasn't tall, dark and handsome, because he was medium height, light-haired and clean-cut-looking without being pretty about it, but if I'd had any dreams left he coulda moved right into them. Well, I didn't, so I headed for the dressing-room to count up my ticket stubs while the stretch was on; see how I was making out. Two cents out of every dime when you turn them in.

They were standing there sizing the barn up, and they'd called Marino over to them. Then the three of them turned around and looked at me just as I made the door, and Marino thumbed me. I headed over to find out what was up. Duke's next was a rhumba, and I said to myself, If I draw the kewpie, I'm going to have kittens all over the floor.

Marino said, "Get your things, Ginger." I thought one of them was going to take me out; they're allowed to do that, you know, only they've got to make it up with the management for taking you out of circulation. It's not as bad as it sounds, you can still stay on the up and up, sit with them in some laundry and listen to their troubles. It's all up to you yourself.

I got the back-yard sable and got back just in time to hear Marino say something about, "Will I have to go bail for her?"

Fat said, "Naw, naw, we just want her to build up the background a little for us."

Then I tumbled, got jittery, squawked: "What is this, a pinch? What've I done? Where you taking me?"

Marino soothed: "They just want to go with them, Ginger. You be a good girl and do like they ast." Then he said something to them I couldn't figure. "Try to keep the place here out of it, will you, fellas?

I been in the red for six months as it is."

I cowered along between them like a lamb being led to the slaughter, looking from one to the other. "Where you taking me?" I wailed, going down the stairs.

Maiden's Prayer answered, in the cab, "To Julie Bennett's, Ginger." They'd gotten my name from Marino, I guess.

"What's she done?" I half sobbed.

"May as well tell her now, Nick," Fat suggested. "Otherwise she'll take it big when we get there."

Nick said, quietly as he could, "Your friend Julie met up with some tough luck, babe." He took his finger and he passed it slowly across his neck.

I took it big right there in the cab, Fat to the contrary. "Ah, no!" I whispered, holding my head. "She was on the floor with me only last night! Just this time last night we were in the dressing-room together having a smoke, having some laughs! No! She was my only friend." And I started to bawl like a two-year-old, straight down my make-up on to the cab floor.

Finally this Nick, after acting embarrassed as hell, took a young tent out of his pocket, said, "Have yourself a time on this, babe."

I was still working on it when I went up the boarding-house stairs sandwiched between them. I recoiled just outside the door. "Is she – is she still in there?"

"Naw, you won't have to look at her," Nick assured me.

I didn't, because she wasn't in there any more, but it was worse than if she had been. Oh God, that sheet, with one tremendous streak down it as if a chicken had been —! I swivelled, played puss-in-the-corner with the first thing I came up against, which happened to be this Nick guy's chest. He sort of stood still like he liked the idea. Then he growled, "Turn that damn thing over out of sight, will you?"

The questioning, when I was calm enough to take it, wasn't a grill; don't get that idea. It was just, as they'd said, to fill out her background. "When was the last time you saw her alive? Did she go around much – y'know what we mean? She have any particular steady?"

"I left her outside the house door downstairs at one-thirty this morning, last night, or whatever you call it," I told them. "We walked home together from Joyland right after the session wound up. She didn't go around at all. She never dated the boys afterwards, and neither did I."

The outside half of Nick's left eyebrow hitched up at this, like when a terrier cocks its ear at something. "Notice anyone follow the two of you?"

"In our racket they always do; it usually takes about five blocks to wear them out, though, and this is ten blocks from Joyland."

"You walk after you been on your pins all night?" Fats asked, aghast.

"We should take a cab, on our earnings! About last night, I can't swear no one followed us, because I didn't look around. That's a come-on, if you do that."

Nick said, "I must remember that," absent-mindedly.

I got up my courage, faltered, "Did it – did it happen right in here?"

"Here's how it went: She went out again after she left you the first time —"

"I knew her better than that!" I yipped. "Don't start that, Balloon Lungs, or I'll let you have this across the snout!" I swung my cat-piece at him.

He grabbed up a little box, shook it in my face. "For this," he said. "Aspirin! Don't try to tell us different, when we've already checked with the all-night drugstore over on Sixth!" He took a couple of heaves, cooled off, sat down again. "She went out, but instead of locking the house door behind her, she was too lazy or careless; shoved a wad of paper under it to hold it open a crack till she got back. In that five minutes or less somebody who was watching from across the street slipped in and lay in wait for her in the upper hallway out here. He was too smart to go for her on the open street, where she might have had a chance to yell."

"How'd he know she was coming back?"

"The unfastened door woulda told him that; also the drug clerk tells us she showed up there fully dressed, but with her bare feet stuck in a pair of carpet slippers to cool 'em. The killer musta spotted that too."

"Why didn't she yell out here in the house, with people sleeping all around her in the different rooms?" I wondered out loud.

"He grabbed her too quick for that, grabbed her by the throat just as she was opening her room door, dragged her in, closed the door, finished strangling her on the other side of it. He remembered later to come out and pick up the aspirins which had dropped and rolled all over out there. All but one, which he overlooked and we found. She wouldn't 've stopped to take one outside her door. That's how we know about that part of it."

I kept seeing that sheet, which was hidden now, before me all over again. I couldn't help it; I didn't want to know, but still I had to know. "But if he strangled her, where did all that blood" – I gestured sickly – "come from?"

Fat didn't answer, I noticed. He shut up all at once, as if he didn't want to tell me the rest of it, and looked kind of sick himself. His eyes gave him away. I almost could have been a detective myself, the way I pieced the rest of it together just by following his eyes around the room. He didn't know I was reading them, or he wouldn't have let them stray like that.

First they rested on the little portable phonograph she had there on a table. By using bamboo needles she could play it late at night, soft, and no one would hear it. The lid was up and there was a record on the turntable, but the needle was worn down half way, all shredded, as though it had been played over and over.

Then his eyes went to a flat piece of paper, on which were spread out eight or ten shiny new dimes; I figured they'd been put aside like that, on paper for evidence. Some of them had little brown flecks on them, bright as they were. Then lastly his eyes went down to the rug; it was all pleated up in places, especially along the edges, as though something heavy, inert, had been dragged back and forth over it.

My hands flew up to my head and I nearly went wacky with horror. I gasped it out because I hoped he'd say no, but he didn't, so it was yes. "You mean he danced with her *after* she was gone? Gave her dead body a dime each time, stabbed her over and over while he did?"

There was no knife, or whatever it had been, left around, so either they'd already sent it down for prints or *he'd* taken it out with him again.

The thought of what must have gone on here in this room, of the death dance that must have taken place . . . All I knew was that I wanted to get out of here into the open, couldn't stand it any more. Yet before I lurched out, with Nick holding me by the elbow, I couldn't resist glancing at the label of the record on the portable: 'Poor Butterfly'.

Stumbling out the door, I managed to say: "She didn't put that on there. She hated that piece, called it a drip. I remember once I was up here with her and started to play it, and she snatched it off, said she couldn't stand it, wanted to bust it then and there, but I kept her from doing it. She was off love and men, and it's a sort of mushy piece, that was why. She didn't buy it, they were all thrown in with the machine when she picked it up second-hand."

"Then we know his favourite song, if that means anything. If she couldn't stand it, it would be at the bottom of the stack of records, not near the top. He went to the trouble of skimming through them to find something he liked."

"With her there in his arms, already!" That thought was about the finishing touch, on top of all the other horror. We were on the stairs going down, and the ground floor seemed to come rushing up to meet me. I could feel Nick's arm hook around me just in time, like an anchor, and then I did a clothes-pin act over it. And that was the first time I didn't mind being pawed.

When I could see straight again, he was holding me propped up on a stool in front of a lunch counter a couple of doors down, holding a cup of coffee to my lips.

"How's Ginger?" he said gently.

"Fine," I dribbled mournfully all over my lap. "How's Nick?"

And on that note the night of Julie Bennett's murder came to an end.

Joyland dance hall was lonely next night. I came in late, and chewing cloves, and for once Marino didn't crack his whip over me. Maybe even he had a heart. "Ginger," was all he said as I went hurrying by, "don't talk about it while you're on the hoof, get me? If anyone asks you, you don't know nothing about it. It's gonna kill business."

Duke, the front man, stopped me on my way to the dressing-room. "I hear they took you over there last night," he started.

"Nobody took nobody nowhere, schmaltz," I snapped. He wore feathers on his neck, that's why I called him that; it's the word for long-haired musicians in our lingo.

I missed her worse in the dressing-room than I was going to later on out in the barn; there'd be a crowd out there around me, and noise and music, at least. In here it was like her ghost was powdering its nose alongside me at the mirror the whole time. The peg for hanging up her things still had her name pencilled under it.

Mom Henderson was having herself a glorious time; you couldn't hear yourself think, she was jabbering away so. She had two tabloids with her tonight, instead of just one, and she knew every word in all of them by heart. She kept leaning over the gals' shoulders, puffing down their necks. "And there was a dime balanced on each of her eyelids when they found her, and another one across her lips, and he stuck one in each of her palms and folded her fingers over it, mind ye! D'ye ever hear of anything like it? Boy, he sure must've been down on you taxis —"

I yanked the door open, planted my foot where it would do the most good, and shot her out into the barn. She hadn't moved that fast from one place to another in twenty years. The other girls just looked at me, and then at one another, as much as to say, "Touchy, isn't she?"

"Get outside and break it down; what do I pay you for anyway?" Marino yelled at the door. A gob-stick tootled plaintively; out we trooped like prisoners in a lock-step and another damn night had started in.

I came back in again during the tenth stretch ('Dinah' and 'Have You Any Castles, Baby?') to take off my kicks a minute and have a smoke. Julie's ghost came around me again. I could still hear her voice in my ears, from night-before-last! "Hold that match, Gin. I'm trying to duck a cement-mixer out there. Dances like a slap-happy pug. Three little steps to the right, as if he were priming for a standing broad-jump. I felt like screaming, 'For Pete's sake, if you're gonna jump, jump!' "

And me: "What're you holding your hand for; been dancing upside-down?"

"It's the way he holds it. Bends it back on itself, and folds it under. Like this, look. My wrist's nearly broken. And look what his ring did to me!" She had shown me a strawberry-sized bruise.

Sitting there alone, now, in the half-light, I said to myself, "I bet *he* was the one! I bet *that's* who it was! Oh, if I'd only gotten a look at him, if I'd only had her point him out to me! If he enjoyed hurting her that much while she was still alive, he'd have enjoyed dancing with her after she was dead." My cigarette tasted rotten. I threw it down and got out of there in a hurry, back into the crowd.

A ticket was shoved at me and I ripped it without looking up. Gliding backward, all the way around on the other side of the barn, a voice finally said a little over my ear, "How's Ginger?"

I looked up and saw who it was, said, "What're you doing here?"

"Detailed here," Nick said.

I shivered to the music. "Do you expect him to show up *again*, after what he's done already?"

"He's a dance-hall killer," Nick said. "He killed Sally Arnold and the Fredericks girl, both from this same mill, and he killed a girl in Chicago in between. The prints on Julie Bennett's phonograph records match those in two of the other cases, and in the third case – where there were no prints – the girl was holding a dime clutched in her hand. He'll show up again sooner or later. There's one of us cops detailed to every one of these mills in the metropolitan area tonight, and we're going to keep it up until he does."

"How do you know what he looks like?" I asked.

He didn't answer for a whole bar. "We don't," he admitted finally. "That's the hell of it. Talk about being invisible in a crowd! We only know he isn't through yet, he'll keep doing it until we get him!"

I said, "He was here that night, he was right up here on this floor with her that night, before it happened; I'm sure of it!" And I sort of moved in closer. Me, who was always griping about being held too tight. I told him about the impression the guy's ring had left on the hand, and the peculiar way he'd held it, and the way he'd danced.

"You've got something there," he said, and left me flat on the floor and went over to phone it in.

Nick picked me up again next dance.

He said, shuffling off: "That was him all right who danced with her. They found a freshly made impression still on her hand, a little offside from the first, which was almost entirely obliterated by then. Meaning the second had been made after death, and therefore stayed uneffaced, just like a pinhole won't close up in the skin after death. They made an impression of it with moulage, my lieutenant just tells me. Then they filled that up with wax, photographed it through a magnifying lens, and now we know what kind of ring he's wearing. A seal ring shaped like a shield, with two little jewel splinters, one in the upper right-hand corner, the other in the lower left."

"Any initials on it?" I gaped, awe-stricken.

"Nope, but something just as good. He can't get it off, unless he has a jeweller or locksmith file it off, and he'll be afraid to do that now. The fact that it would press so deeply into her hand proves that he can't get it off, the flesh of his finger has grown around it; otherwise it would have had a little give to it, the pressure would have shifted the head of it around a little."

He stepped all over my foot, summed up, "So we know how he dances, know what his favourite song is – 'Poor Butterfly', know what kind of a ring he's wearing. And we know he'll be back sooner or later."

That was all well and good, but I had my own health to look out for; the way my foot was throbbing! I hinted gently as I could, "You can't do very much watching out for him, can you, if you keep dancing around like this?"

"Maybe you think I can't. And if I just stand there with my back to the wall it's a dead give-away. He'd smell me a mile away and duck out again. Keep it quiet what I'm doing here, don't pass it around. Your boss knows, of course, but it's to his interest to co-operate. A screwball like that can put an awful dent in his receipts."

"You're talking to the original sphinx," I assured him. "I don't pal with the rest of these twists, anyway. Julie was the only one I was ever chummy with."

When the session closed and I came downstairs to the street, Nick was hanging around down there with the other lizards. He came over to me and took my arm and steered me off like he owned me.

"What's this?" I said.

He said, "This is just part of the act, and make it look like the McCoy."

"Are you sure?" I said to myself, and I winked to myself without him seeing me.

All the other nights from then on were just a carbon copy of that one, and they started piling up by sevens. Seven, fourteen, twenty-one. Pretty soon it was a month since Julie Bennett had died. And not a clue as to who the killer was, where he was, what he looked like. Not a soul had noticed him that night at Joyland, too heavy a crowd. Just having his prints on file was no good by itself.

She was gone from the papers long ago, and she was gone from the dressing-room chatter, too, after a while, as forgotten as though she'd never lived. Only me, I remembered her, because she'd been my pal. And Nick Ballestier, he did because that was his job. I suppose Mom Henderson did too, because she had a morbid mind and loved to linger on gory murders. But outside of us three, nobody cared.

They did it the wrong way around – Nick's superiors at Homicide, I mean. I didn't try to tell him that, because he would have laughed at me. He would have said, "Sure! A dance-mill pony knows more about running the police department than the commissioner does himself!

Why don't you go down there and show 'em how to do it?"

But what I mean is, the dance mills didn't need all that watching in the beginning, the first few weeks after it happened, like they gave them. Maniac or not, anyone would have known he wouldn't show up *that* soon after. They needn't have bothered detailing anyone at all to watch the first few weeks. He was lying low then. It was only after a month or so that they should have begun watching real closely for him. Instead they did it just the reverse. For a whole month Nick was there nightly. Then after that he just looked in occasionally, every second night or so, without staying through the whole session.

Then finally I tumbled that he'd been taken off the case entirely and was just coming for – er – the atmosphere. I put it up to him unexpectedly one night. "Are you still supposed to come around here like this?"

He got all red, admitted: "Naw, we were all taken off this duty long ago. I – er – guess I can't quit because I'm in the habit now or something."

"Oh yeah?" I said to myself knowingly. I wouldn't have minded that so much, only his dancing didn't get any better, and the wear and tear on me was something awful. It was like trying to steer a steamroller around the place.

"Nick," I finally pleaded one night, when he pinned me down flat with one of his size twelves and then tried to push me out from under with the rest of him, "be a detective all over the place, only please don't ask me to dance any more, I can't take it."

He looked innocently surprised. "Am I that bad?"

I tried to cover up with a smile at him. He'd been damn nice to me even if he couldn't dance.

When he didn't show up at all next night, I thought maybe I'd gone a little too far, offended him maybe. But the big hulk hadn't looked like the kind that was sensitive about his dancing, or anything else for that matter. I brought myself up short with a swift, imaginary kick in the pants at this point. What the heck's the matter with *you*? I said to myself. You going soft? Didn't I tell you never to do that! And I reached for the nearest ticket, and tore it, and I gonna-gooed with a 'Grab yourself an armful, mister, it's your dime.'

I got through that night somehow, but I had that same spooky feeling the next night like I'd had *that* night – like tonight was going to be a bad night. Whenever I get that spooky feeling, it turns out to be a bad night all right. I tried to tell myself it was because Nick wasn't around. I'd got used to him, that was all, and now he'd quit coming, and the hell with it. But the feeling wouldn't go away. Like something was going to happen before the night was over. Something bad.

Mom Henderson was sitting in there reading tomorrow morning's tab. "There hasn't been any good juicy murders lately," she mourned over the top of it. "Damn it, I like a good murder y'can get your teeth into wanst in a while!"

"Ah, dry up, you ghoul!" I snapped. I took off my shoes and dumped powder into them, put them on again. Marino came and knocked on the door. "Outside, freaks! What do I pay you for anyway?"

Someone jeered, "I often wonder!" and Duke, the front man, started to gliss over the coffin, and we all came out single file, me last, to a fate worse than death.

I didn't look up at the first buyer, just stared blindly at a triangle of shirt-front level with my eyes. It kept on like that for a while; always that same triangle of shirt-front. Mostly white, but sometimes blue, and once it was lavender, and I wondered if I ought to lead. The pattern of the tie across it kept changing too, but that was all.

> "Butchers and barbers and rats from the harbours
> Are the sweethearts my good luck has brought me."

"Why so downcast, Beautiful?"

"If you were standing where I am, looking where you are, you'd be downcast too."

That took care of him. And then the stretch.

Duke went into a waltz, and something jarred for a minute. My time-table. This should have been a gut bucket (low-down swing music), and it wasn't. He'd switched numbers on me, that's what it was. Maybe a request. For waltzes they killed the pash lights and turned on a blue circuit instead, made the place cool and dim with those flecks of silver from the mirror-top raining down.

I'd had this white shirt-triangle with the diamond pattern before; I remembered the knitted tie, with one tier unravelled on the end. I didn't want to see the face, too much trouble to look up. I hummed the piece mentally, to give my blank mind something to do. Then words seemed to drop into it, fit themselves to it, of their own accord, without my trying, so they must have belonged to it. 'Poor butterfly by the blossoms waiting.'

My hand ached, he was holding it so darned funny. I squirmed it, tried to ease it, but he held on all the tighter. He had it bent down and back on itself.

'The moments pass into hours. . . .'

Gee, if there's one thing I hate it's a guy with a ring that holds your mitt in a straitjacket! And he didn't know the first thing about waltzing. Three funny little hops to the right, over and over and over. It was getting my nerves on edge. "If you're gonna jump, jump!" Julie's voice came back to me from long ago. She'd run into the same kind of a —

'I just must die, poor butterfly!'

Suddenly I was starting to get a little scared and a whole lot excited. I kept saying to myself, Don't look up at him, you'll give yourself away. I kept my eyes on the knitted tie that had one tier unravelled. The lights went white and the stretch came on. We separated, he turned his back on me and I turned mine on him. We walked away from each other without a word. They don't thank you, they're paying for it.

I counted five and then I looked back over my shoulder, to try to see what he was like. He looked back at me at the same time, and we met each other's looks. I managed to slap on a smile as though I'd only looked back because he'd made a hit with me, and that I hoped he'd come around again.

There was nothing wrong with his face, not just to look at, anyway. It was no worse than any of the others around. He was about forty, maybe forty-five, hair still dark. Eyes speculative, nothing else, as they met mine. But he didn't answer my fake smile, maybe he could see through it. We both turned away again and went about our business.

I looked down at my hand, to see what made it hurt so. Careful not to raise it, careful not to bend my head, in case he was still watching. Just dropped my eyes to it. There was a red bruise the size of a small strawberry on it, from where his ring had pressed into it the whole time. I knew enough not to go near the box. I caught Duke's eye from where I was and hitched my head at him, and we got together sort of casually over along the wall.

"What'd you play 'Poor Butterfly' for that last time?" I asked.

"Request number," he said.

I said, "Don't point, and don't look around, but whose request was it?"

He didn't have to. "The guy that was with you the last two times. Why?" I didn't answer, so then he said, "I get it." He didn't at all. "All right, chiseller," he said, and handed me two dollars and a half, splitting the fiver the guy had slipped him to play it. Duke thought I was after a kick-back.

I took it. It was no good to tell him. What could he do? Nick Ballestier was the one to tell. I broke one of the singles at the orangeade concession – for nickles. Then I started to work my way over toward the phone, slow and aimless. I was within a yard of it when the cats started up again!

And suddenly *he* was right next to me, he must have been behind me the whole time.

"Were you going any place?" he asked.

I thought I saw his eyes flick to the phone, but I wasn't positive. One thing sure: there wasn't speculation in them any more, there was – decision.

"No place," I said meekly. "I'm at your disposal." I thought, If I can only hold him here long enough, maybe Nick'll show up.

Then just as we got to the ropes, he said: "Let's skip this. Let's go out to a laundry and sit awhile."

I said, smooth on the surface, panic-stricken underneath, "But I've already torn your ticket, don't you want to finish this one out at least?" and tried to gonna-goo him for all I was worth, but it wouldn't take. He turned around and flagged Marino, to get his O.K.

His back was to me, and across his shoulder I kept shaking my head, more and more violently, to Marino – No, no, I don't want to go with him! Marino just ignored me. It meant more money in his pocket this way.

When I saw that the deal was going through. I turned like a streak, made the phone, got my buffalo in. It was no good trying to tell Marino, he wouldn't believe me, he'd think I was just making it up to get out of going out with the guy. Or if I raised the alarm on my own, he'd simply duck down the stairs before anyone could stop him and vanish again. Nick was the only one to tell, Nick was the only one who'd know how to nail him here.

I said, "Police headquarters, quick! Quick!" and turned and looked over across the barn. But Marino was already alone out there. I couldn't see where the guy had gone, they were milling around so, looking over their prospects for the next one.

A voice came on and I said: "Is Nick Ballestier there? Hurry up, get him for me."

Meanwhile Duke had started to break it down again; real corny. It must have carried over the open wire. I happened to raise my eyes, and there was a shadow on the wall in front of me, coming across my shoulders from behind me. I didn't move, held steady, listening.

I said, "All right, Peggy, I just wanted to know when you're gonna pay me back that five bucks you owe me," and I killed it.

Would he get it when they told him? They'd say, "a girl's voice asked for you, Nick, from somewhere where there was music going on, and we couldn't make any sense out of what she said, and she hung up without waiting." A pretty slim thread to hold all your chances on.

I stood there afraid to turn. His voice said stonily: "Get your things, let's go. Suppose you don't bother any more tonight about your five dollars." There was a hidden meaning, a warning, in it.

There was no window in the dressing-room, no other way out but the way I'd come in, and he was right there outside the door. I poked around all I could, mourning, 'Why don't Nick come?' and, boy, I was scared A crowd all around me and no one to help me. He wouldn't stay; the only way to hang on to him for Nick was to go with him and pray for luck. I kept casing him through the crack of the door every minute or so. I didn't think he saw me, but he must have. Suddenly his heel scuffed at it brutally, and made me jump about an inch off the floor.

"Quit playing peek-a-boo, I'm waiting out here!" he called in sourly.

I grabbed up Mom Henderson's tab and scrawled across it in lipstick: *Nick: He's taking me with him, and I don't know where to. Look for my ticket stubs. Ginger.*

Then I scooped up all the half tickets I'd accumulated all night long and shoved them loose into the pocket of my coat. Then I came sidling out to him. I thought I heard the phone on the wall starting to ring, but the music was so loud I couldn't be sure. We went downstairs and out on the street.

A block away I said, "There's a joint. We all go there a lot from our place," and pointed to Chan's. He said "Shut up!" I dropped one of the dance tickets on the sidewalk. Then I began making a regular trail of them.

The neon lights started to get fewer and fewer, and pretty soon we were in a network of dark lonely side-streets. My pocket was nearly empty now of tickets. My luck was he didn't take a cab. He didn't want anyone to remember the two of us together, I guess.

I pleaded, "Don't make me walk any more, I'm awfully tired."

He said, "We're nearly there, it's right ahead." The sign on the next corner up fooled me; there was a chop-suey joint there, only a second-class laundry, but I thought that was where we were going.

But in between us and it there was a long dismal block, with tumbledown houses and vacant lots on it. And I'd run out of dance tickets. All my take gone, just to keep alive. He must have worked out the whole set-up carefully ahead of time, known I'd fall for that sign in the distance that we *weren't* going to.

Sure, I could have screamed out at any given step of the way, collected a crowd around us. But you don't understand. Much as I wanted to get away from him, there was one thing I wanted even more: to hold him for Nick. I didn't just want him to slip away into the night, and then do it all over again at some future date. And that's what would happen if I raised a row. They wouldn't believe me in a pinch, they'd think it was some kind of a shake-down on my part. He'd talk himself out of it or scram before a cop came.

You have to live at night like I did to know the real callousness of passers-by on the street, how seldom they'll horn in, lift a finger to help you. Even a harness-cop wouldn't be much good, would only weigh my story against his, end up by sending us both about our business.

Maybe the thought came to me because I spotted a cop ahead just then, loitering towards us. I could hardly make him out in the gloom, but the slow steady walk told me. I didn't really think I was going to do it until we came abreast of him.

The three of us met in front of a boarded-up condemned house.

Then, as though I saw my last chance slipping away – because Nick couldn't bridge the gap between me and the last of the dance checks any more, it was too wide – I stopped dead.

I began in a low tense voice, "Officer, this man here —"

Julie's murderer had involuntarily gone on a step without me. That put him to the rear of the cop. The whole thing was so sudden, it must have been one of those knives that shot out of their own hilts. The cop's eyes rolled, I could see them white in the darkness, and he coughed right in my face, warm, and he started to come down on top of me, slow and lazy. I side-stepped and he fell with a soft thud and rocked a couple of times with his own fall and then lay still.

But the knife was already out of him long ago, and its point was touching my side. And where the cop had been a second ago, *he* was now. We were alone together again.

He said in a cold, unexcited voice, "Go ahead, scream, and I'll give it to you to right across him."

I didn't, I just pulled in all my breath.

He said, "Go ahead, down there," and steered me with his knife down a pair of steps into the dark areaway of the boarded-up house it had happened in front of. "Stand there, and if you make a sound – you know what I told you." Then he did something to the cop with his feet, and the cop came rolling down into the areaway after me.

I shrank back and my back was against the boarded-up basement door. It moved a little behind me. I thought. This must be where he's taking me. If it is, then it's open. I couldn't get out past him, but maybe I could get *in* away from him.

I turned and clawed at the door, and the whole framed barrier swung out a little, enough to squeeze in through. He must have been hiding out in here, coming and going through here, all these weeks. No wonder they hadn't found him.

The real basement door behind it had been taken down out of the way. He'd seen what I was up to, and he was already wriggling through the gap after me. I was stumbling down a pitch-black hallway by then.

I found stairs going up by falling down on top of them full length. I sobbed, squirmed up the first few on hands and knees, straightened up as I went.

He stopped to light a match. I didn't have any, but his helped me too, showed me the outline of things. I was on the first-floor hall now, flitting down it. I didn't want to go up too high, he'd only seal me in some dead end up there, but I couldn't stand still down here.

A broken-down chair grazed the side of my leg as I went by, and I turned, swung it up bodily, went back a step and pitched it down over the stair-well on top of him. I don't know if it hurt him at all, but his match went out.

He said a funny thing then. "You always had a temper, Muriel."

I didn't stand there listening. I'd seen an opening in the wall farther ahead, before the match went out. Just a blackness. I dived through it and all the way across with swimming motions, until I hit a jutting mantel slab over some kind of fireplace. I crouched down and tucked myself in under it. It was one of those huge old-fashioned ones. I groped over my head and felt an opening there, lined with rough brickwork and furry with cobwebs, but it wasn't wide enough to climb up through. I squeezed into a corner of the fireplace and prayed he wouldn't spot me.

He'd lit another match, and it came into the room after me, but I could only see his legs from the fireplace opening, it cut him off at the waist. I wondered if he could see me; he didn't come near where I was.

The light got a little stronger, and he'd lit a candle stump. But still his legs didn't come over to me, didn't bend down, or show his face peering in at me. His legs just kept moving to and fro around the room. It was awfully hard, after all that running, to keep my breath down.

Finally he said out loud, "Chilly in here," and I could hear him rattling newspapers, getting them together. It didn't sink in for a minute what was going to happen next. I thought: Has he forgotten me? Is he that crazy? Am I going to get away with it? But there'd been a malicious snicker in his remark; he was crazy like a fox.

Suddenly his legs came over straight to me; without bending down to look he was stuffing the papers in beside me. I couldn't see out any more past them. I heard the scrape of a match against the floorboards. Then there was the momentary silence of combustion. I was sick, I wanted to die quick, but I didn't want to die that way. There was the hum of rising flame, and a brightness before me, the papers all turned gold. I thought, Oh, Nick! Nick! Here I go!

I came plunging out, scattering sparks and burning newspapers.

He said, smiling, pleased with himself, casual: "Hello, Muriel. I thought you didn't have any more use for me. What are you doing in my house?" He still had the knife – with the cop's blood on it.

I said: "I'm not Muriel, I'm Ginger Allen from the Joyland. Oh, mister, please let me get out of here, please let me go!" I was so scared and so sick I went slowly to my knees. "Please!" I cried up at him.

He said, still in that casual way: "Oh, so you're not Muriel! You didn't marry me the night before I embarked for France, thinking I'd be killed, that you'd never see me again, that you'd get my soldier's pension?" And then, getting a little more vicious: "But I fooled you. I was shell-shocked but I didn't die. I came back even if it was on a stretcher. And what did I find? You hadn't even waited to find out! You'd married another guy and you were both living on my pay. You tried to make it up to me, though, didn't you, Muriel? Sure; you visited me in the hospital, bringing me jelly. The man in the next cot died from eating it. Muriel, I've looked for you high and low ever since, and now I've found you."

He moved backwards, knife still in hand, and stood aside, and there was an old battered relic of a phonograph standing there on an empty packing-case. It had a great big horn to it, to give it volume. He must have picked it up off some ash-heap, repaired it himself. He released the catch and cranked it up a couple of times and laid the needle into the groove.

"We're going to dance, Muriel, like we did that night when I was in my khaki uniform and you were so pretty to look at. But it's going to have a different ending this time.

He came back toward me. I was still huddled there, shivering. "No!" I moaned. "Not me! You killed her, you killed her over and over again. Only last month; don't you remember?"

He said with pitiful simplicity, like the tortured thing he was, "Each time I think I have, she rises up again." He dragged me to my feet and caught me to him, and the arm with the knife went around me, and the knife pressed into my side.

The horrid thing over there was blaring into the emptiness loud enough to be heard out on the street, 'Poor Butterfly.' It was horrible, it was ghastly.

And in the candle-lit pallor, with great shadows of us looming on the wall, like two crazed things we started to go round and round. I couldn't hold my head up on my neck; it hung way back over my shoulders like an over-ripe apple. My hair got loose and went streaming out as he pulled me and turned me and dragged me around. . . .

'I just must die, poor butterfly!'

Still holding me to him, he reached in his pocket and brought out a palmful of shiny dimes, and flung them in my face.

Then a shot went off outside in front of the house. It sounded like right in the areaway where the knifed cop was. Then five more in quick succession. The blare of the music must have brought the stabbed cop to. He must've got help.

He turned his head toward the boarded-up windows to listen. I tore myself out of his embrace, stumbled backwards, and the knife-point seemed to leave a long circular scratch around my side, but he didn't jam it in, in time – let it trail off me.

I got out into the hall before he could grab me again, and the rest of it was just kind of a flight-nightmare. I don't remember going down the stairs to the basement; I think I must have fallen down them without hurting myself – just like a drunk does.

Down there a headlight came at me from the tunnel-like passage. It must have been just a pocket torch, but it got bigger and bigger, then went hurling on by. Behind it a long succession of serge-clothed figures brushed by me.

I kept trying to stop each one, saying: "Where's Nick? Are you Nick?"

Then a shot sounded upstairs. I heard a terrible death-cry. "Muriel!" and that was all.

When I next heard anything it was Nick's voice. His arm was around me and he was kissing the cobwebs and tears off my face.

"How's Ginger?" he asked.

"Fine," I said, "and how's Nick?"

The Light in the Window

Night, and the soldier stood under the lamp-post watching. High up over his head the arc-light was like a motionless flare-shell, blinding, dazzling, sending out rays; but standing still up there, not settling slowly to the ground the way a flare-shell would. And then down where he was, on the pavement, there was a big round disc of ghost-light, like a thin dusting of talcum on the ground, with him standing in the middle of it, like a phantom spotlight. Half way down the tall post, between the two, the arc-lamp and him, two flanges stuck out, like a clothes-peg spread wide open. One said '14th Avenue', and it pointed behind his back. One said 'Second Street', and it pointed the way he was looking.

He stood there like a statue. Only statues don't feel. He stood there like a chunk of wood. Only chunks of wood don't hurt so much.

His back was pressed up against the post; the post was what was keeping it up straight. He had one arm looped behind him, giving him an added grip on the post. The other hung slack. He was young, as soldiers are. But not a boy any more. There were lines on his face that had come too soon. His cheekbones were too pronounced; his jaw needed a little easing. His eyes were steady, and slitted with distant sighting. They never moved, they never wavered. They were on a certain window, diagonally opposite, a number of houses down. They never once left it.

On the ground at his feet there lay a number of things. Things that must have fallen, that didn't belong there. A cone of thin green tissue paper. The paper was so flimsy it had burst a seam with its own fall, and the head of a rose and a sprig of fern were peering out through the rent. Then there was an oblong box lying there too, also wrapped in paper, with a tinselled string securing it, the way a candy-box is secured. Then there were two or three cigarettes. The peculiar thing about them was they were all still full-length; that is, unconsumed. The tip of each was just a little charred from the first touch of flame. As though they had been dropped by awkward handling in the very act of lighting them, before they had served their purpose, and not just been thrown away.

He didn't seem to notice that they had fallen. His eyes never left that window.

It was the ground-floor window. It lay alongside the door. Over it there were others in a straight line, a second, a third, a fourth, but he paid no heed to them; it was that one, and that one alone, that held his fixed gaze – his haunted stare.

It was dark, dead, lifeless. It gave him back nothing, not a sign. The one over it, on the second, was lit, was cheerful, was alive. There was even a pot of geraniums on the sill of that one, as if to dress it. But that wasn't the one he was watching, that couldn't do anything for him. Then over that, the third was dark again. And then the fourth in turn was lighted. They seemed to alternate. One floor light, the next dark. But those weren't the ones he was watching. The first, the ground-floor one, was dark.

She was out. But she'd come home soon. He'd watch for her to come home. And then just as she was about to enter he'd call to her and say . . .

No, that would frighten her. Too sudden, too unexpected after three years; out here in the dark, on the empty street. She'd think she was seeing a ghost. Well, she was; there are ghosts of flesh and blood, just as well as the other kind. Who should know that better than he? He'd wait for her to go inside. He'd let her get in first. He'd know when she was in by the way the window lit up. That would tell him. Then he'd go in after her and knock on the door. Softly, quietly, in order not to alarm her. Then she'd open. Then she'd see him. Then hurting would stop.

He should have told her that they'd brought him back. He should have written and let her know, all these weeks, that he was already over here, in a hospital on this side. But he'd wanted to wait until he was all right, to make it even better, to make it more complete. They'd told him he would be. And now finally he was.

She'd come along soon. Better get ready. He'd have to pick up the candy first, he'd have to pick up the flowers. He started to; he started to bend over slowly towards them. He couldn't quite make it, though. He went back flat against the post again. Well, not right now, then; in another minute or two, instead. He'd rest up some more first, before doing it. Funny how tired you got. Battle fatigue, they called it at the hospital. They said it would wear off; they said, "You'll be all right now."

Under the lamp-post the soldier stood watching.

A car horn gave a sharp tweak as it glided past behind him, and he recoiled against the lamp-post, his head went back and hit it, and the hollow stem sounded with a lazy brazen *bong*. Then he let out his breath slowly, and it made a soft hiss. He moved his arm, he drew his sleeve across his forehead, and he was all right again.

He said to himself: 'I think I'll try again. I'll try lighting another of those. So that by the time she comes I can show her I have it licked.'

He had only one of each left, one cigarette, one match. He took the cigarette out and put it in his mouth. That part he could always get. Then he pulled off the match and struck it. That part he could do all right too. It was bringing the two of them together.

He started to move the flame closer. He was afraid of it. It was like that one that had burst right in front of him up front that day. It touched the tip of the cigarette, and he couldn't help it, his face jerked back. The cigarette dropped.

'I guess I won't smoke right now,' he decided ruefully. 'She'll light one for me when she comes, and we're in there together. Like she used to. Only in those days I didn't *have* to have it done for me.'

She ought to be home soon now. She ought to be home soon. *Please*. Out here alone in the dark.

Suddenly his eyes were wide. Something had happened to the house front. The window, *the* window, had bloomed yellow. And she hadn't come in from the street. No one had gone in. He'd been right here watching. His eyes hadn't once left it. She must have – she must have been in there all the time.

In the dark?

There was no other room, only that one overlooking the front; no second room for her to have been in. He'd been in there lots of times before he went away.

It must be – not there. He blinked to make it go away. It stayed bright yellow. He backed his hand across his eyes and held it off a moment, then took it away and looked again. It stayed bright yellow. The one above had gone out by now, but *it*, the one that mattered, it stayed bright yellow.

It even made a pale reflection out before it on the street, and only real things can make reflections. Something can fool you itself, but if it has a reflection it's *there*.

The front door swung out, dropped back, and a man was standing there in front of it.

I'll wait until he's out of the way, the soldier said to himself, then I'll start for over there. He'll go away in a minute.

The man just stood there, enjoying himself. You could tell he was enjoying himself. You could see his head go back and his chest go out, while he took a deep breath of the fresh air, and held it for a while appreciatively, and then let it go again.

He gave his hat a little shift to make it sit more jauntily. He straightened the shoulders of his coat to make them fit more closely. Then he straightened his tie conceitedly. Then at last he struck out and came down the steps to the sidewalk.

He turned towards the corner the soldier watched from, instead of the other. He was still on the opposite side at first. Then he left it. He was crossing diagonally towards the soldier now, approaching that pallid spotlight of his vigil.

The soldier didn't move, he stayed there, back to post. He'd be out of the way in a minute, this passer-by, and behind him the window still waited.

He passed behind the soldier, to the rearward of the post, for that was out at the edge.

The footsteps stopped short. Then they came back a pace or two, as if to regain perspective from the side.

"Hey, wait a minute —"

The soldier hadn't moved, it was just rhetorical.

"Aren't you Mitchell Clark? Sure. Mitch; that was it. They used to call you Mitch."

The soldier turned his head and he was standing there right beside him looking at him.

"I thought I knew your face," he exulted. Then a momentary shade of concern crossed his own. "Don't you remember me? Art Shearer, from the old neighborhood." He held out his hand.

"Oh," the soldier said. He did now; he hadn't at first. "Oh, sure." He shook the other's hand.

"How long is it now? Must be four, five years." He didn't wait for the answer. "You're looking good. Must have agreed with you. Rugged grind, hunh?" He didn't wait for the answer. "Back for good, or just temporary?" He didn't wait for the answer. "What are you doing around here, holding up this post?" He glanced briefly up towards the flanges. "Oh, waiting for a bus, I guess. I don't envy you, brother; you're going to have *some* wait, these days."

He brought out cigarettes, as a spur to sociability.

"Have one."

They had black bands encircling their waists, up near the tips.

"What are they?" the soldier asked curiously.

"They're called 'Black-and-Whites.' Funny brand, hunh? You don't often run into them. I stick to them because I got used to them."

He was prodding into his pockets.

"Gee, I lost my lighter. Or left it somewhere. Can't find it." He clicked his tongue worriedly. "What d'you think of that? Never mind, I think I've got a match. Yeah, here's one."

The small flame, bedded in Shearer's two hands, yellowed both their faces for a moment as they inclined towards it. The soldier's eyes came to rest on Shearer's cheek, at a point offside to his mouth, remained fixed there.

"There's something on your face."

"Where?"

"Right there. No, there."

Shearer took a handkerchief out, touched it with the tip of his tongue, dug at his face. Then he peered at the handkerchief. The smear had transferred itself.

"That stuff gets all over the map," he smirked, pleased with himself.

Mitch Clark tilted his nose slightly and sniffed. "What's that?" Then he looked dubiously at the cigarette he was holding.

"What? Oh, that. That's not the cigarette. It's probably on me." He hoisted his coat lapel up towards his own nose, sniffed in turn. "Yeah, it's all over me," he admitted ruefully. "Whew! It's called 'One Hour Alone.' Can you imagine; so strong it even gets on you secondhand." He wagged his head deprecatingly, but he was still pleased, none the less.

Mitch Clark kept his eyes down. He didn't want to look at the other man. He didn't want to look at the window, lighted, waiting, there in the background behind him.

He edged his foot forward. The candy box went over the edge of the kerb and into the gutter below. It was damp there. The paper stained dark in patches as it soaked in the moisture. It was no good now.

"What was that?" Shearer asked, glancing down. "Something for the garbage-collector's truck, I guess."

"Yeah," Mitch Clark answered dully. "Something for the garbage-collector's truck." He kept looking down.

"What're you looking at?" Shearer asked finally, following the direction of the look with his own eyes a second time.

Mitch Clark's mouth twisted briefly, then resumed its normal outline. "You've got your – left shoe on your right foot and your right on your left. The hollows are on the outside."

Shearer chuckled. He waited deliberately for the soldier to look up at him, meet his eyes. Then when he had, he winked portentously at him. "I have?" he drawled, with complete lack of discomfiture. "Well, what d'ya know?"

Mitch Clark shivered a little, bunched his shoulders defensively. "Chilly tonight, isn't it?" he mumbled.

"Chilly?" Shearer gave him a look of roguish surprise. "Blamed if I can notice it. Don't ask me to tell you. Not when you've just been treated like I have."

He wanted the soldier to know. He wanted him to get it. He wanted to brag about it. He wanted to hammer it into him, by every means except the direct statement.

He even turned his head and glanced briefly over his shoulder, towards where he'd come from. Then when he'd brought his face forward again, there was that smirk of self-esteem all over it.

It faded slowly. His audience wasn't appreciative enough. This conversation hadn't been any fun.

"You've changed some, haven't you?" he let Clark know critically. He threw his cigarette away rather curtly. "Well, I guess I'll be moving. No use hanging around here all night." He didn't offer his hand in parting. Then, from a pace away: "Hope you get your bus. Take it easy."

The soldier didn't answer, didn't move. He heard the footsteps dilute with distance, blur and expire. Silence all around him now. His back wasn't upright against the post for its entire length any more; the upper part was curved forward, as if it had started to peel off it. But he hadn't answered; didn't move.

Only his thoughts moved. But not in a straight line; circularly, round and round, like wisps of bunting caught in the wings of an electric fan. I'm more tired than I was before. I've got to get away from this post. I've got to go. But where? Turn, go back, before you know. You don't know yet. Turn, go back, before you do. No, it's too far away. And they don't want you to come back, they said you were all right. You'll have to – go forward, across the street, that's much nearer. But then you're liable to *know*. Isn't there *any* place where you can go except just those two, forward and back? No, none. Some people have so many places to go, and you have just two, and you don't want to go to either one of them. Why did you, how did you, happen to run out of places, get lost like this? . . . I'm more tired than I was before. I've got to get away from this post. Like this. That's it. Now *pull*. Pull hard —

He broke from it, and was on his own. He went the way the other man had come, diagonally towards the far side. He staggered twice, but he made it. He got up on to the opposite kerb. He wanted to stop again, but there was no post handy. He went over to the steps that led up to the door and stopped there, bending his stomach over the ornamental iron knob that flanked them.

He stopped a long time. I've got to get away from these steps. I've got to go *in*. In there, right in front of me. He went up the three or four steps and then he stopped again, this time leaning against the door embrasure, head down as if he were listening to the stone.

Then suddenly he made a neat, deft little move, an economical half-turn, on one shoulder against the stone, and went in, slipped in like a shadow. Like a shadow when the light changes on a stone facing and drives it away.

The door was white. A pure colour, an innocent colour. The push button beside it was white too; of bone. His finger, held rigid to the push button, was white – with pressure, with strain. The nail was white, all the blood had been forced away from under it. Across the knuckle were livid white cicatrices, ugly to look at, produced by the flattening tension.

The sound of a bell ringing mutedly came through the wood; it was curiously like the whimpering of a sick, puny child.

Over the button there was a card held fast in a rack. On it was printed 'Miss Constance Sterling.' It, the card, would have been a blameless white too, but for one single blemish. The print of somebody's grimy thumb had been left on it; had soiled it, marred it, stained it. It stood out across the 'Constance', dimming it somewhat. It was large, could only have been the print of a man's thumb.

His finger trailed off the push button; his whole arm dropped to his side, and swayed with its own weight, then hung inert. The puling sound behind the wood stopped.

He let his head sink forward until his forehead touched the door. It was as though he were saying a prayer.

He heard something and drew it back.

The door opened and a girl stood there, her face now where his had been only a moment ago.

Her hair was dishevelled. On one side of her face it stood too far forward, almost enclouding one eye. On the other side it was pushed too far back. It was as though her head had been reclining sideways upon a pillow, in sleep or – indolent dalliance. The lower part of her form was enshrouded in soft clinging drapery, that fell too slack, overhanging even the tip of her foot; that had not yet been adjusted properly to her figure, for above it failed to cover one shoulder entirely, and clung to the outermost curve of the other by sheer grace of accident. Her hand was busy with it, trying to support it, to retrieve it.

Two fever-spots of red stood out upon her cheeks that were not rouge, for they were too sharply defined, not graduated enough about their edges.

Her eyes were large with fright. White ships pierced with tremendous black holes, and about to sink at any moment.

They danced about, trying to get in step with his, the man's, as though there were a form of dancing performed by the eyes alone, in which, just as in the bodily form, the man led, the woman followed. She was out of step in this dance.

They stood there, faces close. So close that only a kiss could have brought them closer. There was no kiss.

"Why don't you speak to Mitch?" he said poignantly. "Why don't you say hello to Mitch?"

"Mitch," she answered. She was all out of breath, even with just that one word, so it must have been something else that had robbed her of it.

She panted a little, lightly. "For a minute I thought I was seeing a ghost."

"Maybe you are," he said quietly. "I don't know." His jaw was still tight, and it made the words come out flat. Everything he said had a toneless, pressed quality to it.

"Are we – just going to stand like this?" he said.

She moved backward, and drew the door with her. Two sides of a room expanded into view, like a strip of picture postcards being opened to form a single scene.

In the corner stood the bed. It was tortured, had been used. One pillow overhung the side, as if all but swept off with the sudden inquiring departure of its occupant. The other was reared slightly upward against the headboard, in opposite direction to the first. Orange light leered dimly over it, from under the silk shade of a lamp that stood low beside it. This shade had a single rent or 'run', as in a taut silk stocking, close beside one of its supporting ribs, and there the light came through less dissembling, less evasive, in a clearer tone of yellow.

A still-kindled cigarette lay under the lamp, causing the orange light to seem to flicker at times as its invisible exudation filmed it. A book lay there too, on its face in sudden discard, pocket-sized and paper-covered, its backbone reared and not heavy enough to force itself flat.

"I shouldn't let you in," she said. "Like this, the way I am. But you've been away to war. You've been hurt."

"You shouldn't let anybody in," he said tightly. "Not just me; anybody."

He moved slowly past her, through the gap she allowed him, she offered him, and then she closed the door behind him.

"Here, sit down here," she said, and her hand speared at a chair, sketchily readying it for him. Some pinkish garment that had been slung across its back whipped rearward from sight and never reappeared again, as though done away with by sleight of hand.

"Just let me – fix this," she said, and sat down before the mirror of a dresser, at the opposite wall from the bed. She drew the garment higher about her shoulders and fastened it with something, some pin or something, in front, out of his sight – her back was to him – so that it stayed primly secured from then on.

She took a comb and touched it to her hair in a place or two, then set it down, and touched the places she had touched with it with her hand instead.

"Why didn't you tell me?" she said. "The last letter, you were still over there. Why did you walk in like this?"

He was fumbling for a cigarette. He didn't answer.

She must have seen him in the mirror. "There are some over there," she said.

He got up and went slowly to the place she had pointed out. He found the package. There was only one left in it. He took that one out. But then he kept looking at the package, even though it was now worthless, empty. He did everything very slowly, as though he were infinitely tired and had scarcely the energy to do it.

Again, she must have seen him in the mirror, for she didn't turn her head.

"What's the matter?"

"Do you always smoke this brand?" he said thoughtfully. " 'Black-and-Whites'?"

"Oh, those —" The way she stopped, for a moment he had an impression she was almost as surprised as he at their being there. "No, I —" Then she said: "It's the first time. They were all I could get. I had to take what he'd give me. There's been a shortage, you know."

He picked up an ashtray and looked at it pensively.

"Why are you doing that?"

He put it down again. He said dully, as though it were entirely unimportant: "You must have smoked some with your lipstick on – and some without it. Some are pinkish at their tips. And some are still white."

She turned round and looked at him over her shoulder, ingenuously blank. "Some must be from earlier in the evening, when I first came home and still had it on. Then after I cleaned it off I went ahead smoking, and those are the others." She laughed apologetically. "I should have emptied it out."

"That's a good answer," he said sadly. And then he agreed wistfully, "Yes, you should have." His fist slowly closed, and the empty cigarette package pleated into a curlicued pod, and then dropped from it.

He watched it intently even after that, as though expecting it to re-form and fill out to its original shape again. Then he seemed to notice that he was still holding the cigarette in his hand. For he looked at it, in a rather helpless, dubious sort of way, as though wondering what it was there for, wondering what was meant to be done with it.

"Wait," she said eagerly. She jumped up from the mirror. "Let me. Like I used to. Remember? You go and sit down. I'll do it for you."

He returned to the chair.

"I was trying to outside on the street before, and I —"

She was standing before him now, holding a small enamelled lighter. She bent over towards him with fond intentness, flicked her thumb against it a number of times. Only an arid spark resulted.

"Oh," she said impatiently, "it's always out of fuel just when I want it. Wait, here's another." She had gone, was back again. A generous, spiralling flame leaped up this time.

"That's a man's, isn't it?" he said indifferently.

It was squat, bulky, coated with rough-grained simulated leather.

He smiled astringently, raised sleepy, heavy-lidded eyes towards her. "What are you doing with it?"

"I don't know whose it is. I found it. I was coming home one night, and it was lying there, big as life, outside my door there in the hall. So I picked it up and brought it in with me. There's nothing on it to show whom it belongs to."

"No, there isn't, is there?" he agreed forlornly. "Not a thing, not the slightest." He shook his head, as if in melancholy accord with her negation.

He had neglected to raise the cigarette to proper position. She was waiting, inquiringly. "I don't want to smoke," he said muffledly. He let that fall from his fingers, as the package had before. Then he stroked them unnoticeably against the side of his thigh, as if he were wiping them, or removing some foreign, unworthy tincture from them.

She quenched the flame with a click and put the little implement aside. Then she turned her face back towards him again, querulously worried.

"I know we're a little strange to each other yet. Just at first. They told me it might be like – But – we'll be all right, won't we, Mitch?" She brought her face closer, her lips towards his. "Don't you want to – say hello to me, the right way? Our old way? You haven't yet, since you first came in, you know."

Her hand went up and traced his hair back, lingeringly. Then when it rose a second time to repeat it, his head wasn't under it any more; it had shifted or swerved somehow, without her actually seeing it do so. She was stroking barren space.

Again her lips diffidently approached his. He drew in his breath, sharply. "What is that?"

"What?"

He drew in breath a second time.

"Oh, that. 'One Hour Alone'."

"So strong," he said, as if repeating something from memory, "it even gets on you secondhand." She saw his eyes go up towards the ceiling, as if trying to determine whether he had recited it right.

"I may have used too much," she admitted. "Just now I was so excited, seeing you sitting there in front of me, by way of the mirror."

"Just now?" was all he said.

She withdrew herself slowly from him, reluctantly straightened to her feet. "You're tired," she said mournfully. "We'll have to get used to each other all over again. But we will. I'm going to make you some coffee, that'll help. I have it right here."

"I don't want anything," he said, with a dull, sightless shake of his head, staring before him towards where she had been until now.

She stopped again, baffled. "What is it, Mitch, what is it?" she pleaded in a low, coaxing voice. "What have they done to you?"

"I ask that," he said absently.

They remained without speaking for a moment after that. She, standing in arrested departure, sideways and rearward of him, looking back at him. He, seated, vacant-eyed, looking forward at nothing.

Then suddenly, as if revivified, he stood, went over to the bed. He picked up the paper-backed book, reversed it, glanced into the two exposed pages.

"I saw your light go on, about ten or fifteen minutes ago," he said, without raising his eyes towards her, continuing to scan the page.

"I'd been lying awake in the dark," she said. "Worrying about you, as I always do. I couldn't sleep. So I got sick of it finally, and put on the light and tried to read."

"This?" He raised the book slightly with both hands, lowered it again. But without taking his eyes off it, seeming to peruse it absorbedly.

"Yes, that."

"What was the last line you read, just as my knock came? What was the last thing of all?"

"Oh, Mitch —" she laughed reproachfully.

He kept staring at the book. "I'd like to find the place. To put my finger on it, and say: 'Up to here, she was alone. And then I came in.' "

Her hand sought her hair, strayed into it baffledly. "I can't," she said. "Your knock drove it out of my mind, and now it won't come back. I wasn't interested in it, anyway."

"But you *were* reading," he said placidly, as if in reminder of something she herself had forgotten, and was supposed not to.

"Yes, I was reading it."

"Can't you give me just the sense of it? Just a word?"

"Oh, but Mitch, this is childish." She smiled, but again her hand went to her hair. "I can't think for the life of me. . . . No, wait, I have it! He was asking her if she remembered a woman in the theatre-audience wearing the same kind of hat she herself had on." She chuckled with a mischievous sort of satisfaction. "It just came back to me now."

"That's not here," he said stonily. "Not on here anywhere." He began to turn the pages. Endlessly, he seemed to go on turning them in reverse, from back to front. Suddenly he stopped again, retraced his course by a single page. "It is in here," he said. "I see it. It's the chapter before. You must have been reading it some other night. Not tonight."

"No, I read it tonight. I'm sure of it now. When I threw the book down, the pages must have slipped over and carried my place too far forward."

He turned it in his hands so that it was now face down; he parted his hands and let it fall that way, so that it fell from a greater height than if one had merely discarded it in haste at reading level.

Then he took it up and looked.

"It's still at the same place," he said, with all the objectivity of a physicist.

Then he closed it for good, and thus arbitrarily ended the story it held.

Her face had sobered. "I'll fix that coffee," she said.

"There won't be time." He put his hand out towards her, dissuadingly, but in a lazy, enervated sort of way. And yet the half-hearted gesture was enough to stop her, hold her there, half in, half out of the little recess or wall alcove she had evidently intended using for the purpose.

There was a moment's pause, while he seemed to be thinking what to say, his head held contemplatively downward. "I've been standing out there ever since half past nine. You didn't go by. I didn't see you come in."

"But I was here already. I've been here since nine, a little after. Why didn't you come to the door and —"

Like a drowning man grasping at straws he suddenly blurted out, "You've been visiting somebody upstairs. Somebody in the house that you know, you ran up there first, like girls do, when you first came home . . ." and beat out a sort of agonized time to it by striking his own knee with his clenched fist, once to almost every word, as if by repetition, by rhythm, he could rid himself of pain. "Some girl-friend, some chum, that lives in the building . . . *Then* you came down here, after that." And made a bitter mouth, through which, all incongruously, emerged a throb of happy, almost vacant, laughter.

"I don't know anyone upstairs."

"You've been visiting on the third or fourth, then. *Way* up. Think."

"I don't know anybody in the house. Not a soul in the entire house."

"*Say* you've been visiting somebody upstairs," he pleaded. "*Say* it."

"Why should I, when I haven't?"

He got up from the chair suddenly, started towards the door, as if in desperate urgency to get out, to leave her. Then the impulse wavered, and he stopped and turned towards her, parenthetically. As if still intent on carrying out the idea of departure, but only waiting to be reassured on some point first before doing so.

"Say you haven't waited. Say you haven't been true to me, Constance, and I'll go. I'll go right now. Without a word, without a whimper. Only don't fool me. Respect me, even if I am – what I am now. Say it."

Her eyes were brimming, but she gave no other sign of stress. She shook her head, but with such leniency of motion that the gesture was scarcely discernible at all. As though the phantom of a contradiction was even too substantial to give to such a non-existent idea. "I haven't looked at another man since you've been gone."

A retch of risibility seemed to course from his stomach, and he even placed his hand towards it for a moment as if to quell the pain implicit in it. "I *forgive* you, Constance. I overlook it. I – I understand. The war was long and – and hopeless. What am I now – and what was I before? It's happened to others, why not to me? Only just say it with your own mouth. Is that asking too much? Hurry up, Constance, while I can still take it."

She came towards him slowly. Her voice was choked with compassion. "You're so sick. Oh, what is it, what've they done —?"

Her arms went towards him, and she slowly twined them about his neck, and looked into his face. Then she tried to bring her own closer, to find his lips with hers, and kiss them in consolation.

He breathed heavily. "So strong it even gets on you secondhand," he whispered stonily. He swerved his head violently aside, without otherwise moving, and she was left there pendant, unable to reach him with her lips.

The embrace unravelled, and her arms slipped over his shoulders and fell down like loose ropes.

"I'd better make that coffee," she said almost inaudibly. "There doesn't seem to be – anything else I can do for you."

She turned away and went into the alcove, passing from sight for a moment. A tin container clashed briefly, as it was shifted from a higher to a lower level. There was the scratch of a matchstick against sandpaper, the feathery puff of ignited gas.

His hands went towards his waist, and with a sort of introspective leisureliness he began to separate the fastening of his belt.

She had come back to the alcove opening, was staring at him.

"Mitch, what are you doing? I don't like that. Don't do that here. I don't like that here. Mitch, what are doing that for?"

He had withdrawn it now from the loops that held it. His wrists moved with the sort of absent dexterity one gives to the act of disrobing. Mechanical, oft-repeated, with the thoughts elsewhere. "I'm making it small. I'm making a loop of it. So it'll go around you." He had made a slipknot of it. The horror was in the way he looked at it, not at her. As though his whole preoccupation were with it, to see if it were satisfactory or not, and she were just an onlooker, an admiring feminine observer to his typical masculine skill at such problems as this.

"Will you say you haven't been faithful?"

She didn't answer. She moved suddenly, and to move was death. She darted forward to get to the outer door, swerving outward to get past the place he stood.

He, on the contrary, didn't move from it. Simply pivoted on his heels to face the other way, while she made the longer outward progress. Like a ringmaster halting some small animal prancing about him on a given radius that cannot be altered.

It dropped over her head just as she reached the door. Her outstretched hand, one moment inches from the knob, was drawn slowly backward, as the pressure of the throng arched her back away from it. The second hand, futilely reaching out to take the other's place, was again too late. It likewise fell short, strained tremblingly against inexorable backward draw, stretched out on empty air, then at last receded to a distance that could no longer hope to be bridged.

Then, no longer their own masters, they both flew up to ease the stricture, like mechanical things that, once bent back that way, could no longer open out again.

She dropped to her knees, close up against his legs. He kept doing something with his wrists, with deft economy of movement. Her face turned towards him, but whether puppeted by his hands or in last despairing plea of her own volition, it was no longer possible to determine. They were too inextricably entwined. They were what he had wanted them to be: one.

Death came sectionally, not totally.

Her arms died first. Then her legs died, dancing against air. Then her heaving breast. Her eyes died last, after everything else was gone. The lights went out, but they stayed open.

He bent his head slowly. He found her agonizedly parted lips with his and kissed them. Lingeringly, devoutly. The kiss of homecoming, the kiss of parting.

Then he let go of the belt, that he was gripping behind her head, holding her up as by a halter, and she seemed to fall away from him. She dropped suddenly on to the bed. The bed shook and she seemed to shake with it, but it was only the bed shaking, not she.

"Now I'm alone," he whispered, baffled. "Now she's not here any more. Now I'm without her anyway." A puzzled expression creased his forehead. "What good did that do?" Then the answer he was groping for seemed to come to him, belatedly, and it partially eased him. "Now she has to be true to me, whether she wants to or not." The lover that had her now, he never gave them back again.

He wanted the belt back. There was some sort of dim precaution involved in this; but it wasn't at all coherent to him. Don't leave your belt on her, was all it seemed to say; don't leave your belt on her. He wasn't sure why, but it nudged at him insistently in the twilight of his reflexes.

It was hard to get it off. He'd stop each time, afraid that he was hurting her; then he'd remember that she couldn't feel it now, and go ahead a little more.

It was hard to straighten, too, even after it was off.

He paid it off in a straight line along the floor, and then he smoothed it by treading on it with his foot, and drawing his foot slowly along it, as if he were pressing it with an iron. Then he picked it up.

He turned his back on her, with some dim instinct of delicacy, and inserted it through the loops of his waistband. And then buckled it.

Now he was very tired, now he could sit down and rest.

He sat down on the chair, and supported his head for a while with one hand. It was quiet in the room, soothing. His eyelids started to droop closed once or twice, but he would blink them open again, go on resting again, contemplative, motionless.

She stared at the ceiling, he at the floor. It was as though they had had a quarrel and were sulking, pretending indifference to each other.

After a while something bothered him. There was something still wrong, something left undone. He couldn't think what it was at first. He looked over at her. "My belt is not around her throat."

Then suddenly he knew what it was. "I am still in here with her. I am still in the same room with her. I should be outside somewhere, away from here."

Questions, that was all he was afraid of. Too many questions. He was too tired.

He struck the arms of the chair with his hands, as the preliminary stage of rising. Then enervated, tired, did nothing else.

(More than that, that's not enough. You just moved your hands. You've got to pull your whole body up.)

He thrust one foot backward, under the chair seat, to gain leverage for rising. Then followed it with the second. Then again did nothing further.

(Still not enough. Now this is the hard part. This comes next. *Want to*, like they told you at the hospital. *Want to bad.*)

He pulled himself erect. He stood there just forward of the chair. He swayed. He sought backward-flailing support of the chair-arms and found himself sitting again.

He grimaced and his eyes got wet.

(All right then, do it over. You'll have to start in from the beginning and do it over again. Ready? Rested? Now.)

He was standing again. He fixed his eyes on the door.

(Now go over *there.*)

Midway to it he stopped. Looked back.

(But why do I have to leave her? There *was* some reason, but I've forgotten.) He half turned, about to retrace his steps. (No, keep going, and try to remember it on the outside, if you must. It won't come to you here. The air's clearer out there.)

He got to the doorknob, and punched it into his stomach with both hands, and that held him for a while, as though he'd skewered himself on to it bodily. Then he got the door open and crept around it to the outside.

He closed the door with infinite, tender slowness, holding her face fixed within view to the last. "Little Connie," he whispered, as if reassuring her of his fondness. "We've known each other such a long time, haven't we?"

He touched two fingers to his lips, in what, had it been completed, would have been the gesture of wafting a kiss.

But the kiss faltered, and the fingers dropped, and the door closed.

Outside in the open, it was cool and still and dark. The only sound was the scrape of his foot on the steps of the house. He stood there for a moment on them, as he remembered once having seen some other man do – he couldn't remember who, couldn't remember when – on leaving a house that he had stood watching.

The freshness of the air helped him. He felt a little less tired. He knew the respite was temporary, it would come back again. He knew that when it did, this time it would be for good. He knew, somehow, that before it did he must get as far away from here as he could.

He would have liked to stay there in the doorway, but he forced himself to leave it. He crossed to the other side of the street, at a rather faltering, shaky gait. There was about the way he lifted and set down his feet (almost seeming to free them with a lingering shake each time) a faint suggestion of a struggling fly, already trapped but still able to move, trailing over flypaper.

He stopped and looked back from there. The light was still on in her window. He knew that she was dead in there. He knew that he should go away from it as far as he could. Those two things were clear and distinct. They were all that were.

Then he looked up higher, to see if anyone was looking out. No one was. The last thing he saw was the geraniums, on the window-sill over hers. They were black, but he could still see their outline.

They should be down below, he thought vaguely. Flowers are for death.

The first block wasn't so difficult. He was conscious of going steadily forward. Though he didn't know in what direction forward lay, still he did not stand still, and he kept going away from where he had been. That much was a gain.

Fatigue began creeping back. Not fatigue of the limbs, that can be overcome by resting; fatigue of the senses, that leads into nonawareness, into nothingness. His mind was like an exposed photographic plate, still clear in the centre but beginning to blur all around the edges. In the clear patch in the centre there remained but one sharply defined image or message: Keep going, keep going far away.

The second block he was stopping more frequently now, coming to an erratic standstill every so often, then going on again. As though an enormous hand had been cupped upon him suddenly, holding him where he was; then lifted again, as inexplicably, letting him continue. He was like a mannikin, or something wound with a key, that follows a mechanical trajectory. He would even continue stiffly facing in the one set direction, while the halt lasted; even though it might be on the bias to the guiding-lines of pavement edge and building base. Then continue on it when he resumed going.

It was fairly horrible; night charitably covered most of it.

Once he passed a sentry, and the man studied him suspiciously, but there was no challenge, so he gave no recognition. No halting shot followed, either, though his neck was bent defensively for some time after. He went on until he was past that arca.

The swirling blur had all but closed over the clear space in the centre now. One twinkling point of light remained, like a glimmering star. Keep on, farther away.

He stumbled over some hidden kerbstone hazard, went down. A screaming shell went by just then, trailing blinding light. He could feel the air flurry of its passage, so the fall must have saved him. There was no concussion; it never exploded. It simply whined itself out into far distance. It seemed to skim the surface of the earth without ever descending to it to detonate, without its arc ever coming to an end. He'd never experienced a shell like that before.

He dropped the protective arm with which he'd shielded his eyes, and picked himself up, and went on.

Another one came at him, this time from the opposite direction. He must be in the centre of a cross-fire. Again on a blinding trail of light that *preceded* it. He stood still, paralysed. It swerved violently to one side of him, snaking its comet-like glare with it, skimmed past, then straightened back upon its former trajectory. A smouldering red spark marked its recession. Again there was no thud. His nerves cried out for it, and it never came.

These were the worst kind; there was no sundering of tension after them. They never hit anywhere.

He began to run now, at a sort of tottering trot, to get away from them. No more came for a minute. He stopped, panting and clutching at his stomach with both hands to keep it from rejecting.

Suddenly a voice said: "Anything wrong? Anything I can do for you, buddy?"

His lieutenant, giving him an order.

"Yes sir," he said crisply, and saluted mechanically, and went forward, walking rapidly in a straight, unerring line.

He went face first into a wall, and felt it blindly with the flats of his hands for an opening, then, finding none, and not knowing how to overcome it, lieutenant or no lieutenant, allowed it to deflect him and followed it instead. They often sent you places like that, where there was no way through. You had to go, though, just the same.

The wall turned, and he did with it. Then it left him, and he was on his own again.

They were starting to come around him thick again. Some of them screeched, and some of them hummed, and some of them gave ear-slitting honks, like flying metal geese. He'd better hurry and get a hole dug.

He dropped to his hands and knees, keeping his head low, as he had learned to do, and raked with his bare nails, in long strokes in two parallel rows.

The surface was hard, he couldn't seem to break it, to get through to the fill. He tried harder, faster. His arms flailed in and out.

They kept dropping around him. The flash would come, but then it wouldn't go out again. It would sort of slide to a stop, to one side of him, and then just stay there with a sort of purring throb, that even shook the ground he was grovelling on.

Voices came from them, and doors cracked, and feet thrust suddenly down into view from on high, then took root.

"What is it? What's he doing?"

"I don't know. I been following him for several blocks. Something wrong."

"Oh, my God, Charlie! Don't just stand there *watching* him. Help him. Look at his hands."

There were narrow, dark, glistening tracks appearing now in the wake of his fingers, freshly renewed each minute.

Arms went round his middle. The arms of medicos, they must have been. He was lifted up, held propped. Hands fumbled with the buttons of his shirt, and he could feel his dog-tag being twisted, drawn out through the opening.

"From – Convalescent Hospital," a muffled voice said. "Better get him back there, right away."

His hand groped upward, trying to find his forehead in a salute.

"I couldn't make it," he sighed inaudibly.

"Easy, easy," a sympathetic, sob-thick voice murmured. "The war's over, soldier."

The war's over, soldier. He took that with him down into the long sleep that follows battles. Constance was his girl, safe, waiting, three thousand miles away. Someone to go back to. . . .

It was warm in the sun, on the park bench. It went through your clothes, and found your skin, and felt good; you didn't hurt any more. There were green leaves, and under them a film of pale-blue shade, off that way in the distance, but it was even better here, out in the open, out in full sun.

You just sat, and the blue shade slowly circled round on the ground under the trees, from one side all the way over to the other. Let the shade move. You didn't. You just sat. There was nowhere to go but here. He knew now all the places to go – he wasn't lost or uncertain any more, his mind was clear – and he knew there was no other place but this to go.

There was no going back now, either. He knew that too. He was all right now. You couldn't always go back. He could light a cigarette now. Watch. See? He could walk as long as he wanted to without stopping. And that was all-right. That was all it would ever be from now on. If there had been other things, there weren't any now.

There was no place to go, nothing to do. Sit in the sun, watch the shade go round. You grew old, like the shade. You had to wait for it, what else could you do? It was an order, from a lieutenant. A different one, you never saw. But He'd given it just the same; you had to obey.

The man over at the other end of the bench got up, left his newspaper lying there behind him.

After a while he reached over and picked it up. He rearranged it and started to pore over it patiently. It took a long time, it said so many things. It helped the shade go quicker; it helped in carrying out the lieutenant's order.

It said so many things. Some of them were large, some of them small. He got to even the smallest eventually, after the large ones were done.

It said: 'Forecast for Thursday: Clear and warm, with variable winds, lowered humidity. Maximum temperature —'

It said: 'Extraordinary Values! Mail and phone orders filled while quantities last. Come early to be sure of a full selection —'

It said: 'Cards Strike Out in Second —'

It said: 'Killer Pays Penalty. Orville Johns, 32, went to his death last night in the execution chamber of the State Penitentiary at – for the murder of Constance Sterling, in June of last year. Johns was the janitor of the building in which the slain girl lived; a number of her belongings were found in his basement apartment shortly after the discovery of the crime. He disappeared at the time, and was not apprehended for some months afterwards . . . Protesting his innocence to the last, the condemned man entered the chamber at 11.10 and was pronounced dead at 11.15. # # # For acid indigestion, use Bell-ans. Twenty-five cents at all drugstores."

I did that, he said to himself, squinting thoughtfully up at the sun. That was me.

He'd known he'd done it, for some time now.

The Corpse Next Door

Harlan's wife turned away quickly, trying to hide the can-opener in her hand. "What's the idea?" he asked. She hadn't expected him to look across the top of his morning paper just then. The can of evaporated milk she had been holding in her other hand slipped from her grasp in her excitement, hit the floor with a dull whack, and rolled over. She stooped quickly, snatched it up, but he had seen it.

"Looks like somebody swiped the milk from our door again last night," she said with a nervous little laugh. Harlan had a vicious temper. She hadn't wanted to tell him, but there had not been time to run out to the store and get another bottle.

"That's the fifth time in two weeks!" He rolled the paper into a tube and smacked it viciously against the table-leg. She could see him starting to work himself up, getting whiter by the minute even under his shaving talcum. "It's somebody right in the house!" he roared. "No outsider could get in past that locked street-door after twelve!" He bared his teeth in a deceptive grin. "I'd like to get my hands on the fellow!"

"I've notified the milkman and I've complained to the superintendent, but there doesn't seem to be any way of stopping it," Mrs Harlan sighed. She punched a hole in the top of the can, tilted it over his cup.

He pushed it aside disgustedly and stood up. "Oh, yes, there is," he gritted, "and I'm going to stop it!" A suburban commuter's train whistled thinly in the distance. "Just lemme get hold of whoever —!" he muttered a second time with suppressed savagery as he grabbed his hat, bolted for the door. Mrs Harlan shook her head with worried foreboding as it slammed behind him.

He came back at six bringing something in a paper-bag, which he stood on the kitchen-shelf. Mrs Harlan looked at it and saw a quart of milk.

"We don't need that. I ordered a bottle this afternoon from the grocer," she told him.

"That's not for our use," he answered grimly. "It's a decoy."

At eleven, in bathrobe and slippers, she saw him carry it out to the front door and set it down. He looked up and down the hall, squatted down beside it, tied something invisible around its neck below the cardboard cap. Then he strewed something across the sill and closed the door.

"What on earth —?" said Mrs Harlan apprehensively.

He held up his index-finger. A coil of strong black sewing-thread was plaited around it. It stood out clearly against the skin of his finger, but trailed off invisibly into space and under the door to connect with the bottle. "Get it?" he gloated vindictively. "You've got to look twice to see this stuff once, especially in a shadowy doorway. But it cuts the skin if it's pulled tight. See? One tug should be enough to wake me up, and if I can only get out there in time —"

He left the rest of it unfinished. He didn't have to finish it, his wife knew just what he meant. She was beginning to wish he hadn't found out about the thefted milk. There'd only be a brawl outside their door in the middle of the night, with the neighbors looking on —

He paid out the thread across their living-room floor into the bedroom beyond, got into bed, and left the hand it was attached to outside the covers. Putting out the lights after him, she was tempted to clip the thread then and there, as the safest way out, even picked up a pair of scissors and tried to locate it in the dark. She knew if she did, he'd be sure to notice it in the morning and raise cain.

"Don't walk around in there so much," he called warningly. "You'll snarl it up."

Her courage failed her. She put the scissors down and went to bed. The menacing thread, like a powder-train leading to a high explosive, remained intact.

In the morning it was still there, and there were two bottles of milk at the door instead of one, the usual delivery and the decoy. Mrs Harlan sighed with relief. It would have been very short-sighted of the guilty person to repeat the stunt two nights in succession; it had been happening at the rate of every third night so far. Maybe by the time it happened again, Harlan would cool down.

But Harlan was slow at cooling down. The very fact that the stunt wasn't repeated immediately only made him boil all the more. He wanted his satisfaction out of it. He caught himself thinking about it on the train riding to and from the city. Even at the office, when he should have been attending to his work. It started to fester and rankle. He was in a fair way to becoming hipped on the subject, when at last the thread paid off one night about four.

He was asleep when the warning tug came. Mrs Harlan slept soundly in the adjoining bed. He knew right away what had awakened him, jumped soundlessly out of bed with a bound, and tore through the darkened flat toward the front door.

He reached it with a pattering rush of bare feet and tore it open. It was sweet. It was perfect. He couldn't have asked for it any better! Harlan caught him red-handed, in the very act. The bottle of milk cradled in his arm, he froze there petrified and stared guiltily at the opening door. He'd evidently missed feeling the tug of the thread altogether – which wasn't surprising, because at his end the bottle had received it and not himself. And to make it even better than perfect, pluperfect, he was someone that by the looks of him Harlan could handle without much trouble. Not that he would have hung back even if he'd found himself outclassed. He was white-hot with thirty-six hours' pent-up combustion, and physical cowardice wasn't one of his failings, whatever else was.

He just stood there for a split second, motionless, to rub it in. "Nice work, buddy!" he hissed.

The hijacker cringed, bent lopsidedly to put the bottle on the floor without taking his terrified eyes off Harlan. He was a reedy sort of fellow in trousers and undershirt, a misleading tangle of hair showing on his chest.

"Gee, I've been so broke," he faltered apologetically. "Doctor-bills, an' – an' I'm outa work. I needed this stuff awfully bad, I ain't well —"

"You're in the pink of condish compared to what you're gonna be in just about a minute more!" rumbled Harlan. The fellow could have gotten down on his knees, paid for the milk ten times over, but it wouldn't have cut any ice with Harlan. He was going to get his satisfaction out of this the way he wanted it. That was the kind Harlan was.

He waited until the culprit straightened up again, then breathed a name at him fiercely and swung his arm like a shot-putter.

Harlan's fist smashed the lighter man square in the mouth. He went over like a paper cut-out and lay just as flat as one. The empty hallway throbbed with his fall. He lay there and miraculously still showed life. Rolling his head dazedly from side to side, he reached up vaguely to find out where his mouth had gone. Those slight movements were like waving a red flag at a bull. Harlan snorted and flung himself down on the man. Knee to chest, he grabbed the fellow by the hair of the head, pulled it upward and crashed his skull down against the flagged floor.

When the dancing embers of his rage began to thin out so that he was able to see straight once more, the man wasn't rolling his head dazedly any more. He wasn't moving in the slightest. A thread of blood was trickling out of each ear-hollow, as though something had shattered inside.

Harlan stiff-armed himself against the floor and got up slowly like something leaving its kill. "All right, you brought it on yourself!" he growled. There was an undertone of fear in his voice. He prodded the silent form reluctantly. "Take the lousy milk," he said. "Only next time ask for it first!" He got up on his haunches, squatting there ape-like. "Hey! Hey, you!" He shook him again. "Matter with you? Going to lie there all night? I said you could take the —"

The hand trying to rouse the man stopped suddenly over his heart. It came away slowly, very slowly. The color drained out of Harlan's face. He sucked in a deep breath that quivered his lips. It stayed cold all the way down like menthol.

"Gone!" The hoarsely-muttered word jerked him to his feet. He started backing, backing a step at a time, toward the door he'd come out of. He could not take his eyes off the huddled, shrunken form lying there close beside the wall.

"Gee, I better get in!" was the first inchoate thought that came to him. He found the opening with his back, even retreated a step or two through it, before he realized the folly of what he was doing. Couldn't leave him lying there like that right outside his own door. They'd know right away who had – and they weren't going to if he could help it.

He glanced behind him into the darkened flat. His wife's peaceful, rhythmic breathing was clearly audible in the intense stillness. She'd slept through the whole thing. He stepped into the hall again, looked up and down. If she hadn't heard, with the door standing wide open, then surely nobody else had with theirs closed.

But one door was not closed! The next one down the line was open a crack, just about an inch, showing a thin line of white inner-frame. Harlan went cold all over for a minute, then sighed with relief. Why that was where the milk-thief came from. Sure, obviously. He'd been heading back in that direction when Harlan came out and caught him. It was the last door down that way. The hall, it was true, took a right-angle turn when it got past there, and there were still other flats around the other side, out of sight. That must be the place. Who else would leave their door off the latch like that at four in the morning, except this guy who had come out to prowl in the hallway?

This was one time when Mrs Harlan would have come in handy. She would have known for sure whether the guy lived in there or not, or just where he did belong. He himself wasn't interested in their neighbors, didn't know one from the other, much less which flats they hung out in. But it was a cinch he wasn't going to wake her and drag her out here to look at a dead man, just to find out where to park him. One screech from her would put him behind the eight-ball before he knew it.

Then while he was hesitating, sudden, urgent danger made up his mind for him. A faint whirring sound started somewhere in the bowels of the building. Along with it the faceted glass knob beside the automatic elevator panel burned brightly red. Somebody was coming up!

He jumped for the prostrate form, got an under-arm grip on it, and started hauling it hastily toward that unlatched door. Legs splayed out behind it, the heels of the shoes ticked over the cracks between the flagstones like train-wheels on a track.

The elevator beat him to it, slow-moving though it was. He had the guy at the door, still in full view, when the triangular porthole in the elevator door-panel bloomed yellow with its arrival. He whirled, crouching defiantly over the body, like something at bay. He would be caught with the goods, just as he himself had caught this guy, if the party got out at this floor. But they didn't. The porthole darkened again as the car went on up.

He let out a long, whistling breath like a deflating tire, pushed the door carefully open. It gave a single rebellious click as the latch cleared the socket altogether. He listened, heart pounding. Might be sixteen kids in there for all he knew, a guy that stole milk like that.

"I'll drop him just inside," Harlan thought grimly. "Let them figure it out in the morning!"

He tugged the fellow across the sill with an unavoidable wooden thump of the heels, let him down, tensed, listened again, silhouetted there against the orange light from the hall – if anyone was inside looking out. But there was an absence of breathing-sounds from within. It seemed too good to be true. He felt his way forward, peering into the dark, ready to jump back and bolt for it at the first alarm.

Once he got past the closed-in foyer, the late moon cast enough light through the windows to show him that there was no one living in the place but the guy himself. It was a one-room flat and the bed, which was one of those that come down out of a closet, showed white and vacant.

"Swell!" said Harlan. "No one's gonna miss you right away!"

He hauled him in, put him on the bed, turned to soft-shoe out again when he got a better idea. Why not make it really tough to find him while he was about it? This way, the first person that stuck his head in was bound to spot the man. He tugged the sheet clear of the body lying on it and pulled it over him like a shroud. He tucked it in on both sides, so that it held him in a mild sort of grip.

He gripped the foot of the bed. It was hard to lift, but once he got it started the mechanism itself came to his aid. It began swinging upward of its own accord. He held onto it to keep it from banging. It went into the closet neatly enough but wouldn't stay put. The impediment between it and the wall pushed it down each time. But the door would probably hold it. He heard a rustle as something shifted, slipped further down in back of the bed. He didn't have to be told what that was.

He pushed the bed with one arm and caught the door with the other. Each time he took the supporting arm away, the bed tipped out and blocked the door. Finally at the sixth try he got it to stand still and swiftly slapped the door in place over it. That held it like glue and he had nothing further to worry about. It would have been even better if there'd been a key to lock it, take out, and throw away. There wasn't. This was good enough, this would hold – twenty-four hours, forty-eight, a week even, until the guy's rent came due and they searched the place. And by that time he could pull a quick change of address, back a van up to the door, and get out of the building. Wouldn't look so hot, of course, but who wanted to stay where there was a permanent corpse next door? They'd never be able to pin it on him anyway, never in a million years. Not a living soul, not a single human eye, had seen it happen. He was sure of that.

Harlan gave the closet door a swipe with the loose end of his pajama jacket, just for luck, up where his hand had pushed against it. He hadn't touched either knob.

He reconnoitered, stepped out, closed the flat up after him. The tumbler fell in the lock. It couldn't be opened from the outside now except by the super's passkey. Back where it had happened, he picked up the lethal bottle of milk and took it into his own flat. He went back a second time, got down close on hands and knees and gave the floor a careful inspection. There were just two spots of blood, the size of two-bit pieces, that must have dripped from the guy's ears before he picked him up. He looked down at his pajama coat. There were more than two spots on that, but that didn't worry him any.

He went into his bathroom, stripped off the jacket, soaked a handful of it under the hot water and slipped into the hall with it. The spots came up off the satiny flagstones at a touch without leaving a trace. He hurried down the corridor, opened a door, and stepped into a hot, steamy little whitewashed alcove provided with an incinerator chute. He balled the coat up, pulled down the flap of the chute, shoved the bundle in like a letter in a mail box and then sent the trousers down after it too, just to make sure. That way he wouldn't be stuck with any odd pair of trousers without their matching jacket. Who could swear there had ever been such a pair of pajamas now? A strong cindery odor came up the chute. The fire was going in the basement right now. He wouldn't even have to worry about the articles staying intact down there until morning. Talk about your quick service!

He slipped back to his own door the way he was without a stitch on him. He realized it would have been a bum joke if somebody had seen him like that, after the care he'd taken about all those little details. But they hadn't. So what?

He shut the door of his apartment, and put on another pair of pajamas. Slipping quietly into the bed next to the peacefully-slumbering Missis, he lit a cigarette. Then the let-down came. Not that he got jittery, but he saw that he wasn't going to sleep any more that night. Rather than lie there tossing and turning, he dressed and went out of the house to take a walk.

He would have liked a drink, but it was nearly five, way past closing-time for all the bars, so he had to be satisfied with a cup of coffee at the counter lunch. He tried to put it to his mouth a couple of times, finally had to call the waiter back.

"Bring me a black one," he said. "Leave the milk out!" That way it went down easy enough.

The sun was already up when he got back, and he felt like he'd been pulled through a wringer. He found Mrs Harlan in the kitchen, getting things started for his breakfast.

"Skip that," he told her irritably. "I don't want any – and shove that damn bottle out of sight, will you?"

He took time off during his lunch-hour to look at a flat in the city and paid a deposit for it. When he got home that night he told Mrs Harlan abruptly, "Better get packed up, we're getting out of here the first thing in the morning."

"Wha-at?" she squawked. "Why we can't do that. We've got a lease! What's come over you?"

"Lease or no lease," he barked. "I can't stand it here any more. We're getting out after tonight, I tell you!"

They were in the living-room and his eyes flicked toward the wall that partitioned them off from the flat next door. He didn't want to do that, but he couldn't help himself. She didn't notice, but obediently started to pack. He called up a moving-van company.

In the middle of the night he woke up from a bad dream and ran smack into something even worse. He got up and went into the living-room. He didn't exactly know why. The moon was even brighter than the night before and washed that dividing wall with almost a luminous calsomine. Right in the middle of the wall there was a hideous black, blurred outline, like an X-ray showing through from the other side. Right about where that bed would be. Stiff and skinny the hazy figure was with legs and arms and even a sort of head on it. He pitched the back of his arm to his mouth just in time to douse the yell struggling to come out, went wet all over as though he were under a shower-bath. He managed to turn finally and saw the peculiar shape of one of Mrs Harlan's modernistic lamps standing in the path of the moon, throwing its shadow upon the wall. He pulled down the shade and tottered back inside. He took his coffee black again next morning, looked terrible.

She rang him at the office just before closing-time. "You at the new place?" he asked eagerly.

"No," she said, "they wouldn't let me take the stuff out. I had a terrible time with the renting-agent. Ed, we'll just have to make the best of it. He warned me that if we go, they're going to garnishee your salary and get a judgment against you for the whole two-years' rent. Ed, we can't afford to keep two places going at once and your firm will fire you the minute they find out. They won't stand for anything like that. You told me so yourself. He told me any justified complaint we have will be attended to, but we can't just walk out on our lease. You'd better think twice about it. I don't know what's wrong with the flat anyway."

He did, but he could not tell her. He saw that they had him by the short hairs. If he went, it meant loss of his job, destitution; even if he got another, they'd attach the wages of that too. Attracting this much attention wasn't the best thing in the world, either. When he got home, the agent came up to find out what was the trouble, what his reasons were, he didn't know what to answer, couldn't think of a legitimate kick he had coming. He was afraid now even to bring up about the chiseling of the milk. It would have sounded picayune at that.

"I don't have to give you my reasons!" he said surlily. "I'm sick o' the place, and that's that!"

Which he saw right away was a tactical error, not only because it might sow suspicion later, but because it antagonized the agent now. "You can go just as soon as you've settled for the balance of your lease. I'm not trying to hold you!" he fumed. "If you try moving your things out without that, I'll call the police!"

Harlan slammed the door after him like a six-gun salute. He had a hunch the agent wouldn't be strictly within his legal rights in going quite that far, but he was in no position to force a showdown and find out for sure. No cops, thanks.

He realized that his own blundering had raised such a stink that it really didn't matter now any more whether he stayed or went. They'd make it their business to trace his forwarding address, and they'd have that on tap when disclosure came. So the whole object of moving out would be defeated. The lesser of two evils now was to stay, lie very low, hope the whole incident would be half-forgotten by the time the real excitement broke. It may have been lesser, but it was still plenty evil. He didn't see how he was going to stand it. Yet he had to.

He went out and came back with a bottle of rye, told his wife he felt a cold coming on. That was so he wouldn't run into any more hallucinations during the night like that phantom X-ray on the wall. When he went to bed the bottle was empty. He was still stony sober, but at least it put him through the night somehow.

On his way across the hall toward the elevator that morning, his head turned automatically to look up at that other door. He couldn't seem to control it. When he came back that evening the same thing happened. It was locked, just as it had been for the past two nights and two days now. He thought, "I've got to quit that. Somebody's liable to catch me at it and put two and two together."

In those two days and two nights he changed almost beyond recognition. He lost all his color; was losing weight almost by the hour; shelves under his eyes you could have stacked books on; appetite shot to smithereens. A backfire on the street made him leave his shoes without unlacing them, and his office-work was starting to go haywire. Hooch was putting him to sleep each night, but he had to keep stepping it up. He was getting afraid one of these times he'd spill the whole thing to his wife while he was tanked without knowing it. She was beginning to notice there was something the matter and mentioned his seeing a doctor about himself once or twice. He snapped at her and shut her up.

The third night, which was the thirty-first of the month, they were sitting there in the living-room. She was sewing. He stared glassy-eyed through the paper, pretending to read, whisky-tumbler at his elbow, sweat all over his ashen forehead, when she started sniffling.

"Got a cold?" he asked tonelessly.

"No," she said, "there's a peculiar musty odor in here, don't you get it? Sickly-sweet. I've been noticing it off and on all day, it's stronger in this room than in —"

"Shut up!" he rasped. The tumbler shook in his hand as he downed its contents, refilled it. He got up, opened the windows as far as they would go. He came back, killed the second shot, lit a cigarette unsteadily, deliberately blew the first thickly fragrant puff all around her head. "No, I don't notice anything," he said in an artificially steady voice. His face was almost green in the lamplight.

"I don't see how you can miss it," she said innocently. "It's getting worse every minute. I wonder if there's something wrong with the drains in this building?"

He didn't hear the rest of it. He was thinking: 'It'll pay off, one way or the other, pretty soon – thank goodness for that! Tomorrow's the first, they'll be showing up for his rent, that'll be the finale.'

He almost didn't care now which way it worked out – anything so long as it was over with, anything but this ghastly suspense. He couldn't hold out much longer. Let them suspect him even, if they wanted to; the complete lack of proof still held good. Any lawyer worth his fee could get him out of it with one hand tied behind his back.

But then when he snapped out of it and caught sight of her over the inter-house phone, realized what she was about, he backed water in a hurry. All the bravado went out of him. "What're you doing?" he croaked.

"I'm going to ask the superintendent what that is, have him come up here and —"

"Get away from there!" he bellowed. She hung up as though she'd been bitten, turned to stare.

A second later he realized what a swell out that would have been to have the first report of the nuisance come from them themselves; he wished he had let her go ahead. It should have come from them. They were closest to the death-flat. If it came from somebody else further away – and they seemed not to have noticed it – that would be one more chip stacked up against him.

"All right, notify him if you want to," he countermanded.

"No, no, not if you don't want me to." She was frightened now. He had her all rattled. She moved away from the phone.

To bridge the awkward silence he said the one thing he didn't want to, the one thing of all he'd intended not to say. As though possessed of perverse demons, it came out before he could stop it: "Maybe it's from next-door." Then his eyes hopelessly rolled around in their sockets.

"How could it be?" she contradicted mildly. "That flat's been vacant for the past month or more —"

A clock they had in there in the room with them ticked on hollowly, resoundingly, eight, nine, ten times. Clack, clack, clack, as though it were hooked up to a loudspeaker. What a racket it was making! Couldn't hear yourself think.

"No one living in there, you say?" he said in a hoarse whisper after what seemed an hour ticked by.

"No, I thought you knew that. I forgot, you don't take much interest in the neighbors —"

Then who was he? Where had he come from? Not from the street, because he had been in his undershirt. "I dragged the guy back into the wrong apartment!" thought Harlan. He was lucky it was vacant! It gave him the shivers, even now, to think what might have happened if there had been somebody else in there that night! The more he puzzled over it, the cloudier the mystery got. That particular door had been ajar, the bed down out of the closet, and the guy had been pussyfooting back toward there. Then where did he belong, if not in there? He was obviously a lone wolf, or he would have been missed by now. Those living with him would have sent out an alarm the very next morning after it had happened. Harlan had been keeping close tabs on the police calls on his radio and there hadn't been anything of the kind. And even if he had lived alone in one of the other flats, the unlatched door left waiting for his return would have attracted attention from the hall by now.

What was the difference where he came from anyway; it was where he was now that mattered! All he could get out of it was this: there would be no pay-off tomorrow after all. The agony would be prolonged now indefinitely – until prospective tenants were shown the place and sudden discovery resulted. He groaned aloud, took his next swig direct from the bottle without any tumbler for a go-between.

In the morning he could tell breakdown was already setting in. Between the nightly sousing, the unending mental strain, the lack of food, he was a doddering wreck when he got out of bed and staggered into his clothes. Mrs Harlan said, "I don't think you'd better go to the office today. If you could see yourself —!" But he had to, anything was better than staying around here!

He opened the living-room door (he'd closed it on the two of them the night before) and the fetid air from inside seemed to hit him in the face, it was so strong. He reeled there in that corrupt, acrid draft, not because it was so difficult to breathe but because it was so difficult for *him* to breathe, knowing what he did about it. He stood there gagging, hand to throat; his wife had to come up behind him and support him with one arm for a minute, until he pulled himself together. He couldn't, of course, eat anything. He grabbed his hat and made for the elevator in a blind hurry that was almost panic. His head jerked toward that other door as he crossed the hall; it hadn't missed doing that once for three days and nights.

This time there was a difference. He swung back again in time to meet the superintendent's stare. The latter had just that moment come out of the elevator with a wad of rent receipts in his hand. You couldn't say that Harlan paled at the involuntary betrayal he had just committed because he hadn't been the color of living protoplasm in thirty-six hours now.

The super had caught the gesture, put his own implication on it. "That bothering you folks too?" he said. "I've had complaints from everyone else on this floor about it so far. I'm going in there right now and invest —"

The hallway went spinning around Harlan like a cyclorama. The superintendent reached out, steadied him by the elbow. "See that, it's got you dizzy already! Must be some kind of sewer-gas." He fumbled for a passkey. "That why you folks wanted to move earlier in the week?"

Harlan still had enough presence of mind left, just enough, to nod. "Why didn't you say so?" the super went on. Harlan didn't have enough left to answer that one. What difference did it make. In about a minute more it would be all over but the shouting. He groped desperately to get himself a minute more time.

"I guess you want the rent," he said with screwy matter-of-factness. "I got it right here with me. Better let me give it to you now. I'm going in to town —"

He paid him the fifty bucks, counted them three times, purposely let one drop, purposely fumbled picking it up. But the passkey still stayed ready in the super's hand. He leaned against the wall, scribbled a receipt, and handed it to Harlan. "Thanks, Mr Harlan." He turned, started down the hall toward that door. That damnable doorway to hell!

Harlan was thinking: "I'm not going to leave him now. I'm going to stick with him when he goes in there. He's going to make the discovery, but it's never gonna get past him! I can't let it. He saw me look at that door just now. He'll read it all over my face. I haven't got the juice left to bluff it out. I'm going to kill him in there – with my bare hands." He let the rent receipt fall out of his hand, went slowly after the man like somebody walking in his sleep.

The passkey clicked, the super pushed the door open, light came out into the dimmer hallway from it, and he passed from sight. Harlan slunk through the doorframe after him and pushed the door back the other way, partly closing it after the two of them. It was only then that Harlan made an imcomprehensible discovery. The air was actually clearer in here than in his own place – clearer even than out in the hall! Stale and dust-laden from being shut up for days, it was true, but odorless, the way air should be!

"Can't be in here, after all," the super was saying, a few paces ahead.

Harlan took up a position to one side of the bedcloset, murmuring to himself: "He lives – until he opens that!"

The super had gone into the bath. Harlan heard him raise and slap down the wooden bowl cover in there, fiddle with the washbasin stopper. "Nope, nothing in here!" he called out. He came out again, went into the postage-stamp kitchen, sniffed around in there, examining the sink, the gas-stove. "It *seemed* to come from in here," he said, showing up again, "I can't make head or tail out of it!"

Neither could Harlan. The only thing he could think of was: the bedding and the mattress, which were on *this* side of what was causing it, must have acted as a barricade, stuffing up the closet-door, and must have kept that odor from coming out into this room, sending it through the thin porous wall in the other direction instead, into his own place and from there out into the hall.

The super's eye roved speculatively on past him and came to rest on the closet-door. "Maybe it's something behind that bed," he said.

Harlan didn't bat an eyelash, jerky as he had been before out in the hall. "You just killed yourself then, Mister," was his unheard remark. "This is it. Now!" He gripped the floor-boards with the soles of his feet through the shoe-leather, tensed, crouched imperceptibly for the spring.

The super stepped over, so did Harlan, diagonally, toward him. The super reached down for the knob, touched it, got ready to twist his wrist —

The house-phone in the entry-way buzzed like an angry hornet. Harlan went up off his heels, coming down again on them spasmodically. "Paging me, I guess. I told them I was coming in here," said the super, turning to go out there and answer it. "Okay, Molly," he said, "I'll be right down." He held the front door ready to show Harlan he wanted to leave and lock up again. "Somebody wants to see an apartment," he explained. The door clicked shut, the odors of decay swirled around them once more on the outside of it, and they rode down together in the car.

Something was dying in Harlan by inches – his reason maybe. "I can never go through that again," he moaned. The sweat did not start coming through his paralyzed pores until after he was seated in the train, riding in. Everything looked misshapen and out of focus.

He came back at twilight. In addition to the dusky amber hall lights, there was a fan of bright yellow spilling out of the death-door. Open again, and voices in there. Lined up along the wall outside the door were a radio cabinet, a bridge lamp, a pair of chairs compacted together seat to seat. An expressman in a dirty blue blouse came out, picked them up effortlessly with one arm, and slung them inside after him.

Harlan sort of collapsed against his own door. He scratched blindly for admittance, forgetting he had a key, too shell-shocked to use it even if he had taken it out.

Mrs Harlan let him in, too simmering with the news she had to tell to notice his appearance or actions. "We've got new neighbors," she said almost before she had the door closed. "Nice young couple, they just started to move in before you got here —"

He was groping desperately for the bottle on the shelf, knocked down a glass and broke it. Then they hadn't found out yet; they hadn't taken down the bed yet! It kept going through his battered brain like a demoniac rhythm. He nearly gagged on the amount of whisky he was swallowing from the neck of the bottle all at one time. When room had been cleared for his voice, he panted: "What about that odor? You mean they took that place the way it —?"

"I guess they were in a hurry, couldn't be choosy. He sent his wife up to squirt deodorant around in the hall before they got here. What does he care, once he gets them signed up? Dirty trick, if you ask me."

He had one more question to ask. "Of course you sized up every stick of stuff they have. Did they – did they bring their own bed with them?"

"No, I guess they're going to use the one in there —"

Any minute now? His brain was fifty per cent blind unreasoning panic, unable to get the thing in the right perspective any more. That discovery itself wasn't necessarily fatal, but his own possible implication in it no longer seemed to register with him. He was confusing one with the other, unable to differentiate between them any more. Discovery had to be prevented, discovery had to be forestalled! Why? Because his own corrosive guilty conscience knew the full explanation of the mystery. He was forgetting that they didn't – unless he gave it to them himself.

Still sucking at the bottle, he edged back to the front door, turned sidewise to it, put his ear up against it.

"T'anks very much, buddy," he heard the moving man say gruffly, and the elevator-slide closed.

He opened the door, peered out. The last of the furniture had gone inside, the hall was clear now. The fumes of the disinfectant the super's wife had used were combating that other odor, but it was still struggling through – to his acute senses, at least. They had left their door open. Their voices were clearly audible as he edged further out. Two living people unsuspectingly getting settled in a room with an unseen corpse!

"Move that over a little further," he heard the woman say. "The bed has to come down here at nights. Oh, that reminds me! He couldn't get it open when he wanted to show it to me today. The door must be jammed. He promised to come back, but I guess he forgot —"

"Let's see what I can do with it," the husband's voice answered.

Harlan, like something drawn irresistibly toward its own destruction, was slinking nearer and nearer, edgewise along the corridor-wall. A tom-tom he carried with him was his heart.

A sound of bare hands pounding wood came through the bright-yellow gap in the wall ahead. Then a couple of heavier impacts, kicks with the point of a shoe.

"It's not locked, is it?"

"No, when I turn the knob I can see the catch slip back under the lock. Something's holding it jammed in there. The bed must be out of true or somebody closed it too hard the last time."

"What're we going to sleep on?" the woman wailed.

"If I can hit it hard enough, maybe the vibration'll snap it back. Run down a minute and borrow a hammer from the super, like a good girl."

Harlan turned and vanished back where he had come from. Through the crack of the door he saw the woman come out into the hall, standing waiting for the car, go down in it. He said to his wife, "Where's that hammer we used to have?" He found it in a drawer and went out with it.

He was no longer quite sane when he knocked politely alongside that open door down the hall. He knew what he was doing, but the motivation was all shot. The man, standing there in the middle of the lighted room staring helplessly at the fast closet-door, turned his head. He was just an ordinary man, coat off, tie off, suspenders showing; Harlan had never set eyes on him before, their paths were just now crossing for the first time. But discovery had to be prevented, discovery had to be prevented!

Harlan, smiling sleepily, said, "Excuse me. I couldn't help overhearing you ask your wife for a hammer. I'm your next-door neighbor. Having trouble with that bed-closet, I see. Here, I brought you mine."

The other man reached out, took it shaft-first the way Harlan was holding it. "Thanks, that's real swell of you," he grinned appreciately. "Let's see what luck I have with it this time."

Harlan got in real close. The tips of his fingers kept feeling the goods of his suit. The other man started tapping lightly all up and down the joint of the door. "Tricky things, these beds," he commented.

"Yeah, tricky," agreed Harlan with that same sleepy, watchful smile. He came in a little closer. Something suddenly gave a muffled "Zing!" behind the door, like a misplaced spring or joint jumping back in place.

"That does it!" said the man cheerfully. "Now let's see how she goes. Better stand back a little," he warned. "It'll catch you coming out." He turned the knob with one hand and the door started opening. He passed the hammer back to Harlan, to free the other. Harlan moved around to the same side he was on until he was right at his neighbor's elbow. The door swung flat against the wall. The bed started to come down. The man's two arms went out and up to ease it, so it wouldn't fall too swiftly.

Just as the top-side of it got down to eye-level the hammer rose in Harlan's fist, described a swift arc, fell, crashed into the base of the other man's skull. He went down so instantaneously that the blow seemed not to have been interrupted, to have continued all the way to the floor in one swing. Again the red motes of anger, call them self-preservation this time —

A dull boom came through them first – the bed hitting the floor. They swirled thicker than ever; then screams and angry, frightened voices pierced them. They began to dissipate. He found himself kneeling there alongside the bed, gory hammer poised in his hand, facing them across it. There must have been other blows.

A woman lay slumped there by the door, moaning, "My husband, my husband!" They were picking her up to carry her out. Another woman further in the background was staring in, all eyes. Wait, he knew her – his wife. Someone out in the hall was saying, "Hurry up, hurry up! This way! In here!" and two figures in dark-blue flashed in, moving so swiftly that before he knew it they were behind him holding his arms. They took the hammer away. Nothing but voices, a welter of voices, heard through cotton-batting.

"This man is dead!"

"He didn't even know him. They just moved in. Went crazy, I guess."

He was being shaken back and forth from behind, like a terrier. "What'd you do it for? What'd you do it for?"

Harlan pointed at the bed. "So he wouldn't find out —"

"Find out what?" He was being shaken some more. "Find out what? Explain what you mean!"

Didn't they understand, with it staring them right in the face? His eyes came to rest on it. The bed was empty.

"God, I think I understand!" There was such sheer horror in the voice that even Harlan turned to see where it had come from. It was the superintendent. "There was a down-and-outer, a friend of mine. He didn't have a roof over his head – I know I had no right to, but I let him hang out in here nights the past couple weeks, while the apartment was vacant. Just common, ordinary charity. Then people started complaining about losing their milk, and I saw I'd get into trouble, so I told him to get out. He disappeared three days ago, I figured he'd taken me at my word, and then this morning I found out he was in the hospital with a slight head-concussion. I even dropped in for a few minutes to see how he was getting along. He wouldn't tell me how it happened, but I think I get it now. *He* must have done it to him, thought he'd killed him, hidden him there in that folding-bed. My friend got such a fright that he lammed out the minute he came to —"

Harlan was mumbling idiotically, "Then I didn't kill anyone?"

"You went to town on this one, all right," one of the men in blue said. He turned to the second one, scornfully. "To cover up a justified assault-and-battery, he pulls a murder!"

When another man, in mufti, took him out in the hall at the end of two or three short steel links, he recoiled from the putrid odor still clinging out there. "I thought they said he wasn't dead —"

Somewhere behind him he heard the super explaining to one of them: "Aw, that's just some sloppy people on the floor below cooking corned-beef and cabbage alla time, we gave 'em a dispossess for creating a nuisance in the building! He musta thought it was —"

You'll Never See Me Again

It was the biscuits started it. How he wished, afterward, that she'd never made those biscuits! But she made them, and she was proud of them. Her first try. Typical bride-and-groom stuff. The gag everyone's heard for years, so old it has whiskers down to here. So old it isn't funny any more. No, it isn't funny; listen while it's told.

He wasn't in the mood for playing house. He'd been working hard all day over his drafting-board. Even if they'd been good he probably would have grunted, "Not bad," and let it go at that. But they weren't good, they were atrocious. They were as hard as gravel, they tasted like lye, she'd put in too much of something and left out too much of something else, and life was too short to fool around with them.

"Well, I don't hear you saying anything about them," she pouted.

All he said was: "Take my advice, Smiles, and get 'em at the corner bakery after this."

"That isn't very appreciative," she said. "If you think it was much fun bending over that hot oven —"

"If you think it's much fun eating them – I've got a blueprint to do tomorrow; I can't take punishment like this!"

One word led to another. By the time the meal was over, her fluffy golden head was down inside her folded arms on the table and she was making broken-hearted little noises.

Crying is an irritant to a tired man. He kept saying things he didn't want to. "I could have had a meal in any restaurant without this. I'm tired. I came home to get a little rest, not the death scene from 'Camille' across the table from me."

She raised her head at that. She meant business now. "If I'm annoying you, that's easily taken care of! You want it quiet; we'll see that you *get* it quiet. No trouble at all about that."

She stormed into the bedroom and he could hear drawers slamming in and out. So she was going to walk out on him, was she? For a minute he was going to jump up and go in there after her and put his arms around her and say: "I'm sorry, Smiles; I didn't mean what I said." And that probably would have ended the incident then and there.

But he checked himself. He remembered a well-meaning piece of advice a bachelor friend of his had given him before his marriage. And bachelors always seem to know so much about marriage rules! "If she should ever threaten to walk out on you, and they all do at one time or another," this sage had counseled him, "there's only one way for you to handle that. Act as though you don't care; let her go. She'll come back fast enough, don't worry. Otherwise, if you beg her not to, she'll have the upper hand over you from then on."

He scratched himself behind one ear. "I wonder if he was right?" he muttered. "Well, the only way to find out is to try it."

So he left the table, went into the living-room, snapped on a reading-lamp, sprawled back in a chair, and opened his evening paper, perfectly unconcerned to all appearances. The only way you could tell he wasn't, was by the little glances he kept stealing over the top of the paper every once in a while to see if she was really going to carry out her threat.

She acted as if she were. She may have been waiting for him to come running in there after her and beg for forgiveness, and when he didn't, forced herself to go through with it. Stubborn pride on both their parts. And they were both so young, and this was so new to them. Six weeks the day after tomorrow.

She came bustling in, set down a little black valise in the middle of the room, and put on her gloves. Still waiting for him to make the first overtures for reconciliation. But he kept making the breach worse every time he opened his mouth, all because of what some fool had told him. "Sure you've got everything?" he said quietly.

She was so pretty even when she was angry. "I'm glad you're showing your true colors; I'd rather find out now than later."

Someone should have pushed their two heads together, probably. But there wasn't anyone around but just the two of them. "You're making a mountain out of a molehill. Well, pick a nice comfortable hotel while you're at it."

"I don't have to go to a hotel. I'm not a waif. I've got a perfectly good mother who'll receive me with open arms."

"Quite a trip in the middle of the night, isn't it?" And to make matters worse, he opened his wallet as if to give her the money for her fare.

That put the finishing touch to her exasperation. "I'll get up there without any help from you, Mr Ed Bliss! And I don't want any of the things you ever gave me, either! Take your old silver-fox piece!" *Fluff.* "And take your old diamond ring!" *Plink.* "And take your old pin money!" *Scuff-scuff-slap.* "And you can take back that insurance policy you took out on me, too! Simon Legree! Ivan the Terrible!"

He turned the paper back to where the boxscores were. He only hoped that bachelor was right. "See you day after tomorrow, or whenever you get tired playing hide-and-seek," he said calmly.

"You'll never see me again as long as you live!" It rang in his ears for days afterwards.

She picked up the valise, the front door went *boom*! and he was single again.

The thing to do now was to pretend he didn't care, and then she'd never try anything like this again. Otherwise his life would be made miserable. Every time they had the least little argument, she'd threaten to go back to her mother.

That first night he did all the things he'd always wanted to do, but they didn't stack up to so much after all. Took off his socks and walked around in his bare feet, let the ashes lie wherever they happened to drop off, drank six bottles of cold beer through their mouths and let them lie all over the room, and went to bed without bothering to shave.

He woke up about four in the morning, and it felt strange knowing she wasn't in the house with him, and he hoped she was all right wherever she was, and he finally forced himself to go back to sleep again. In the morning there wasn't anyone to wake him up. Her not being around didn't seem so strange then simply because he didn't have time to notice; he was exactly an hour and twenty-two minutes late for work.

But when he came back that night, it did seem strange, not finding anyone there waiting for him, the house dark and empty, and beer bottles rolling all around the living-room floor. Last night's meal, their last one together, was still strewn around on the table after twenty-four hours. He poked his finger at one of the biscuits, thought remorsefully, *I should have kept quiet. I could have pretended they were good, even if they weren't*. But it was too late now, the damage had been done.

He had to eat out at a counter by himself, and it was very depressing. He picked up the phone twice that evening, at 10:30 and again at 11:22, on the point of phoning up to her mother's place and making up with her, or at least finding out how she was. But each time he sort of slapped his own hand, metaphorically speaking, in rebuke and hung up without putting the call through. *I'll hold out until tomorrow*, he said to himself. *If I give in now, I'm at her mercy*.

The second night was rocky. The bed was no good; they needed to be made up about once every twenty-four hours, he now found out for the first time. A cop poked him in the shoulder with his club at about three in the morning and growled, "What's your trouble, bud?"

"Nothing that's got anything to do with what's in your rule book," Bliss growled back at him. He picked himself up from the curb and went back inside his house again.

He would have phoned her as soon as he woke up in the morning, but he was late again – only twelve minutes behind, this time, though – and he couldn't do it from the office without his fellow draftsmen getting wise she had left him.

He finally did it when he came back that evening, the second time, after eating. This was exactly 8:17 p.m. Thursday, two nights after she'd gone.

He said, "I want to talk to Mrs Belle Alden, in Denby, this State. I don't know her number. Find it for me and give it to me." He'd never met Smiles's mother, incidentally.

While he was waiting for the operator to ring back, he was still figuring how to get out of it; find out how she was without seeming to capitulate. Young pride! *Maybe I can talk the mother into not letting on I called to ask about her, so she won't know I'm weakening. Let it seem like she's the first one to thaw out.*

The phone rang and he picked it up fast, pride or no pride.

"Here's your party."

A woman's voice got on, and he said, "Hello, is this Mrs Alden?"

The voice said it was.

"This is Ed, Smiles's husband."

"Oh, how is she?" she said animatedly.

He sat down at the phone. It took him a minute to get his breath back again. "Isn't she there?" he said finally.

The voice was surprised. "Here? No. Isn't she *there*?"

For a minute his stomach had felt all hollow. Now he was all right again. He was beginning to get it. Or thought he was. He winked at himself, with the wall in front of him for a reflector. So the mother was going to bat for her. They'd cooked up this little fib between them, to punish him. They were going to throw a little fright into him. He'd thought he was teaching her a lesson, and now she was going to turn the tables on him and teach him one. He was supposed to go rushing up there tearing at his hair and foaming at the mouth. "Where's Smiles? She's gone! I can't find her!" Then she'd step out from behind the door, crack her whip over his head, and threaten: "Are you going to behave? Are you ever going to do that again?" And from then on, she'd lead him around with a ring in his nose.

"You can't fool me, Mrs Alden," he said self-assuredly. "I know she's there. I know she told you to say that."

Her voice wasn't panicky, it was still calm and self-possessed, but there was no mistaking the earnest ring to it. Either she was an awfully good actress, or this wasn't any act. "Now listen, Ed. You ought to know I wouldn't joke about a thing like that. As a matter of fact, I wrote her a long letter only yesterday afternoon. It ought to be in your mailbox by now. If she's not there with you, I'd make it my business to find out where she is, if I were you. And I wouldn't put it off, either!"

He still kept wondering: *Is she ribbing me or isn't she?* He drawled undecidedly, "Well, it's damned peculiar."

"I certainly agree with you," she said briskly.

He just chewed the inner tube of his cheek.

"Well, will you let me know as soon as you find out where she is?" she concluded. "I don't want to worry, and naturally I won't be able to help doing so until I hear that she's all right."

He hung up, and first he was surer than ever that it wasn't true she wasn't there. For one thing, the mother hadn't seemed *worried* enough to make it convincing. He thought, *I'll be damned if I call back again, so you and she can have the laugh on me. She's up there with you right now.*

But then he went outside and opened the mailbox, and there was a letter for Smiles with her mother's name on the envelope, and post-marked 6:30 the evening before.

He opened it and read it through. It was bona fide, all right; leisurely, chatty, nothing fake about it. One of those letters that are written over a period of days, a little at a time. There was no mistaking it; up to the time it had been mailed, she hadn't seen her daughter for months. And Smiles had left him the night before; if she'd gone up there at all, she would have been there long before then.

He didn't feel so chipper any more, after that. She wouldn't have stayed away this long if she'd been here in town, where she could walk or take a cab back to the house. There was nothing to be that sore about. And she'd intended going up there. The reason he felt sure of that was this. With her, it wasn't a light decision, lightly taken and lightly discarded. She hadn't been living home with her mother when he married her. She'd been on her own down here for several years before then. They corresponded regularly, they were on good terms, but the mother's remarriage had made a difference. In other words, it wasn't a case of flying straight back to the nest the first time she'd lost a few feathers. It was not only a fairly lengthy trip up there, but they had not seen each other for several years. So if she'd said she was going up there, it was no fleeting impulse, but a rational, clear-cut decision, and she was the kind of girl who would carry it out once she had arrived at it.

He put his hat on, straightened his tie, left the house, and went downtown. There was only one way she could get anywhere near Denby, and that was by bus. It wasn't serviced by train.

Of the two main bus systems, one ran an express line that didn't stop anywhere near there; you had to go all the way to the Canadian border and then double back nearly half of the way by local, to get within hailing distance. The smaller line ran several a day, in each direction, up through there to the nearest large city beyond; they stopped there by request. It was obvious which of the two systems she'd taken.

That should have simplified matters greatly for him; he found out it didn't. He went down to the terminal and approached the ticket seller.

"Were you on duty here Tuesday night?"

"Yeah, from six on. That's my shift every night."

"I'm trying to locate someone. Look. I know you're selling tickets all night long, but maybe you can remember her." He swallowed a lump in his throat. "She's young, only twenty, with blond hair. So pretty you'd look at her twice, if you ever saw her the first time; I know you would. Her eyes are sort of crinkly and smiling. Even when her mouth isn't smiling, her eyes are. She – she bought a ticket to Denby."

The man turned around and took a pack of tickets out of a pigeon-hole and blew a layer of dust off them. "I haven't sold a ticket to Denby in over a month." They had a rubber band around them. All but the top one. That blew off with his breath.

That seemed to do something to his powers of memory. He ducked down out of sight, came up with it from the floor. "Wait a minute," he said, prodding his thumbnail between two of his teeth. "I don't remember anything much about any eyes or smile, but there *was* a young woman came up and priced the fare to Denby. I guess it was night before last, at that. Seeing this one ticket pulled loose out of the batch reminded me of it. I told her how much it was, and I snagged out a ticket – this loose one here. But then she couldn't make it; I dunno, she didn't have enough money on her or something. She looked at her wrist watch, and asked me how late the pawnshops stay open. I told her they were all closed by then. Then she shoveled all the money she could round up across the counter at me and asked me how far that would take her. So I counted and told her, and she told me to give her a ticket to that far."

Bliss was hanging onto his words, hands gripping the counter until his knuckles showed white. "Yes, but where to?"

The ticket's seller's eyelids drooped deprecatingly. "That's the trouble," he said, easing the back of his collar. "I can't remember that part of it. I can't even remember how much the amount came to, now, any more. If I could, I could get the destination by elimination."

If I only knew how much she had in her handbag when she left the house, Bliss thought desolately, *we could work it out together, him and me*. He prodded: "Three dollars? Four? Five?"

The ticket vendor shook his head baffedly. "No use, it won't come back. I'm juggling so many figures all night long, every night in the week —"

Bliss slumped lower before the sill. "But don't you keep a record of what places you sell tickets to?"

"No, just the total take for the night, without breaking it down."

He was as bad off as before. "Then you can't tell me for sure whether she did get on the bus that night or not?"

Meanwhile an impatient line had formed behind Bliss, and the ticket seller was getting fidgety.

"No. The driver might remember her. Look at it this way: she only stood in front of me for a minute or two at the most. If she got on the bus at all, she sat in back of him for anywhere from an hour to four hours. Remember, I'm not even guaranteeing that the party I just told you about is the same one you mean. It's just a vague incident to me."

"Would the same one that made Tuesday night's run be back by now?"

"Sure, he's going out tonight again." The ticket man looked at a chart. "Go over there and ask for No. 27. Next!"

No. 27 put down his coffee mug, swiveled around on the counter stool, and looked at his questioner.

"Yare, I made Tuesday night's upstate run."

"Did you take a pretty blond girl, dressed in a gray jacket and skirt, as far as Denby?"

No. 27 stopped looking at him. His face stayed on in the same direction, but he was looking at other things. "Nawr, I didn't."

"Well, was she on the bus at all?"

No. 27's eyes remained at a tangent from the man he was answering. "Nawr, she wasn't."

"What're you acting so evasive about? I can tell you're hiding something, just by looking at you."

"I said, 'Nawr, I didn't.' "

"Listen. I'm her husband. I've got to know. Here, take this, only tell me, will you? I've got to know. It's an awful feeling!"

The driver took a hitch in his belt. "I get good wages. A ten-dollar bill wouldn't make me say I sawr someone when I didn't. No, nor a twenty, nor a century either. That's an old one. It would only make me lose my rating with the company." He swung around on his stool, took up his coffee mug again. "I only sawr the road," he said truculently. "I ain't supposed to see who's riding in back of me."

"But you can't help seeing who gets off each time you stop."

This time No. 27 wouldn't answer at all. The interview was over, as far as he was concerned. He flung down a nickel, defiantly jerked down the visor of his cap, and swaggered off.

Bliss slouched forlornly out of the terminal, worse off than before. The issue was all blurred now. The ticket seller vaguely thought some girl or other had haphazardly bought a ticket for as much money as she had on her person that night, but without guaranteeing that she fitted his description of Smiles at all. The driver, on the other hand, definitely denied anyone like her had ridden with him, as far as Denby or anywhere else. What was he to think? Had she left, or hadn't she left?

Whether she had or not, it was obvious that she had never arrived. He had the testimony of her own mother, and that letter from her from upstate, to vouch for that. And who was better to be believed than her own mother?

Had she stayed here in the city then? But she hadn't done that, either. He knew Smiles so well. Even if she had gone to the length of staying overnight at a hotel that first night, Tuesday, she would have been back home with him by Wednesday morning at the very latest. Her peevishness would have evaporated long before then. Another thing, she wouldn't have had enough money to stay for any longer than just one night at even a moderately priced hotel. She'd flung down the greater part of her household expense money on the floor that night before walking out.

All I can do, he thought apprehensively, *is make a round of the hotels and find out if anyone like her was at any of them Tuesday night, even if she's not there now.*

He didn't check every last hotel in town, but he checked all the ones she would have gone to, if she'd gone to one at all. She wouldn't have been sappy enough to go to some rundown lodginghouse near the freight yards or longshoremen's hostelry down by the piers. That narrowed the field somewhat.

He checked on her triply: by name first, on the hotel registers for Tuesday night; then by her description, given to the desk clerks; and lastly by any and all entries in the registers, no matter what name was given. He knew her handwriting, even if she'd registered under an assumed name.

He drew a complete blank. No one who looked like her had come to any of the hotels, Tuesday night, or at any time since. No one giving her name. No one giving another name, who wrote like her. What was left? Where else could she have gone? Friends? She didn't have any. Not close ones, not friends she knew well enough to walk in on unannounced and stay overnight with.

Where was she? She wasn't in the city. She wasn't in the country, up at Denby. She seemed to have vanished completely from the face of the earth.

It was past two in the morning by the time he'd finished checking the hotels. It was too late to get a bus any more that night, or he would have gone up to Denby then and there himself. He turned up his coat collar against the night mist and started disconsolately homeward. On the way he tried to buck himself up by saying: *Nothing's happened to her. She's just hiding out somewhere, trying to throw a scare into me. She'll show up, she's bound to.* It wouldn't work, much. It was two whole days and three nights now. Marriage is learning to know another person, learning to know by heart what he or she'd do in such-and-such a situation. They'd only been married six weeks, but, after all, they'd been going together nearly a year before that; he knew her pretty well by now.

She wasn't vindictive. She didn't nurse grievances, even imaginary ones. There were only two possible things she would have done. She would have either gotten on that bus red-hot, been cooled off long before she got off it again, but stayed up there a couple of days as long as she was once there. Or if she hadn't taken the bus, she would have been back by twelve at the latest right that same night, with an injured air and a remark like: "You ought to be ashamed of yourself letting your wife walk the streets like a vagrant!" or something to that effect. She hadn't, so she must have gone up there. Then he thought of the letter from her mother, and he felt good and scared.

The phone was ringing when he got back. He could hear it even before he got the front door open. He nearly broke the door down in his hurry to get at it. For a minute he thought —

But it was only Mrs Alden. She said, "I've been trying to get you ever since ten o'clock. I didn't hear from you, and I've been getting more and more worried." His heart went down under his shoelaces. "Did you locate her? Is it all right?"

"I can't find her," he said, so low he had to say it over again so she could catch it.

She'd been talking fast until now. Now she didn't say anything at all for a couple of minutes; there was just an empty hum on the wire. Something came between them. They'd never seen each other face to face, but he could sense a change in her voice, a different sound to it the next time he heard it. It was as though she were drawing away from him. Not moving from where she stood, of course, but rather withdrawing her confidence. The beginnings of suspicion were lurking in it somewhere or other.

"Don't you think it's high time you got in touch with the police?" he heard her say. And then, so low that he could hardly get it: "If you don't, I will." *Click*, and she was gone.

He didn't take it the way he, perhaps, should have.

As he hung up, he thought, *Yes, she's right, I'll have to. Nothing else left to be done now. It's two full days now; no use kidding myself any more.*

He put on his hat and coat again, left the house once more. It was about three in the morning by this time. He hated to go to them. It seemed like writing finis to it. It seemed to make it so final, tragic, in a way. As though, once he notified them, all hope of her returning to him unharmed, of her own accord, was over. As though it stopped being just a little private, domestic matter any more and became a police matter, out of his own hands. Ridiculous, he knew, but that was the way he felt about it. But it had to be done. Just sitting worrying about her wasn't going to bring her back.

He went in between two green door lamps and spoke to a desk sergeant. "I want to report my wife missing." They sent a man out, a detective, to talk to him. Then he had to go down to the city morgue, to see if she was among the unidentified dead there, and that was the worst experience he'd had yet. It wasn't the sight of the still faces one by one; it was the dread, each time, that the next one would be hers. Half under his breath, each time he shook his head and looked at someone who had once been loved, he added, "No, thank God." She wasn't there.

Although he hadn't found her, all he could give when he left the place of the dead was a sigh of unutterable relief. She wasn't among the *found* dead, that was all this respite marked. But he knew, although he tried to shut the grisly thought out, that there are many dead who are *not* found. Sometimes not right away, sometimes never.

They took him around to the hospitals then, to certain wards, and though this wasn't quite so bad as the other place, it wasn't much better either. He looked for her among amnesia victims, would-be suicides who had not yet recovered consciousness, persons with all the skin burned off their faces, mercifully swathed in gauze bandaging and tea leaves. They even made him look in the alcoholic wards, though he protested strenously that *she* wouldn't be there, and in the psychopathic wards.

The sigh of relief he gave when this tour was over was only less heartfelt than after leaving the morgue. She wasn't dead. She wasn't maimed or injured or out of her mind in any way. And still she wasn't to be found.

Then they turned it over to Missing Persons, had her description broadcast, and told him there wasn't anything he could do for the present but go home.

He didn't even try to sleep when he got back the second time. Just sat there waiting – for the call that didn't come and that he somehow knew wouldn't come, not if he waited for a week or a month.

It was starting to get light by that time. The third day since she'd been swallowed up bodily was dawning. She wasn't in the city, alive or dead, he was convinced. Why sit there waiting for them to locate her when he was sure she wasn't here? He'd done all he could at this end. He hadn't done anything yet at the other end. The thing was too serious now; it wasn't enough just to take the word of a *voice* over a telephone wire that she wasn't up there. Not even if the voice was that of her own mother, who was to be trusted if anyone was, who thought as much of her as he did. He decided he'd go up there himself. Anything was better than just sitting here waiting helplessly.

He couldn't take the early-morning bus, the way he wanted to. Those building plans he was finishing up had to be turned in today; there was an important contractor waiting for them. He stood there poring over the blueprints, more dead than alive between worry and lack of sleep, and when they were finally finished, turned in, and O.K.'d, he went straight from the office to the terminal and took the bus that should get in there about dark.

Denby wasn't even an incorporated village, he found when the bus finally got there, an hour late. It was just a place where a turnpike crossed another road, with houses spaced at lengthy intervals along the four arms of the intersection. Some of them a quarter of a mile apart, few of them in full view of one another due to intervening trees, bends in the roads, rises and dips of the ground. A filling-station was the nearest thing to the crossroads, in one direction. Up in the other was a store, with living-quarters over it. It was the most dispersed community he had ever seen.

He chose the store at random, stopped in there, and asked, "Which way to the Alden house?"

The storekeeper seemed to be one of those people who wear glasses for the express purpose of staring over instead of through them. Or maybe they'd slipped down on the bridge of his nose. "Take that other fork, to your right," he instructed. "Just keep going till you think there ain't going to be no more houses, and you're sure I steered you wrong. Keep on going anyway. When you least expect it, one last house'll show up, round the turn. That's them. Can't miss it. You'll know it by the low brick barrier wall runs along in front of it. He put that up lately, just to keep in practice, I reckon."

Bliss wondered what he meant by that, if anything, but didn't bother asking. The storekeeper was evidently one of these loquacious souls who would have rambled on forever given the slightest encouragement, and Bliss was tired and anxious to reach his destination. He thanked him and left.

The walk out was no picayune city block or two; it was a good stiff hike. The road stretched before him like a white tape under the velvety night sky, dark-blue rather than black, and stars twinkled down through the openings between the roadside-tree branches. He could hear countryside night noises around him, crickets or something, and once a dog barked 'way off in the distance, it sounded like miles away. It was lonely, but not particularly frightening; nature rarely is, it is man that is menacing.

Just the same, if she had come up here – and of course she hadn't – it wouldn't have been particularly prudent for a young girl alone like her to walk this distance at that hour of the night. She probably would have phoned out to them to come in and meet her at the crossroads, from either the store of that filling-station. And yet if both had been closed up by then – her bus wouldn't have passed through here until one or two in the morning – she would have had to walk it alone. But she hadn't come up so why conjure up additional dangers?

Thinking which, he came around the slow turn in the road and a low, elbow-height boundary wall sprang up beside him and ran down the road past a pleasant, white-painted two-story house, with dark gables, presumably green. They seemed to keep it in good condition. As for the wall itself, he got what the storekeeper's remark had intended to convey when he saw it. It looked very much as though Alden had put it up simply to kill time, give himself something to do, add a fancy touch to his property. For it seemed to serve no useful purpose. It was not nearly high enough to shut off the view, so it had not been built for privacy. It only ran along the front of the parcel, did not extend around the sides or to the back, so it was not even effective as a barrier against poultry or cattle, or useful as a boundary mark. It seemed to be purely decorative. As such, it was a neat, workmanlike job; you could tell Alden had been a mason before his marriage. It was brick, smoothly, painstakingly plastered over.

There was no gate in it, just a gap, with an ornamental willow wicket arched high over it. He turned in through there. They were up yet, though perhaps already on the point of retiring. One of the upper-floor windows held a light, but with a blind discreetly drawn down over it.

He rang the bell, then stepped back from the door and looked up, expecting to be interrogated first from the window, particularly at this hour. Nothing of the kind happened; they evidently possessed the trustfulness that goes with a clear conscious. He could hear steps start down the inside stairs. A woman's steps, at that, and a voice that carried out to where he was with surprising clarity said, "Must be somebody lost their way, I guess."

A hospitable little lantern up over the door went on from the inside, and a moment later he was looking at a pleasant-faced, middle-aged woman with soft gray eyes. Her face was long and thin, but without the hatchet-sharp features that are so often an accompaniment of that contour of face. Her hair was a graying blond, but soft and wavy, not scraggly. Knowing who she was, he almost thought he could detect a little bit of Smiles in her face: the shape of the brows and the curve of the mouth, but that might have been just autosuggestion.

"Hm-m-m?" she said serenely.

"I'm Ed, Mrs Alden."

She blinked twice, as though she didn't get it for a minute. Or maybe wasn't expecting it.

"Smiles's husband," he said, a trifle irritatedly. You're supposed to know your own in-laws. It wasn't their fault, of course, that they didn't. It wasn't his, either. He and Smiles had been meaning to come up here on a visit as soon as they could, but they'd been so busy getting their own home together, and six weeks is such a short time. Her mother had been getting over a prolonged illness at the time of their wedding, hadn't been strong enough for the trip down and back.

Both her hands came out toward his now, after that momentary blankness. "Oh, come in, Ed," she said heartily. "I've been looking forward to meeting you, but I *wish* it had been under other circumstances." She glanced past his shoulder. "She's not with you, I see. No word yet, Ed?" she went on worriedly.

He looked down and shook his head glumly.

She held her hand to her mouth in involuntary dismay, then quickly recovered her self-control, as though not wishing to add to his distress. "Don't know what to think," she murmured half audibly. "It's not like her to do a thing like that. Have you been to the police yet, Ed?"

"I reported it to them before daylight this morning. Had to go around to the different hospitals and places." He blew out his breath at the recollection. "Huff, it was ghastly."

"Don't let's give up yet, Ed. You know the old saying, 'No news is good news.' " Then: "Don't let me keep you standing out here. Joe's upstairs; I'll call him down."

As he followed her inside, his whole first impression of Smiles's mother was that she was as nice, wholesome, inartificial a woman as you could find anywhere. And first impressions are always half the battle.

She led him along a neat, hardwood-floored hall, varnished to the brightness of a mirror. An equally spotless white staircase rose at the back of it to the floor above.

"Let me take your hat," she said thoughtfully, and hung it on a peg. "You look peaked, Ed; I can tell you're taking it hard. That trip up is strenuous, too. It's awful; you know you read about things like this in the papers nearly every day, but it's only when it hits home you realize —"

Talking disconnectedly like that, she had reached the entrance to the living-room. She thrust her hand around to the inside of the door frame and snapped on the lights. He was standing directly in the center of the opening as she did so. There was something a little unexpected about the way they went on, but he couldn't figure what it was; it must have been just a subconscious impression on his part. Maybe they were a little brighter than he'd expected, and after coming in out of the dark – The room looked as though it had been painted fairly recently, and he supposed that was what it was, the walls and woodwork gave it back with unexpected dazzle. It was too small a detail even to waste time on. Or is any detail ever too small?

She had left him for a moment to go as far as the foot of the stairs. "Joe, Smiles's husband is here," he heard her call.

A deep rumbling voice answered, "She with him?"

She tactfully didn't answer that, no doubt to spare Bliss's feelings; she seemed to be such a considerate woman. "Come down, dear," was all she said.

He was a thick, heavy-set man, with a bull neck and a little circular fringe of russet-blond hair around his head, the crown of it bald. He was going to be the blunt, aggressive type, Bliss could see. With eyes too small to match it. Eyes that said, *Try and get past us.*

"So you're Bliss." He reached out and shook hands with him. It was a hard shake, but not particularly friendly. His hands were calloused to the lumpiness of alligator hide. "Well, you're taking it pretty calmly, it seems to me."

Bliss looked at him. "How do you figure that?"

"Joe!" the mother had remonstrated, but so low neither of them paid any attention.

"Coming up here like this. Don't you think it's your business to stick close down there, where you could do some good?"

Mrs Alden laid a comforting hand on Bliss's arm. "Don't, Joe. You can tell how the boy feels by looking at him. I'm Smiles's mother and I know how it is; if she said she was coming up here, why, naturally —"

"I know you're Teresa's mother," he said emphatically, as if to shut her up.

A moment of awkward silence hung suspended in the air above their three heads. Bliss had a funny "lost" feeling for a minute, as though something had eluded him just then, something had been a little askew. It was like when there's a word you are trying desperately to remember; it's on the tip of your tongue, but you can't bring it out. It was such a small thing, though —

"I'll get you something to eat, Ed," she said, and as she turned to go out of the room, Bliss couldn't help overhearing her say to her husband in a stage whisper: "Talk to him. Find out what really happened."

Alden had about as much finesse as a trained elephant doing the gavotte among ninepins. He cleared his throat judically. "D'ja do something you shouldn't, that how it come about?"

"What do you mean?"

"Wull, *we* have no way of knowing what kind of a disposition you've got. Have you got a pretty bad temper, are you a little too quick with the flat of your hand?"

Bliss looked at him incredulously. Then he got it. "That's hardly a charge I expected to have to defend myself on. But if it's required of me – I happen to worship the ground my wife walks on. I'd sooner have my right arm wither away than —"

"No offense," said Alden lamely. "It's been known to happen before, that's all."

"Not in my house," Bliss said, and gave him a steely look.

Smiles's mother came in again at this point, with something on a tray. Bliss didn't even bother looking up to see what it was. He waved it aside, sat there with his arms dangling out over his knees, his head bent way over, looking straight down through them.

The room was a vague irritant. He kept getting it all the time, at least every time he raised his head and looked around, but he couldn't figure what was doing it. There was only one thing he was sure of, it wasn't the people in it. So that left it up to the room. Smiles's mother was the soothing, soft-moving type that it was pleasant to have around you. And even the husband, in spite of his brusqueness, was the stolid emotionless sort that didn't get on your nerves.

What was it, then? Was the room furnished in bad taste? It wasn't; it was comfortable and homey-looking. And even if it hadn't been, that wouldn't have done it. He was no interior decorator, allergic to anything like that. Was it the glare from the recent paint job? No, not that, either; now that he looked, there wasn't any glare. It wasn't even glossy paint, it was the dull kind without high lights. That had just been an optical illusion when the lights first went on.

He shook his head a little to get rid of it, and thought, *What's annoying me in here?* And he couldn't tell.

He was holding a lighted cigarette between his dangling fingers, and the ash was slowly accumulating.

"Pass him an ash tray, Joe," she said in a watery voice. She was starting to cry, without any fuss, unnoticeably, but she still had time to think of their guest's comfort. Some women are like that.

He looked and a whole cylinder of ash had fallen to the rug. It looked like a good rug, too. "I'm sorry," he said, and rubbed it out with his shoe. Even the rug bothered him in some way.

Pattern too loud? No, it was quiet, dark-colored, and in good taste. He couldn't find a thing the matter with it. But it kept troubling him just the same.

Something went *clang*. It wasn't in the same room with them, some other part of the house, faint and muffled, like a defective pipe joint settling or swelling.

She said, "Joe, when are you going to have the plumber in to fix that water pipe? It's sprung out of line again. You'll wait until we have a good-sized leak on our hands."

"Yeah, that's right," he said. It sounded more like an original discovery than a recollection of something overlooked. Bliss couldn't have told why, it just did. More of his occultism, he supposed.

"I'll have to get a fresh handkerchief," she said apologetically, got up and passed between them, the one she had been using until now rolled into a tight little ball at her upper lip.

"Take it easy," Alden said consolingly.

His eyes went to Bliss, then back to her again, as if to say: *Do you see that she's crying, as well as I do?* So Bliss glanced at her profile as she went by, and she was. She ought to have been, she was the girl's mother.

When she came in again with the fresh handkerchief she'd gone to get, he got to his feet.

"This isn't bringing her back. I'd better get down to the city again. They might have word for me by now."

Alden said, "Can I talk to you alone a minute, Bliss, before you go?"

The three of them had moved out into the hall. Mrs Alden went up the stairs slowly. The higher up she got the louder her sobs became. Finally a long wail burst out, and the closing of a door cut it in half.

A minute later bedsprings protested, as if someone had dropped on them full length.

"D'you hear that?" Alden said to him. Another of those never-ending nuances hit Bliss; he'd said it as if he were proud of it.

Bliss was standing in the doorway, looking back into the room. He felt as if he were glad to get out of it. And he still couldn't understand why, any more than any of the rest of it.

"What was it you wanted to say to me on the side?"

Blunt as ever, Alden asked, "Have you told us everything, or have you left out part of it? Just what went on between you and Teresa anyway?"

"One of those tiffs."

Alden's small eyes got even smaller, they almost creased out in his face. "It must have been *some* tiff, for her to walk out on you with her grip in her hand. She wasn't the kind —"

"How did you know she took her grip with her? I didn't tell you that."

"You didn't have to. She was coming up here, wasn't she? They always take their grips when they walk out on you."

There wasn't pause enough between their two sentences to stick a bent comma. One just seemed to flow out of the other, only with a change of speakers. Alden's voice had gone up a little with the strain of the added pace he'd put into it, that was all. He'd spoken it a little faster than his usual cadence. Small things. Damn those small things to hell, torturing him like gnats, like gnats that you can't put your finger on!

Right under Bliss's eyes, a bead of sweat was forming between two of the reddish tufts of hair at the edge of Alden's hair line. He could see it oozing out of the pore. What was that from? Just from discussing what time his bus would get him back to the city, as they were doing now? No, it must have been from saying that sentence too fast a while ago – the one about the grip. The effects were only coming out now.

"Well," Bliss said, "I'd better get a move on, to catch the bus back."

Her door, upstairs, had opened again. It might have been just coincidental, but it was timed almost as though she'd been listening.

"Joe," she called down the stair well. "Don't let Ed start back down again right tonight. Two trips in one day is too much; he'll be a wreck. Why not have him stay over with us tonight, and take the early morning one instead?"

Bliss was standing right down there next to him. She could have spoken to him directly just as easily. Why did she have to relay it through her husband?

"Yeah," Alden said up to her, "that's just what I was thinking myself." But it was as though he'd said: *I get you.*

Bliss had a funny feeling they'd been saying something to one another right in front of his face without his knowing what it was.

"No," he said dolefully, "I'm worried about her. The sooner I get down there and get to the bottom of it —"

He went on out the door, and Alden came after him.

"I'll walk you down to the bus stop," he offered.

"Not necessary," Bliss told him curtly. After all, twice now this other man had tried to suggest he'd abused or maltreated his wife; he couldn't help resenting it. "I can find my way back without any trouble. You're probably tired and want to turn in."

"Just as you say," Alden acquiesced.

They didn't shake hands at parting. Bliss couldn't help noticing that the other man didn't even reach out and offer to. For his part, that suited him just as well.

After he'd already taken a few steps down the road, Alden called out after him, "Let us know the minute you get good news; I don't want my wife to worry any more than she has to. She's taking it hard."

Bliss noticed he didn't include himself in that. He didn't hold that against him, though; after all, there was no blood relationship there.

Alden turned as if to go back inside the house again, but when Bliss happened to glance back several minutes later, just before taking the turn in the road that cut the house off from sight, he could still detect a narrow up-and-down band of light escaping from the doorway, with a break in it at one point as though a protruding profile were obscuring it.

Wants to make sure I'm really on my way to take that bus, he said to himself knowingly. But suspicion is a two-edged sword that turns against the wielder as readily as the one it is wielded against. He only detected the edge that was turned toward him, and even that but vaguely.

He reached the crossroads and took up his position. He still had about five minutes to wait, but he'd hardly arrived when two yellow peas of light, swelling until they became great hazy balloons, came down the turnpike toward him. He thought it was the bus at first, ahead of its own schedule, but it turned out to be a coupé with a Quebec license. It slowed long enough for the occupant to lean out and ask:

"Am I on the right road for the city?"

"Yeah, keep going straight, you can't miss," Bliss said dully. Then suddenly, on an impulse he was unable to account for afterward, he raised his voice and called out after him, "Hey! I don't suppose you'd care to give me a lift in with you?"

"Why not?" the Canuck said amiably, and slowed long enough for Bliss to catch up to him.

Bliss opened the door and sidled in. He still didn't know what had made him change his mind like this, unless perhaps it was the vague thought that he might make better time in with a private car like this than he would have with the bus.

The driver said something about being glad to have someone to talk to on the way down, and Bliss explained briefly that he'd been waiting for the bus, but beyond those few introductory remarks, they did not talk much. Bliss wanted to think. He wanted to analyze his impression of the visit he had just concluded.

It was pretty hopeless to do much involved thinking with a stranger at his elbow, liable to interrupt his train of thought every once in a while with some unimportant remark that had to be answered for courtesy's sake, so the most he could do was marshal his impressions, sort of document them for future reference when he was actually alone:

1. The lights seemed to go on in an unexpected way, when she first pressed the switch.

2. The room bothered him. It hadn't been the kind of room you feel at ease in. It hadn't been *restful.*

3. There had been some sort of faulty vocal co-ordination when she said, "I'm Smiles's mother," and he said, "I know you're Teresa's mother."

4. There had also been nuances in the following places: When Alden's eyes sought his, as if to assure himself that he, Bliss, saw that she was crying almost unnoticeably there in the room with them. When she ran whimpering up the stairs and threw herself on the bed, and he said, "Hear that?" And lastly when she called down and addressed her overnight invitation to Alden, instead of Bliss himself, as though there were some intangible kernel in it to be extracted first before he passed on the dry husk of the words themselves to Bliss.

At this point, before he got any further, there was a thud, a long-drawn-out reptilian hiss, and a tire went out. They staggered to a stop at the side of the road.

"Looks like I've brought you tough luck," Bliss remarked.

"No," his host assured him, "that thing's been on its ninth life for weeks; I'm only surprised it lasted this long. I had it patched before I left Three Rivers this morning, thought maybe I could make the city on it, but it looks like no soap. Well, I have a spare, and now I *am* glad I hitched you on; four hands are better than two."

The stretch of roadway where it had happened was a particularly bad one, Bliss couldn't help noticing as he slung off his coat and jumped down to lend a hand; it was crying for attention, needled with small jagged rock fragments, either improperly crushed in the first place or else loosened from their bed by some recent rain. He supposed it hadn't been blocked off because there was no other branch road in the immediate vicinity that could take its place as a detour.

They'd hardly gotten the jack out when the bus overtook and passed them, wiping out his gain of time at a stroke. And then, a considerable time later, after they'd already finished the job and wiped their hands clean, some other anonymous car went steaming by, this time at a rate of speed that made the bus seem to have been standing still in its tracks. The Canadian was the only one in sight by the stalled car as its cometlike headlights flicked by. Bliss happened to be farther in off the road just then. He turned his head and looked after it, however, at the tornado-like rush of air that followed in its wake, and got a glimpse of it just before it hurtled from sight.

"That fellow's *asking* for a flat," the Canadian said, "passing over a stretch of fill like this at such a clip."

"He didn't have a spare on him, either," Bliss commented.

"Looked like he was trying to beat that bus in." Just an idle phrase, for purposes of comparison. It took on new meaning later, though, when Bliss remembered it.

They climbed in and started off again. The rest of the ride passed uneventfully. Bliss spelled his companion at the wheel, the last hour in, and let him take a little doze. He'd been on the road steadily since early that morning, he'd told Bliss.

Bliss woke him up and gave the car back to him when they reached the city limits. The Canadian was heading for a certain hotel all the way downtown, so Bliss wouldn't let him deviate from his course to take him over to his place; he got out instead at the nearest parallel point to it they touched, thanked him, and started over on foot.

He had a good stiff walk ahead of him, but he didn't mind that, he'd been sitting cramped up for so long. He still wanted to think things over as badly as ever, too, and he'd found out by experience that solitary walking helped him to think better.

It didn't in this case, though. He was either too tired from the events of the past few days, or else the materials he had were too formless, indefinite, to get a good grip on. He kept asking himself, *What was wrong up there? Why am I dissatisfied?* And he couldn't answer for the life of him. *Was anything wrong,* he was finally reduced to wondering, *or was it wholly imaginary on my part?* It was like a wrestling bout with shadows.

The night around him was dark-blue velvet, and as he drew near his own isolated semisuburban neighborhood, the silence was at least equal to that up at Denby. There wasn't a soul stirring, not even a milkman. He trudged onward under a leafy tunnel of sidewalk trees that all but made him invisible.

Leaving the coupé where he had, and coming over in a straight line this way, brought him up to his house from behind, on the street in back of it instead of the one running directly before it, which was an approach he never took at other times, such as when coming home from downtown. Behind it there was nothing but vacant plots, so it was a short-cut to cross diagonally behind the house next door and go through from the back instead of going all the way around the corner on the outside. He did that now, without thinking of anything except to save a few extra steps.

As he came out from behind the house next door, treading soundless on the well-kept backyard grass, he saw a momentary flash through one of his own windows that could only have been a pocket torch. He stopped dead in his tracks. *Burglars* was the first thought that came to him.

He advanced a wary step or two. The flash came again, but from another window this time, nearer the front. They were evidently on their way out, using it only intermittently to help find their way. He'd be able to head them off at the front door, as they stole forth.

There was a partition hedge between the two houses, running from front to back. He scurried along that, on his neighbor's side of it, keeping head and shoulders down, until he was on a line with his own front door. He crouched there, peering through.

They had left a lookout standing just outside his door. He could see the motionless figure. And then, as his fingers were about to part the hedge, to aid him in crashing through, the still form shifted a little, and the uncertain light struck a glint from a little wedge on its chest. At the same instinct Bliss caught the outline of a visor above the profile. A cop!

One hand behind him, Bliss ebbed back again on his heels, thrown completely off balance by the unexpected revelation.

His own front door opened just then and two men came out, one behind the other. Without visors and without metallic gleams on their chests. But the cop turned and flipped up his nightstick toward them in semisalute; so, whatever they were, they weren't burglars, although one was unmistakably carrying something out of the house with him.

They carefully closed the front door behind them, even tried it a second time to make sure it was securely fastened. A snatch of guarded conversation drifted toward him as they made their way down the short front walk to the sidewalk. The uniformed man took no part in it, only the two who had been inside.

"He's hot, all right," Bliss heard one say.

"Sure, he's hot, and he already knows it. You notice he wasn't on that bus when it got in. I'll beat it down and get the Teletype busy. You put a case on this place. Still, he might try to sneak back in again later."

Bliss had been crouched there on his heels. He went forward and down now on the flats of his hands, as stunned as though he'd gotten a rabbit punch at the back of the neck.

Motionless there, almost dazed, he kept shaking his head slightly, as though to clear it. They were after *him*, they thought he'd – Not only that, but they'd been tipped off what bus he was supposed to show up on. That could mean only one person, Joe Alden.

He wasn't surprised. He could even understand his doing a thing like that; it must seem suspicious to them up there the way she'd disappeared, and Bliss's own complete lack of any plausible explanation for it. He'd probably have felt the same way about it himself, if he'd been in their place. But he did resent the sneaky way Alden had gone about it, waiting until he was gone and then denouncing him the minute his back was turned. Why hadn't he tried to have him held by the locals while he was right up there with them? He supposed, now, that was the esoteric meaning in her invitation to him to stay over; so Alden could go out and bring in the cops while he was asleep under their roof. It hadn't worked because he'd insisted on leaving.

Meanwhile, he continued watching these men before him who had now, through no fault of his own, become his deadly enemies. They separated. One of them, with the uniformed cop trailing along with him, started down the street away from the house. The other drifted diagonally across to the opposite side. The gloom of an overshadowing tree over there swallowed him, and he failed to show up again on the other side of it, where there was a little more light.

There was hardly any noise about the whole thing, hardly so much as a footfall. They were like shadows moving in a dream world. A car engine began droning stealthily, slurred away, from a short distance farther down the street, marking the point of departure of two out of the three. A drop of sweat, as cold as mercury, toiled sluggishly down the nape of Bliss's neck, blotted itself into his collar.

He stayed there where he was, on all fours behind the hedge, a few minutes longer. The only thing to do was go out and try to clear himself. The only thing *not* to do was turn around and slink off – though the way lay open behind him. But at the same time he had a chill premonition that it wasn't going to be so easy to clear himself; that once they got their hands on him —

But I've got to, he kept telling himself over and over. *They've got to help me, not go after me. They can't say I – did anything like that to Smiles! Maybe I can hit one of them that's fair minded, will listen to me.*

Meanwhile he had remained in the crouched position of a track runner waiting for the signal to start. He picked himself up slowly and straightened to his full height behind the hedge. That took courage, alone, without moving a step farther. "Well, here goes," he muttered, tightened his belt, and stuck a cigarette in his mouth. It was a crawly sort of feeling. He knew, nine chances to one, his freedom of movement was over the minute he stepped out from behind this hedge and went over toward that inky tree shadow across the street that was just a little too lumpy in the middle. He didn't give a rap about freedom of movement in itself, but his whole purpose, his one aim from now on, was to look for and find Smiles. He was afraid losing it would hamper him in that. She was his wife, he wanted to look for her himself, he didn't want other guys to do it for him whether they were professionals or not.

He lighted the cigarette when halfway across the street, but the tree shadow didn't move. The detective evidently didn't know him by sight yet, was on the lookout for someone coming from the other direction on his way to the house.

Bliss stopped right in front of him and said, "Are you looking for me? I'm Ed Bliss and I live over there."

The shadow up and down the tree trunk detached itself, became a man. "How'd you know anyone was looking for you?" It was a challenge, as though that were already an admission of guilt in itself.

Bliss said, "Come inside, will you? I want to talk to you."

They crossed over once more. Bliss unlocked the door for him, with his own key this time, and put on the lights. They went into the living-room. It was already getting dusty from not being cleaned in several days.

He looked Bliss over good. Bliss looked him over just as good. He wanted a man in this, not a detective.

The detective spoke first, repeated what he'd asked him outside on the street. "How'd you know we'd be looking for you when that bus got in?"

"I didn't. I just happened to take a lift down instead."

"What's become of your wife, Bliss?"

"I don't know."

"We think you do."

"I wish you were right. But not in the way you mean."

"Never mind what you wish. You know another good word for that? Remorse."

The blood in Bliss's face thinned a little. "Before you put me in the soup, just let me talk here quietly with you a few minutes. That's all I ask."

"When she walked out of here Tuesday night, what was she wearing?"

Bliss hesitated a minute. Not because he didn't know – he'd already described her outfit to them when he reported her missing – but because he could sense a deeper import lurking behind the question.

The detective took the hesitancy for an attempt at evasion, went on: "Now every man knows his wife's clothes by heart. You paid for every last one of them, you know just what she owned. Just tell me what she had on."

There was danger in it somewhere. "She had on a gray suit – jacket and skirt, you know. Then a pink silk shirtwaist. She threw her fur piece back at me, so that's about all she went out in. A hat, of course. One of those crazy hats."

"Baggage?"

"A black valise with tan binding. Oh, about the size of a typewriter case."

"Sure of that?"

"Sure of that."

The detective gave a kind of soundless whistle through his teeth. "Whe-ew!" he said, and he looked at Bliss almost as if he felt sorry for him. "You've sure made it tough for yourself this time! I didn't have to ask you that, because we know just as well as you what she had on."

"How?"

"Because we found every last one of those articles you just mentioned in the furnace downstairs in this very house, less than twenty minutes ago. My partner's gone down to headquarters with them. And a guy don't do that to his wife's clothes unless he's done something to his wife, too. What've you done with her, Bliss?"

The other man wasn't even in the room with him any more, so far as Bliss was concerned. A curtain of foggy horror had dropped down all around him. "My God!" he whispered hoarsely. "Something's happened to her, somebody's done something to her!" And he jumped up and ran out of the room so unexpectedly, so swiftly, that if his purpose had been to escape, he almost could have eluded the other man. Instead he made for the cellar door and ran down the basement steps. The detective had shot to his feet after him, was at his heels by the time he got down to the bottom. Bliss turned on the light and looked at the furnace grate, yawning emptily open – as though that could tell him anything more.

He turned despairingly to the detective. "Was there any blood on them?"

"Should there have been?"

"Don't! Have a heart," Bliss begged in a choked voice, and shaded his eyes. "Who put them in there? Why'd they bring them back here? How'd they get in while I was out?"

"Quit that," the headquarters man said dryly. "Suppose we get started. Our guys'll be looking all over for you, and it'll save them a lot of trouble."

Every few steps on the way back up those basement stairs, Bliss would stop, as though he'd run down and needed winding up again. The detective would prod him forward, not roughly, just as a sort of reminder to keep going.

"Why'd they put them *there*?" he asked. "Things that go in there are meant for fuel. That's what you came back for, to finish burning them, isn't it? Too late in the year to make a fire in the daytime without attracting attention."

"Listen. We were only married six weeks."

"What's that supposed to prove? Do you think there haven't been guys that got rid of their wives six *days* after they were married, or even six *hours*?"

"But those are fiends – monsters. *I* couldn't be one of them!"

And the pitiless answer was: "How do we know that? We can't tell, from the outside, what you're like on the inside. We're not X-ray machines."

They were up on the main floor again by now.

"Was she insured?" the detective questioned.

"Yes."

"You tell everything, don't you?"

"Because there's nothing to hide. I didn't just insure *her*, I insured us both. I took out twin policies, one on each of us. We were each other's beneficiaries. She wanted it that way."

"But you're here and she's not," the detective pointed out remorselessly.

They passed the dining-room entrance. Maybe it was the dishes still left on the table from that night that got to him. She came before him again, with her smiling crinkly eyes. He could see her carrying in a plate covered with a napkin. "Sit down there, mister, and don't look. I've got a surprise for you."

That finished him. That was a blow below the belt. He said, "You gotta let me alone a minute." And he slumped against the wall with his arm up over his face.

When he finally got over it, and it took some getting over, a sort of change had come over the detective. He said tonelessly, "Sit down a minute. Get your breath back and pull yourself together." He didn't sound like he meant that particularly, it was just an excuse.

He lighted a cigarette and then he threw the pack over at Bliss. Bliss let it slide off his thigh without bothering with it.

The detective said, "I've been a dick going on eight years now, and I never saw a guy who could fake a spell like you just had, and make it so convincing." He paused, then went on: "The reason I'm saying this is, once you go in you stay in, after what we found here in the house tonight. And, then, you did come up to me outside of your own accord, but of course that could have been just self-preservation. So I'm listening, for just as long as it takes me to finish this cigarette. By the time I'm through, if you haven't been able to tell me anything that changes the looks of things around, away we go." And he took a puff and waited.

"There's nothing I can tell you that I haven't already told you. She walked out of here Tuesday night at supper time. Said she was going to her mother's. She never got there. I haven't seen her since. Now you fellows find the things I saw her leave in, stuffed into the furnace in the basement." He pinched the bridge of his nose and kept it pinched.

The detective took another slow pull at his cigarette. "You've been around to the morgue and the hospitals. So she hadn't had any accident. Her things are back here again. So it isn't just a straight disappearance, or amnesia, or anything like that. That means that whatever was done to her or with her, was done against her will. Since we've eliminated accident, suicide, voluntary and involuntary disappearance, that spells murder."

"Don't!" Bliss said.

"It's got to be done." The detective took another puff. "Let's get down to motive. Now, you already have one, and a damned fine one. You'll have to dig up one on the part of somebody else that'll be stronger than yours, if you expect to cancel it out."

"Who could want to hurt her? She was so lovely, she was so beautiful —"

"Sometimes it's dangerous for a girl to be too lovely, too beautiful. It drives a man out of his mind, the man that can't have her. Were there any?"

"You're talking about Smiles now," Bliss growled dangerously, tightening his fist.

"I'm talking about a *case*. A case of suspected murder. And to us cases aren't beautiful, aren't ugly, they're just punishable." He puffed again. "Did she turn anyone down to marry you?"

Bliss shook his head. "She once told me I was the first fellow she ever went with."

The detective took another puff at his cigarette. He looked at it, shifted his fingers back a little, then looked at Bliss. "I seldom smoke that far down," he warned him. "I'm giving you a break. There's one more drag left in it. Anyone else stand to gain anything, financially, by her death, outside of yourself?"

"No one I know of."

The detective took the last puff, dropped the buff, ground it out. "Well, let's go," he said. He fumbled under his coat, took out a pair of handcuffs. "Incidentally, what was her real name? I have to know when I bring you in."

"Teresa."

"Smiles was just your pet name for her, eh?" The detective seemed to be just talking aimlessly, to try to take the sting out of the pinch, keep Bliss's mind off the handcuffs.

"Yeah," Bliss said, holding out his wrist without being told to. "I was the first one called her that. She never liked to be called Teresa. Her mother was the one always stuck to that."

He jerked his wrist back in again.

"C'mon, don't get hard to handle," the detective growled, reaching out after it.

"Wait a minute," Bliss said excitedly, and stuck his hand behind his back. "Some things have been bothering me. You brought one of them back just then. I nearly had it. Let me look, before I lose it again. Let me look at that letter a minute that her mother sent her yesterday. It's here in my pocket."

He stripped it out of the envelope. *Smiles, dear*, it began.

He opened his mouth and looked at the other man. "That's funny. Her mother never called her anything but Teresa. I know I'm right about that. How could she? It was *my* nickname. And I'd never seen her until last night and – and Smiles hadn't been home since we were married."

The detective, meanwhile, kept trying to snag his other hand – he was holding the letter in his left – and bring it around in front of him.

"Wait a minute, wait a minute," Bliss pleaded. "I've got one of those things now. There was like a hitch in the flow of conversation, an air pocket. She said, 'I'm Smiles's mother,' and he said, 'You're *Teresa*'s mother,' like he was reminding her what she always called Smiles. Why should he have to remind her of what she always called Smiles herself?

"And that's supposed to clear you of suspicion, because her mother picks up your nickname for your wife, after she's been talking to you on the phone two or three days in a row? Anyone would be liable to do that. She did it to sort of accommodate you. Didn't you ever hear of people doing that before? That's how nicknames spread."

"But she caught it *ahead of time*, before she heard me call it to her. This letter heading shows that. She didn't know Smiles had disappeared yet, when she sent this letter. Therefore she hadn't spoken to me yet."

"Well, then, she got it from the husband, or from your wife's own letters home."

"But she never used it before; she disliked it until now. She wrote Smiles and told her openly it sounded too much like the nickname of a chorus girl. I can prove it to you. I can show you. Wait a minute, whatever your name is. Won't you let me see if I can find some other letter from her, just to convince myself?"

My name is Stillman, and it's too small a matter to make any difference one way or the other. Now, come on Bliss; I've tried to be fair with you until now —"

"Nothing is too small a matter to be important. You're a detective, do I have to tell you that? It's the little things in life that count, never the big ones. The little ones go to make up the big ones. Why should she suddenly call her by a nickname she never used before and disapproved of? Wait, let me show you. There must be one of her old letters upstairs yet, left around in one of the bureau drawers. Just let me go up and hunt for it. It'll take just a minute."

Stillman went up with him, but Bliss could tell he was slowly souring on him. He hadn't changed over completely yet, but he was well under way. "I've taken all the stalling I'm going to from you," he muttered tight-lipped. "If I've got to crack down on you to get you out of here with me, I'll show you that I can do that, too."

Bliss was pawing through his wife's drawers meanwhile, head tensely lowered, knowing he had to beat his captor's change of mood to the punch, that in another thirty seconds at the most the slow-to-anger detective was going to yank him flat on the floor by the slack of the collar and drag him bodily out of the room after him.

He found one at last, almost when he'd given up hope. The same medium-blue ink, the same note paper. They hadn't corresponded with any great frequency, but they had corresponded regularly, about once every month or so.

"Here," he said relievedly, "here, see?" And he spread it out flat on the dresser top. Then he spread the one from his pocket alongside it, to compare. "See? 'Dearest Teresa.' What did I tell —"

He never finished it. They both saw it at once. It would have been hard to miss, the way he'd put both missives edge to edge. Bliss looked at the detective, then back at the dresser again.

Stillman was the first to put it into words. An expression of sudden concentration had come over his face. He elbowed Bliss a little aside, to get a better look. "See if you can dig up some more samples of her writing," he said slowly. "I'm not an expert, but, unless I miss my guess, these two letters weren't written by the same person."

Bliss didn't need to be told twice. He was frantically going through everything of Smiles's he could lay his hands on, all her keepsakes, mementos, accumulated belongings, scattering them around. He stopped as suddenly as he'd begun, and Stillman saw him standing there staring fixedly at something in one of the trinket boxes he had been plumbing through.

"What's the matter? Did you find some more?"

Bliss acted scared. His face was pale. "No, not writing," he said in a bated voice. "Something even – Look."

The detective's chin thrust over his shoulder. "Who are they?"

"That's evidently a snapshot of her and her mother, taken at a beach when she was a girl. I've never seen it before, but —"

"How do you know it's her mother? It could be some other woman, a friend of the family's."

Bliss had turned it over right while he was speaking. On the back, in schoolgirlish handwriting, was the notation: *Mamma and I, at Sea Crest, 19—*

Bliss reversed it again, right side forward.

"Well, what're you acting so scared about?" Stillman demanded impatiently. "You look like you've seen a ghost."

"Because this woman on the snapshot isn't the same woman I spoke to as her mother up at Denby tonight!"

"Now, wait a minute; hold your horses. You admit yourself you had never set eyes on her before until tonight; eight years is eight years.

She's in a bathing-suit in this snapshot. She may have dyed or bleached her hair since, or it may have turned gray on her."

"That has nothing to do with it! I'm not looking at her hair or her clothes. The whole shape of her face is different. The bone structure is different. The features are different. This woman has a broad, round face. The one in Denby has a long, oval one. I tell you, it's not the same woman at all!"

"Gimme that, and gimme those." Stillman pocketed letters and snapshot. "Come on downstairs. I think I'll smoke another cigarette." His way of saying: *You've got yourself a reprieve.*

When they were below again, he sat down, with a misleading air of leisure. "Gimme your wife's family background, as much of it as you can, as much of it as she told you."

"Smiles was down here on her own when I met her. Her own father died when she was a kid, and left them comfortably well off, with their own house up in —"

"Denby?"

"No, it was some other place; I can't think of it offhand. While she was still a youngster, her mother gave Smiles her whole time and attention. But when Smiles had finished her schooling, about two years ago, the mother was still an attractive woman, young for her years, lively, good-hearted. It was only natural that she should marry again. Smiles didn't resent that, she'd expected her to. When the mother fell for this mason, Joe Alden, whom she first met when they were having some repairs made to the house, Smiles tried to like him. He'd been a good man in his line, too, but she couldn't help noticing that after he married her mother, he stopped dead, never did a stroke of work from then on; pretending he couldn't find any – when she knew for a fact that there was work to be had. That was the first thing she didn't like. Maybe he sensed she was onto him, but anyway they didn't rub well together. For her mother's sake, to avoid trouble, she decided to clear out, so her mother wouldn't have to choose between them. She was so diplomatic about it, though, that her mother never guessed what the real reason was.

"She came on down here, and not long ago Alden and her mother sold their own house and moved to a new one in Denby. Smiles said she supposed he did it to get away from the gossipy neighbors as much as anything else; they were probably beginning to criticize him for not at least making a stab at getting a job after he was once married."

"Did they come down when you married Smiles?"

"No. Smiles didn't notify them ahead; just sent a wire of announcement the day we were married. Her mother had been in poor health, and she was afraid the trip down would be more than she could stand. Well, there's the background."

"Nothing much there to dig into, at first sight."

"There never is, anywhere – at first sight," Bliss let him know. "Listen, Stillman. I'm going back up there again. Whatever's wrong is up at that end, not at this."

"I was detailed here to bring you in for questioning, you know." But he didn't move.

"Suppose I hadn't gone up to you outside in the street just now. Suppose I hadn't shown up around here for, say, another eight or ten hours. Can't you give me those extra hours? Come up there with me, never leave me out of your sight, put the bracelet on me, do anything you want, but at least let me go up there once more and confront those people. If you lock me up down at this end, then I've lost her sure as anything. I'll never find out what became of her – and you won't either. Something bothered me up there. A whole lot of things bothered me up there, but I've only cleared up one of them so far. Let me take a crack at the rest.

"You don't want much," Stillman said grudgingly. "D'ya know what can happen to me for stepping out of line like that? D'ya know I can be broken for anything like that?"

"You mean you're ready to ignore the discrepancy in handwriting in those two letters, and my assurance that there's someone up there that doesn't match the woman on that snapshot?"

"No, naturally not; I'm going to let my lieutenant know about both those things."

"And by that time it'll be too late. It's already three days since she's been gone."

"Tell you what," Stillman said. "I'll make a deal with you. We'll start out for headquarters now, and on the way we'll stop in at that bus terminal. If I can find any evidence, the slightest shred, that she started for Denby that night, I'll go up there with you. If not, we go over to headquarters."

All Bliss said was: "I know you'll find out she did leave."

Stillman took him without handcuffing him, merely remarking, "If you try anything, you'll be the loser, not me."

The ticket seller again went as far as he had with Bliss the time before, but still couldn't go any further than that. "Yeah, she bought a ticket for as far as the money she had on her would take her, but I can't remember where it was to."

"Which don't prove she ever hit Denby," Stillman grunted.

"Tackle the bus driver," Bliss pleaded. "No. 27. I know he was holding out on me. I could tell by the way he acted. She rode with him, all right, but for some reason he was cagey about saying so."

But they were out of luck. No. 27 was up at the other end, due to bring the cityward bus in the following afternoon.

Stillman was already trying to steer his charge out of the place and on his way over to headquarters, but Bliss wouldn't give up. "There must be someone around here that saw her get on that night. One of the attendants, one of the concessionaires that are around here every night. Maybe she checked her bag, maybe she drank a cup of coffee at the counter."

She hadn't checked her bag; the checkroom attendant couldn't remember anyone like her. She hadn't stopped at the lunch counter, either; neither could the counterman recall her. Nor the Negro that shined shoes. They even interrogated the matron of the restroom, when she happened to appear outside the door briefly. No, she hadn't noticed anyone like that, either.

"All right, come on," Stillman said, hooking his arm around Bliss's.

"One more spin. How about him, over there, behind the magazine stand?"

Stillman only gave in because it happened to be near the exit; they had to pass it on their way out.

And it broke! The fog lifted, if only momentarily, for the first time since the previous Tuesday night. "Sure I do," the vendor said readily. "How could I help remembering? She came up to me in such a funny way. She said, 'I have exactly one dime left, which I overlooked when I was buying my ticket because it slipped to the bottom of my handbag. Let me have a magazine.' Naturally, I asked her which one she wanted. 'I don't care,' she said, 'so long as it lasts until I get off the bus. I want to be sure my mind is taken up.' Well, I've been doing business here for years, and it's gotten so I can clock the various stops. I mean, if they're riding a long distance, I give them a good thick magazine; if they're riding a short distance, I give them a skinny one. I gave her one for a medium distance – Denby; that was where she told me she was going."

All Stillman said was: "Come on over to the window while I get our tickets."

Bliss didn't say "Thanks." He didn't say anything. He didn't have to. The grateful look he gave the detective spoke for itself.

"Two to Denby, round," Stillman told the ticket seller. It was too late for the morning bus; the next one left in the early afternoon.

As they turned from the window, Bliss wondered aloud:

"Still and all, why was that driver so reluctant to admit she rode on the bus with him that night? And the ticket man claims she didn't buy a ticket to Denby, but to some point short of there."

"It's easy to see what it adds up to," Stillman told him. "She had a ticket for only part of the distance. She coaxed the driver into letting her ride the rest of the way to Denby. Probably explained her plight to him, and he felt sorry for her. That explains his reluctance to let you think she was on the bus at all. He must have thought you were a company spotter and naturally what he did would be against the regulations."

Tucking away the tickets in his inside coat pocket, the detective stood there a moment or two undecidedly. Then he said, "We may as well go back to your house. I might be able to turn up something else while we're waiting, and you can catch a nap. And, too, I'm going to call in, see if I can still make this detour up there and back legitimate while I'm about it."

When they got back to his house Bliss, exhausted, fell asleep in the bedroom. He remained oblivious to everything until the detective woke him up a half hour before bus time.

"Any luck?" Bliss asked him, shrugging into his coat.

"Nope, nothing more," Stillman said. Then he announced, "I've given my word to my lieutenant I'll show up at headquarters and have you with me, no later than nine tomorrow morning. He doesn't know you're with me right now; I let him think I got a tip where I could lay my hands on you. Leaving now, we will get up there around sunset, and we'll have to take the night bus back. That gives us only a few hours up there to see if we can find any trace of her. Pretty tight squeeze, if you ask me."

They boarded the bus together and sat down in one of the back seats. They didn't talk much during the long, monotonous ride up.

"Better take another snooze while you've got the chance," Stillman said.

Bliss thought he wouldn't be able to again, but, little by little, sheer physical exhaustion, combined with the lulling motion of the bus, overcame him and he dropped off.

It seemed like only five minutes later that Stillman shook him by the shoulder, rousing him. The sun was low in the west; he'd slept through nearly the entire trip. "Snap out of it, Bliss; we get off in another couple of minutes, right on time."

"I dreamed about her," Bliss said dully. "I dreamed she was in some kind of danger, needed me bad. She kept calling to me, 'Ed! Hurry up, Ed!'

Stillman dropped his eyes. "I heard you say her name twice in your sleep: 'Smiles, Smiles,' " he remarked quietly. "Damned if you act like any guilty man I ever had in my custody before. Even in your sleep you sound like you were innocent."

"Denby!" the driver called out.

As the bus pulled away and left them behind at the crossroads, Stillman said, "Now that we're up here, let's have an understanding with each other. I don't want to haul you around on the end of a handcuff with me, but my job is at stake; I've got to be sure that you're still with me when I start back."

"Would my word of honor that I won't try to give you the slip while we're up here be worth anything to you?"

Stillman looked at him square in the eye. "Is it worth anything to *you*?"

"It's about all I've got. I know I've never broken it."

Stillman nodded slowly. "I think maybe it'll be worth taking a chance on. All right, let me have it."

They shook hands solemnly.

Dusk was rapidly falling by now; the sun was already gone from sight and its afterglow fading out.

"Come on, let's get out to their place," Bliss said impatiently.

"Let's do a little inquiring around first. Remember, we have no evidence so far that she actually got off the bus here at all, let alone reached their house. Just her buying that magazine and saying she was coming here is no proof in itself. Now, let's see, she gets off in the middle of the night at this sleeping hamlet. Would she know the way out to their house, or would she have to ask someone?"

"She'd have to ask. Remember, I told you they moved here *after* Smiles had already left home. This would have been her first trip up here."

"Well, that ought to cinch it for us, if she couldn't get out there without asking directions. Let's try our luck at that filling-station first; it would probably have been the only thing open any more at the hour she came."

The single attendant on duty came out, said, "Yes, gents?"

"Look," Stillman began. "The traffic to and from here isn't exactly heavy, so this shouldn't be too hard. Think back to Tuesday night, the last bus north. Did you see anyone get off it?"

"I don't have to see 'em get off, I got a sure-fire way of telling whether anyone gets off or not."

"What's that?"

"Anyone that does get off, at least anyone that's a stranger here, never fails to stop by me and ask their way. That's as far as the last bus is concerned. The store is closed before then. And no one asked their way of me Tuesday night, so I figure no strangers got off."

"This don't look so good," murmured Stillman in an aside to Bliss. Then he asked the attendant, "Did you hear it go by at all? You must have, it's so quiet here."

"Yeah, sure, I did. It was right on time, too."

"Then you could tell if it stopped to let anyone down or went straight through without stopping, couldn't you?"

"Yeah, usually I can," was the disappointing answer. "But just that night, at that particular time, I was doing some repair work on a guy's car, trying to hammer out a bent fender for him, and my own noise drowned it out. As long as no one stopped by, though, I'm pretty sure it never stopped."

"Damn it," Stillman growled, as they turned away, "she couldn't have been more unseen if she was a ghost!"

After they were out of earshot of the filling-station attendant, Bliss said, "If Alden, for instance, had known she was coming and waited to meet her at the bus, that would do away with her having to ask anyone for directions. She may have telephoned ahead, or sent a wire up."

"If she didn't even have enough money to buy a ticket all the way, she certainly wouldn't have been able to make a toll call. Anyway, if we accept that theory, that means we're implicating them directly in her disappearance, and we have no evidence so far to support that. Remember, she may have met with foul play right here in Denby, along the road to their house, without ever having reached it."

It was fully dark by the time they rounded the bend in the road and came in sight of that last house of all, with the low brick wall in front of it. This time not a patch of light showed from any of the windows, upstairs or down, and yet it was earlier in the evening than when Bliss himself had arrived.

"Hello?" the detective said. "Looks like nobody home."

They turned in under the willow arch, rang the bell, and waited. Stillman pommeled the door and they waited some more. This was just perfunctory, however; it had been obvious to the two of them from the moment they first looked at the place that no one was in.

"Well, come on. What're we waiting for?" Bliss demanded. "I can get in one of the windows without any trouble."

Stillman laid a restraining hand on his arm. "No, you don't; that's breaking and entering. And I'm out of jurisdiction up here to begin with. We'll have to go back and dig up the local law; maybe I can talk him into putting the seal of official approval on it. Let's see if we can tell anything from the outside, first. I may be able to shine my torch in through one of the windows."

He clicked it on, made a white puddle against the front of the house, walked slowly in the wake of that as it moved along until it leaped in through one of the black window embrasures. They both edged up until their noses were nearly pressed flat against the glass, trying to peer through. It wouldn't work. The blinds were not down, but the closely webbed net curtains that hung down inside of the panes effectively parried its rays. They coursed slowly along the side of the house, trying it at window after window, each time with the same results.

Stillman turned away finally, but left his torch on. He splashed it up and down the short length of private dirt lane that ran beside the house, from the corrugated tin shack at the back that served Alden as a garage to the public highway in front. He motioned Bliss back as the latter started to step out onto it. "Stay off here a minute. I want to see if I can find out something from these tire prints their car left. See 'em?"

It would have been hard not to. The road past the house was macadamized, but there was a border of soft, powdery dust along the side of it, as with most rural roads. "I want to see if I can make out which way they turned," Stillman explained, strewing his beam of light along them and following offside. "If they went in to the city, to offer their co-operation to us down there, that would take them off to the right; no other way they could turn from here. If they turned to the left, up that way, it was definitely a lam, and it changes the looks of things all around."

The beam of his light, coursing along the prints like quicksilver in a channel, started to curve around *toward the right* as it followed them up out of sight on the hard-surfaced road. There was his answer.

He turned aimlessly back along them, light still on. He stopped parallel to the corner of the house, strengthened the beam's focus by bringing the torch down closer to the ground. "Here's something else," Bliss heard him say. "Funny how you can notice every little thing in this fine floury dust. His front left tire had a patch on it, and a bad one, too. See it? You can tell just what they did. Alden evidently ran the car out of the shed alone, ahead of his wife. She got in here at the side of the house, to save time, instead of going out the front way; they were going down the road the other way, anyway. His wheel came to rest with the patch squarely under it. That's why it shows so plain in this one place. Then he took his brake off and the car coasted back a little with the tilt of the ground. When he came forward again, the position of his wheel diverged a little, missed erasing its own former imprint. Bet they have trouble with that before the night's over."

He spoke as though it were just a trivial detail. But is anything, Bliss was to ask himself later, a trivial detail?

"Come on," Stillman concluded, pocketing his light, "let's go get the law and see what it looks like on the inside."

The constable's name was Cochrane, and they finally located him at his own home. "Evening," Stillman introduced himself, "I'm Stillman of the city police. I was wondering if there's some way we could get a look inside that Alden house. Their – er – stepdaughter has disappeared down in the city; she was supposed to have started for here, and this is just a routine check. Nothing against them. They seem to be out, and we have to make the next bus back."

Cochrane plucked at his throat judiciously. "Well, now, I guess I can accommodate you, as long as it's done in my presence. I'm the law around here, and if they've got nothing to hide, there's no reason why they should object. I'll drive ye back in my car. This feller here your subordinate, I s'pose?"

Stillman said, "Um," noncommittally, favored Bliss with a nudge. The constable would have probably balked at letting a man already wanted by the police into these people's house, they both knew, even if he was accompanied by a bona fide detective.

He stopped off at his office first to get a master key, came back with the remark: "This ought to do the trick." They were back at the Alden place once more inside of ten minutes, all told, from the time they had first left it.

Cochrane favored them with a sly grimace as they got out and went up to the house. "I'm sort of glad you fellers asked me to do this, at that. Fact is, we've all been curious about them folks ourselves hereabouts for a long time past. Kind of unsociable; keep to themselves a lot. This is as good a time as any to see if they got any skeletons in the closet."

Bliss shuddered involuntarily at the expression.

The constable's master key opened the door without any great difficulty, and the three of them went in.

They looked in every room in the place from top to bottom, and in every closet of every room, and not one of the "skeletons" the constable had spoken of turned up, either allegorical or literal. There wasn't anything out of the way, and nothing to show that anything had ever been out of the way, in this house.

In the basement, when they reached it, were a couple of sagging, half-empty bags of cement in one corner, and pinkish traces of brick dust and brick grit on the floor, but that was easily accounted for. "Left over from when he was putting up that wall along the roadside a while back, I guess," murmured Cochrane.

They turned and went upstairs again. The only other discovery of any sort they made was not of a guilty nature, but simply an indication of how long ago the occupants had left. Stillman happened to knuckle a coffeepot standing on the kitchen range, and it was still faintly warm from the residue of liquid left in it.

"They must have only just left before we got here," he said to Bliss. "Missed them just by minutes."

"Funny; why did they wait until after dark to start on a long trip like that? Why didn't they leave sooner?"

"That don't convict them of anything, just the same," Stillman maintained obdurately. "We haven't turned up a shred of evidence that your wife ever saw the inside of this house. Don't try to get around that."

The local officer, meanwhile, had gone outside to put some water in his car. "Close the door good after you as you come out," he called out to them.

They were already at the door, but Bliss unaccountably turned and went back inside again. When Stillman followed him a moment later, he was sitting there in the living-room raking his fingers perplexedly through his hair.

"Come on," the detective said, as considerately as he could, "let's get going. He's waiting for us."

Bliss looked up at him helplessly. "Don't you get it? Doesn't this room bother you?"

Stillman looked around vaguely. "No. In what way? What's wrong with it? To me it seems clean, well kept, and comfortable. All you could ask for."

"There's something about it annoys me. I feel ill at ease in it. It's not *restful*, for some reason. And I have a peculiar feeling that if I could figure out *why* it isn't restful, it would help to partly clear up this mystery about Smiles."

Stillman sliced the edge of his hand at him scornfully. "Now you're beginning to talk plain crazy, Bliss. You say this room isn't restful. The room has nothing to do with it. It's you. You're all tense, jittery, about your wife. Your nerves are on edge, frayed to the breaking point. That's why the room don't seem restful to you. Naturally it don't. No room would."

Bliss kept shaking his head baffledly. "No. No. That may sound plausible, but I know that isn't it. It's not *me*, it's the room itself. I'll admit I'm all keyed up, but I noticed it already the other night when I wasn't half so keyed up. Another thing, I don't get it in any of the other rooms in this house, I only get it in here."

"I don't like the way you're talking; I think you're starting to crack up under the strain," Stillman let him know, but he hung around in the doorway for a few minutes, watching him curiously, while Bliss sat there motionless, clasped hands hanging from the back of his neck now.

"Did you get it yet?"

Bliss raised his head, shook it mutely, chewing the corner of his mouth. "It's one of those things; when you try too hard for it, it escapes you altogether. It's only when you're sort of not thinking about it, that you notice it. The harder I try to pin it down, the more elusive it becomes."

"Sure," said Stillman with a look of sympathetic concern, "and if you sit around in here brooding about it much more, I'll be taking you back with me in a straitjacket. Come on, we've only got ten more minutes to make that bus."

Bliss got reluctantly to his feet. "There it goes," he said. "I'll never get it now."

"Ah, you talk like these guys that keep trying to communicate with spirits through a ouija board," Stillman let him know, locking up the front door after them. "The whole thing was a wild-goose chase."

"No, it wasn't."

"Well, what'd we get out of it?"

"Nothing. But that doesn't mean it isn't around here waiting to be seen. It's just that we've missed seeing it, whatever it is."

"There's not a sign of her around that house. Not a sign of her ever having been there. Not a sign of violence."

"And I know that, by going away from here, we're turning our backs on whatever there is to be learned about what became of her. We'll never find out at the other end, in the city. I nearly had it, too, when I was sitting in there. Just as I was about to get it, it would slip away from me again. Talk about torture!"

Stillman lost his temper. "Will you lay off that room! If there was anything the matter with it, I'd notice it as well as you. My eyes are just as good, my brains are just as good. What's the difference between you and me?" The question was only rhetorical.

"You're a detective and I'm an architect," Bliss said inattentively, answering it as asked.

"Are you fellows going to stand there arguing all night?" the constable called from the other side of the wall.

They went out and got into the open car, started off. Bliss felt like groaning: "Good-bye, Smiles." Just as they reached the turn of the road that would have swept the house out of sight once they rounded it, Stillman happened to glance back for no particular reason, at almost the very last possible moment that it could still be seen in a straight line behind them.

"Hold it," he ejaculated, thumbing a slim bar of light narrowed by perspective. "We left the lights on in that last room we were in."

The constable braked promptly. "Have to go back and turn them off, or they'll—"

"We haven't time now, we'll miss the bus," Stillman cut in. "It's due in six more minutes. Drive us down to the crossroads first, and then you come back afterward and put them out yourself."

"No!" Bliss cried out wildly, jumping to his feet. "This has a meaning to it! I'm not passing this up! I want another look at those lights; they're asking me to, they're begging me to!" Before either one of them could stop him, he had jumped down from the side of the car without bothering to unlatch the door. He started to run back up the road, deaf to Stillman's shouts and imprecations.

"Come back here, you welsher! You gave me your word of honor!"

A moment later the detective's feet hit the ground and he started after his prisoner. But Bliss had already turned in through the opening in the wall, was flinging himself bodily against the door, without waiting for any master key this time. The infuriated detective caught him by the shoulder, swung him violently around, when he had reached him.

"Take your hands off me!" Bliss said hoarsely. "I'm going to get in there!"

Stillman swung at him and missed. Instead of returning the blow, Bliss threw his whole weight against the door for the last time. There was a rendering and splintering of wood, and it shot inward, leaving the whole lock intact against the frame. Bliss went flailing downward on his face into the hallway. He scrambled erect, reached the inner doorway, put his hand inside, and put the lights out without looking into the room.

"It's when they go on that counts," he panted.

The only reason Stillman wasn't grappling with him was that he couldn't locate him for a minute in the dark. The switch clicked a second time. Light flashed from the dazzingly calcimined ceiling. Bliss was standing directly in the middle of the opening as it did so, just as he had been the first night.

Stillman was down the hall a few steps, couldn't see his face for a minute. "Well?" he asked.

Bliss turned to him without saying anything. The look on his face answered for him. He'd gotten what he wanted.

"Why, they're not in the center of the ceiling! They're offside That's what made them seem glaring, unexpected. They took my eyes by surprise. I've got professionally trained eyes, remember. They didn't go on where I expected them to, but a little farther over. And now that I have that much, I have it all." He gripped Stillman excitedly by the biceps. "Now I see what's wrong with the room. Now I see why I found it so unrestful. It's out of true."

"What?"

"Out of proportion. Look. Look at that window. It's not in the center of that wall. And d'you see how cleverly they've tried to cover the discrepancy? A thin, skinny, up-and-down picture on the short side; a big, wide, fat one on the longer side. That creates an optical illusion, makes both sides seem even. Now come over here and look this way." He pulled the detective in after him, turned him around by the shoulder. "Sure, same thing with the door frame; that's not dead center, either. But the door opens inward into the room, swings to that short side and partly screens it, throws a shadow over it, so that takes care of that. What else? What else?"

He kept pivoting feverishly, sweeping his glance around on all sides. "Oh, sure, the rug. I was sitting here and I dropped some ashes and looked down at the floor. See what bothered me about that? Again there's an unbalance. See the margin of polished woodwork running around on three sides of it? And on the fourth side it runs right smack up against the baseboard of the wall. Your eye wants proportion, symmetry; it's got to have it in all things. If it doesn't get it, it's uncomfortable. It wants that dark strip of woodwork on all *four* sides, or else the rug should touch all four baseboards, like a carpet –"

He was talking slower and slower, like a record that's running down. Some sort of tension was mounting in him, gripping him, Stillman could tell by looking at him. He panted the last few words out, as if it took all his strength to produce them, and then his voice died away altogether, without a period.

"What're you getting so white around the gills for?" the detective demanded. "Suppose the room is lopsided, what then? Your face is turning all green –"

Bliss had to grab him by the shoulder for a minute for support. His voice was all furry with dawning horror. "Because – because – don't you see what it means? Don't you see *why* it's that way? One of these walls is a dummy wall, built out *in front* of the real one." His eyes were dilated with unbelieving horror. He clawed insensately at his own hair. "It all hangs together so damnably! He was a mason before he married her mother, I told you that. The storekeeper down at the crossroads said that Alden built a low brick wall in front of the house, 'just to keep in practice,' he guessed. No reason for it. It wasn't high enough for privacy, it didn't even run around all four sides of the plot.

"He didn't build it just to keep in practice! He did it to get the bricks in here from the contractor. More than he needed. He put it up just to have an excuse to order them. Who's going to count – Don't stand there! Get an ax, a crowbar; help me break this thing down! Don't you see what this dummy wall is for? Don't you see what we'll find –"

The detective had been slower in grasping it, but he finally got it, too. His own face went gray. "Which one is it?"

"It must be on this side, the side that's the shortest distance from the window, door, and light fixture." Bliss rushed up to it, began to pound it with his clenched fists, up and down, sounding it out. Sweat flew literally off his face like raindrops in a stiff wind.

The detective bolted out of the room, sent an excited yell at the open front door:

"Cochrane! Come in here, give us a hand, bring tools!"

Between the two of them they dug up a hatchet, a crowbar, cold chisel, and bung starter. "That wall," the detective explained tersely for the constable's benefit, without going into details. Cochrane didn't argue; one look at both their faces must have told him that some unspeakable horror was on the way to revelation.

Bliss was leaning sideways against it by now, perfectly still, head lowered almost as though he were trying to hear something through it. He wasn't. His head was lowered with the affliction of discovery. "I've found it," he said stifledly. "I've found – the place. Listen." He pounded once or twice. There was the flat impact of solidity. He moved farther over, pounded again. This time there was the deeper resonance of a partly, or only imperfectly, filled orifice. "Half bricks, with a hollow behind them. Elsewhere, whole bricks, mortar behind them."

Stillman stripped his coat off, spit on his hands. "Better get out of the room – in case you're right," he suggested, flying at it with the hatchet, to knock off the plaster. "Wait outside the door; we'll call you –"

"No! I've got to know, I've got to see. Three of us are quicker than two." And he began chipping off the plaster coating with the cutting edge of the chisel. Cochrane cracked it for them with the bung starter. A cloud of dust hovered about them while they hacked away. Finally, they had laid bare an upright, *coffin-shaped* segment of pinkish-white brickwork in the plaster finish of the wall.

They started driving the chisel in between the interstices of the brick ends, Stillman steadying it, Cochrane driving it home with the bung starter. They changed to the crowbar, started to work that as a lever, when they'd pierced a big enough space.

"Look out. One of them's working out."

A fragment of brick ricocheted halfway across the room, dropped with a thud. A second one followed. A third. Bliss started to claw at the opening with his bare nails, to enlarge it faster.

"You're only impeding us, we can get at it faster this way," Stillman said, pushing him aside. A gray fill of imperfectly dried clayey mortar was being laid bare. It was only a shell; flakes of it, like dried mud, had begun dropping off and out, some of their own weight, others with the impact of their blows, long before they had opened more than a "window" in the brickwork façade.

"Get back," Stillman ordered. His purpose was to protect Bliss from the full impact of discovery that was about to ensue.

Bliss obeyed him at last, staggered over to the other end of the room, stood there with his back to them as if he were looking out of the window. Only the window was farther over. A spasmodic shiver went down his back every so often. He could hear the pops and thuds as brick fragments continued to drop out of the wall under the others' efforts, then a sudden engulfing silence.

He turned his head just in time to see them lowering something from the niche in the wall. An upright something. A rigid, mummified, columnar something that resembled nothing so much as a log covered with mortar. The scant remainder of bricks that still held it fast below, down toward the floor, shattered, spilled down in a little freshet as they wrenched it free. A haze of kindly concealing dust veiled them from him. For a minute or two they were just white shadows working over something, and then they had this thing lying on the floor. A truncated thing without any human attributes whatever, like the mold around a cast metal statue – but with a core that was something else again.

"Get out of here, Bliss," Stillman growled. "This is no place for you!"

Wild horses couldn't have dragged Bliss away. He was numbed beyond feeling now, anyway. The whole scene had been one that could never again be forgotten by a man who had once lived through it.

"Not with that!" he protested, as he saw the crouching. Stillman flick open the large blade of a penknife.

"It's the only thing I *can* use! Go out and get us some water, see if we can soften this stuff up a little, dissolve it."

When Bliss came back with a pail of it, Stillman was working away cautiously at one end of the mound, shaving a little with the knife blade, probing and testing with his fingers. He desisted suddenly, flashed the constable a mutely eloquent look, shifted up to the opposite end. Bliss, staring with glazed eyes, saw a stubby bluish-black wedge peering through where he had been working – the tip of a woman's shoe.

"Upside down at that," grunted Cochrane, trying not to let Bliss overhear him. The latter's teeth were chattering with nervous shock.

"I told you to get out of here!" Stillman flared for the third and last time. "Your face is driving me crazy!" With as little effect as before.

Fine wires seemed to hold some of it together, even after he had pared it with the knife blade. He wet the palms of his hands in the pail of water, kneaded and crumbled it between them in those places. What had seemed like stiff wires was strands of human hair.

"That's enough," he said finally in a sick voice. "There's someone there; that's all I wanted to be sure of. I don't know how to go about the rest of it, much; an expert'll have to attend to that."

"Them devils," growled Cochrane deep in his throat.

Bliss suddenly toppled down between them, so abruptly they both thought he had fainted for a minute. "Stillman!" he said in a low throbbing voice. He was almost leaning across the thing. "These wisps of hair – Look! They show through dark, bluish-black! *She was blond!* Like an angel. It's somebody else!"

Stillman nodded, held his forehead dazedly. "Sure, it must be. I don't have to go by that; d'you know what should have told me from the beginning? Your wife's only been missing since Tuesday night, three days ago. The condition of the mortar shows plainly that this job's been up for weeks past. Why, the paint on the outside of the wall would have hardly been dry yet, let alone the fill in back of it. Apart from that, it would have been humanly impossible to put up such a job single-handed in three days. We both lost our heads; it shows you it doesn't pay to get excited.

"It's the mother, that's who it is. There's your answer for the discrepancy in the handwriting on the two notes, the snapshot, and that business about the nickname that puzzled you. Come on, stand up and lean on me, we're going to find out where he keeps his liquor. You need a drink if a man ever did!"

They found some in a cupboard out in the kitchen, sat down for a minute. Bliss looked as if he'd been pulled through a knothole. The constable had gone out on wobbly legs to get a breath of fresh air.

Bliss put the bottle down and started to look alive again.

"I think I'll have a gulp myself," Stillman said. "I'm not a drinking man, but that was one of the nastiest jobs in there just now I've ever been called on to participate in."

The constable rejoined them, his face still slighly greenish. He had a drink, too.

"How many of them were there when they first moved in here?" Stillman asked him.

"Only two. Only him and his wife, from first to last."

"Then you never saw her; they hid her from sight, that's all."

"They've been kind of stand-offish, no one's ever been inside the place until tonight."

"It's her, all right, the real mother," Bliss said, as soon as he'd gotten his mental equilibrium back. "I don't have to see the face, I know I'm right. No, no more. I'm O.K. now, and I want to be able to think clearly. Don't you touch any more of it, either, Still. That's who it must be. Don't you see how the whole thing hangs together? Smiles *did* show up here Tuesday night, or rather in the early hours of Wednesday morning; I'm surer than ever of it now. You asked me, back at my house, for a motive that would overshadow that possible insurance one of mine. Well, here it is; this is it. She was the last one they expected to see, so soon after her own marriage to me. She walked in here and found an impostor in the place of her own mother, a stranger impersonating her. They had to shut her up quick, keep her from raising an alarm. There's your motive as far as Smiles is concerned."

"And it's a wow," concurred Stillman heartily. "The thing is, what've they done with her, where is she? We're no better off than before. She's not around here; we've cased the place from cellar to attic. Unless there's another of those trick walls that we've missed spotting."

"You're forgetting that what you said about the first one still goes. There hasn't been time enough to rig up anything that elaborate."

"I shouldn't have taken that drink," confessed Stillman.

"I'm convinced she *was* here, though, as late as Thursday night, and still alive in the place. Another of those tantalizing things just came back to me. There was a knock on one of the water pipes somewhere; I couldn't tell if it was upstairs or down. I bet she was tied up someplace, the whole time I was sitting here."

"Did you hear one or more than one?"

"Just one. The woman got right up and went out, I noticed, giving an excuse about getting a fresh handkerchief. They probably had her doped, or under some sedative."

"That's then, but now?"

"There's a lot of earth around outside, acres of it, miles of it," Cochrane put in morbidly.

"No, now wait a minute," Stillman interjected. "Let's get this straight. If their object was just to make her disappear, clean vanish, as in the mother's case, that would be one thing. Then I'm afraid we might find her lying somewhere around in that earth you speak of. But you're forgetting that her clothes turned up in your own furnace at home, Bliss – showing they didn't want her to disappear, they wanted to pin her death definitely on you."

"Why?"

"Self-preservation, pure and simple. With a straight disappearance, the investigation would have never been closed. In the end it might have been directed up this way, resulted in unearthing the first murder, just as we did tonight. Pinning it on you would have not only obviated that risk, but eliminated you as well – cleaned the slate for them. A second murder to safeguard the first, a legal execution to clinch the second. But – to pin it successfully on you, that body has to show up down around where you are, and not up here at all. The clothes were a forerunner of it."

"But would they risk taking her back to my place, knowing it was likely to be watched by you fellows, once they had denounced me to you themselves? That would be like sticking their own heads in a noose. They might know it would be kept under surveillance."

"No, it wouldn't have been. You see, your accidental switch to that hitchhike from the bus resulted in two things going wrong. We not only went out to your house to look for you when you didn't show up at the terminal, but, by going out there, we found the clothes in the furnace sooner than they wanted us to. I don't believe they were meant to be found until – the body was also in position."

"Then why make two trips, instead of just one? Why not take poor Smiles at the same time they took her clothes?"

"He had to make a fast trip in, the first time, to beat that bus. They may have felt it was too risky to take her along then. He also had to familiarize himself with your premises, find some way of getting in, find out if the whole thing was feasible or not before going ahead with it. They felt their call to us – it wasn't an accusation at all, by the way, but simply a request that we investigate – would get you out of the way, clear the coast for them. They expected you to be held and questioned for twenty-four, forty-eight hours, straight. They thought they'd given themselves a wide enough margin of safety. But your failure to take the bus telescoped it."

Bliss rose abruptly. "Do you think she's – yet?" He couldn't bring himself to mention the word.

"It stands to reason that they'd be foolish to do it until the last possible moment. That would increase the risk of transporting her a hundred-fold. And they'd be crazy to do it anywhere else but on the exact spot where they intend her to be found eventually. Otherwise it would be too easy for us to reconstruct the fact that she was killed somewhere else and taken there afterward."

"Then the chances are she was still alive when they left here with her! There may still be time even now; she may still be alive! What are we sitting here like this for?"

They both bolted out together, but Bliss made for the front door, Stillman headed for the phone in the hall.

"What're you doing that for?"

"Phone in an alarm to city headquarters. How else can we hope to save her? Have them throw a cordon around your house –"

Bliss pulled the instrument out of his hands. "Don't! You'll only be killing her quicker that way! If we frighten them off, we'll never save her. They'll lose their heads, kill her anywhere and drop her off just to get rid of her. This way, at least we know it'll be in or somewhere around my house."

"But, man, do you realize the head start they've had?"

"We only missed them by five or ten minutes. Remember that coffeepot on the stove?"

"Even so, even with a State police escort, I doubt if we can get in under a couple of hours."

"And I say that we've got to take the chance! You noticed their tire treads before. He has a walloping bad patch, and he's never going to make that bad stretch on the road with it. I saw his car last night when it raced past, and he had no spares up. There's no gas station for miles around there. All that will cut down their head start."

"You're willing to gamble your wife's life against a flat tire?"

"There isn't anything else I *can* do. I'm convinced if you send an alarm ahead and have a dragnet thrown around my house, they'll scent it and simply shy away from there and go off someplace else with her where we *won't* be able to get to her in time, because we won't know where it is. Come on, we could be miles away already, for the time we've wasted talking."

"All right," snapped the detective, "we'll play it your way! Is this car of yours any good?" he asked Cochrane, hopping in.

"Fastest thing in these parts," said the constable grimly, slithering under the wheel.

"Well, you know what you've got to do with it: cut down their head start to nothing flat; less than nothing, you've got to get us there five minutes to the good."

"Just get down low in your seats and hang onto your back teeth," promised Cochrane. "What we just turned up in there happened in my jurisdiction, don't forget – and the law of the land gives this road to us tonight!"

It was an incredible ride; incredible for the fact that they stayed right side up on the surface of the road at all. The speedometer needle clung to stratospheric heights throughout. The scenery was just a blurred hiss on both sides of them. The wind pressure stung the pupils of their eyes to the point where they could barely hold them open. The constable, luckily, used glasses for reading and had happened to have them about him when they started. He put them on simply in order to make sure of staying on the road at all.

They had to take the bad stretch at a slower speed in sheer self-defense, in order not to have the same thing happen to them that they were counting on having happened to the Alden car. An intact tire could possibly get over it unharmed, but one that was already defective was almost sure to go out.

"Wouldn't you think he'd have remembered about this from passing over it last night, and taken precautions?" Stillman yelled above the wind at Bliss.

"He took a chance on it just like we're doing now. Slow up a minute at the first gas station after here, see if he got away with it or not." He knew that if he had, that meant they might just as well turn back then and there; Smiles was as good as dead already.

It didn't appear for another twenty minutes even at the clip they had resumed once the bad stretch was past. With a flat, or until a tow car was sent out after anyone, it would have taken an hour or more to make it.

"Had a flat to fix, coming from our way, tonight?" Stillman yelled out at the attendant.

"And how!" the man yelled back, jogging over to them. "That was no flat! He wobbled up here with ribbons around his wheel. Rim all flattened, too, from riding so long on it."

"*He?*" echoed Stillman. "Wasn't there two women or anyway one, with him?"

"No, just a fellow alone."

"She probably waited for him up the road out of sight with Smiles," Bliss suggested in an undertone, "to avoid being seen; then he picked them up again when the job was finished. Or if Smiles was able to walk, maybe they detoured around it on foot and rejoined the car farther down."

"Heavy-set man with a bull neck, and little eyes, and scraggly red hair?" the constable asked the station operator.

"Yeah."

"That's him. How long ago did he pull out of here?"

"Not more than an hour ago, I'd say."

"See? We've already cut their head start plenty," Bliss rejoiced.

"There's still too damn much of it to suit me," was the detective's answer.

"One of you take the wheel for the next lap," Cochrane said. "The strain is telling on me. Better put these on for goggles." He handed Stillman his reading-glasses.

The filling-station and its circular glow of light whisked out behind them and they were on the tear once more. They picked up a State police motorcycle escort automatically within the next twenty minutes, by their mere speed in itself; simply tapered off long enough to show their badges and make their shouts of explanation heard. This was all to the good, it cleared their way through such towns and restricted-speed belts as lay in their path. Just to give an idea of their pace, there were times, on the straightaway, when their escort had difficulty in keeping up with them. And even so, they weren't making good enough time to satisfy Bliss. He alternated between fits of optimism, when he sat crouched forward on the edge of the seat, fists clenched, gritting: "We'll swing it; we'll get there in time; I know it!" and fits of despair, when he slumped back on his shoulder blades and groaned, "We'll never make it! I'm a fool, I should have let you phone in ahead like you wanted to! Can't you make this thing *move* at all?"

"Look at that speedometer," the man at the wheel suggested curtly. "There's nowhere else for the needle to go but off the dial altogether! Take it easy, Bliss. They can't possibly tear along at this clip; we're official, remember. Another thing, once they get there, they'll do a lot of cagey reconnoitering first. That'll eat up more of their head start. And finally, even after they get at it, they'll take it slow, make all their preparations first, to make it look right. Don't forget, they think they've got all night; they don't know we're on their trail."

"And it's still going to be an awful close shave," insisted Bliss through tightly clenched teeth.

Their State police escort signed off at the city limits with a wave of the arm, a hairpin turn, and left them on their own. They had to taper down necessarily now, even though traffic was light at this night hour. Bliss showed Stillman the shortcut over that would bring them up to his house from the rear. A block and a half away Stillman choked off their engine, coasted to a stealthy stop under the overshadowing trees, and the long grueling race against time was over – without their knowing as yet whether it had been successful or not.

"Now follow me," Bliss murmured, hopping down. "I hope we didn't bring the car in too close; sounds carry so at an hour like this."

"They won't be expecting us." One of Stillman's legs gave under him from his long motionless stint at the wheel; he had to hobble along slapping at it until he could get the circulation back into it. Cochrane brought up at the rear.

When they cleared the back of the house next door to Bliss's and could look through the canal of separation to the street out in front, Bliss touched his companions on the arm, pointed meaningly. The blurred outline of a car was visible, parked there under the same leafy trees where Stillman himself had hidden when he was waiting for Bliss. They couldn't make out its interior.

"Someone in it," Cochrane said, breathing hard. "I think it's a woman, too. I can see the white curve of a bare arm on the wheel."

"You take that car, we'll take the house; he must be in there with her long ago at this stage of the game," Stillman muttered. "Can you come up on it quietly enough so she won't have time to sound the horn or signal him in any way?"

"I'll see to it I do!" was the purposeful answer. Cochrane turned back like a wraith, left the two of them alone.

They couldn't go near the front of the house because of the lookout, and there was no time to wait for Cochrane to incapacitate her. "Flatten out and do like I do," Bliss whispered. "She's probably watching the street out there more than this lot behind the house." He crouched, with his chin nearly down to his knees, darted across the intervening space to the concealment provided by the back of his own house.

"We can get in through the kitchen window," Bliss instructed, when Stillman had made the switch-over after him. "The latch never worked right. Give me a folder of matches, and make a footrest with your hands."

When he was up with one foot on the outside of the sill, his companion supporting the other, Bliss tore off and discarded the sandpaper and matches adhering to it, used the cardboard remainder as a sort of impromptu jimmy, slipping it down into the seam between the two window halves, and pushing the fastening back out of the way with it. A moment later he had the lower pane up and was inside the room, stretching down his hands to Stillman to help him up after him.

They both stood perfectly still there for a minute in the gloom, listening for all they were worth. Not a sound reached them, not a chink of light showed. Bliss felt a cold knife of doubt stab at his heart.

"Is he in here at all?" He breathed heavily. "That may be somebody else's car out there across the way."

At that instant there was the blurred but unmistakable sound that loose, falling earth makes, dropping back into a hollow or cavity. You hear it on the streets when a drainage ditch is being refilled. You hear it in a cemetery when a grave is being covered up. In the silence of this house, in the dead of night, it had a knell-like sound of finality. *Burial.*

Bliss gave a strangled gasp of horror, lurched forward in the darkness. "He's already – through!"

The sound had seemed to come from somewhere underneath them. Bliss made for the basement door. Stillman's heavy footfalls pounded after him, all thought of concealment past.

Bliss clawed open the door that gave down to the cellar, flung it back. For a split second, and no more, dull-yellow light gleamed up from below. Then it snuffed out, too quickly to show them anything. There was pitch blackness below them, as above, and an ominous silence.

Something clicked just over Bliss's shoulder, and the pale moon of Stillman's torch glowed out from the cellar floor below them, started traveling around, looking for something to center on. Instantly a vicious tongue of flame spurted toward the parent orb, the reflector, and something flew past Bliss, went *spat* against the wall, as a thunderous boom sounded below.

Bliss could sense, rather than tell, that Stillman was raising his gun behind his. He clawed out, caught the cuff of the detective's sleeve, brought it down. "Don't! She may be down there somewhere in the line of fire!"

Something shot out over his shoulder. Not a gun or slug, but the torch itself. Stillman was trying to turn it into a sort of readymade star shell, by throwing it down there still lighted. The light pool on the floor streaked off like a comet, flicked across the ceiling, dropped down on the other side, and steadied itself against the far wall – with a pair of trouser legs caught squarely in the light, from the knees down. They buckled to jump aside out of the revealing beam, but not quickly enough. Stillman sighted his gun at a kneecap and fired. The legs jolted, wobbled, folded up forward toward the light, bringing a torso and head down into view on the floor. When the fall ended, the beam of the torch was weirdly centered on the exact crown of a bald head surrounded by a circular fringe of reddish hair. It rolled from side to side like a giant ostrich egg, screaming agonizedly into the cellar floor.

"I'll take him," Stillman grunted. "You put on that light!"

Bliss groped for the dangling light cord that had proved such a hindrance to them just now by being down in the center of the basement instead of up by the doorway where they could get at it. He snagged it, found the finger switch, turned it. Horror flooded the place at his touch, in piebald tones of deep black shadow and pale yellow. The shovel Alden had just started to wield when he heard them coming lay half across a mound of freshly disinterred earth. Near it were the flat flagstones that had topped it, flooring the cellar, and the pickax that had loosened them. He must have brought the tools with him in the car, for they weren't Bliss's.

And on the other side of that mound – the short but deep hole the earth had come out of. Alden must have been working away down here for some time, to get so much done singlehanded. And yet, though they had arrived before he'd finished, they were still too late – for in the hole, filling it to within an inch or two of the top, and fitting the sides even more closely, rested a deep old-fashioned trunk that had probably belonged to Smiles's mother and come down in the trunk compartment of the car. And four-square as it was, it looked ominously small for anyone to fit into – whole.

Bliss pointed down at it, moaned sickly. "She – she –"

He wanted to fold up and let himself topple inertly across the mound of earth before it. Stillman's sharp, whiplike command kept him upright. "Hang on! Coming!"

He had clipped the back of Alden's skull with his gun butt, to put him out of commission while their backs were turned. He leaped up on the mound of earth, and across the hole to the opposite side, then dropped down by the trunk, tugging at it.

"There's no blood around; he may have put her in alive. Hurry up, help me to get the lid up! Don't waste time trying to lift the whole thing out; just the lid. Get some air into it –"

It shot up between the two of them, and within lay a huddled bulk of sacking, pitifully doubled around on itself. *It was still moving feebly.* Fluttering spasmodically, rather than struggling any more.

The blade of the penknife Stillman had already used once before tonight flew out, slashed furiously at the coarse stuff. A contorted face was revealed through the rents, but not recognizable as Smiles's any more – a face black with suffocation, in which the last spark of life had been about to go out. And still might, if they didn't coax it back in a hurry.

They got her up out of it between them and straightened her out flat on the floor. Stillman sawed away at the short length of rope cruelly twisted around her neck, the cause of suffocation, severed it after seconds that seemed like centuries, unwound it, flung it off. Bliss, meanwhile, was stripping off the tattered remnants of the sacking. She was in a white silk slip.

Stillman straightened up, jumped for the stairs. "Breathe into her mouth like they do with choking kids. I'll send out a call for a Pulmotor."

But the battle was already won by the time he came trooping down again; they could both tell that, laymen though they were. The congested darkness was leaving her face little by little, her chest was rising and falling of its own accord, she was coughing distressedly, and making little whimpering sounds of returning consciousness. They carried her up to the floor above when the emergency apparatus arrived, nevertheless, just to make doubly sure. It was while they were both up there, absorbed in watching the Pulmotor being used on her, that a single shot boomed out in the basement under them, with ominous-finality.

Stillman clapped a hand to his hip. "Forgot to take his gun away from him. Well, there goes one of Cochrane's prisoners!"

They ran for the basement stairs, stopped halfway down them, one behind the other, looking at Alden's still form lying there below. It was still face-down, in the same position as before. One arm, curved under his own body at chest level, and a lazy tendril of smoke curling up around his ribs, told the difference.

"What a detective I am!" Stillman said disgustedly.

"It's better this way," Bliss answered, tight lipped. "I think I would have killed him with my own bare hands, before they got him out of here, after what he tried to do to her tonight!"

By the time they returned upstairs again, Cochrane had come in with the woman. They were both being iodined and bandaged by an intern.

"What happened?" Stillman asked dryly. "Looks like she gave you more trouble than he gave us."

"Did you ever try to hang onto the outside of a wild car while the driver tried to shake you off? I'd gotten up to within one tree length of her, when the shots down in the basement tipped her off Alden was in for it. I just had time to make a flying tackle for the baggage rack before she was off a mile a minute. I had to work my way forward along the running-board, with her swerving and flinging around corners on two wheels. She finally piled up against a refuse-collection truck; dunno how it was we both weren't killed."

"Well, she's all yours, Cochrane," Stillman said. "But first I'm going to have to ask you to let me take her over to headquarters with me. You, too, Bliss." He looked at his watch. "I promised my lieutenant I'd be in with you by nine the latest, and I'm a stickler for keeping a promise. We'll be a little early, but unforeseen circumstances came up."

At headquarters, in the presence of Bliss, Stillman, Cochrane, the lieutenant of detectives, and the necessary police stenographer, Alden's accomplice was prevailed on to talk.

"My name is Irma Gilman," she began, "and I'm thirty-nine years old. I used to be a trained nurse on the staff of one of the large metropolitan hospitals. Two of my patients lost their lives through carelessness on my part, and I was discharged.

"I met Joe Alden six months ago. His wife was in ill health, so I moved in with them to look after her. Her first husband had left her well off, with slews of negotiable bonds. Alden had already helped himself to a few of them before I showed up, but now that I was there, he wanted to get rid of her altogether, so that we could get our hands on the rest. I told him he'd never get away with anything there, where everybody knew her; he'd have to take her somewhere else first. He went looking for a house, and when he'd found one that suited him, the place in Denby, he took me out to inspect it, without her, and palmed me off on the agent as his wife.

"We made all the arrangements, and when the day came to move, he went ahead with the moving van. I followed in the car with her after dark. That timed it so that we reached there late at night; there wasn't a soul around any more to see her go in. And from then on, as far as anyone in Denby knew, there were only two of us living in the house, not three. We didn't keep her locked up, but we put her in a bedroom at the back, where she couldn't be seen from the road, and put up a fine-meshed screen on the window. She was bed-ridden a good part of the time, anyway, and that made it easier to keep her presence concealed.

"He started to make his preparations from the moment we moved in. He began building this low wall out in front, as an excuse to order the bricks and other materials that he needed for the real work later on. He ordered more from the contractor than he needed, of course.

"Finally it happened. She felt a little better one day, came downstairs, and started checking over her list of bonds. He'd persuaded her when they were first married not to entrust them to a bank; she had them in an ordinary strongbox. She found out some of them were already missing. He went in there to her, and I listened outside the door. She didn't say very much, just: 'I thought I had more of these thousand-dollar bonds.' But that was enough to show us that she'd caught on. Then she got up very quietly and went out of the room without another word.

"Before we knew it, she was on the telephone in the hall – trying to get help, I suppose. She didn't have a chance to utter a word, he was too quick for her. He jumped out after her and pulled it away from her. He was between her and the front door, and she turned and went back upstairs, still without a sound, not even a scream. Maybe she still did not realize she was in bodily danger, thought she could get her things on and get out of the house.

"He said to me, 'Go outside and wait in front. Make sure there's no one anywhere in sight, up and down the road or in the fields.' I went out there, looked, raised my arm and dropped it, as a signal to him to go ahead. He went up the stairs after her.

"You couldn't hear a thing from inside. Not even a scream, or a chair falling over. He must have done it very quietly. In a while he came down to the door again. He was breathing a little fast and his face was a little pale, that was all. He said, 'It's over. I smothered her with one of the bed pillows. She didn't have much strength.' Then he went in again and carried her body down to the basement. We kept her down there while he went to work on this other wall; as soon as it was up high enough, he put her behind it and finished it. He repainted the whole room so that one side wouldn't look too new.

"Then, without a word of warning, the girl showed up the other night. Luckily, just that night Joe had stayed down at the hotel late having a few beers. He recognized her as she got off the bus and brought her out with him in the car. That did away with her having to ask her way of anyone. We stalled her for a few minutes by pretending her mother was fast asleep, until I had time to put a sedative in some tea I gave her to drink.

After that it was easy to handle her; we put her down in the basement and kept her doped down there.

"Joe remembered, from one of her letters, that she'd said her husband had insured her, so that gave us our angle. The next day I faked a long letter to her and mailed it to the city, as if she'd never shown up here at all. Then when Bliss came up looking for her, I tried to dope him, too, to give us a chance to transport her back to his house during his absence, finish her off down there, and pin it on him. He spoiled that by passing the food up and walking out on us. The only thing left for us to do after that was for Joe to beat the bus in, plant her clothes ahead of time, and put a bee in the police's bonnet. That was just to get Bliss out of the way, so the coast would be left clear to get her in down there.

"We called his house from just inside the city limits when we got down here with her tonight. No one answered, so it seemed to have worked. But we'd lost a lot of time on account of that blowout. I waited outside in the car, with her covered up on the floor, drugged. When Joe had the hole dug, he came out and took her in with him.

"We thought all the risk we had to run was down at this end. We were sure we were perfectly safe up at the other end; Joe had done such a bang-up job on that wall. I still can't understand how you caught onto it so quick."

"I'm an architect, that's why," Bliss said grimly. "There was something about that room that bothered me. It wasn't on the square."

Smiles was lying in bed when Bliss went back to his own house, and she was pretty again. When she opened her eyes and looked up at him, they were all crinkly and smiling just as they used to be.

"Honey," she said, "it's so good to have you near me. I've learned my lesson. I'll never walk out on you again."

"That's right, you stay where you belong, with Ed," he said soothingly, "and nothing like that'll ever happen to you again."

The Screaming Laugh

A call came into constabulary headquarters, at the county seat, about seven one morning. It was from Milford Junction, a local doctor named Johnson reporting the death of one Eleazar Hunt sometime during the night. Just a routine report, as required by law.

"And have you ascertained the causes?" asked the sheriff.

"Yes, I just got through examining him. I find he had burst a blood vessel – laughing too hard. Nothing out of the usual about it, but of course that's for you to decide."

"Well, I'll send a man over to check." The sheriff turned to Al Traynor, one of the members of his constabulary, who had just come in. "Drive down Milford Junction way, Al. Local resident near there, name of Eleazar Hunt, died from laughing too hard. Look things over just for the record."

"Laughing too hard?" Traynor looked at him when he heard that. Then he shrugged. "Well, I suppose if you've got to go, it's better to go laughing than crying."

He returned to his car and started off for Milford Junction. It was about three quarters of an hour's drive by the new State highway that had been completed only two or three years before, although the hamlet itself wasn't directly on this, had to be reached by a dirt feeder road that branched off it. The Hunt place was about half a mile on the other side of it, near a point where the highway curved back again to rejoin the shortcut, cutting a corner off the late Mr Hunt's acreage.

The white painted farmhouse with its green shutters gleamed dazzlingly in the early morning sunshine. Peach trees, bursting into bloom before it, hid the roof and cast blue shade on the ground. A wire fence at the back enclosed a poultry yard, and beyond that were hen houses, a stall from which a black and white cow looked plaintively forth, a toolshed, a roofed well, a vegetable garden. It was an infinitely pleasant-looking little property, and if death had struck there at all, there was no outward sign.

There was a coupé standing in the road before the house, belonging to the doctor who had reported the death, presumably. Traynor coasted up behind it, braked, got out, and went in through the gate. He had to crouch to pass under some of the low hanging peach boughs. There was a cat sunning itself on the lower doorstep. He reached down to tickle it and a man came around the corner of the house just then, stood looking at him.

He was sunburned, husky, and about thirty. He wore overalls and was carrying an empty millet sack in his hand. Judging by the commotion audible at the back, he had just finished feeding the poultry. His eyes were shrewd and lidded in a perpetual squint that had nothing to do with the sun.

"You the undertaker already?" he wanted to know.

"Sheriff's office," snapped Traynor, none to pleased at the comparison. "You work here?"

"Yep. Hired man."

"How long?"

" 'Bout six months."

"What's your name?"

"Dan Fears."

"He keep anybody else on?"

Fears answered indirectly, with a scornful gesture toward the back. "Not enough to keep one man busy as it is. Tend one cow and pick up a few eggs."

It occurred to Traynor if there was that little to do, why hadn't the cow been led out to pasture by now and the poultry fed earlier? He went on in, stepping high over the cat. She looked indolently upward at his heel as it passed over her.

A shaggy, slow moving man was coming toward the screen door to meet Traynor as he pushed through it with a single cursory knock at its frame. Johnson was a typical country doctor, of a type growing scarcer by the year. You could tell by looking at him that he'd never hurried or got excited in his life. You could surmise that he'd never refused a middle-of-the-night call from miles away in the dead of winter either. He was probably highly competent, in spite of his misleading rusticity.

"Hello, son." He nodded benignly. "You from the sheriff's office? I was just going back to my own place to make out the death certificate."

"Can I see him?"

"Why, shore. Right in here." The doctor parted a pair of old-fashioned sliding doors and revealed the "front-parlor" of the house. Across the top of each window was stretched a valance of faded red plush, ending in a row of little plush balls. On a table stood an oil lamp – there was no electricity this far out – with a frosted glass dome and a lot of little glass prisms dangling from it.

There was an old-fashioned reclining chair with an adjustable back near the table and lamp. Just now it was tilted only slightly, at a comfortable reading position. It was partly covered over with an ordinary bed sheet, like some furniture is in summertime, only the sheet bulged in places and a clawlike hand hung down from under it, over the arm of the chair. Traynor reached down, turned back the upper edge of the sheet. It was hard not to be jolted. The face was a cartoon of frozen hilarity. It wasn't just that death's-head grimace that so often, because of bared teeth, faintly suggests a grin. It was the real thing. It was Laughter, permanently photographed in death. The eyes were creased into slits; you could see the dried but still faintly glistening saline traces of the tears that had overflowed their ducts down alongside his nose. The mouth was a vast upturned crescent full of yellowish horse teeth. The whole head was thrown stiffly back at an angle of uncontrollable risibility. It was uncanny only because it was so motionless, so silent, so permanent.

"You found him just like this?"

"Shore. Had to examine him, of course, but rigor had already set in, so I figger nothing I did disturbed him much." Johnson chuckled inside himself, gave Traynor a humorously reproachful look. "Why, son, you don't think this is one of *those* things? Shame on you!"

He saw that he hadn't convinced the younger man by his raillery. "Why, I examined him thoroughly, son," he protested gently. "I know my business as well as the next man. I tell you not a finger was laid on this man. Nothing's happened to him but what I said. He burst a blood vessel from laughing too hard. Course, if you want me to perform a complete autopsy, send his innards and the contents of his stomach down to the State laboratory –" It was said with an air of paternal patience, as if he were humoring a headstrong boy.

"I'm not discrediting your competence, doctor. What's this?" Traynor picked up a little booklet, lying open tent-shaped on the table. "Joe Miller's Joke Book," it said on the cover, and the copyright was 1892.

"That's what he was reading. That's what got him, I reckon. Found it lying on the floor under his right hand. Fell from his fingers at the moment of death, I guess."

"Same page?"

"Same one it's open at now. You want to find the exact joke he was reading when he passed away, that what you're aiming at, son?" More of that paternal condescension.

Traynor evidently did, or at least an approximation of what type of killing humor this was. He stopped doing anything else and stood there stock-still for five minutes, conscientiously reading every joke on the two open pages, about a dozen altogether. The first one read:

Pat: Were you calm and collected when the explosion occurred?
Mike: I wuz calm and Murphy wuz collected.

The others were just about as bad, some even staler.

"Do me a favor, doc," he said abruptly, passing the booklet over. "Read these for yourself."

"Oh, now, here –" protested Johnson, with a rueful glance at the still form in the chair, but he went ahead and did what Traynor requested.

Traynor watched his expression closely. He'd only just met the man, but he could already tell he was full of a dry sort of humor. But not a gleam showed, his face never changed from first to last; it became, if anything, sort of mournful.

"D'you see what I mean?" was all Traynor said, taking the booklet back and tossing it aside.

Johnson shook his head. "No two people have the same sense of humor, remember that, son. What's excruciatingly funny to one man goes right over another's head. Likely, these jokes were new to him, not mossbacked like they are to you and me."

"Did you know him at all, doc?"

"Just to say howdy to on the road."

"Ever see him smile much?"

"Can't say I did. But there's nothing funny about saying howdy. What is it you're driving at, son?"

Traynor didn't answer. He went over to the corpse, unbuttoned its shirt, and scrutinized the under arms and ribs with exhaustive intentness.

The doctor just stood looking on. "You won't find any marks of violence, son. I've been all over that."

Next Traynor squatted down by the feet, drew up one trouser leg to the knees, then the other. Johnson by this time, it was plain to see, considered him a bad case of dementia detectivis. Traynor seemed to see something at last; he smiled grimly. All Johnson could see were a pair of shanks encased in wool socks, supported by garters. Patent garters, sold by the million, worn by the million.

"Found something suspicious?" he asked, but without conviction, it was easy to see.

"Suspicious isn't the word," Traynor murmured low. "Damning."

"Damning whom – and of what?" said Johnson dryly.

Again Traynor didn't answer.

He hurried unlaced both of Hunt's shoes, dropped them off. Then he unfastened one garter and stripped the sock off his foot. Turned it inside out and peered at the sole. Peered at the sole of the foot itself too. He stripped the other one off and went through the same proceeding. Johnson, meanwhile, was shaking his head disapprovingly, as if his patience were being overtaxed.

"You are the most pee-culiar young fellow I ever hope to meet," he sighed.

Traynor balled up the two socks, and thrust one into each pocket of his coat, garter and all. They were black – fortunately. He flipped the sheet back over the bared feet, concealing them. A little wisp of something rose in the air as he did so, disturbed by the draft of his doing that, fluttered, winged downward again. A little bit of fluff, it seemed to be. He went after it, nevertheless, retrieved it, took an envelope out of his pocket, and thrust it in.

Johnson was past even questioning his actions by now; he was convinced they were unaccountable by all rational standards, anyway. "Would you care to talk to Mrs Hunt?" he asked.

"Yes, I sure would," Traynor said curtly.

Johnson went out to the hall, called respectfully up the stairs:

"Mrs Hunt, honey."

She was very ready to come down, Traynor noticed. Her footsteps began to descend almost before the words were out of the doctor's mouth. As though she'd been poised right up above at the head of the staircase, waiting for the summons.

He couldn't help a slight start of surprise as she came into sight; he had expected someone near Hunt's own age. She was about twenty-eight, the buxom blond type. "Second wife," Traynor thought.

She had reached the bottom by now, and the doctor introduced them.

"This is Mr Traynor of the sheriff's office."

"How do you do?" she said mournfully. But her eyes were clear, so she must have stopped crying some time before. "Did you want to talk to me?"

"Just to ask you the main facts, that's all."

"Oh. Well, let's go outdoors, huh? It – it sort of weighs you down in here." She glanced toward the partly open parlor doors, glanced hurriedly away again.

They went outside, began to stroll aimlessly along the front of the house, then around the corner and along the side. He could see Fears out there in the sun, beyond the poultry yard, hoeing the vegetable patch. Fears turned his head, looked over his shoulder at them as they came into sight, then looked down again. Hunt's widow seemed unaware of his existence.

"Well," she was saying, "all I can tell you is, I went upstairs to bed about ten o'clock last night, left him down there reading by the lamp. I'm a sound sleeper, and before I knew it, it was daybreak and the roosters woke me up. I saw he'd never come up to bed. I hurried down, and there he was just like I'd left him, lamp still lit and all, only the book had fallen out of his hand. He had this broad grin on his face and –"

"He did?" he interrupted.

"Yes. Isn't it spooky?" She shuddered. "Did you see it?"

"I did. And spooky," he said slowly, "is a very good word for it."

If he meant anything by that, she seemed to miss it completely.

She wound up the little there was left of her story. "I tried to wake him, and when I couldn't, I knew what it was. I called to Fears, but he was out back some place, so I ran all the way down the road to Doctor Johnson's house myself and brought him back."

"Did he usually stay down alone like that, nights, and read?"

"Yes. Only in the beginning, when I first married him, he used to read things like mail order catalogues and such. Well, I'd tried to liven him up a little lately. I bought that joke book for him and left it lying around, tried to coax him to read it. He wouldn't have any part of it at first, pretended not to be interested, but I think on the sly he began to dip into it after I'd go upstairs at nights. He wasn't used to laughing and he got a stitch or something, I guess. Maybe he was ashamed to have me catch him at it and tried to hold it in – and that's what happened to him."

They were lingering under the parlor windows. He'd stopped unnoticeably, so she had too, perforce. He was gazing blankly around, eyes on the treetops, the fleecy clouds skimming by, everywhere but the right place. He'd seen something on the ground, and the job was to retrieve it right under her eyes without letting her see him do it.

"Do you mind?" he said, and took out a package of cigarettes. It was crumpled from being carried around on his person for days, and in trying to shake one out, he lost nearly the whole contents. He bent down and picked them up again one by one, with a fine disregard for hygiene, and each time something else as well. It was very neatly done. It went over her head completely.

They turned around and went slowly back to the front of the house again. As they were rounding the corner once more, Traynor looked back. He saw Fears raise his head and look after them at that moment. "Very allergic to my being here," Traynor thought to himself.

Johnson came out of the door.

"The undertaker's here."

And he looked questioningly at Traynor; the latter nodded his permission for removal.

She said, "Oh, I'd better get upstairs; I don't want to – see him go," and hurriedly ran inside.

Traynor didn't hang around to watch, either. He drifted back around the side of the house again. He let himself through the poultry yard, and out at the far side of it, where Fears was puttering around. He approached him with a fine aimlessness, like a man who has nothing to do with himself and gravitates toward the nearest person in sight to kill time chatting.

"He had a nice place here," he remarked.

Fears straightened, leaned on his hoe, drew his sleeve across his forehead. "No money in it, though." He was looking the other way, off from Traynor.

"What do you figure she'll do, keep on running it herself now that he's gone?"

The question should have brought the other's head around toward him, at least. It didn't. Fears spat reflectively, still kept looking stubbornly away from him.

"I don't think she's cut out for it, don't think she'd make a go of it."

There's something in this direction, away from where he's looking, that he doesn't want me to notice, Traynor told himself. He subtly jockeyed himself around so that he could look behind him without turning his entire head.

There was a toolshed there. Implements were stacked up against the wall at the back of it. The door was open and the sun shone sufficiently far in to reveal them. It glinted from the working edges of shovels, rakes, spades. But he noted a trowel with moist clayey soil drying out along its wedge; it was drying to a dirty gray white color.

"That looks like the well," he thought. Aloud he said: "Sun's getting hotter by the minute. Think I'll have a drink."

Fears dropped the hoe handle, stooped and got it again.

"I'd advise you to get it from the kitchen," he said tautly. "Well's all stirred up and muddy, 'pears like part of the sides must have crumbled. Have to 'low it to settle."

"Oh, I'm not choosy," Traynor remarked, strolling toward it. It hadn't rained in weeks. He shifted around to the far side of the structure, where he could face Fears while he pretended to dabble with the chained drinking cup.

There could be no mistaking it, the man was suddenly tense, rigid, out there in the sun, even while he went ahead stiffly hoeing. Every part of his shoulders and arms was forced. He wasn't even watching what he was doing, his hoe was damaging some tender young shoots. Traynor didn't bother getting his drink after all. He knew all he needed to know now. What's Fears been up to down there that he don't want me to find out about? – Traynor wondered. And more important still, did it have anything to do with Eleazar Hunt's death? He couldn't answer the first – yet – but he already had more than a sneaking suspicion that the answer to the second was yes.

He sauntered back toward the tiller.

"You're right," he admitted; "it's all soupy."

With every step that took him farther away from the well rim, he could see more and more of the apprehension lift from Fears. It was almost physical, the way he seemed to straighten out, loosen up there under his eyes, until he was all relaxed again.

"Told you so," Fears muttered, and once again he wiped his forehead with a great wide sweep of the arm. But it looked more like relief this time than sweat.

"Well, take it easy." Traynor drifted lethargically back toward the front of the house once more. He knew Fears's eyes were following him every step of the way; he could almost feel them boring into the back of his skull. But he knew that if he turned and looked, the other would lower his head too quickly for him to catch him at it, so he didn't bother.

Hunt's body had been removed now and Doctor Johnson was on the point of leaving. They walked out to the roadway together toward their cars.

"Well, son," the doctor wanted to know, "still looking for something ornery in this or are you satisfied?"

"Perfectly satisfied now," Traynor assured him grimly, but he didn't say in which way he meant it. "Tell the truth, doc," he added. "Did you ever see a corpse grin that broadly before?"

"There you go again," sighed Johnson. "Well, no, can't say I have. But there is such a thing as cadaveric spasm, you know."

"There is," Traynor agreed. "And this isn't it. In fact this is so remarkable I'm going to have it photographed before I let the undertaker put a finger to him. I'd like to keep a record of it."

"Shucks," the doctor scoffed as he got in his coupé. "Why, I bet there never was a normal decease yet that couldn't be made to 'pear onnatural if you tried hard enough."

"And there never was an unnatural one yet," Traynor answered softly, "that couldn't be made to appear normal – if you were willing to take things for granted."

After he had arranged for the photographs to be taken, he dropped in at the general store. A place like that, he knew, was the nerve center, the telephone exchange, of the village, so to speak. The news of Eleazar Hunt's death had spread by now, and the cracker barrel brigade were holding a post-mortem. Traynor, who was not known by sight to anyone present, for his duties had not brought him over this way much, did not identify himself for fear of making them self-conscious in the presence of the law. He hung around, trying to make up his mind between two brands of plug tobacco, neither of which he intended buying, meanwhile getting an earful.

"Waal," said one individual, chewing a straw, "guess we'll never know now whether he actually did git all that money from the highway commission folks claim he did, for slicin' off a corner of his propitty to run that new road through."

"He always claimed he didn't. Not a penny of it ever showed up in the bank. My cousin works there and he'd be the first one to know it if it did."

"They say he tuck and hid it out at his place, that's why. Too mean to trust the bank, and he didn't want people thinking he was rich."

An ancient of eighty stepped forth, right angled over a hickory stick, and tapped it commandingly to gain the floor. "Shows ye it don't pay to teach an old dog new tricks! I've knowed Eleazar Hunt since he was knee-high to a grasshopper, and this is the first time I ever heard tell of him even smiling, let alone laughing fit to kill like they claim he done. Exceptin' just once, but that were beyond his control and didn't count."

"When was that?" asked Traynor, chiming in carefully casual. He knew by experience the best way to bring out these villagers' full narrative powers was to act bored stiff.

The old man fastened on him eagerly, glad of an audience. "Why, right in here where we're standing now, 'bout two years ago. Him and me was both standing up to the counter to git waited on, and Andy took me first and asked me what I wanted. So I raised this here stick of mine to point up at the shelf and without meaning to, I grazed Eleazar's side with the tip of it – I can't see so good any more, you know. Well, sir, for a minute I couldn't believe my ears. Here he was, not only laughing, but giggling like a girl, clutching at his ribs and shying away from me. Then the minute he got free of the stick, he changed right back to his usual self, mouth turned down like a horseshoe, snapped, 'Careful what you're doing, will you!' Ticklish, that's all it was. Some's more so than others."

"Anyone else see that but you?"

"I saw it," said the storekeeper. "I was standing right behind the counter when it happened. I never knew that about him until then myself. Funny mixture, to be ticklish with a glum disposition like he had."

"And outside of that, you say you never saw him smile?"

"Not even as a boy!" declared the old man vehemently.

"*She* was livening him up, though, lately," qualified the storekeeper. "Heard she was making right smart progress too."

"Who told you?" asked Traynor, lidding his eyes.

"Why, she did herself."

Traynor just nodded to himself. Buildup beforehand, he was thinking.

"Yes, and that's what killed him!" insisted the garrulous old man. "Way I figger it, he'd never used them muscles around the mouth that you shape smiles with and so they'd gone useless on him from lack of practice. Just like if you don't use your right arm for fifty years, it withers on you. Then she comes along and starts him to laughing at joke books and whatnot, and the strain was too much for him. Like I said before, you can't teach an old dog new tricks! These old codgers that marry young chickens!"

All Traynor did, after the old man had stumped out with an accurate shot at the brass receptacle inside the door, was get his name from the storekeeper and jot it down in his notebook, without letting anyone see him do it. The ancient one just might come in handy as a witness, if a murder trial was to come up – provided of course that he lasted that long.

"Well, how does it look?" the sheriff asked Traynor when he finally got back to headquarters.

"It doesn't look good," was the grim answer. "It was murder."

The sheriff drew in his breath involuntarily. "Got any evidence?" he said finally.

His eyes opened wide in astonishment as a small joke book, a handful of chicken feathers, and a pair of black socks with garters still attached, descended upon his desk. "What've these got to do with it?" he asked in stupefaction. "You don't mean to tell me – this is your evidence, do you?"

"It certainly is," said Traynor gloomily. "It's all the evidence there is or ever will be. This, and photographs I've had taken of his face. It's the cleverest thing that was ever committed under the sun. But not quite clever enough."

"Well, don't you think you'd better at least tell me what makes you so sure? What did you see?"

"All right," said Traynor irritably, "here's what I saw – and I know you're going to say right away it didn't amount to a row of pins. I saw a dead man with a broad grin on his face, too broad to be natural. I saw chicken feathers lying scattered around the ground –"

"It's a poultry farm, after all; they raise chickens there."

"But their tips are all bent over at right angles to the quill; show me the chicken that can do that to itself. And they were lying *outside* the wired enclosure, under the window of the room in which the dead man was."

"And?" said the sheriff, pointing to the socks.

"A few fibers of the same chicken feathers, adhering to the soles. The socks are black, luckily! I could see them with my naked eye."

"But isn't it likely that this Hunt might potter around in his stocking feet, even outdoors – where there are chicken feathers lying around?"

"Yes. But these fibers are on the linings of the socks, not the outside of the soles. I reversed them pulling them off his feet."

"Anything else?"

"Not directly bearing on the commission of the murder itself, but involved in it. I saw a trowel with white clay drying on its edges, and a pair of thick gauntlets, used for spraying something on the peach trees, hanging up in the toolshed. Now tell me all this is no good to us."

"It certainly isn't!" declared the sheriff emphatically. "Why, I'd be laughed out of office if I moved against anyone on the strength of evidence such as this! You're talking in riddles, man! I can't make anything out of this. You not only haven't told me whom you suspect, but you haven't even given me the method used, or the motive."

Traynor drummed his finger tips on the desk. "And yet I'm dead sure. I'm as sure of it right now as if I'd seen it with my own eyes. I can give you the method right now, but what's the use? You'd only laugh at me, I can tell by the look on your face. I could name the motive and the suspects too, but until I've got the one, there's no use bringing in the others; there wouldn't be enough to hold them on."

"Well" – his superior shrugged, turning up his palms – "what do you want me to do?"

"Very little," muttered Traynor, "except lend me a waterproof pocket flashlight, if you've got one. And stick around till I come back; I've got an idea I won't be coming alone. There might be matters discussed that you'd be interested in."

"Where'll you be in the meantime?" the sheriff called after him as he pocketed the light and headed for the door.

"Down in Eleazar Hunt's well," was the cryptic answer. "And not because I'm thirsty, either."

Traynor coasted to a noiseless stop, well down the road from the Hunt place and out of sight of it, at about ten thirty that night. He snapped off his headlights, got out, examined the torch the sheriff had lent him to make sure it was in good working order, then cut across into the trees on foot, and made his way along under them parallel to the road but hidden from it.

There were no lights showing by the time he'd come in sight of the house. Death or no death, people in the country retire early. He knew there was no dog on the place so he didn't hesitate in breaking cover and skirting the house around to the back. The story was Hunt had been too stingy to keep one, begrudging the scraps it would have required to feed it. His sour face, was the general verdict, was enough to frighten away any trespasser.

He found the poultry yard locked, but his business wasn't with that; he detoured around the outside of it in the pale moonlight, treading warily in order not to make his presence known. He played his light briefly on the toolshed door; it was closed but not locked, fortunately. He eased it open, caught up the trowel and rope ladder he had noticed yesterday morning, and hurried over to the well with them. He mightn't need the trowel, but he took it with him to make sure. The clay, incidentally, had been carefully scraped off it now – but too late to do Fears any good; the damage had already been done.

Traynor clamped the iron hooks on the end of the ladder firmly to the rim of the well, paid it out all the way down the shaft until he heard it go in with a muffled splash. It sounded deeper than he enjoyed contemplating, but if Fears had gone down in there, dredging, then he could do it too.

He clicked his light on, tucked it firmly under his left armpit, straddled the well guard, and started climbing down, trowel wedged in his coat pocket. The ladder pivoted lightly from side to side under his weight, but so long as it didn't snarl up altogether, that was all right. He stopped every few rungs to play the light around the shaft in a circle. Nothing showed above the water line, any more than it had yesterday morning, but that trowel hadn't had clay on it, and the water hadn't been all muddied up, for nothing.

The water hit him unexpectedly and he jolted at the knifelike cold of it. He knew he couldn't stay in it very long without numbing, but he kept going down rung by rung. It came up his legs, hit his kidneys, finally rose above the light under his arm. That was waterproof, didn't go out. He stretched one leg downward off the ladder, feeling for the bottom. No bottom; the shaft seemed to go to China. One sure thing was, *he* couldn't – and keep on breathing.

He explored the wall of the well under the water line with his free hand, all around him and down as far as he could reach. The clay was velvet smooth, unmarred. Another rung – they were widely spaced – would take his head under, and he didn't like to risk it; he was already beginning to get numb all over.

Then suddenly the leg that he was using for a depth finder struck something like a plank. But across the shaft, behind him. He'd attached the ladder to the wrong side of the well rim. Still, it was fairly accessible; the circumference of the bore wasn't unduly large. He adjusted his leg to its height and got his heel on it. Tested its sustaining powers and it didn't crumble in spite of the fact that it must have been water-logged for years. It was evidently inserted solidly into the clay, like a sort of shelf, more of it bedded than actually protruding. Still it was a risky thing to trust oneself to; he had an idea it was meant more for a marker than to be used to stand on. He turned his body outward to face it, got across to it without mishap, but bringing the ladder with him over his shoulder as a precaution. He was mostly under water during the whole maneuver, and rapidly chilling to the bone. That Fears before him had been through all this without some good, all powerful reason, he refused to believe.

He found a large cavity on that side of the well almost at once. It was just a few inches above the plank, a large square recess gouged out of the compact clay. It was, as far as his waterlogged finger tips could make out, a large empty biscuit tin wedged in flush with the well wall, open end outward. A sort of handmade but none the less efficient safe-deposit box, so to speak.

But the important thing was that he could feel a heavy rubbery bulk resting within it. Flat, pouch shaped. He drew this out, teeth chattering as the water momentarily rose into his nostrils, and finding it was too bulky to wedge into his pocket, tucked it into his submerged waistband, not caring to run the risk of bringing it up under his arm and perhaps dropping it to the bottom of the well just as he neared the top. The trowel, which he found he had not needed after all, he tossed over his shoulder into watery oblivion. The light, though it hampered him the way he kept it pinned against his side, he retained because it was not his but the sheriff's.

He renewed his grip on the transported ladder, took his feet off the scaffolding, and let the ladder swing back with him to its original side of the well. He didn't feel the slight collision at all, showing how thoroughly numbed he was by now, and showing what a risk he was running every moment of having his hold on it automatically relax and drop him into the depths. Nor could he tell the difference when his body was finally clear of the water. Meaning he'd better get out of there fast.

But it was twice as slow getting up as it had been getting down. He couldn't tell, through shoes and all, when each successive rung was firmly fixed under the arches of his feet, he kept making idiotic pawing gestures with his whole leg each time before it would finally catch on. That should have looked very funny, but not down there where he was.

Finally the cloying dampness of the air began to lift a little and he knew he must be nearing the top. Then a whiff of a draft, that he would never have felt if he'd been dry, struck through his drenched clothes like ice cold needles, and that proved it. His teeth were tapping together like typewriter keys.

There was something else, some faint warning that reached him. Not actually heard so much as sensed. As if someone's breath were coming down the shaft from just over his head, slightly amplified as if by a sounding board. He acted on it instantly, more from instinct than actual realization of danger. Unsheathed the light from under his arm and pointed it upward. He was closer to the top than he'd thought, scarcely a yard below it. The beam illumined Fears's face, bent low above him, contorted into a maniacal grimace of impending destruction, both arms high over his head wielding something. It looked like the flat of a shovel, but there was no time to find out, do anything but get out of its way. It came hissing down in a big arc against the well shaft. It would have smashed his skull like an egg, ground the fragments into the clay – great whipcords of straining muscle stood out on the arms wielding it – but he swerved his body violently sidewise off the ladder, hanging on just by one hand and one foot, and it cycloned by, missing him by fractions of inches, and battered into the clay with a pulpy whack.

Fears had been in too much of a hurry; if he'd let him get up a single rung higher, so that his head showed above the well rim, nothing could have saved him from being brained by the blow. The torch, of course, went skittering down into oblivion with a distant *plink*! The shovel followed it a second later; Fears didn't trouble to bring it up again from striking position, let go of it, perhaps under the mistaken impression that it had served its purpose and the only reason the victim didn't topple was that his stunned body had become tangled in the ropes.

Traynor could feel the ladder jar under him as his would-be destroyer sought to detach the hooks that clasped the well rim and throw the whole structure snaking down to the bottom. The very weight of his own body, on the inside, pinning it down close to the shaft, defeated the first try, gave him an added second's grace. To free the hooks, Fears had to raise the climber's whole weight first, ladder and all, to get enough slack into it.

There wasn't enough time to finish climbing out. Traynor vaulted up one more rung with the agility of desperation, so that his head cleared the shaft rim; he flung up his arm and caught Fears's lowered head, bent down to his task, toward him in a riveted headlock that was like a drowning man's. Fears gave a muffled howl of dismay, tried to arch his slumped back against it. There was a brief equipoise, then gravity and their combined topheavy positions had their way. Fears came floundering over into the mouth of the well, nearly broke Traynor's back by the shift of weight to the other side of him, tore him off his own precarious foothold, and they both went plunging sickeningly down off the ladder together. Their two yells of approaching destruction blended hollowly into one.

Numb and half frozen as Traynor already was, the shock of submersion was evidently less for him than for Fears, plunging in with his pores wide open and possibly overheated from hurrying out to the well from a warm bed. Traynor had been in the water once already, felt it less than he would have the first time. The way people condition their bodies to frigid water by wetting themselves before they dive off a board, for instance.

He never touched bottom, even now. He came up alone – the fall must have loosened the bear hug he'd had on the other man – struck out wildly all around him, aware that if he went down again – The radius of the confining wall was luckily narrow. He contacted the ladder, sealed his hands to it in a hold that blow torches couldn't have pried off, got on it again, and quickly pulled himself up above the water.

He waited there a minute, willing to stretch out a hand, but unable to do more than that. Fears never came up. Not a sound broke the inky black silence around Traynor but the slow heave of the disturbed water itself. The shock had either made the man lose consciousness or he'd struck his head against his own shovel at the bottom. If there was a bottom, which Traynor was beginning to doubt.

Go in again after him and try to find him, he couldn't. He got the warning from every cramped muscle in his body, and his restricted lungs and pounding heart. It meant his own sure death, inevitably. There are times one can tell. He wasn't even sure that he could get up any more, unaided.

But he finally did, tottering painfully rung by rung and feeling as if he'd been doing this all night. He flung himself across the well rim, crawled clear of it on his belly like some half drowned thing, then turned over on his back and did nothing else much but just breathe. Gusts of uncontrollable shivering swept over him every once in a while. Finally he sat up, pulled off his soaked coat, shirt, and even undershirt, and began beating himself all over the body with them to bring back the circulation.

It was only when he'd started it going again that he remembered to feel for the rubber pouch that had cost two lives so far, and nearly a third – his own. If he'd lost it down there, he'd had all his trouble for nothing. But instead of falling out, it had slipped down under his waistband and become wedged in the top of one trouser leg, too bulky to go any farther. There wasn't enough sensation left in his leg to tell him it was there until he'd pried it out with both hands.

"Money," he murmured, when he'd finally stripped it open and examined it. He turned his head and looked toward that sinister black opening in the ground. "I thought it was that. It almost always is."

There were seventy-five thousand dollars in it, so well protected they weren't even damp after three years' immersion.

He put on his coat and made his way back toward the house. One of the upper story window sashes eased up and a voice whispered cautiously down in the stillness:

"Did you get him, Dan?"

"No, Dan didn't get him, Mrs Hunt," he answered in full speaking tone. "Put on something and come down; I'm taking you in to the sheriff's office with me. And don't keep me waiting around down here; I'm chilled to the bone."

The sheriff awoke with a start when Traynor thrust open his office door and ushered Mrs Hunt in ahead of him.

"Here's one," he said, "and the other one's at the bottom of the well with the rest of the slimy things where he belongs. Sit down, Mrs Hunt, while I run through the facts for the benefit of my superior here.

"I'll begin at the beginning. The State built a spanking fine concrete highway that sliced off a little corner of Eleazar Hunt's property. He had the good luck – or bad luck, as it now turns out to have been – to collect seventy-five thousand dollars for it. Here it is." He threw down the waterlogged package. "There's your motive. First of all, it got him a second wife, almost before he knew it himself. Then, through the wife, it got him a hired man. Then, through the hired man *and* the wife, it got him – torture to the death."

He turned to the prisoner, who was sitting nervously shredding her handkerchief. "You want to tell the rest of it, or shall I? I've got it on the tip of my tongue, you know – and I've got it straight."

"I'll tell it," she said dully. "You seem to know it anyway."

"How'd you catch on he was hypersensitive to tickling?"

"By accident. I was sitting on the arm of his chair one evening, trying to vamp it out of him – where the money was, you know. I happened to tickle him under the chin, and he jumped a mile. Dan saw it happen and that gave him the idea. He built it up to me for weeks. 'If he was tied down,' he said, 'in one place so he couldn't get away from it, he couldn't hold out against it very long, he'd have to tell you. It'd be like torture, but it wouldn't hurt him.' It sounded swell, so I gave in.

"But, honest, I didn't know Dan meant to kill him. He was the one did it. I didn't! I thought he only meant for us to take the money and lam, and leave El tied up."

"Never mind that; go ahead."

"Dan had it all thought out beautiful. He had me go around the village first building it up that I was getting El to laugh and liven up. He even had me buy the joke book at the general store. Then last night about ten thirty when El was sitting by the lamp reading some seed catalogues, I gave the signal and Dan came up behind him with rope and pillows from the bed and insect spray gauntlets. He held him while I put the gauntlets on him – they're good thick buckram, you know – so no rope burns would show from his struggles, and then he tied his hands to the arms of the chair, over the gauntlet. The pillows we used over his waist and thighs, for the same reason, to deaden the ropes. Then he let the chair back down nearly flat, and he took off El's shoes and socks, and brought in a handful of chicken feathers from the yard, and squatted down in front of him like an Indian, and started to slowly stroke the soles of his feet back and forth. It was pretty awful to watch and listen to: I hadn't thought it would be. But that screaming laugh! Tickling doesn't sound so bad, you know.

"Every time Dan blunted a feather, he'd throw it away and start in using a new one. And he said in his sleepy way: 'Care to tell us where it is now? No? Wa'al, mebbe you know best.' I wanted to bring him water once, but Dan wouldn't let me, said that would only help him hold out longer.

"El was such a stubborn fool. He didn't once say he didn't have the money, he only said he'd see us both in hell before he told us where it was. He fainted away, the first time, about twelve. After that he kept getting weaker all the time, couldn't laugh any more, just heave his ribs.

"Finally he gave in, whispered it was in a tin box plastered into the well, below the water line. He told us there was a rope ladder he'd made himself to get down there, hidden in the attic. Dan lowered himself down, and got it out, brought it up, and counted it. I wanted to leave right away, but he talked me out of it. He said: 'We'll only give ourselves away if we do that. We know where it is now. Let's leave it there a mite longer; he mayn't live *as long as you'd expect.*' I see now what he meant; I still didn't then. Well, I listened to him; he seemed to have the whole thing lined up so cleverly. He climbed back with it and left it down there. Then we went back to the house. I went upstairs, and I no sooner got there than I heard El start up this whimpering and cooing again, like a little newborn baby. I quickly ran down to try and stop him, but it was too late. Just as I got there, El overstrained himself and suddenly went limp. That little added extra bit more killed him, and Dan Fears had known it would, that's why he did it!

"I got frightened, but he told me there was nothing to worry about, everything was under control, and they'd never tumble in a million years. We took the ropes and pillows and gauntlets off him, of course, and no marks were left. We raised the chair back to reading position, and dropped the joke book by his hand, and I put on his shoes and socks. The only thing was, after he'd been dead a little while, his face started to relapse to that sour, scowly look he always had all his life, and that didn't match the joke book. Well, Dan took care of that too. He waited until just before he was starting to stiffen, and then he arranged the lips and mouth with his hands so it looked like he'd been laughing his head off; and they hardened and stayed that way. Then he sent me out to fetch the doctor." She hung her head. "It seemed so perfect. I don't know how it is it fell through."

"How did you catch on so quick, Al?" the sheriff asked Traynor, while they were waiting for a stenographer to come and take down her confession.

"First of all, the smile. You could see his features had been rearranged after death. Before rigor sets in, there's a relaxation to the habitual expression. Secondly, the jokes were no good. Fears may have thought a sour puss wouldn't match them, but it would have matched them lots better than the one they gave him. Thirdly, when I hitched up the cuffs of his trousers, I saw that his socks had been put on wrong, as if in a hurry by someone who wasn't familiar with things like that – therefore presumably it was a woman. The garter clasps were fastened at the insides of the calves, but the original indentations still showed on the outsides. Fourthly, the bent chicken feathers. I still didn't quite get it, though, until I learned this afternoon at the general store that he was supersensitive to tickling. That gave me the whole picture, intact. I'd already seen the clay on the trowel, and Fears did his level best to keep me away from the well, so it didn't take much imagination to figure where the money was hidden. The marks of the ropes may not have shown on his hands, but the gauntlets were scarred by their friction, I could see that plainly even by the light of the torch when I went back to the toolshed tonight.

"It was pretty good, I'll give it that. If they'd only left his face alone. I don't think my suspicions would have been awakened in the first place. They spoiled it by overdoing it; just a mere inference of how he'd died wasn't enough – they had guilty consciences, so they wanted to make sure of getting their point across, hitting the onlooker in the eye with it. And that was the one thing he'd never had in life – a sense of humor. The joke wasn't really in the book after all. The joke was on them."

Dead On Her Feet

"And another thing I've got against these non-stop shindigs," orated the chief to his slightly bored listeners, "is they let minors get in 'em and dance for days until they wind up in a hospital with the D.T.'s, when the whole thing's been fixed ahead of time and they haven't a chance of copping the prize anyway. Here's a Missus Mollie McGuire been calling up every hour on the half-hour all day long, and bawling the eardrums off me because her daughter Toodles ain't been home in over a week and she wants this guy Pasternack arrested. So you go over there and tell Joe Pasternack I'll give him until tomorrow morning to fold up his contest and send his entries home. And tell him for me he can shove all his big and little silver loving-cups –"

For the first time his audience looked interested, even expectant, as they waited to hear what it was Mr P. could do with his loving-cups, hoping for the best.

"– back in their packing-cases," concluded the chief chastely, if somewhat disappointingly. "He ain't going to need 'em any more. He has promoted his last marathon in this neck of the woods."

There was a pause while nobody stirred. "Well, what are you all standing there looking at me for?" demanded the chief testily. "You, Donnelly, you're nearest the door. Get going."

Donnelly gave him an injured look. "Me, Chief? Why, I've got a red-hot lead on that payroll thing you were so hipped about. If I don't keep after it it'll cool off on me."

"All right, then you Stevens!"

"Why, I'm due in Yonkers right now," protested Stevens virtuously. "Machine-gun Rosie has been seen around again and I want to have a little talk with her –"

"That leaves you, Doyle," snapped the merciless chief.

"Gee, Chief," whined Doyle plaintively, "gimme a break, can't you? My wife is expecting –" Very much under his breath he added: " – me home early tonight."

"Congratulations," scowled the chief, who had missed hearing the last part of it. He glowered at them. "I get it!" he roared. "It's below your dignity, ain't it! It's too petty-larcency for you! Anything less than the St. Valentine's Day massacre ain't worth going out after, is that it? You figure it's a detail for a bluecoat, don't you?" His open palm hit the desk-top with a sound like a firecracker going off. Purple became the dominant color of his complexion. "I'll put you all back where you started, watching pickpockets in the subway! I'll take some of the high-falutinness out of you! I'll – I'll –" The only surprising thing about it was that foam did not appear at his mouth.

It may have been that the chief's bark was worse than his bite. At any rate no great amount of apprehension was shown by the culprits before him. One of them cleared his throat inoffensively. "By the way, Chief, I understand that rookie, Smith, has been swiping bananas from Tony on the corner again, and getting the squad a bad name after you told him to pay for them."

The chief took pause and considered this point.

The others seemed to get the idea at once. "They tell me he darned near wrecked a Chinese laundry because the Chinks tried to pass him somebody else's shirts. You could hear the screeching for miles."

Doyle put the artistic finishing touch. "I overheard him say he wouldn't be seen dead wearing the kind of socks you do. He was asking me did I think you had lost an election bet or just didn't know any better."

The chief had become dangerously quiet all at once. A faint drumming sound from somewhere under the desk told what he was doing with his fingers. "Oh he did, did he?" he remarked, very slowly and very ominously.

At this most unfortunate of all possible moments the door blew open and in breezed the maligned one in person. He looked very tired and at the same time enthusiastic, if the combination can be imagined. Red rimmed his eyes, blue shadowed his jaws, but he had a triumphant look on his face, the look of a man who has done his job well and expects a kind word. "Well, Chief," he burst out, "it's over! I got both of 'em. Just brought 'em in. They're in the back room right now –"

An oppressive silence greeted him. Frost seemed to be in the air. He blinked and glanced at his three pals for enlightenment.

The silence didn't last long, however. The chief cleared his throat. "*Hrrrmph*. Zat so?" he said with deceptive mildness. "Well now, Smitty, as long as your engine's warm and you're hitting on all six, just run over to Joe Pasternack's marathon dance and put the skids under it. It's been going on in that old armory on the west side –"

Smitty's face had become a picture of despair. He glanced mutely at the clock on the wall. The clock said four – a.m., not p.m. The chief, not being a naturally hard-hearted man, took time off to glance down at his own socks, as if to steel himself for this bit of cruelty. It seemed to work beautifully. "An election bet!" he muttered cryptically to himself, and came up redder than ever.

"Gee, Chief," pleaded the rookie, "I haven't even had time to shave since yesterday morning." In the background unseen nudgings and silent strangulation were rampant.

"You ain't taking part in it, you're putting the lid on it," the chief reminded him morosely. "First you buy your way in just like anyone else and size it up good and plenty, see if there's anything against it on moral grounds. Then you dig out one Toodles McGuire from under, and don't let her stall you she's of age either. Her old lady says she's sixteen and she ought to know. Smack her and send her home. You seal everything up tight and tell Pasternack and whoever else is backing this thing with him it's all off. And don't go 'way. You stay with him and make sure he refunds any money that's coming to anybody and shuts up shop good and proper. If he tries to squawk about there ain't no ordinance against marathons just lemme know. We can find an ordinance against anything if we go back far enough in the books –"

Smitty shifted his hat from northeast to southwest and started reluctantly toward the great outdoors once more. "Anything screwy like this that comes up, I'm always It," he was heard to mutter rebelliously. "Nice job, shooing a dancing contest. I'll probably get bombarded with powder-puffs –"

The chief reached suddenly for the heavy brass inkwell on his desk, whether to sign some report or to let Smitty have it, Smitty didn't wait to find out. He ducked hurriedly out the door.

"Ah me," sighed the chief profoundly, "what a bunch of crumbs. Why didn't I listen to me old man and join the fire department instead!"

Young Mr Smith, muttering bad language all the way, had himself driven over to the unused armory where the peculiar enterprise was taking place.

"Sixty cents," said the taxi-driver.

Smitty took out a little pocket account-book and wrote down – *Taxi-fare – $1.20.* "Send me out after nothing at four in the morning, will he!" he commented. After which he felt a lot better.

There was a box-office outside the entrance but now it was dark and untenanted. Smitty pushed through the unlocked doors and found a combination porter and doorman, a gentleman of color, seated on the inside, who gave him a stub of pink pasteboard in exchange for fifty-cents, then promptly took the stub back again and tore it in half. "Boy," he remarked affably, "you is either up pow'ful early or up awful late."

"I just is plain up," remarked Smitty, and looked around him.

It was an hour before daylight and there were a dozen people left in the armory, which was built to hold two thousand. Six of them were dancing, but you wouldn't have known it by looking at them. It had been going on nine days. There was no one watching them any more. The last of the paid admissions had gone home hours ago, even the drunks and the Park Avenue stay-outs. All the big snow-white arc lights hanging from the rafters had been put out, except one in the middle, to save expenses. Pasternack wasn't in this for his health. The one remaining light, spitting and sizzling way up overhead, and sending down violet and white rays that you could see with the naked eye, made everything look ghostly, unreal. A phonograph fitted with an amplifier was grinding away at one end of the big hall, tearing a dance-tune to pieces, giving it the beating of its life. Each time the needle got to the end of the record it was swept back to the beginning by a sort of stencil fitted over the turn-table.

Six scarecrows, three men and three girls, clung ludicrously together in pairs out in the middle of the floor. They were not dancing and they were not walking, they were tottering by now, barely moving enough to keep from standing still. Each of the men bore a number on his back. 3, 8, and 14 the numbers were. They were the "lucky" couples who had outlasted all the others, the scores who had started with them at the bang of a gun a week and two days ago. There wasn't a coat or vest left among the three men – or a necktie. Two of them had replaced their shoes with carpet-slippers to ease their aching feet. The third had on a pair of canvas sneakers.

One of the girls had a wet handkerchief plastered across her forehead. Another had changed into a chorus-girl's practice outfit – shorts and a blouse. The third was a slip of a thing, a mere child, her head hanging limply down over her partner's shoulder, her eyes glazed with exhaustion.

Smitty watched her for a moment. There wasn't a curve in her whole body. If there was anyone here under age, it was she. She must be Toodles McGuire, killing herself for a plated loving-cup, a line in the newspapers, a contract to dance in some cheap honky-tonk, and a thousand dollars that she wasn't going to get anyway – according to the chief. He was probably right, reflected Smitty. There wasn't a thousand dollars in the whole set-up, much less three prizes on a sliding scale. Pasternack would probably pocket whatever profits there were and blow, letting the fame-struck suckers whistle. Corner-lizards and dance-hall belles like these couldn't even scrape together enough to bring suit. Now was as good a time as any to stop the lousy racket.

Smitty sauntered over to the bleachers where four of the remaining six the armory housed just then were seated and sprawled in various attitudes. He looked them over. One was an aged crone who acted as matron to the female participants during the brief five-minute rest-periods that came every half-hour. She had come out of her retirement for the time being, a towel of dubious cleanliness slung over her arm, and was absorbed in the working-out of a crossword puzzle, mumbling to herself all the while. She had climbed halfway up the reviewing stand to secure privacy for her occupation.

Two or three rows below her lounged a greasy-looking counterman from some one-arm lunchroom, guarding a tray that held a covered tin pail of steaming coffee and a stack of waxpaper cups. One of the rest periods was evidently approaching and he was ready to cash in on it.

The third spectator was a girl in a dance dress, her face twisted with pain. Judging by her unkempt appearance and the scornful bitter look in her eyes as she watched the remaining dancers, she had only just recently disqualified herself. She had one stockingless foot up before her and was rubbing the swollen instep with alcohol and cursing softly under her breath.

The fourth and last of the onlookers (the fifth being the darky at the door) was too busy with his arithmetic even to look up when Smitty parked before him. He was in his shirt-sleeves and wore blue elastic armbands and a green celluloid eye-shade. A soggy-looking stogie protruded from his mouth. A watch, a megaphone, a whistle, and a blank-cartridge pistol lay beside him on the bench. He appeared to be computing the day's receipts in a pocket notebook, making them up out of his head as he went along. "Get out of my light," he remarked ungraciously as Smitty's shadow fell athwart him.

"You Pasternack?" Smitty wanted to know, not moving an inch.

"Naw, he's in his office taking a nap."

"Well, get him out here, I've got news for him."

"He don't wanna hear it," said the pleasant party on the bench.

Smitty turned over his lapel, then let it curl back again. "Oh, the lor," commented the auditor, and two tens left the day's receipts and were left high and dry in Smitty's right hand. "Buy yourself a drop of schnapps," he said without even looking up. "Stop in and ask for me tomorrow when there's more in the kitty –"

Smitty plucked the nearest armband, stretched it out until it would have gone around a piano, then let it snap back again. The business manager let out a yip. Smitty's palm with the two sawbucks came up flat against his face, clamped itself there by the chin and bridge of the nose, and executed a rotary motion, grinding them in. "Wrong guy," he said and followed the financial wizard into the sanctum where Pasternack lay in repose, mouth fixed to catch flies.

"Joe," said the humbled side-kick, spitting out pieces of ten-dollar-bill, "the lor."

Pasternack got vertical as though he worked by a spring. "Where's your warrant?" he said before his eyes were even open. "Quick, get me my mouth on the phone, Moe!"

"You go out there and blow your whistle," said Smitty, "and call the bally off – or do I have to throw this place out in the street?" He turned suddenly, tripped over something unseen, and went staggering halfway across the room. The telephone went flying out of Moe's hand at one end and the sound-box came ripping off the baseboard of the wall at the other. "*Tch, tch* excuse it please," apologized Smitty insincerely. "Just when you needed it most, too!"

He turned back to the one called Moe and sent him headlong out into the auditorium with a hearty shove at the back of the neck. "Now do like I told you," he said, "while we're waiting for the telephone repairman to get here. And when their dogs have cooled, send them all in here to me. That goes for the cannibal and the washroom dame, too." He motioned toward the desk. "Get out your little tin box, Pasternack. How much you got on hand to pay these people?"

It wasn't in a tin box but in a briefcase. "Close the door," said Pasternack in an insinuating voice. "There's plenty here, and plenty more will be coming in. How big a cut will square you? Write your own ticket."

Smitty sighed wearily. "Do I have to knock your front teeth down the back of your throat before I can convince you I'm one of these old-fashioned guys that likes to work for my money?"

Outside a gun boomed hollowly and the squawking of the phonograph stopped. Moe could be heard making an announcement through the megaphone. "You can't get away with this!" stormed Pasternack. "Where's your warrant?"

"Where's your license," countered Smitty, "if you're going to get technical? C'mon, don't waste any more time, you're keeping me up! Get the dough ready for the pay-off." He stepped to the door and called out into the auditorium: "Everybody in here. Get your things and line up." Two of the three couples separated slowly like sleepwalkers and began to trudge painfully over toward him, walking zig-zag as though their metabolism was all shot.

The third pair, Number 14, still clung together out on the floor, the man facing toward Smitty. They didn't seem to realize it was over. They seemed to be holding each other up. They were in the shape of a human tent, their feet about three feet apart on the floor, their faces and shoulders pressed closely together. The girl was that clothes-pin, that stringbean of a kid he had already figured for Toodles McGuire. So she was going to be stubborn about it, was she? He went over to the pair bellicosely. "C'mon, you heard me, break it up!"

The man gave him a frightened look over her shoulder. "Will you take her off me please, Mac? She's passed out or something, and if I let her go she'll crack her conk on the floor." He blew out his breath. "I can't hold her up much longer!"

Smitty hooked an arm about her middle. She didn't weigh any more than a discarded topcoat. The poor devil who had been bearing her weight, more or less, for nine days and nights on end, let go and folded up into a squatting position at her feet like a shriveled Buddha. "Just lemme stay like this," he moaned, "it feels so good." The girl, meanwhile, had begun to bend slowly double over Smitty's supporting arm, closing up like a jackknife. But she did it with a jerkiness, a deliberateness, that was almost grisly, slipping stiffly down a notch at a time, until her upside-down head had met her knees. She was like a walking doll whose spring has run down.

Smitty turned and barked over one shoulder at the washroom hag. "Hey you! C'mere and gimme a hand with this girl! Can't you see she needs attention? Take her in there with you and see what you can do for her –"

The old crone edged fearfully nearer, but when Smitty tried to pass the inanimate form to her she drew hurriedly back. "I – I ain't got the stren'th to lift her," she mumbled stubbornly. "You're strong, you carry her in and set her down –"

"I can't go in there," he snarled disgustedly. "That's no place for me! What're you here for if you can't –"

The girl who had been sitting on the sidelines suddenly got up and came limping over on one stockingless foot. "Give her to me," she said. "I'll take her in for you." She gave the old woman a long hard look before which the latter quailed and dropped her eyes. "Take hold of her feet," she ordered in a low voice. The hag hurriedly stooped to obey. They sidled off with her between them, and disappeared around the side of the orchestra-stand, toward the washroom. Their burden sagged low, until it almost touched the floor.

"Hang onto her," Smitty thought he heard the younger woman say. "She won't bite you!" The washroom door banged closed on the weird little procession. Smitty turned and hoisted the deflated Number 14 to his feet. "C'mon, he said. "In you go, with the rest!"

They were all lined up against the wall in Pasternack's "office," so played-out that if the wall had suddenly been taken away they would have all toppled flat like a pack of cards. Pasternack and his shill had gone into a huddle in the opposite corner, buzzing like a hive of bees.

"Would you two like to be alone?" Smitty wanted to know, parking Number 14 with the rest of the droops.

Pasternack evidently believed in the old adage, "He who fights and runs away lives to fight, etc." The game, he seemed to think, was no longer worth the candle. He unlatched the briefcase he had been guarding under his arm, walked back to the desk with it, and prepared to ease his conscience. "Well folks," he remarked genially, "on the advice of this gentleman here" (big pally smile for Smitty) "my partner and I are calling off the contest. While we are under no legal obligation to any of you" (business of clearing his throat and hitching up his necktie) "we have decided to do the square thing, just so there won't be any trouble, and split the prize money among all the remaining entries. Deducting the rental for the armory, the light bill, and the cost of printing tickets and handbills, that would leave –"

"No you don't!" said Smitty. "That comes out of your first nine-days profits. What's on hand now gets divvied without any deductions. Do it your way and they'd all be owing you money!" He turned to the doorman. "You been paid, sunburnt?"

"Nossuh! I'se got five dolluhs a night coming at me –"

"Forty-five for you," said Smitty.

Pasternack suddenly blew up and advanced menacingly upon his partner. "That's what I get for listening to you, know-it-all! So New York was a sucker town, was it! So there was easy pickings here, was there! Yah!"

"Boys, boys," remonstrated Smitty, elbowing them apart.

"Throw them a piece of cheese, the rats," remarked the girl in shorts. There was a scuffling sound in the doorway and Smitty turned in time to see the lamed girl and the washroom matron each trying to get in ahead of the other.

"You don't leave me in there!"

"Well I'm not staying in there alone with her. It ain't my job! I resign!"

The one with the limp got to him first. "Listen, mister, you better go in there yourself," she panted. "We can't do anything with her. I think she's dead."

"She's cold as ice and all stiff-like," corroborated the old woman.

"Oh my God, I've killed her!" someone groaned. Number 14 sagged to his knees and went out like a light. Those on either side of him eased him down to the floor by his arms, too weak themselves to support him.

"Hold everything!" barked Smitty. He gripped the pop-eyed doorman by the shoulder. "Scram out front and get a cop. Tell him to put in a call for an ambulance, and then have him report in here to me. And if you try lighting out, you lose your forty-five bucks and get the electric chair."

"I'se pracktilly back inside again," sobbed the terrified darky as he fled.

"The rest of you stay right where you are. I'll hold you responsible, Pasternack, if anybody ducks."

"As though we could move an inch on these howling dogs," muttered the girl in shorts.

Smitty pushed the girl with one shoe ahead of him. "You come and show me," he grunted. He was what might be termed a moral coward at the moment; he was going where he'd never gone before.

"Straight ahead of you," she scowled, halting outside the door. "Do you need a road-map?"

"C'mon, I'm not going in there alone," he said and gave her a shove through the forbidden portal.

She was stretched out on the floor where they'd left her, a bottle of rubbing alcohol that hadn't worked uncorked beside her. His face was flaming as he squatted down and examined her. She was gone all right. She was as cold as they'd said and getting more rigid by the minute. "Overtaxed her heart most likely," he growled. "That guy Pasternack ought to be hauled up for this. He's morally responsible."

The cop, less well-brought-up than Smitty, stuck his head in the door without compunction.

"Stay by the entrance," Smitty instructed him, "Nobody leaves." Then, "This was the McGuire kid, wasn't it?" he asked his feminine companion.

"Can't prove it by me," she said sulkily. "Pasternack kept calling her Rose Lamont all through the contest. Why don't-cha ask the guy that was dancing with her? Maybe they got around to swapping names after nine days. Personally," she said as she moved toward the door, "I don't know who she was and I don't give a damn!"

"You'll make a swell mother for some guy's children," commented Smitty following her out. "In there," he said to the ambulance doctor who had just arrived, "but it's the morgue now, and not first-aid. Take a look."

Number 14, when he got back to where they all were, was taking it hard and self-accusing. "I didn't mean to do it, I didn't mean to!" he kept moaning.

"Shut up, you sap, you're making it tough for yourself," someone hissed.

"Lemme see a list of your entries," Smitty told Pasternack.

The impresario fished a ledger out of the desk drawer and held it out to him. "All I got out of this enterprise was kicks in the pants! Why didn't I stick to the sticks where they don't drop dead from a little dancing? Ask me, why didn't I!"

"Fourteen," read Smitty. "Rose Lamont and Gene Monahan. That your real name, guy? Back it up." 14 jerked off the coat that someone had slipped around his shoulders and turned the inner pocket inside out. The name was inked onto the label. The address checked too. "What about her, was that her real tag?"

"McGuire was her real name," admitted Monahan, "Toodles McGuire. She was going to change it anyway, pretty soon, if we'dda won that thousand" – he hung his head – "so it didn't matter."

"Why'd you say you did it? Why do you keep saying you didn't mean to?"

"Because I could feel there was something the matter with her in my arms. I knew she oughtta quit, and I wouldn't let her. I kept begging her to stick it out a little longer, even when she didn't answer me. I went crazy, I guess, thinking of that thousand dollars. We needed it to get married on. I kept expecting the others to drop out any minute, there were only two other couples left, and no one was watching us any more. When the rest-periods came, I carried her in my arms to the washroom door, so no one would notice she couldn't make it herself, and turned her over to the old lady in there. She couldn't do anything with her either, but I begged her not to let on, and each time the whistle blew I picked her up and started out from there with her –"

"Well, you've danced her into her grave," said Smitty bitterly. "If I was you I'd go out and stick both my feet under the first trolley-car that came along and hold them there until it went by. It might make a man of you!"

He went out and found the ambulance doctor in the act of leaving. "What was it, her heart?"

The A.D. favored him with a peculiar look, starting at the floor and ending at the top of his head. "Why wouldn't it be? Nobody's heart keeps going with a seven- or eight-inch metal pencil jammed into it."

He unfolded a handkerchief to reveal a slim coppery cylinder, tapering to needle-like sharpness at the writing end, where the case was pointed over the lead to protect it. It was aluminum – encrusted blood was what gave it its copper sheen. Smitty nearly dropped it in consternation – not because of what it had done but because he had missed seeing it.

"And another thing," went on the A.D. "You're new to this sort of thing, aren't you? Well, just a friendly tip. No offense, but you don't call an ambulance that long after they've gone, our time is too val –"

"I don't getcha," said Smitty impatiently. "She needed help; who am I supposed to ring in, potter's field, and have her buried before she's quit breathing?"

This time the look he got was withering. "She was past help hours ago." The doctor scanned his wrist. "It's five now. She's been dead since three, easily. I can't tell you when exactly, but your friend the medical examiner'll tell you whether I'm right or not. I've seen too many of 'em in my time. She's been gone two hours anyhow."

Smitty had taken a step back, as though he were afraid of the guy. "I came in here at four thirty," he stammered excitedly, "and she was dancing on that floor there – I saw her with my own eyes – fifteen, twenty minutes ago!" His face was slightly sallow.

"I don't care whether you saw her dancin' or saw her doin' double-hand-springs on her left ear, she was dead!" roared the ambulance man testily. "She was celebrating her own wake then, if you insist!" He took a look at Smitty's horrified face, quieted down, spit emphatically out of one corner of his mouth, and remarked: "Somebody was dancing with her dead body, that's all. Pleasant dreams, kid!"

Smitty started to burn slowly. "Somebody was," he agreed, gritting his teeth. "I know who Somebody is, too. His number was Fourteen until a little while ago; well, it's Thirteen from now on!"

He went in to look at her again, the doctor whose time was so valuable trailing along. "From the back, eh? That's how I missed it. She was lying on it the first time I came in and looked."

"I nearly missed it myself," the interne told him. "I thought it was a boil at first. See this little pad of gauze? It had been soaked in alcohol and laid over it. There was absolutely no external flow of blood, and the pencil didn't protrude, it was in up to the hilt. In fact I had to use forceps to get it out. You can see for yourself, the clip that fastens to the wearer's pocket, which would have stopped it halfway, is missing. Probably broken off long before."

"I can't figure it," said Smitty. "If it went in up to the hilt, what room was there left for the grip that sent it home?"

"Must have just gone in an inch or two at first and stayed there," suggested the interne. "She probably killed herself on it by keeling over backwards and hitting the floor or the wall, driving it the rest of the way in." He got to his feet. "Well, the pleasure's all yours." He flipped a careless salute, and left.

"Send the old crow in that had charge in here," Smitty told the cop.

The old woman came in fumbling with her hands, as though she had the seven-day itch.

"What's your name?"

"Josephine Falvey – Mrs Josephine Falvey." She couldn't keep her eyes off what lay on the floor.

"It don't matter after you're forty," Smitty assured her drily. "What'd you bandage that wound up for? D'you know that makes you an accessory to a crime?"

"I didn't do no such a –" she started to deny whitely.

He suddenly thrust the postage-stamp of folded gauze, rusty on one side, under her nose. She cawed and jumped back. He followed her retreat. "You didn't stick this on? C'mon, answer me!"

"Yeah, I did!" she cackled, almost jumping up and down, "I did, I did – but I didn't mean no harm. Honest, mister, I –"

"When'd you do it?"

"The last time, when you made me and the girl bring her in here. Up to then I kept rubbing her face with alcohol each time he brought her back to the door, but it didn't seem to help her any. I knew I should of gone out and reported it to Pasternack, but he – that feller you know – begged me not to. He begged me to give them a break and not get them ruled out. He said it didn't matter if she acted all limp that way, that she was just dazed. And anyway, there wasn't so much difference between her and the rest any more, they were all acting dopy like that. Then after you told me to bring her in the last time, I stuck my hand down the back of her dress and I felt something hard and round, like a carbuncle or berl, so I put a little gauze application over it. And then me and her decided, as long as the contest was over anyway, we better go out an tell you –"

"Yeah," he scoffed, "and I s'pose if I hadn't shown up she'd still be dancing around out there, until the place needed disinfecting! When was the first time you noticed anything the matter with her?"

She babbled: "About two thirty, three o'clock. They were all in here – the place was still crowded – and someone knocked on the door. He was standing out there with her in his arms and he passed her to me and whispered, 'Look after her, will you?' That's when he begged me not to tell anyone. He said he'd –" She stopped.

"Go on!" snapped Smitty.

"He said he'd cut me in on the thousand if they won it. Then when the whistle blew and they all went out again, he was standing there waiting to take her back in his arms – and off he goes with her. They all had to be helped out by that time, anyway, so nobody noticed anything wrong. After that, the same thing happened each time – until you came. But I didn't dream she was dead." She crossed herself. "If I'da thought that, you couldn't have got me to touch her for love nor money –"

"I've got my doubts," Smitty told her, "about the money part of that, anyway. Outside – and consider yourself a material witness."

If the old crone was to be believed, it had happened outside on the dance floor under the bright arclights, and not in here. He was pretty sure it had, at that. Monahan wouldn't have dared try to force his way in here. The screaming of the other occupants would have blown the roof off. Secondly, the very fact that the floor had been more crowded at that time than later, had helped cover it up. They'd probably quarreled when she tried to quit. He'd whipped out the pencil and struck her while she clung to him. She'd either fallen and killed herself on it, and he'd picked her up again immediately before anyone noticed, or else the Falvey woman had handled her carelessly in the washroom and the impaled pencil had reached her heart.

Smitty decided he wanted to know if any of the feminine entries had been seen to fall to the floor at any time during the evening. Pasternack had been in his office from ten on, first giving out publicity items and then taking a nap, so Smitty put him back on the shelf. Moe, however, came across beautifully.

"Did I see anyone fall?" he echoed shrilly. "Who didn't! Such a commotion you never saw in your life. About half-past two. Right when we were on the air, too."

"Go on, this is getting good. What'd he do, pick her right up again?"

"Pick her up! She wouldn't get up. You couldn't go near her! She just sat there swearing and screaming and throwing things. I thought we'd have to send for the police. Finally they sneaked up behind her and hauled her off on her fanny to the bleachers and disqualified her –"

"Wa-a-ait a minute," gasped Smitty. "Who you talking about?"

Moe looked surprised. "That Standish dame, who else? you saw her, the one with the bum pin. That was when she sprained it and couldn't dance any more. She wouldn't go home. She hung around saying she was framed and gypped and we couldn't get rid of her –"

"Wrong number," said Smitty disgustedly. "Back where you came from." And to the cop: "Now we'll get down to brass tacks. Let's have a crack at Monahan –"

He was thumbing his notebook with studied absorption when the fellow was shoved in the door. "Be right with you," he said offhandedly, tapping his pockets, "soon as I jot down – Lend me your pencil a minute, will you?"

"I – I had one, but I lost it," said Monahan dully.

"How come?" asked Smitty quietly.

"Fell out of my pocket, I guess. The clip was broken."

"This it?"

The fellow's eyes grew big, while it almost touched their lashes, twirling from left to right and right to left. "Yeah, but what's the matter with it, what's it got on it?"

"You asking me that?" leered Smitty. "Come on, show me how you did it!"

Monahan cowered back against the wall, looked from the body on the floor to the pencil, and back again. "Oh no," he moaned, "no. Is that what happened to her? I didn't even know –"

"Guys as innocent as you rub me the wrong way," said Smitty. He reached for him, hauled him out into the center of the room, and then sent him flying back again. His head bonged the door and the cop looked in inquiringly. "No, I didn't knock," said Smitty, "that was just his dome." He sprayed a little of the alcohol into Monahan's stunned face and hauled him forward again. "The first peep out of you was, 'I killed her.' Then you keeled over. Later on you kept saying 'I'm to blame, I'm to blame.' Why try to back out now?"

"But I didn't mean I did anything to her," wailed Monahan, "I thought I killed her by dancing too much. She was all right when I helped her in here about two. Then when I came back for her, the old dame whispered she couldn't wake her up. She said maybe the motion of dancing would bring her to. She said, 'You want that thousand dollars, don't you? Here, hold her up, no one'll be any the wiser.' And I listened to her like a fool and faked it from then on."

Smitty sent him hurling again. "Oh, so now it's supposed to have happened in here – with your pencil, no less! Quit trying to pass the buck!"

The cop, who didn't seem to be very bright, again opened the door, and Monahan came sprawling out at his feet. "Geez, what a hard head he must have," he remarked.

"Go over and start up that phonograph over there," ordered Smitty. "We're going to have a little demonstration – of how he did it. If banging his conk against the door won't bring back his memory, maybe dancing with her will do it." He hoisted Monahan upright by the scruff of the neck. "Which pocket was the pencil in?"

The man motioned toward his breast. Smitty dropped it in point-first. The cop fitted the needle into the groove and threw the switch. A blare came from the amplifier. "Pick her up and hold her," grated Smitty.

An animal-like moan was the only answer he got. The man tried to back away. The cop threw him forward again. "So you won't dance, eh?"

"I won't dance," gasped Monahan.

When they helped him up from the floor, he would dance.

"You held her like that dead, for two solid hours," Smitty reminded him. "Why mind an extra five minutes or so?"

The moving scarecrow crouched down beside the other inert scarecrow on the floor. Slowly his arms went around her. The two scarecrows rose to their feet, tottered drunkenly together, then moved out of the doorway into the open in time to the music. The cop began to perspire.

Smitty said: "Any time you're willing to admit you done it, you can quit."

"God forgive you for this!" said a tomb-like voice.

"Take out the pencil," said Smitty, "without letting go of her – like you did the first time."

"This is the first time," said that hollow voice. "The time before – it dropped out." His right hand slipped slowly away from the corpse's back, dipped into his pocket.

The others had come out of Pasternack's office, drawn by the sound of the macabre music, and stood huddled together, horror and unbelief written all over their weary faces. A corner of the bleachers hid both Smitty and the cop from them; all they could see was that grisly couple moving slowly out into the center of the big floor, alone under the funeral heliotrope arc light. Monahan's hand suddenly went up, with something gleaming in it; stabbed down again and was hidden against his partner's back. There was an unearthly howl and the girl with the turned ankle fell flat on her face amidst the onlookers.

Smitty signaled the cop; the music suddenly broke off. Monahan and his partner had come to a halt again and stood there like they had when the contest first ended, upright, tent-shaped, feet far apart, heads locked together. One pair of eyes was as glazed as the other now.

"All right break, break!" said Smitty.

Monahan was clinging to her with a silent, terrible intensity as though he could no longer let go.

The Standish girl had sat up, but promptly covered her eyes with both hands and was shaking all over as if she had a chill.

"I want that girl in here," said Smitty. "And you, Moe. And the old lady."

He closed the door on the three of them. "Let's see that book of entries again."

Moe handed it over jumpily.

"Sylvia Standish, eh?" The girl nodded, still sucking in her breath from the fright she'd had.

"Toodles McGuire was Rose Lamont – now what's your real name?" He thumbed at the old woman. "What are you two to each other?"

The girl looked away. "She's my mother, if you gotta know," she said.

"Might as well admit it, it's easy enough to check up on," he agreed. "I had a hunch there was a tie-up like that in it somewhere. You were too ready to help her carry the body in here the first time." He turned to the cringing Moe. "I understood you to say she carried on like nobody's never-mind when she was ruled out, had to be hauled off the floor by main force and wouldn't go home. Was she just a bum loser, or what was her grievance?"

"She claimed it was done purposely," said Moe. "Me, I got my doubts. It was like this. That girl the feller killed, she had on a string of glass beads, see? So the string broke and they rolled all over the floor under everybody's feet. So this one, she slipped on 'em, fell and turned her ankle and couldn't dance no more. Then she starts hollering blue murder." He shrugged. "What should we do, call off the contest because she couldn't dance no more?"

"She did it purposely," broke in the girl hotly, "so she could hook the award herself! She knew I had a better chance than anyone else –"

"I suppose it was while you were sitting there on the floor you picked up the pencil Monahan had dropped," Smitty said casually.

"I did like hell! It fell out in the bleachers when he came over to apolo-" She stopped abruptly. "I don't know what pencil you're talking about."

"Don't worry about a little slip-up like that," Smitty told her. "You're down for it anyway – and have been ever since you folded up out there just now. You're not telling me anything I don't know already."

"Anyone woulda keeled over; I thought I was seeing her ghost –"

"That ain't what told me. It was seeing him pretend to do it that told me he never did it. It wasn't done outside at all, in spite of what your old lady tried to hand me. Know why? The pencil didn't go through her dress. There's no hole in the back of her dress. Therefore she had her dress off and was cooling off when it happened. Therefore it was done here in the restroom. For Monahan to do it outside he would have had to hitch her whole dress up almost over her head in front of everybody – and maybe that wouldn't have been noticed!

"He never came in here after her; your own mother would have been the first one to squawk for help. You did, though. She stayed a moment after the others. You came in the minute they cleared out and stuck her with it. She fell on it and killed herself. Then your old lady tried to cover you by putting a pad on the wound and giving Monahan the idea she was stupefied from fatigue. When he began to notice the coldness, if he did, he thought it was from the alcohol-rubs she was getting every rest-period. I guess he isn't very bright anyway – a guy like that, that dances for his coffee-and. He didn't have any motive. He wouldn't have done it even if she wanted to quit, he'd have let her. He was too penitent later on when he thought he'd tired her to death. But you had all the motive I need – those broken beads. Getting even for what you thought she did. Have I left anything out?"

"Yeah," she said curtly, "look up my sleeve and tell me if my hat's on straight!"

On the way out to the Black Maria that had backed up to the entrance, with the two Falvey women, Pasternack, Moe, and the other four dancers marching single file ahead of him, Smitty called to the cop: "Where's Monahan? Bring him along!"

The cop came up mopping his brow. "I finally pried him loose," he said, "when they came to take her away, but I can't get him to stop laughing. He's been laughing ever since. I think he's lost his mind. Makes your blood run cold. Look at that!"

Monahan was standing there, propped against the wall, a lone figure under the arclight, his arms still extended in the half-embrace in which he had held his partner for nine days and nights, while peal after peal of macabre mirth came from him, shaking him from head to foot.

Waltz

She was sitting there in white, cool and crisp and pure-looking, with ten young men around her, waiting for the next number to begin. She knew what it was going to be because only a short while ago she had requested the orchestra leader to play it. 'The Blue Danube'. She knew whom it was going to be with too.

As the opening bars were struck, a preamble started all around her. She laughed and kept shaking her head and saying, "Reserved, reserved. The next one, maybe." But the joke was, there wasn't going to be any next one. She knew that and they didn't.

When she saw him coming for her all the way across the enormous room, she stood up expectantly. There seemed to be a star twinkling behind both of her eyes. The strains of Strauss' lovely lilting music found an echo in her heart. The disappointed men put on long faces and drifted back to the stag line that stretched unbroken across one entire side of the ballroom, ruler-straight, like a regiment on dress parade: black shoulders, white shirt-fronts, pink faces. Under the sparkling crystal chandeliers, figures in blue and yellow and pink were slowly beginning to turn all over the room, like tops, each with its black-garbed complement.

The girl in white and the man she'd been waiting for met, stood poised for a moment, started off with a slow spin, their forms reflected upside down on the glass floor. Her voice was eager, confidential:

"This is the first chance I've had to say a word to you alone all evening, they've been watching me so. Especially mother. . . . You've got your car outside, of course? . . . Right after this dance? Yes, that's as good a time as any. They'll be going upstairs then. They'll let the party go ahead under its own momentum. She's starting to yawn already. . . .

"Yes, I'm all set. I sneaked up and finished my packing while the last dance was going on. Imagine me doing my own packing! I wasn't taking any chances on the maid giving me away to the family. I even carried my bags down the back stairs myself. They're hidden in a little closet off the servants' entrance. Just as soon as this piece is over, you slip out the front way, bring your car around to the back, and I'll meet you there. We'll be miles away before we're even missed. . . .

"I still can't believe it, it's all been so sudden. . . . The family'll probably throw fits, when they find out I've only known you ten days. . . .

They think you have to know a person years before you can trust them. And even then, you're supposed to play safe and not trust them anyway, half the time. Anyone you know less than six months, to them, is an utter stranger. I guess it's our money that made them that way. . . .

"Well, suppose they do think it's that? Let them. We know better, don't we, Wes? . . . Oh, shall I? I never thought of that. I never stop to think of money. Well, about how much shall I bring along? There's a lot of it lying scattered around in my bureau drawer upstairs. I just throw it in and then forget about it. . . . I've never bothered counting. Maybe a thousand or two. Will that be enough? I mean, I haven't the faintest idea what things cost, gasoline and hotels and things like that. I've never had to pay for anything myself. . . . Oh, don't apologize, Wes – I understand perfectly. Of course, just until you can cash a check tomorrow or the next day. What difference does money make anyway when two people are as much in love as we are? . . . If you don't think two thousand will be enough, I could go to Father maybe and ask him – . . . No, I guess you're right, I'd better not. He *might* think it was a strange time, right in the middle of the party like this, and start asking all kinds of questions. . . .

"My jewels? Why, of course, I'm bringing them. They're in one of the valises right now. . . . Yes, I suppose they are worth a lot. . . . No, I haven't the faintest idea; seventy-five, a hundred thousand, somewhere around there, don't you think? . . . A lot? Why, I thought every girl had about that amount of jewelry. I mean, except *servant* girls and people like that. Don't they? Everyone I know has at least that much. . . .

"Oh, here we're wasting this whole lovely music talking about money and jewels and uninteresting things like that! It's the last time I'll ever dance in my own home, with people around me that I've known all my life, who have sheltered and protected me. By morning we'll be hundreds of miles away, without leaving a trace. No one'll know where I am, what's become of me. They'll never see me again. Isn't that romantic, dropping from sight in the middle of a big party right under your own roof?

"Regret it? Feel sorry? No, how can I, when I think what I do of you? No, these other men don't mean a thing to me. I grew up with most of them. I know every one of those twenty-five men on that stag line, and there's not one of them I – . . . Well, yes, there are twenty-six, but that third one from the end doesn't count. He's only a detective. . . .

"Oops, you went out of step there. My fault I guess, I'm so excited tonight. . . .

"No, I don't mean that kind of a *hired* detective, that you just have around to see that no valuables are stolen during a big party like this. This one's some special kind of a detective, who's hunting somebody.

Imagine looking for somebody *here*! Isn't that rich? . . .

"There we go again; it must be these high heels of mine. . . . I didn't really bother listening. I just happened to overhear Father bawling him out as I was passing the door; that was all. . . . Father nearly had a fit. He wanted to have him thrown out bodily, from what I could gather. But you know how nervous Mother is. As soon as she heard about it, she insisted that Father let him stay – just in case. . . .

"No, not a thief. He gave it a funny word. Wait'll I see if I can remember. Oh yes – con-congenital murderer! That was it. What's a congenital murderer anyway, Wes? . . . Darling, have we been dancing too hard? Your forehead's all wet. . . . Now isn't that preposterous? I don't believe a word of it. I think he's just trying to sound important and frighten us. Well anyway, Mother talked Father into letting him hang around, as long as he minded his business and didn't spoil the looks of the party. She made him give his word that he wouldn't start any rough stuff inside the house here – that he'd wait until the person – if there is such a person – left, and he'd get him outside. . . .

"Oh no, he's not alone. I think he's brought a whole battery of others with him. They're probably spread out lurking outside around the house somewhere. Something asinine like that. Father put his foot down. He said one inside the house was all he'd stand for – the rest would have to stay out. I guess they're all out there right now, thick as bees. . . .

"There we go again. My, but I'm clumsy tonight! . . .

"No, of course not, Wes; why should they interfere with us? They wouldn't dare! They'll just stop this man, when and if they see him coming out. . . . He might be here at that. When you throw a large party like this and invite dozens and dozens of people, almost anyone can slip in unannounced. Like you did yourself, that night I first met you at Sylvia's party, ten nights ago. Only of course you did it just for the fun of it. I asked her who you were afterwards, and she said she didn't know herself. . . . You know, if I weren't so excited about what *we*'re going to do, I'd have myself a perfectly swell time trying to figure out just who it could be. . . . Isn't it thrilling? Somebody here at this party is a congenital murderer! Somebody right out on this floor dancing like we are this very minute! I wouldn't want to be in his partner's shoes. . . . Let's see now, Tommy Turner, over there with that girl in yellow, has always had a perfectly vile temper. Why he half killed a man once just for – but Tommy and I have been playmates since we were seven. He wouldn't have the time to go around murdering people. He's always too busy playing polo. . . . Or maybe it's that Argentine sheik that's been rushing Kay Landon so all season. I always did think he had kind of a murderous face. . . .

"Don't stare at him like that, Wes – the detective, I mean. He'll know I told you something, and he asked us not to. I know you're highly interested, but you haven't taken your eyes off him *once* the past five minutes. No, he's not looking at us. Why should he be? . . . Well, if he is, it's because you've been looking at *him* so hard. You're like all the men. You seem to think a detective is wonderful. Personally I find them very stupid and uninteresting. This one talks out of the side of his mouth. I wish you could hear – . . .

"Wes, you're breathing so hard. I must be difficult to lead. . . .

"So they know what he looks like? I'm not sure. They do and they don't. I mean, what they're counting on is a certain scar across the back of his hand. That seems to be one of the few definite facts they know about him. They're positive he has it. I suppose they'll make every man that leaves here tonight hold up his hand before his face or something before they let him through. Which just goes to show you how very stupid they are. As though there couldn't be two people with a scar – . . . What am I laughing at? Why, there are! I just remembered you yourself have one. *You* know, that scald you got trying to unscrew the overheated cap of your radiator. Don't you remember my asking you about it at Sylvia's that night, when you still had tape around it? Incidentally, how is it getting – . . . Wes, don't pull your hand away like that! You nearly tore my arm out of my socket! . . . Silly, are you afraid they'll mistake *you* for this murderer? As though *you* could be a congenital murderer! Why, I'd know one in a minute. At least I think I would. Of course I never saw one, but they're sort of pale and hollow-eyed and suspicious looking, aren't they? . . . Wes, what a peculiar smile you just gave me! . . . Darling, is it too warm for you in here? You've gotten so white. . . .

"Oh, let's forget this stupid detective and his murderer! How'd we ever start talking about him anyway? . . . There, Father and Mother are saying good night. They'll be starting upstairs in a minute. Now just as soon as this waltz is over, I'll make a beeline out of here before that bunch of stags jump on my neck again. I'll get the money I told you about, throw something over this dress, and meet you by the rear entrance. . . . Father's private library? Why the library? Well all right, anything you say. You wait for me in there then. Keep the door closed so no one'll see you. . . . What? Why yes, I think Father *does* keep some kind of a gun in the table drawer in there. I remember seeing it once or twice, but how on earth did *you* know about it? . . . I still can't understand why you want me to follow you in there. The library is in the exact center of the whole house. There's only one door to it and no windows. And we'll be cut off, walled up, in there; it'll be terribly hard for us to get out again without being seen. . . . Well, you know best, Wes. It'd be terribly unlucky for me to start arguing with my future husband the very first night. . . .

"The waltz is ending. Lead me over toward the stairs, so I can make a quick getaway. . . . That stupid detective keeps watching so; he must have intended asking me for the next dance. Well, he'll have another guess! I bet he dances like a Mack truck. . . . One minute more. . . .

"There, it's over! Wasn't that a lovely waltz? I'll never forget it as long as I live. Maybe that won't be as long as I think it will – I'll leave you for just this minute, and then I'll never leave you again. Till death do us part."

The two shots came so close together they sounded like one; they shattered the after-the-waltz stillness. A girl or two bleated fearfully. Then with a patter like rain on the polished dancing floor the crowd began herding toward a single point, converging on the partly open library door, where a man was standing. There was a wisp of smoke just over his head. Then it blew away.

Beyond him a man's face was visible, chin on the long, narrow table. Then that too disappeared, like the smoke, and a dull sound came from the carpeted floor.

The detective was saying, to those behind him in the doorway: "Search me, I headed over for this private liberry to bum another of the old man's cigars – they're the finest I ever smoked. I open the door and he's standing there perfectly still on the other side on that table, with the drawer open and his hand in it. He don't say anything, just looks at me like I'm a ghost. So I reach out my paw to help myself from the big humidor standing there between us. With that, he jerks up this gun, misses my ear by an eighth of an inch, turns it to his own dome, and gives it the works!"

Voices cried excitedly, "He must be that murderer you wanted!" The story had evidently already gotten around in some way.

"How could he be?" the detective shrugged. "We got him over an hour ago – nabbed him outside the house as he was on his way in with some swell-looking dame that was next on his list. He's been safely in custody ever since ten o'clock, and the guys I had watching the place all went with him. Why did I come back and hang around like that afterwards? Well I'll tell you frankly, the punch and the sanwidges and the cigars were the best I ever tried, and does anybody feel like complaining?"

The Book that Squealed

The outside world never intruded into the sanctum where Prudence Roberts worked. Nothing violent or exciting ever happened there, or was ever likely to. Voices were never raised above a whisper, or at the most a discreet murmur. The most untoward thing that could possibly occur would be that some gentleman browser became so engrossed he forgot to remove his hat and had to be tactfully reminded. Once, it is true, a car backfired violently somewhere outside in the street and the whole staff gave a nervous start, including Prudence, who dropped her date stamp all the way out in the aisle in front of her desk; but that had never happened again after that one time.

Things that the papers printed, holdups, gang warfare, kidnappings, murders, remained just things that the papers printed. They never came past these portals behind which she worked.

Just books came in and went out again. Harmless, silent books.

Until, one bright June day –

The Book showed up around noon, shortly before Prudence Roberts was due to go off duty for lunch. She was on the Returned Books desk. She turned up her nose with unqualified inner disapproval at first sight of the volume. Her taste was severely classical; she had nothing against light reading in itself, but to her, light reading meant Dumas, Scott, Dickens. She could tell this thing before her was trash by the title alone, and the author's pen name: *Manuela Gets Her Man*, by Orchid Ollivant.

Furthermore it had a lurid orange dust cover that showed just what kind of claptrap might be expected within. She was surprised a city library had added such worthless tripe to its stock; it belonged more in a candy-store lending library than here. She supposed there had been a great many requests for it among a certain class of readers; that was why.

Date stamp poised in hand she glanced up, expecting to see one of these modern young hussies, all paint and boldness, or else a faded middle-aged blonde of the type that lounged around all day in a wrapper, reading such stuff and eating marshmallows. To her surprise the woman before her was drab, looked hardworking and anything but frivolous. She didn't seem to go with the book at all.

Prudence Roberts didn't say anything, looked down again, took the book's reference card out of the filing drawer just below her desk, compared them.

"You're two days overdue with this," she said; "it's a one-week book. That'll be four cents."

The woman fumbled timidly in an old-fashioned handbag, placed a nickel on the desk.

"My daughter's been reading it to me at nights," she explained, "but she goes to night school and some nights she couldn't; that's what delayed me. Oh, it was grand." She sighed. "It brings back all your dreams of romance."

"Humph," said Prudence Roberts, still disapproving as much as ever. She returned a penny change to the borrower, stamped both cards. That should have ended the trivial little transaction.

But the woman had lingered there by the desk, as though trying to summon up courage to ask something. "Please," she faltered timidly when Prudence had glanced up a second time, "I was wondering, could you tell me what happens on page 42? You know, that time when the rich man lures her on his yasht?"

"Yacht," Prudence corrected her firmly. "Didn't you read the book yourself?"

"Yes, my daughter read it to me, but Pages 41 and 42 are missing, and we were wondering, we'd give anything to know, if Ronald got there in time to save her from that awful –"

Prudence had pricked up her official ears at that. "Just a minute," she interrupted, and retrieved the book from where she had just discarded it. She thumbed through it rapidly. At first glance it seemed in perfect condition; it was hard to tell anything was the matter with it. If the borrower hadn't given her the exact page number – but Pages 41 and 42 were missing, as she had said. A telltale scalloping of torn paper ran down the seam between Pages 40 and 43. The leaf had been plucked out bodily, torn out like a sheet in a notebook, not just become loosened and fallen out. Moreover, the condition of the book's spine showed that this could not have happened from wear and tear; it was still too new and firm. It was a case of out-and-out vandalism. Inexcusable destruction of the city's property.

"This book's been damaged," said Prudence ominously. "It's only been in use six weeks, it's still a new book, and this page was deliberately ripped out along its entire length. I'll have to ask you for your reader's card back. Wait here, please."

She took the book over to Miss Everett, the head librarian, and showed it to her. The latter was Prudence twenty years from now, if nothing happened in between to snap her out of it. She sailed back toward the culprit, steel-rimmed spectacles glittering balefully.

The woman was standing there cringing, her face as white as though she expected to be executed on the spot. She had the humble person's typical fear of anyone in authority. "Please, lady, I didn't do it," she whined.

"You should have reported it before taking it out," said the inexorable Miss Everett. "I'm sorry, but as the last borrower, we'll have to hold you responsible. Do you realize you could go to jail for this?"

The woman quailed. "It was that way when I took it home," she pleaded; "I didn't do it."

Prudence relented a little. "She did call my attention to it herself, Miss Everett," she remarked. "I wouldn't have noticed it otherwise."

"You know the rules as well as I do, Miss Roberts," said her flinty superior. She turned to the terrified drudge. "You will lose your card and all library privileges until you have paid the fine assessed against you for damaging this book." She turned and went careering off again.

The poor woman still hovered there, pathetically anxious. "Please don't make me do without my reading," she pleaded. "That's the only pleasure I got. I work hard all day. How much is it? Maybe I can pay a little something each week."

"Are you sure you didn't do it?" Prudence asked her searchingly. The lack of esteem in which she held this book was now beginning to incline her in the woman's favor. Of course, it was the principle of the thing, it didn't matter how trashy the book in question was. On the other hand, how could the woman have been expected to notice that a page was gone, in time to report it, *before* she had begun to read it?

"I swear I didn't," the woman protested. "I love books, I wouldn't want to hurt one of them."

"Tell you what I'll do," said Prudence, lowering her voice and looking around to make sure she wasn't overheard. "I'll pay the fine for you out of my own pocket, so you can go ahead using the library meanwhile. I think it's likely this was done by one of the former borrowers, ahead of you. If such proves not to be the case, however, then you'll simply have to repay me a little at a time."

The poor woman actually tried to take hold of her hand to kiss it. Prudence hastily withdrew it, marked the fine paid, and returned the card to her.

"And I suggest you try to read something a little more worth while in future," she couldn't help adding.

She didn't discover the additional damage until she had gone upstairs with the book, when she was relieved for lunch. It was no use sending it back to be rebound or repaired; with one entire page gone like that, there was nothing could be done with it; the book was worthless. Well, it had been that to begin with, she thought tartly.

She happened to flutter the leaves scornfully and light filtered through one of the pages, in dashes of varying length, like a sort of

Morse code. She looked more closely, and it was the forty-third page, the one immediately after the missing leaf. It bore innumerable horizontal slashes scattered all over it from top to bottom, as though some moron had underlined the words on it, but with some sharp-edged instrument rather than the point of a pencil. They were so fine they were almost invisible when the leaf was lying flat against the others, white on white; it was only when it was up against the light that they stood revealed. The leaf was almost threadbare with them. The one after it had some too, but not nearly so distinct; they hadn't pierced the thickness of the paper, were just scratches on it.

She had heard of books being defaced with pencil, with ink, with crayon, something visible at least – but with an improvised stylus that just left slits? On the other hand, what was there in this junky novel important enough to be emphasized – if that was why it had been done?

She began to read the page, to try to get some connected meaning out of the words that had been underscored. It was just a lot of senseless drivel about the heroine who was being entertained on the villain's yacht. It couldn't have been done for emphasis, then, of that Prudence was positive.

But she had the type of mind that, once something aroused its curiosity, couldn't rest again until the matter had been solved. If she couldn't remember a certain name, for instance, the agonizing feeling of having it on the tip of her tongue but being unable to bring it out would keep her from getting any sleep until the name had come back to her.

This now took hold of her in the same way. Failing to get anything out of the entire text, she began to see if she could get something out of the gashed words in themselves. Maybe that was where the explanation lay. She took a pencil and paper and began to transcribe them one by one, in the same order in which they came in the book. She got:

hardly anyone going invited merrily

Before she could go any farther than that, the lunch period was over, it was time to report down to her desk again.

She decided she was going to take the book home with her that night and keep working on it until she got something out of it. This was simply a matter of self-defense; she wouldn't be getting any sleep until she did. She put it away in her locker, returned downstairs to duty, and put the money with which she was paying Mrs Trasker's fine into the till. That was the woman's name, Mrs Trasker.

The afternoon passed as uneventfully as a hundred others had before it, but her mind kept returning to the enigma at intervals. "There's a reason for everything in this world," she insisted to herself, "and I want to know the reason for this: why were certain words in this utterly unmemorable novel underscored by slashes as though they were Holy Writ or something? And I'm going to find out if it takes me all the rest of this summer!"

She smuggled the book out with her when she left for home, trying to keep it hidden so the other members of the staff wouldn't notice. Not that she would have been refused permission if she had asked for it, but she would have had to give her reasons for wanting to take it, and she was afraid they would all laugh at her or think she was becoming touched in the head if she told them. After all, she excused herself, if she could find out the meaning of what had been done, that might help the library to discover who the guilty party really was and recover damages, and she could get back her own money that she had put in for poor Mrs Trasker.

Prudence hurried up her meal as much as possible, and returned to her room. She took a soft pencil and lightly went over the slits in the paper, to make them stand out more clearly. It would be easy enough to erase the pencil marks later. But almost as soon as she had finished and could get a comprehensive view of the whole page at a glance, she saw there was something wrong. The underscorings weren't flush with some of the words. Sometimes they only took in half a word, carried across the intervening space, and then took in half of the next. One of them even fell where there was absolutely no word at all over it, in the blank space between two paragraphs.

That gave her the answer; she saw in a flash what her mistake was. She'd been wasting her time on the wrong page. It was the leaf before, the missing Page 41, that had held the real meaning of the slashed words. The sharp instrument used on it had simply carried through to the leaf under it, and even, very lightly, to the third one following. No wonder the scorings overlapped and she hadn't been able to make sense out of them! Their real sense, if any, lay on the page that had been removed.

Well, she'd wasted enough time on it. It probably wasn't anything anyway. She tossed the book contemptuously aside, made up her mind that was the end of it. A moment or so later her eyes strayed irresistibly, longingly over to it again. "I know how I *could* find out for sure," she tempted herself.

Suddenly she was putting on her things again to go out. To go out and do something she had never done before: buy a trashy, frothy novel. Her courage almost failed her outside the bookstore window, where she finally located a copy, along with bridge sets, ash trays, statuettes of Dopey, and other gew-gaws. If it had only had a less . . . er . . . compromising title. She set her chin, took a deep breath, and plunged in.

"I want a copy of *Manuela Gets Her Man*, please," she said, flushing a little.

The clerk was one of these brazen blonds painted up like an Iroquios. She took in Prudence's shell-rimmed glasses, knot of hair, drab clothing. She smirked a little, as if to say "So you're finally getting wise to yourself?" Prudence Roberts gave her two dollars, almost ran out of the store with her purchase, cheeks flaming with embarrassment.

She opened it the minute she got in and avidly scanned Page 41. There wasn't anything on it, in itself, of more consequence than there had been on any of the other pages, but that wasn't stopping her this time. This thing had now cost her over three dollars of her hard-earned money, and she was going to get something out of it.

She committed an act of vandalism for the first time in her life, even though the book was her own property and not the city's. She ripped Pages 41 and 42 neatly out of the binding, just as the leaf had been torn from the other book. Then she inserted it in the first book, the original one. Not *over* Page 43, where it belonged, but under it. She found a piece of carbon paper, cut it down to size, and slipped that between the two. Then she fastened the three sheets together with paper clips, carefully seeing to it that the borders of the two printed pages didn't vary by a hair's breadth. Then she took her pencil and once more traced the gashes on Page 43, but this time bore down heavily on them. When she had finished, she withdrew the loose Page 41 from under the carbon and she had a haphazard array of underlined words sprinkled over the page. The original ones from the missing page. Her eye traveled over them excitedly. Then her face dropped again. They didn't make sense any more than before. She opened the lower half of the window, balanced the book in her hand, resisted an impulse to toss it out then and there. She gave herself a fight talk instead. "I'm a librarian. I have more brains than whoever did this to this book, I don't care who they are! I can get out whatever meaning they put into it, if I just keep cool and keep at it." She closed the window, sat down once more.

She studied the carbon-scored page intently, and presently a belated flash of enlightenment followed. The very arrangement of the dashes showed her what her mistake had been this time. They were too symmetrical, each one had its complement one line directly under it. In other words they were really double, not single lines. Their vertical alignment didn't vary in the slightest. She should have noticed that right away. She saw what it was now. The words hadn't been merely underlined, they had been cut out of the page bodily by four gashes around each required one, two vertical, two horizontal, forming an oblong that contained the wanted word. What she had mistaken for dashes had been the top and bottom lines of these "boxes." The faint side lines she had overlooked entirely.

She canceled out every alternate line, beginning with the top one, and that should have given her the real kernel of the message. But again she was confronted with a meaningless jumble, scant as the residue of words was. She held her head distractedly as she took it in:

cure
wait
poor
honey to
grand
her
health
your
fifty
instructions

"The text around them is what's distracting me," she decided after a futile five or ten minutes of poring over them." Subconsciously I keep trying to read them in the order in which they appear on the page. Since they were taken bodily out of it, that arrangement was almost certainly not meant to be observed. It is, after all, the same principle as a jig-saw puzzle. I have the pieces now, all that remains is to put each one in the right place."

She took a small pair of nail scissors and carefully clipped out each boxed word, just as the unknown predecessor had whose footsteps she was trying to unearth. That done, she discarded the book entirely, in order to be hampered by it no longer. Then she took a blank piece of paper, placed all the little paper cut-outs on it, careful that they remained right side up, and milled them about with her finger, to be able to start from scratch.

"I'll begin with the word 'fifty' as the easiest entering wedge," she breathed absorbedly. "It is a numerical adjective, and therefore simply must modify one of those three nouns, according to all the rules of grammar." She separated it from the rest, set to work. Fifty health – no, the noun is in the singular. Fifty honey – no, again singular. Fifty instructions – yes, but it was an awkward combination, something about it didn't ring true, she wasn't quite satisfied with it. Fifty grand? That was it! It was grammatically incorrect, it wasn't a noun at all, but in slang it was used as one. She had often heard it herself, used by people who were slovenly in their speech. She set the two words apart, satisfied they belonged together.

"Now a noun, in any kind of a sentence at all," she murmured to herself, "has to be followed by a verb." There were only two to choose from. She tried them both. Fifty grand wait. Fifty grand cure. Elliptical, both. But that form of the verb had to take a preposition, and there was one there at hand: "to." She tried it that way. Fifty grand to wait. Fifty grand to cure. She chose the latter, and the personal pronoun fell into place almost automatically after it. Fifty grand to cure her. That was almost certainly it.

She had five out of the eleven words now. She had a verb, two adjectives, and three nouns left: wait, your, poor, honey, health instructions. But that personal pronoun already in place was a stumbling block, kept baffling her. It seemed to refer to some preceding proper name, it demanded one to make sense, and she didn't have any in her six remaining words. And then suddenly she saw that she did have. Honey. It was to be read as a term of endearment, not a substance made by bees.

The remaining words paired off almost as if magnetically drawn toward one another. Your honey, poor health, wait instructions. She shifted them about the basic nucleus she already had, trying them out before and after it, until, with a little minor rearranging, she had them satisfactorily in place.

your honey poor health fifty grand to cure her wait instructions

There it was at last. It couldn't be any more lucid than that. She had no mucilage at hand to paste the little paper oblongs down flat and hold them fast in the position she had so laboriously achieved. Instead she took a number of pins and skewered them to the blank sheets of paper. Then she sat back looking at them.

It was a ransom note. Even she, unworldly as she was, could tell that at a glance. Printed words cut bodily out of a book, to avoid the use of handwriting or typewriting that might be traced later. Then the telltale leaf with the gaps had been torn out and destroyed. But in their hurry they had overlooked one little thing, the slits had carried through to the next page. Or else they had thought it didn't matter, no one would be able to reconstruct the thing once the original page was gone. Well, she had.

There were still numerous questions left unanswered. To whom had the note been addressed? By whom? Whose "honey" was it? And why, with a heinous crime like kidnaping for ransom involved, had they taken the trouble to return the book at all? Why not just destroy it entirely and be done with it? The answer to that could very well be that the actual borrower – one of those names on the book's reference card – was someone who knew them, but wasn't aware what they were doing, what the book had been used for, hadn't been present when the message was concocted; had all unwittingly returned the book.

There was of course a question as to whether the message was genuine or simply some adolescent's practical joke, yet the trouble taken to evade the use of handwriting argued that it was anything but a joke. And the most important question of all was: should she go to the police about it? She answered that then and there, with a slow but determined *yes*!

It was well after eleven by now, and the thought of venturing out on the streets alone at such an hour, especially to and from a place like a police station, filled her timid soul with misgivings. She could ring up from here, but then they'd send someone around to question her most likely, and that would be even worse. What would the landlady and the rest of the roomers think of her, receiving a gentleman caller at such an hour, even if he was from the police? It looked so . . . er . . . rowdy.

She steeled herself to go to them in person, and it required a good deal of steeling and even a cup of hot tea, but finally she set out, book and transcribed message under her arm, also a large umbrella with which to defend herself if she were insulted on the way.

She was ashamed to ask anyone where the nearest precinct house was, but luckily she saw a pair of policemen walking along as if they were going off duty, and by following them at a discreet distance, she finally saw them turn and go into a building that had a pair of green lights outside the entrance. She walked past it four times, twice in each direction, before she finally got up nerve enough to go in.

There was a uniformed man sitting at a desk near the entrance and she edged over and stood waiting for him to look up at her. He didn't, he was busy with some kind of report, so after standing there a minute or two, she cleared her throat timidly.

"Well, lady?" he said in a stentorian voice that made her jump and draw back.

"Could I speak to a . . . a detective, please?" she faltered.

"Any particular one?"

"A good one."

He said to a cop standing over by the door: "Go and tell Murph there's a young lady out here wants to see him."

A square-shouldered, husky young man came out a minute later, hopefully straightening the knot of his tie and looking around as if he expected to see a Fifth Avenue model at the very least. His gaze fell on Prudence, skipped over her, came up against the blank walls beyond her, and then had to return to her again.

"You the one?" he asked a little disappointedly.

"Could I talk to you privately?" she said. "I believe I have made a discovery of the greatest importance."

"Why . . . uh . . . sure," he said, without too much enthusiasm. "Right this way." But as he turned to follow her inside, he slurred something out of the corner of his mouth at the smirking desk sergeant that sounded suspiciously like "I'll fix you for this, kibitzer. It couldn't have been Dolan instead, could it?"

He snapped on a cone light in a small office toward the back, motioned Prudence to a chair, leaned against the edge of the desk.

She was slightly flustered; she had never been in a police station before. "Has . . . er . . . anyone been kidnaped lately, that is to say within the past six weeks?" she blurted out.

He folded his arms, flipped his hands up and down against his own sides, "Why?" he asked noncommitally.

"Well, one of our books came back damaged today, and I think I've deciphered a kidnap message from its pages."

Put baldly like that, it did sound sort of far-fetched, she had to admit that herself. Still, he should have at least given her time to explain more fully, not acted like a jackass just because she was prim-looking and wore thick-lensed glasses.

His face reddened and his mouth started to quiver treacherously. He put one hand up over it to hide it from her, but he couldn't keep his shoulders from shaking. Finally he had to turn away altogether and stand in front of the water cooler a minute. Something that sounded like a strangled cough came from him.

"You're laughing at me!" she snapped accusingly. "I come here to help you, and that's the thanks I get!"

He turned around again with a carefully straightened face. "No, ma'am," he lied cheerfully right to her face, "I'm not laughing at you. I . . . we . . . appreciate your co-operation. You leave this here and we . . . we'll check on it."

But Prudence Roberts was nobody's fool. Besides, he had ruffled her plumage now, and once that was done, it took a great deal to smooth it down again. She had a highly developed sense of her own dignity. "You haven't the slightest idea of doing anything of the kind!" she let him know. "I can tell that just by looking at you! I must say I'm very surprised that a member of the police department of this city –"

She was so steamed up and exasperated at his facetious attitude, that she removed her glasses, in order to be able to give him a piece of her mind more clearly. A little thing like that shouldn't have made the slightest difference – after all this was police business, not a beauty contest – but to her surprise it seemed to.

He looked at her, blinked, looked at her again, suddenly began to show a great deal more interest in what she had come here to tell him. "What'd you say your name was again, miss?" he asked, and absently made that gesture to the knot of his tie again.

She hadn't said what it was in the first place. Why, this man was just a common – a common masher; he was a disgrace to the shield he wore. "I am Miss Roberts of the Hillcrest Branch of the Public Library," she said stiffly. "What has that to do with this?"

"Well . . . er . . . we have to know the source of our information," he told her lamely. He picked up the book, thumbed through it, then he scanned the message she had deciphered. "Yeah" – Murphy nodded slowly – "that does read like a ransom note."

Mollified, she explained rapidly the process by which she had built up from the gashes on the succeeding leaf of the book.

"Just a minute, Miss Roberts," he said, when she had finished. "I'll take this in and show it to the lieutenant."

But when he came back, she could tell by his attitude that this superior didn't take any more stock in it than he had himself. "I tried to explain to him the process by which you extracted it out of the book, but . . . er . . . in his opinion it's just a coincidence, I mean the gashes may not have any meaning at all. F'r instance, someone may have been just cutting something out on top of the book, cookies or pie crust and –"

She snorted in outrage. "Cookies or pie crust! I got a coherent message. If you men can't see it there in front of your eyes –"

"But here's the thing, Miss Roberts," he tried to soothe her. "We haven't any case on deck right now that this could possibly fit into. No one's been reported missing. And we'd know, wouldn't we? I've heard of kidnap cases without ransom notes, but I never heard of a ransom note without a kidnap case to go with it."

"As a police officer doesn't it occur to you that in some instances a kidnaped persons' relatives would purposely refrain from notifying the authorities to avoid jeopardizing their loved ones? That may have happened in this case."

"I mentioned that to the lieutenant myself, but he claims it can't be done. There are cases where we purposely hold off at the request of the family until after the victim's been returned, but it's never because we haven't been informed what's going on. You see, a certain length of time always elapses between the snatch itself and the first contact between the kidnapers and the family, and no matter how short that is, the family has almost always reported the person missing in the meantime, before they know what's up themselves. I can check with Missing Persons if you want, but if it's anything more than just a straight disappearance, they always turn it over to us right away, anyway."

But Prudence didn't intend urging or begging them to look into it as a personal favor to her. She considered she'd done more than her duty. If they discredited it, they discredited it. *She* didn't, and she made up her mind to pursue the investigation, single-handed and without their help if necessary, until she had settled it one way or the other. "Very well," she said coldly, "I'll leave the transcribed message and the extra copy of the book here with you. I'm sorry I bothered you. Good evening." She stalked out, still having forgotten to replace her glasses.

Her indignation carried her as far as the station-house steps, and then her courage began to falter. It was past midnight by now, and the streets looked so lonely; suppose – suppose she met a drunk? While she was standing there trying to get up her nerve, this same Murphy came out behind her, evidently on his way home himself. She had put her glasses on again by now.

"You look a lot different without them," he remarked lamely, stopping a step below her and hanging around.

"Indeed," she said forbiddingly.

"I'm going off duty now. Could I . . . uh . . . see you to where you live?"

She would have preferred not to have to accept the offer, but those shadows down the street looked awfully deep and the light posts awfully far apart. "I *am* a little nervous about being out alone so late," she admitted, starting out beside him. "Once I met a drunk and he said, 'H'lo, babe.' I had to drink a cup of hot tea when I got home, I was so upset."

"Did you have your glasses on?" he asked cryptically.

"No. Come to think of it, that was the time I'd left them to be repaired."

He just nodded knowingly, as though that explained everything.

When they got to her door, he said: "Well, I'll do some more digging through the files on that thing, just to make sure. If I turn up anything . . . uh . . . suppose I drop around tomorrow night and let you know. And if I don't, I'll drop around and let you know that too. Just so you'll know what's what."

"That's very considerate of you."

"Gee, you're refined," he said wistfully. "You talk such good English."

He seemed not averse to lingering on here talking to her, but someone might have looked out of one of the windows and it would appear so unrefined to be seen dallying there at that hour, so she turned and hurried inside.

When she got to her room, she looked at herself in the mirror. Then she took her glasses off and tried it that way. "How peculiar," she murmured. "How very unaccountable!"

The following day at the library she got out the reference card on *Manuela Gets Her Man* and studied it carefully. It had been out six times in the six weeks it had been in stock. The record went like this:

Doyle, Helen (address)	Apr. 15-Apr. 22
Caine, Rose	Apr. 22-Apr. 29
Dermuth, Alvin	Apr. 29-May 6
Turner, Florence	May 6-May 18
Baumgarten, Lucille	May 18-May 25
Trasker, Sophie	May 25-June 3

Being a new book, it had had a quick turnover, had been taken out again each time the same day it had been brought back. Twice it had been kept out overtime, the first time nearly a whole week beyond the return limit. There might be something in that. All the borrowers but one, so far, were women; that was another noticeable fact. It was, after all, a woman's book. Her library experience had taught her that what is called a "man's book" will often be read by women, but a "woman's book" is abolutely never, and there are few exceptions to this rule, read by men. That might mean something, that lone male borrower. She must have seen him at the time, but so many faces passed her desk daily she couldn't remember what he was like any more, if she had. However, she decided not to jump to hasty conclusions, but investigate the list one by one in reverse order. She'd show that ignorant, skirt-chasing Murphy person that where there's smoke there's fire, if you only take the trouble to look for it!

At about eight thirty, just as she was about to start out on her quest – she could only pursue it in the evenings, of course, after library hours – the doorbell rang and she found him standing there. He looked disappointed when he saw that she had her glasses on. He came in rather shyly and clumsily, tripping over the threshold and careening several steps down the hall.

"Were you able to find out anything?" she asked eagerly.

"Nope, I checked again, I went all the way back six months, and I also got in touch with Missing Persons. Nothing doing, I'm afraid it isn't a genuine message, Miss Roberts; just a fluke, like the lieutenant says."

"I'm sorry, but I don't agree with you. I've copied a list of the borrowers and I intend to investigate each one of them in turn. That message was not intended to be readily deciphered, or for that matter deciphered at all; therefore it is not a practical joke or some adolescent's prank. Yet it has a terrible coherence; therefore it is not a fluke or a haphazard scarring of the page, your lieutenant to the contrary. What remains? It is a genuine ransom note, sent in deadly earnest, and I should think you and your sup-superiors would be the first to –"

"Miss Roberts," he said soulfully, "you're too refined to . . . to dabble in crime like this. Somehow it don't seem right for you to be talking shop, about kidnapings and –" He eased his collar. "I . . . uh . . . it's my night off and I was wondering if you'd like to go to the movies."

"So that's why you took the trouble of coming around!" she said indignantly. "I'm afraid your interest is entirely too personal and not nearly official enough!"

"Gee, even when you talk fast," he said admiringly, "you pronounce every word clear, like in a po-em."

"Well, you don't. It's poem, not po-em. I intend going ahead with this until I can find out just what the meaning of that message is, and who sent it! And I *don't* go to movies with people the second time I've met them!"

He didn't seem at all fazed. "Could I drop around sometime and find out how you're getting along?" he wanted to know, as he edged through the door backward.

"That will be entirely superfluous," she said icily. "If I uncover anything suspicious, I shall of course report it promptly. It is not my job, after all . . . but . . . ahem . . . other people's."

"Movies! The idea!" She frowned after she had closed the door on him. Then she dropped her eyes and pondered a minute. "It would have been sort of frisky, at that." She smiled.

She took the book along with her as an excuse for calling, and set out, very determined on the surface, as timid as usual underneath. However, she found it easier to get started because the first name on the list, the meek Mrs Trasker, held no terror even for her. She was almost sure she was innocent, because it was she herself who had called the library's attention to the missing page in the first place, and a guilty person would hardly do that. Still there was always a possibility it was someone else in her family or household, and she meant to be thorough about this if nothing else.

Mrs Trasker's address was a small old-fashioned apartment building of the pre-War variety. It was not expensive by any means, but still it did seem beyond the means of a person who had been unable to pay even a two-dollar fine, and for a moment Prudence thought she scented suspicion in this. But as soon as she entered the lobby and asked for Mrs Trasker, the mystery was explained.

"You'll have to go to the basement for her," the elevator boy told her, "she's the janitress."

A young girl of seventeen admitted her at the basement entrance and led her down a bare brick passage past rows of empty trash cans to the living quarters in the back.

Mrs Trasker was sitting propped up in bed, and again showed a little alarm at sight of the librarian, a person in authority. An open book on a chair beside her showed that her daughter had been reading aloud to her when they were interrupted.

"Don't be afraid," Prudence reassured them. "I just want to ask a few questions."

"Sure, anything, missis," said the janitress, clasping and unclasping her hands placatingly.

"Just the two of you live here? No father or brothers?"

"Just mom and me, nobody else," the girl answered.

"Now tell me, are you sure you didn't take the book out with you anywhere, to some friend's house, or lend it to someone else?"

"No, no, it stayed right here!" They both said it together and vehemently.

"Well, then, did anyone call on you down here, while it was in the rooms?"

The mother answered this. "No, no one. When the tenants want me for anything, they ring down for me from upstairs. And when I'm working around the house, I keep our place locked just like anyone does their apartment. So I know no one was near the book while we had it."

"I feel pretty sure of that myself," Prudience said, as she got up to go. She patted Mrs Trasker's toil-worn hand reassuringly. "Just forget about my coming here like this. Your fine is paid and there's nothing to worry about. See you at the library."

The next name on the reference card was Lucille Baumgarten. Prudence was emboldened to stop in there because she noticed the address, though fairly nearby, in the same branch-library district, was in a higher-class neighborhood. Besides, she was beginning to forget her timidity in the newly awaked interest her quest was arousing in her. It occurred to her for the first time that detectives must lead fairly interesting lives.

A glance at the imposing, almost palatial apartment building Borrower Baumgarten lived in told her this place could probably be crossed off her list of suspects as well. Though she had heard vaguely somewhere or other that gangsters and criminals sometimes lived in luxurious surroundings, these were more than that. These spelled solid, substantial wealth and respectability that couldn't be faked. She had to state her name and business to a uniformed houseman in the lobby before she was even allowed to go up.

"Just tell Miss Baumgarten the librarian from her branch library would like to talk to her a minute."

A maid opened the upstairs door, but before she could open her mouth, a girl slightly younger than Mrs Trasker's daughter had come skidding down the parquet hall, swept her aside, and displaced her. She was about fifteen at the most and really had no business borrowing from the adult department yet. Prudence vaguely recalled seeing her face before, although then it had been liberally rouged and lipsticked, whereas now it was properly without cosmetics.

She put a finger to her lips and whispered conspiratorially, "Sh! Don't tell my –"

Before she could get any further, there was a firm tread behind her and she was displaced in turn by a stout matronly lady wearing more diamonds than Prudence had ever seen before outside of a jewelry-store window.

"I've just come to check up on this book which was returned to us in a damaged condition," Prudence explained. "Our record shows that Miss Lucille Baumgarten had it out between –"

"Lucille?" gasped the bediamoned lady. "Lucille? There's no

Lucille –" She broke off short and glanced at her daughter, who vainly tried to duck out between the two of them and shrink away unnoticed. "Oh, so that's it!" she said, suddenly enlightened. "So Leah isn't good enough for you any more!"

Prudence addressed her offspring, since it was obvious that the mother was in the dark about more things than just the book. "Miss Baumgarten, I'd like you to tell me whether there was a page missing when you brought the book home with you." And then she added craftily: "It was borrowed again afterward by several other subscribers, but I haven't got around to them yet." If the girl was guilty, she would use this as an out and claim the page had still been in, implying it had been taken out afterward by someone else. Prudence knew it hadn't, of course.

But Lucille-Leah admitted unhesitatingly: "Yes, there was a page or two missing, but it didn't spoil the fun much, because I could tell what happened after I read on a little bit." Nothing seemed to hold any terrors for her, compared to the parental wrath brewing in the heaving bosom that wedged her in inextricably.

"Did you lend it to anyone else, or take it out of the house with you at any time, while you were in possession of it?"

The girl rolled her eyes meaningly. "I should say not! I kept it hidden in the bottom drawer of my bureau the whole time; and now you had to come around here and give me away!"

"Thank you," said Prudence, and turned to go. This place was definitely off her list too, as she had felt it would be even before the interview. People who lived in such surroundings didn't send kidnap notes or associate with people who did.

The door had closed, but Mrs Baumgarten's shrill, punitive tones sounded all too clearly through it while Prudence stood there waiting for the elevator to take her down. "I'll *give* you Lucille! Wait'll your father hears about this! I'll give you such a *frass*, you won't know whether you're Lucille or Gwendolyn!" punctuated by a loud, popping slap on youthful epidermis.

The next name on the list was Florence Turner. It was already well after ten by now, and for a moment Prudence was tempted to go home, and put off the next interview until the following night. She discarded the temptation resolutely. "Don't be such a 'fraid-cat," she lectured herself. "Nothing's happened to you so far, and nothing's likely to happen hereafter either." And then too, without knowing it, she was already prejudiced; in the back of her mind all along there lurked the suspicion that the lone male borrower, Dermuth, was the one to watch out for. He was next but one on the list, in reverse order. As long as she was out, she would interview Florence Turner, who was probably harmless, and then tackle Dermuth good and early tomorrow night –

and see to it that a policeman waited for her outside his door so she'd be sure of getting out again unharmed.

The address listed for Library Member Turner was not at first sight exactly prepossessing, when she located it. It was a rooming house, or rather that newer variation of one called a "residence club," which has sprung up in the larger cities within the past few years, in which the rooms are grouped into detached little apartments. Possibly it was the sight of the chop-suey place that occupied the ground floor that gave it its unsavory aspect in her eyes; she had peculiar notions about some things.

Nevertheless, now that she had come this far, she wasn't going to let a chop-suey restaurant frighten her away without completing her mission. She tightened the book under her arm, took a good deep breath to ward off possible hatchet men and opium smokers, and marched into the building, whose entrance adjoined that of the restaurant.

She rang the manager's bell and a blowsy-looking, middle-aged woman came out and met her at the foot of the stairs. "Yes?" she said gruffly.

"Have you a Florence Turner living here?"

"No. We did have, but she left."

"Have you any idea where I could reach her?"

"She left very suddenly, didn't say where she was going."

"About how long ago did she leave, could you tell me?"

"Let's see now." The woman did some complicated mental calculation. "Two weeks ago Monday, I think it was. That would bring it to the 17th. Yes, that's it, May 17th."

Here was a small mystery already. The book hadn't been returned until the 18th. The woman's memory might be at fault, of course. "If you say she left in a hurry, how is it she found time to return this book to us?"

The woman glanced at it. "Oh, no, I was the one returned that for her," she explained. "My cleaning maid found it in her room the next morning after she was gone, along with a lot of other stuff she left behind her. I saw it was a liberry book, so I sent Beulah over with it, so's it wouldn't roll up a big fine for her. I'm economical that way. How'd you happen to get hold of it?" she asked in surprise.

"I work at the library," Prudence explained. "I wanted to see her about this book. One of the pages was torn out." She knew enough not to confide any more than that about what her real object was.

"Gee, aren't you people fussy," marveled the manager.

"Well, you see, it's taken out of my salary," prevaricated Prudence, trying to strike a note she felt the other might understand.

"Oh, that's different. No wonder you're anxious to locate her. Well, all I know is she didn't expect to go when she did; she even paid for her room ahead, I been holding it for her ever since, till the time's up. I'm conshenshus that way."

"That's strange," Prudence mused aloud. "I wonder what could have –"

"I think someone got took sick in her family," confided the manager. "Some friends or relatives, I don't know who they was, called for her in a car late at night and off she went in a rush. I just wanted to be sure it wasn't no one who hadn't paid up yet, so I opened my door and looked out."

Prudence picked up her ears. That fatal curiosity of hers was driving her on like a spur. She had suddenly forgotten all about being leery of the nefarious chop-suey den on the premises. She was starting to tingle all over, and tried not to show it. Had she unearthed something at last, or wasn't it anything at all? "You say she left some belongings behind? Do you think she'll be back for them?"

"No, she won't be back herself, I don't believe. But she did ask me to keep them for her; she said she'd send someone around to get them as soon as she was able."

Prudence suddenly decided she'd give almost anything to be able to get a look at the things this Turner girl had left behind her; why, she wasn't quite sure herself. They might help her to form an idea of what their owner was like. She couldn't ask openly; the woman might suspect her of trying to steal something. "When will her room be available?" She asked offhandedly. "I'm thinking of moving, and as long as I'm here, I was wondering –"

"Come on up and I'll show it to you right now," offered the manager with alacrity. She evidently considered librarians superior to the average run of tenants she got.

Prudence followed her up the stairs, incredulous at her own effrontery. This didn't seem a bit like her; she wondered what had come over her.

"Murphy should see me now!" she gloated.

The manager unlocked a door on the second floor.

"It's real nice in the daytime," she said. "And I can turn it over to you day after tomorrow."

"Is the closet good and deep?" asked Prudence, noting its locked doors.

"I'll show you." The woman took out a key, opened it unsuspectingly for her approval.

"My," said the subtle Prudence," she left lots of things behind!"

"And some of them are real good too," agreed the landlady. "I don't know how they do it, on just a hat check girl's tips. And she even gave that up six months ago."

"Hm-m-m," said Prudence absently, deftly edging a silver slipper she noted standing on the floor up against one of another pair, with the tip of her own foot. She looked down covertly; with their heels in true with one another, there was an inch difference in the toes. Two different sizes! She absently fingered the lining of one of the frocks hanging up, noted its size tag. A 34. "Such exquisite things," she murmured, to cover up what she was doing. Three hangers over there was another frock. Size 28.

"Did she have anyone else living here with her?" she asked.

The manager locked the closet, pocketed the key once more. "No. These two men friends or relatives of hers used to visit with her a good deal, but they never made a sound and they never came one at a time, so I didn't raise any objections. Now, I have another room, nearly as nice, just down the hall I could show you."

"I wish there were some way in which you could notify me when someone does call for her things," said Prudence, who was getting better as she went along. "I'm terribly anxious to get in touch with her. You see, it's not only the fine, it might even cost me my job."

"Sure I know how it is," said the manager sympathetically. "Well, I could ask whoever she sends to leave word where you can reach her."

"No, don't do that!" said Prudence hastily. "I'm afraid they . . . er . . . I'd prefer if you didn't mention I was here asking about her at all."

"Anything you say," said the manager amenably. "If you'll leave your number with me, I could give you a ring and let you know whenever the person shows up."

"I'm afraid I wouldn't get over here in time; they might be gone by the time I got here."

The manager tapped her teeth helpfully. "Why don't you take one of my rooms then? That way you'd be right on the spot when they do show up."

"Yes, but suppose they come in the daytime? I'd be at the library, and I can't leave my job."

"I don't think they'll come in the daytime. Most of her friends and the people she went with were up and around at night, more than in the daytime."

The idea appealed to Prudence, although only a short while before she would have been aghast at the thought of moving into such a place. She made up her mind quickly without giving herself time to stop and get cold feet. It might be a wild-goose chase, but she'd never yet heard of a woman who wore two different sizes in dresses like this Florence Turner seemed to. "All right, I will," she decided, "if you'll promise two things. To let me know without fail the minute someone comes to get her things, and not to say a word to them about my coming here and asking about her."

"Why not?" said the manager accommodatingly. "Anything to earn an honest dollar?"

But when the door of her new abode closed on her, a good deal of her new-found courage evaporated. She sat down limply on the edge of the bed and stared in bewilderment at her reflection in the cheap dresser mirror. "I must be crazy to do a thing like this!" she gasped. "What's come over me anyway?" She didn't even have her teapot with her to brew a cup of the fortifying liquid. There was nothing the matter with the room in itself, but that sinister Oriental den downstairs had a lurid red tube sign just under her window and its glare winked malevolently in at her. She imagined felt-slippered hirelings of some Fu-Manchu creeping up the stairs to snatch her bodily from her bed. It was nearly daylight before she could close her eyes. But so far as the room across the hall was concerned, as might have been expected, no one showed up.

Next day at the library, between book returns, Prudence took out the reference card on Manuela and placed a neat red check next to Mrs Trasker's name and Lucille Baumgarten's, to mark the progress of her investigation so far. But she didn't need this; it was easy enough to remember whom she had been to see and whom she hadn't, but she had the precise type of mind that like everything neatly docketed and in order. Next to Florence Turner's name she placed a small red question mark.

She was strongly tempted to call up Murphy on her way home that evening, and tell him she already felt she was on the trail of something. But for one thing, nothing definite enough had developed yet. If he'd laughed at her about the original message itself, imagine how he'd roar if she told him the sum total of her suspicions was based on the fact that a certain party had two different-sized dresses in her clothes closet. And secondly, even in her new state of emancipation, it still seemed awfully forward to call a man up, even a detective. She would track down this Florence Turner first, and then she'd call Murphy up if her findings warranted it. "And if he says I'm good, and asks me to go to the movies with him," she threatened, "I'll . . . I'll make him ask two or three times before I do!"

She met the manager on her way in. "Did anyone come yet?" she asked in an undertone.

"No. I'll keep my promise. I'll let you know; don't worry."

A lot of the strangeness had already worn off her new surroundings, even after sleeping there just one night, and it occurred to her that maybe she had been in a rut, should have changed living quarters more often in the past. She went to bed shortly after ten, and even the Chinese restaurant sign had no power to keep her awake tonight; she fell asleep almost at once, tired from the night before.

About an hour or so later, she had no way of telling how long afterward it was, a surreptitious tapping outside her door woke her. "Yes?" she called out forgetfully, in a loud voice.

The manager stuck her tousled head in.

"Shh!" she warned. "Somebody's come for her things. You asked me to tell you, and I've been coughing out there in the hall, trying to attract your attention. He just went down with the first armful; he'll be up again in a minute. You'd better hurry if you want to catch him before he goes; he's working fast."

"Don't say anything to him," Prudence whispered back. "See if you can delay him a minute or two, give me time to get downstairs."

"Are you sure it's just a liberry book this is all about?" the manager asked searchingly. "Here he comes up again." She pulled her head back and swiftly closed the door.

Prudence had never dressed so fast in her life before. Even so, she managed to find time to dart a glance down at the street from her window. There was a black sedan drawn up in front of the house. "How am I ever going to –" she thought in dismay. She didn't let that hold her up any. She made sure she had shoes on and a coat over her and let the rest go hang. There was no time to phone Murphy, even if she had wanted to, but the thought didn't occur to her.

She eased her room door open, flitted out into the hall and down the stairs, glimpsing the open door of Florence Turner's room as she sneaked by. She couldn't see the man, whoever he was, but she could hear the landlady saying, "Wait a minute, until I make sure you haven't left anything behind."

Prudence slipped out of the street door downstairs looked hopelessly up and down the street. He had evidently come alone in the car; there was no one else in it. He had piled the clothing on the back seat. For a moment she even thought of smuggling herself in and hiding under it, but that was too harebrained to be seriously considered. Then, just as she heard his tread start down the inside stairs behind her, the much-maligned chop-suey joint came to her aid. A cab drove up to it, stopped directly behind the first machine, and a young couple got out.

Prudence darted over, climbed in almost before they were out of the way.

"Where to, lady?" asked the driver.

She found it hard to come out with it, it sounded so unrespectable and fly-by-nightish. Detectives, she supposed, didn't think twice about giving an order like that, but with her it was different. "Er . . . would you mind just waiting a minute until that car in front of us leaves?" she said constrainedly. "Then take me wherever it goes."

He shot her a glance in his rear-sight mirror, but didn't say anything. He was probably used to getting stranger orders than that.

A man came out of the same doorway she had just left herself. She couldn't get a very good look at his face, but he had a batch of clothing slung over his arm. He dumped the apparel in the back of the sedan, got in himself, slammed the door closed, and started off. A moment later the cab was in motion as well.

"Moving out on ya, huh?" said the driver knowingly. "I don't blame ya for follying him."

"That will do," she said primly. This night life got you into more embarrassing situations! "Do you think you can manage it so he won't notice you coming after him?" she asked after a block or two.

"Leave it to me, lady," he promised, waving his hand at her. "I know this game backwards."

Presently they had turned into one of the circumferential express highways leading out of the city. "Now it's gonna be pie!" he exulted. "He won't be able to tell us from anyone else on here. Everyone going the same direction and no turning off."

The stream of traffic was fairly heavy for that hour of the night; homeward-bound suburbanites for the most part. But then, as the city limits were passed and branch road after branch road drained it off, it thinned to a mere trickle. The lead car finally turned off itself, and onto a practically deserted secondary highway.

"Now it's gonna be ticklish," the cabman admitted. "I'm gonna have to hang back as far as I can from him, or he'll tumble to us."

He let the other car pull away until it was merely a red dot in the distance. "You sure must be carryin' some torch," he said presently with a baffled shake of his head, "to come all the way out this far after him."

"Please confine yourself to your driving," was the haughty reproof.

The distant red pin point had suddenly snuffed out. "He must've turned off up ahead some place," said the driver, alarmed. "I better step it up!"

When they had reached the approximate place, minutes later, an even less-traveled bypass than the one they were on was revealed, not only lightless but even unsurfaced. It obviously didn't lead anywhere that the general public would have wanted to go, or it would have been better maintained. They braked forthwith.

"What a lonely-looking road." Prudence shuddered involuntarily.

"Y'wanna chuck it and turn back?" he suggested, as though he would have been only too willing to himself.

She probably would have if she'd been alone, but she hated to admit defeat in his presence. He'd probably laugh at her all the way back. "No, now that I've come this far, I'm not going back until I find out exactly where he went. Don't stand here like this: you won't be able to catch up with him again!"

The driver gave his cap a defiant hitch. "The time has come to tell you

I've got you clocked at seven bucks and eighty-five cents, and I didn't notice any pockybook in your hand when you got in. Where's it coming from?" He tapped his fingers sardonically on the rim of his wheel.

Prudence froze. Her handbag was exactly twenty or thirty miles away, back in her room at the residence club. She didn't have to answer; the driver was an old experienced hand at this sort of thing; he could read the signs.

"I thought so," he said, almost resignedly. He got down, opened the door. "Outside," he said. "If you was a man, I'd take it out of your jaw. Or if there was a cop anywhere within five miles, I'd have you run in. Take off that coat." He looked it over, slung it over his arm. "It'll have to do. Now if you want it back, you know what to do; just look me up with seven-eighty-five in your mitt. And for being so smart, you're gonna walk all the way back from here on your two little puppies."

"Don't leave me all alone, in the dark, in this God-forsaken place! I don't even know where I am!" she wailed after him.

"I'll tell you where you are," he called back remorselessly. "You're on your own!" The cab's taillight went streaking obliviously back the way they had just come.

She held the side of her head and looked helplessly all around her. Real detectives didn't run into these predicaments, she felt sure. It only happened to her! "Oh, why didn't I just mind my own business back at the library!" she lamented.

It was too cool out here in the wilds to stand still without a coat on, even though it was June. She might stand waiting here all night and no other machine would come along. The only thing to do was to keep walking until she came to a house, and then ask to use the telephone. There must be a house somewhere around here.

She started in along the bypath the first car had taken, gloomy and forbidding as it was, because it seemed more likely there was a house some place farther along it, than out on this other one. They hadn't passed a single dwelling the whole time the cab was on the road, and she didn't want to walk still farther out along it; no telling where it led to. The man she'd been following must have had *some* destination. Even if she struck the very house he had gone to, there wouldn't really be much harm to it, because he didn't know who she was, he'd never seen her before. Neither had this Florence Turner, if she was there with him. She could just say she'd lost her way or something. Anyone would have looked good to her just then, out here alone in the dark the way she was.

If she'd been skittish of shadows on the city streets, there was reason enough for her to have St. Vitus's dance here; it was nothing *but* shadows. Once she came in sight of a little clearing, with a scarecrow fluttering at the far side of it, and nearly had heart failure for a minute.

Another time an owl went "Who-o-o" up in a tree over her, and she ran about twenty yards before she could pull herself together and stop again. "Oh, if I ever get back to the nice safe library after tonight, I'll never –" she sobbed nervously.

The only reason she kept going on now was because she was afraid to turn back any more. Maybe that hadn't been a scarecrow after all –

The place was so set back from the road, so half hidden amidst the shrubbery, that she had almost passed it by before she even saw it there. She happened to glance to her right as she came to a break in the trees, and there was the unmistakable shadowy outline of a decrepit house. Not a chink of light showed from it, at least from where she was. Wheel ruts unmistakably led in toward it over the grass and weeds, but she wasn't much of a hand at this sort of lore, couldn't tell if they'd been made recently or long ago. The whole place had an appearance of not being lived in.

It took nearly as much courage to turn aside and start over toward it as it would have to continue on the road. It was anything but what she'd been hoping for, and she knew already it was useless to expect to find a telephone in such a ramshackle wreck.

The closer she got to it, the less inviting it became. True, it was two or three in the morning by now, and even if anyone had been living in it, they probably would have been fast asleep by this time, but it didn't seem possible such a forlorn, neglected-looking place could be inhabited. Going up onto that ink-black porch and knocking for admittance took more nerve than she could muster. Heaven knows what she was liable to bring out on her; bats or rats or maybe some horrible hobos.

She decided she'd walk all around the outside of it just once, and if it didn't look any better from the sides and rear than it did from the front, she'd go back to the road and take her own chances on that some more. The side was no better than the front when she picked her way cautiously along it. Twigs snapped under her feet and little stones shifted, and made her heart miss a beat each time. But when she got around to the back, she saw two things at once that showed her she had been mistaken, there was someone in there after all. One was the car, the same car that had driven away in front of the residence club, standing at a little distance behind the house, under some kind of warped toolshed or something. The other was a slit of light showing around three sides of a ground-floor window. It wasn't a brightly lighted pane by any means; the whole window still showed black under some kind of sacking or heavy covering; there was just this telltale yellow seam outlining three sides of it if you looked closely enough.

Before she could decide what to do about it, if anything, her gaze traveled a little higher up the side of the house and she saw something else that brought her heart up into her throat. She choked back an inadvertent scream just in time. It was a face. A round white face staring down at her from one of the upper windows, dimly visible behind the dusty pane.

Prudence Roberts started to back away apprehensively a step at a time, staring up at it spellbound as she did so, and ready at any moment to turn and run for her life, away from whomever or whatever that was up there. But before she could carry out the impulse, she saw something else that changed her mind, rooted her to the spot. Two wavering white hands had appeared, just under the ghost-like face. They were making signs to her, desperate, pleading signs. They beckoned her nearer, then they clasped together imploringly, as if trying to say, "Don't go away, don't leave me."

Prudence drew a little nearer again. The hands were warning her to silence now, one pointing downward toward the floor below, the other holding a cautioning finger to their owner's mouth.

It was a young girl; Prudence could make out that much, but most of the pantomime was lost through the blurred dust-caked pane. She gestured back to her with upcurved fingers, meaning, "Open the window so I can hear you."

It took the girl a long time. The window was either fastened in some way or warped from lack of use, or else it stuck just because she was trying to do it without making any noise. The sash finally jarred up a short distance, with an alarming creaking and grating in spite of her best efforts. Or at least it seemed so in the preternatural stillness that reigned about the place. They both held their breaths for a wary moment, as if by mutual understanding.

Then as Prudence moved in still closer under the window, a faint sibilance came down to her from the narrow opening.

"Please take me away from here. Oh, please help me to get away from here."

"What's the matter?" Prudence whispered back.

Both alike were afraid to use too much breath even to whisper, it was so quiet outside the house. It was hard for them to make themselves understood. She missed most of the other's answer, all but:

"They won't let me go. I think they're going to kill me. They haven't given me anything to eat in two whole days now."

Prudence inhaled fearfully. "Can you climb out through there and let yourself drop from the sill? I'll get a seat cover from that car and put it under you."

"I'm chained to the bed up here. I've pulled it over little by little to the window. Oh, please hurry and bring someone back with you; that's the only way –"

Prudence nodded in agreement, made hasty encouraging signs as she started to draw away. "I'll run all the way back to where the two roads meet, and stop the first car that comes al –"

Suddenly she froze, and at the same instant seemed to light up yellowly from head to foot, like a sort of living torch. A great fan of light spread out from the doorway before her, and in the middle of it a wavering shadow began to lengthen toward her along the ground.

"Come in, sweetheart, and stay a while," a man's voice said slurringly. He sauntered out toward her with lithe, springy determination. Behind him in the doorway were another man and a woman.

"Naw, don't be bashful," he went on, moving around in back of her and prodding her toward the house with his gun. "You ain't going on nowheres else from here. You've reached your final destination."

A well-dressed, middle-aged man was sitting beside the lieutenant's desk, forearm supporting his head, shading his eyes with outstretched fingers, when Murphy and every other man jack available came piling in, responding to the urgent summons.

The lieutenant had three desk phones going at once, and still found time to say, "Close that door, I don't want a word of this to get out," to the last man in. He hung up – *click, click, clack* – speared a shaking finger at the operatives forming into line before him.

"This is Mr Martin Rapf, men," he said tensely. "I won't ask him to repeat what he's just said to me; he's not in any condition to talk right now. His young daughter, Virginia, left home on the night of May 17th and she hasn't been seen since. He and Mrs Rapf received an anonymous telephone call that same night, before they'd even had time to become alarmed at her absence, informing them not to expect her back and warning them above all not to report her missing to us. Late the next day Mr Rapf received a ransom note demanding fifty thousand dollars. This is it here."

Everyone in the room fastened their eyes on it as he spun it around on his desk to face them. At first sight it seemed to be a telegram. It was an actual telegraph blank form, taken from some office pad, with strips of paper containing printed words pasted on it.

"It wasn't filed, of course; it was slipped under the front door in an unaddressed envelope," the lieutenant went on. "The instructions didn't come for two more days, by telephone again. Mr Rapf had raised the amount and was waiting for them. They were rather amateurish, to say the least. And amateurs are more to be dreaded than professionals at this sort of thing, as you men well know. He was to bring the money along in a cigar box, he was to go all the way out to a certain seldom-used suburban crossroads, and wait there. Then when a closed car with its rear windows down drove slowly by and sounded its horn three times, two short ones and a long one, he was to pitch the cigar box in the back of it through the open window and go home.

"In about a quarter of an hour a closed car with its windows down came along fairly slowly. Mr Rapf was too concerned about his daughter's safety even to risk memorizing the numerals on its license plates, which were plainly exposed to view. A truck going crosswise to it threatened to block it at the intersection, and it gave three blasts of its horn, two short ones and a long one. Mr Rapf threw the cigar box in through its rear window and watched it pick up speed and drive away. He was too excited and overwrought to start back immediately, and in less than five minutes, while he was still there, a second car came along with its windows down and its license plates removed. It gave three blasts of its horn, without there being any obstruction ahead. He ran out toward it to try and explain, but only succeeded in frightening it off. It put on speed and got away from him. I don't know whether it was actually a ghastly coincidence, or whether an unspeakable trick was perpetrated on him, to get twice the amount they had originally asked. Probably just a hideous coincidence, though, because he would have been just as willing to give them one hundred thousand from the beginning.

"At any rate, what it succeeded in doing was to throw a hitch into the negotiations, make them nervous and skittish. They contacted him again several days later, refused to believe his explanation, and breathed dire threats against the girl. He pleaded with them for another chance, and asked for more time to raise a second fifty thousand. He's been holding it in readiness for some time now, and they're apparently suffering from a bad case of fright; they cancel each set of new instructions as fast as they issue them to him. Wait'll I get through, please, will you, Murphy? It's five days since Mr Rapf last heard from them, and he is convinced that –" He didn't finish it, out of consideration for the agonized man sitting there. Then he went ahead briskly: "Now here's Miss Rapf's description, and here's what our fist move is going to be. Twenty years old, weight so-and-so, height so-and-so, light-brown hair –"

"She was wearing a pale-pink party dress and dancing shoes when she left the house," Rapf supplied forlornly.

"We don't pin any reliance on items of apparel in matters of this kind," the lieutenant explained to him in a kindly aside. "That's for amnesia cases or straight disappearances. They almost invariably discard the victim's clothes, to make accidental recognition harder. Some woman in the outfit will usually supply her with her own things."

"It's too late, lieutenant; it's too late," the man who sat facing him murmured grief-strickenly. "I know it; I'm sure of it."

"We have no proof that it is," the lieutenant replied reassuringly.

"But if it is, Mr Rapf, you have only yourself to blame for waiting this long to come to us. If you'd come to us sooner, you might have your daughter back by now –"

He broke off short. "What's the matter, Murphy?" he snapped. "What are you climbing halfway across the desk at me like that for?"

"Will you let me get a word in and tell you, lieutenant?" Murphy exclaimed with a fine show of exasperated insubordination. "I been trying to for the last five minutes! That librarian, that Miss Roberts that came in here the other night – It was this thing she stumbled over accidentally then already. It must have been! It's the same message."

The lieutenant's jaw dropped well below his collar button. "Ho-ly smoke!" he exhaled. "Say, she's a smart young woman all right!"

"Yeah, she's so smart we laughed her out of the place, book and all," Murphy said bitterly. "She practically hands it to us on a silver platter, and you and me, both, we think it's the funniest thing we ever heard of."

"Never mind that now! Go out and get hold of her! Bring her in here fast!"

"She's practically standing in front of you!" The door swung closed after Murphy.

Miss Everett, the hatchet-faced librarian, felt called upon to interfere at the commotion that started up less than five minutes later at the usually placid new-membership desk, which happened to be closest to the front door.

"Will you *kindly* keep your voice down, young man?" she said severely, sailing over. "This is a library, not a –"

"I haven't got time to keep my voice down! Where's Prudence Roberts? She's wanted at headquarters right away."

"She didn't come to work this morning. It's the first time she's ever missed a day since she's been with the library. What is it she's wanted –" But there was just a rush of outgoing air where he'd been standing until then. Miss Everett looked startledly at the other librarian. "What was that he just said?"

"It sounded to me like 'Skip it, toots.'"

Miss Everett looked blankly over her shoulder to see if anyone else was standing there, but no one was.

In a matter of minutes Murphy had burst in on them again, looking a good deal more harried than the first time. "Something's happened to her. She hasn't been at her rooming house all night either, and that's the first time *that* happened too! Listen. There was a card went with that book she brought to us, showing who had it out and all that. Get it out quick; let me have it!"

He couldn't have remembered its name just then to save his life, and it might have taken them until closing time and after to wade through the library's filing system. But no matter how much of a battle-ax this Miss

Everett both looked and was, one thing must be said in her favor: she had an uncanny memory when it came to damaged library property. "The reference card on *Manuela Gets Her Man*, by Ollivant," she snapped succinctly to her helpers. And in no time it was in his hands.

His face lighted. He brought his fist down on the counter with a bang that brought every nose in the place up out of its book, and for once Miss Everett forgot to remonstrate or even frown, "Thank God for her methodical mind!" he exulted. "Trasker, check; Baumgarten, check; Turner, question mark. It's as good as though she left full directions behind her!"

"What was it he said *that* time?" puzzled Miss Everett, as the doors flapped hectically to and fro behind him.

"It sounded to me like 'Keep your fingers crossed.' Only, I'm not sure if it was 'fingers' or –"

"It's getting dark again," Virginia Rapf whimpered frightenedly, dragging herself along the floor toward her fellow captive. "Each time night comes, I think they're going to . . . *you* know! Maybe tonight they *will.*"

Prudence Roberts was fully as frightened as the other girl, but simply because one of them had to keep the other's courage up, she wouldn't let herself show it. "No, they won't; they wouldn't dare!" she said with a confidence she was far from feeling.

She went ahead tinkering futilely with the small padlock and chain that secured her to the foot of the bed. It was the same type that is used to fasten bicycles to something in the owner's absence, only of course the chain had not been left in an open loop or she could simply have withdrawn her hand. It was fastened tight around her wrist by passing the clasp of the lock through two of the small links at once. It permitted her a radius of action of not more than three or four yards around the foot of the bed at most. Virginia Rapf was similarly attached to the opposite side.

"In books you read," Prudence remarked, "women prisoners always seem to be able to open anything from a strong box to a cell door with just a hairpin. I don't seem to have the knack, somehow. This is the last one I have left."

"If you couldn't do it before, while it was light, you'll never be able to do it in the dark."

"I guess you're right," Prudence sighed. "There it goes, out of shape like all the rest, anyway." She tossed it away with a little *plink*.

"Oh, if you'd only moved away from under that window a minute sooner, they wouldn't have seen you out there, you might have been able to –"

"No use crying over spilt milk," Prudence said briskly.

Sounds reached them from outside presently, after they'd been lying silent on the floor for a while.

"Listen," Virginia Rapf breathed. "There's someone moving around down there, under the window. You can hear the ground crunch every once in a while."

Something crashed violently, and they both gave a start.

"What was that, their car?" asked Virginia Rapf.

"No, it sounded like a tin can of some kind; something he threw away."

A voice called out of the back door: "Have you got enough?"

The answer seemed to come from around the side of the house. "No gimme the other one too."

A few moments later a second tinny clash reached their tense ears. They waited, hearts pounding furiously under their ribs. A sense of impending danger assailed Prudence.

"What's that funny smell?" Virginia Rapf whispered fearfully. "Do you notice it? Like –"

Prudence supplied the word before she realized its portent. "Gasoline." The frightful implication hit the two of them at once. The other girl gave a sob of convulsive terror, cringed against her. Prudence threw her arms about her, tried to calm her. "Shh! Don't be frightened. No, they wouldn't do that, they couldn't be that inhuman." But her own terror was half stifling her.

One of their captors' voices sounded directly under them, with a terrible clarity. "All right, get in the car, Flo. You too, Duke, I'm about ready."

They heard the woman answer him, and there was unmistakable horror even in her tones. "Oh, not *that* way, Eddie. You're going to finish them first, aren't you?"

He laughed coarsely. "What's the difference? The smoke'll finish them in a minute or two; they won't suffer none. All right, soft-hearted, have it your own way. I'll go up and give 'em a clip on the head apiece, if it makes you feel any better." His tread started up the rickety stairs.

They were almost crazed with fear. Prudence fought to keep her presence of mind.

"Get under the bed, quick!" she panted hoarsely.

But the other girl gave a convulsive heave in her arms, then fell limp. She'd fainted dead away. The oncoming tread was halfway up the stairs now. He was taking his time, no hurry. Outside in the open she heard the woman's voice once more, in sharp remonstrance.

"Wait a minute, you dope; not yet! Wait'll Eddie gets out first!"

The man with her must have struck a match. "He can make it; let's see him run for it," he answered jeeringly. "I still owe him something for that hot-foot he gave me one time, remember?"

Prudence had let the other girl roll lifelessly out of her arms, and squirmed under the bed herself, not to try to save her own skin but to do the little that could be done to try to save both of them, futile as she knew it to be. She twisted like a caterpillar, clawed at her own foot, got her right shoe off. She'd never gone in for these stylish featherweight sandals with spindly heels, and she was glad of that now. It was a good strong substantial Oxford, nearly as heavy as a man's, with a club heel. She got a grasp on it by the toe, then twisted her body around so that her legs were toward the side the room door gave onto. She reared one at the knee, held it poised, backed up as far as the height of the bed would allow it to be.

The door opened and he came in, lightless. He didn't need a light for a simple little job like this – stunning two helpless girls chained to a bed. He started around toward the foot of it, evidently thinking they were crouched there hiding from him. Her left leg suddenly shot out between his two, like a spoke, tripping him neatly.

He went floundering forward on his face with a muffled curse. She had hoped he might hit his head, be dazed by the impact if only for a second or two. He wasn't; he must have broken the fall with his arm. She threshed her body madly around the other way again, to get her free arm in play with the shoe for a weapon. She began to rain blows on him with it, trying to get his head with the heel. That went wrong too. He'd fallen too far out along the floor, the chain wouldn't let her come out any farther after him. She couldn't reach any higher up than his muscular shoulders with the shoe, and its blows fell ineffectively there.

Raucous laughter was coming from somewhere outside, topped by warning screams. "Eddie, hurry up and get out, you fool! Duke's started it already!" They held no meaning for Prudence; she was too absorbed in this last despairing attempt to save herself and her fellow prisoner.

But he must have heard and understood them. The room was no longer as inky black as before. A strange wan light was beginning to peer up below the window, like a satanic moonrise. He jumped to his feet with a snarl, turned and fired down point-blank at Prudence as she tried to writhe hastily back under cover. The bullet hit the iron rim of the bedstead directly over her eyes and glanced inside. He was too yellow to linger and try again. Spurred by the screamed warnings and the increasing brightness, he bolted from the room and went crashing down the stairs three at a time.

A second shot went off just as he reached the back doorway, and she mistakenly thought he had fired at his fellow kidnaper in retaliation for the ghastly practical joke played on him. Then there was a whole volley of shots, more than just one gun could have fired. The car engine started up with an abortive flurry, then died down again where it was without moving. But her mind was too full of horror at the imminent doom that threatened to engulf both herself and Virginia Rapf, to realize the meaning of anything she dimly heard going on below. Anything but that sullen hungry crackle, like bundles of twigs snapping, that kept growing louder from minute to minute. They had been left hopelessly chained, to be cremated alive!

She screamed her lungs out, and at the same time knew that screaming wasn't going to save her or the other girl. She began to hammer futilely with her shoe at the chain holding her, so slender yet so strong, and knew that wasn't going to save her either.

Heavy steps pounded up the staircase again, and for a moment she thought he'd come back to finish the two of them after all, and was glad of it. Anything was better than being roasted alive. She wouldn't try to hide this time.

The figure that came tearing through the thickening smoke haze toward her was already bending down above her before she looked and saw that it was Murphy. She'd seen some beautiful pictures in art galleries in her time, but he was more beautiful to her eyes than a Rubens portrait.

"All right, chin up, keep cool," he said briefly, so she wouldn't lose her head and impede him.

"Get the key to these locks! The short dark one has them."

"He's dead and there's no time. Lean back. Stretch it out tight and lean out of the way!" He fired and the small chain snapped in two. "Jump! You can't get down the stairs any more." His second shot, freeing Virginia Rapf, punctuated the order.

Prudence flung up the window, climbed awkwardly across the sill, feet first. Then clung there terrified as an intolerable haze of heat rose up under her from below. She glimpsed two men running up under her with a blanket or lap robe from the car stretched out between them.

"I can't; it's . . . it's right under me!"

He gave her an unceremonious shove in the middle of the back and she went hurling out into space with a screech. The two with the blanket got there just about the same time she did. Murphy hadn't waited to make sure; a broken leg was preferable to being incinerated. She hit the ground through the lap robe and all, but at least it broke the direct force of the fall.

They cleared it for the next arrival by rolling her out at one side, and by the time she had picked herself dazedly to her feet, Virginia Rapf was already lying in it, thrown there by him from above.

"Hurry it up, Murph!" she heard one of them shout frighteningly, and instinctively caught at the other girl, dragged her off it to clear the way for him. He crouched with both feet on the sill, came sailing down, and even before he'd hit the blanket, there was a dull roar behind him as the roof caved in, and a great gush of sparks went shooting straight up into the dark night sky.

They were still too close; they all had to draw hurriedly back away from the unbearable heat beginning to radiate from it. Murphy came last, as might have been expected, dragging a very dead kidnaper – the one called Eddie – along the ground after him by the collar of his coat. Prudence saw the other one, Duke, slumped inertly over the wheel of the car he had never had time to make his getaway in, either already dead or rapidly dying. A disheveled blond scarcecrow that had been Florence Turner was apparently the only survivor of the trio. She kept whimpering placatingly, "I didn't want to do *that* to them! I didn't want to do *that* to them!" over and over, as though she still didn't realize they had been saved in time.

Virginia Rapf was coming out of her long faint. It was kinder, Prudence thought, that she had been spared those last few horrible moments; she had been through enough without that.

"Rush her downtown with you, fellow!" Murphy said. "Her dad's waiting for her; he doesn't know yet, I shot out here so fast the minute I located that taxi driver outside the residence club, who remembered driving Miss Roberts out to this vicinity, that I didn't even have time to notify headquarters, just picked up whoever I could on the way."

He came over to where Prudence was standing, staring at the fire with horrified fascination.

"How do you feel? Are you O.K.?" he murmured, brow furrowed with a proprietary anxiety.

"Strange as it may be," she admitted in surprise, "I seem to feel perfectly all right; can't find a thing the matter with me."

Back at the library the following day – and what a world away it seemed from the scenes of violence she had just lived through – the acidulous Miss Everett came up to her just before closing time with, of all things, a twinkle in her eyes. Either that or there was a flaw in her glasses.

"You don't have to stay to the very last minute . . . er . . . toots," she confided. "Your boy-friend's waiting for you outside; I just saw him through the window."

There he was holding up the front of the library when Prudence Roberts emerged a moment or two later.

"The lieutenant would like to see you to personally convey his thanks on behalf of the department," he said. "And afterward I . . . uh . . . know where there's a real high-brow pitcher showing, awful refined."

Prudence pondered the invitation. "No," she said finally. "Make it a nice snappy gangster movie and you're on. I've got so used to excitement in the last few days, I'd feel sort of lost without it."

Death Escapes the Eye

The other night at a party I met my last love again. By last, I don't mean my latest, I mean my final one. He was as taking and as debonair as ever, but not to me any more; a little older maybe; and we said the things you say, with two glasses in our hands to keep us from feeling lonely.

"Hello, Lizzie"; "Hello, Dwight"; "Haven't seen you"; "Nor you either."

Then when there wasn't anything more to say, we moved on. In opposite directions.

It isn't often that I see him any more. But whenever I do, I still think of her. I wonder what really did become of her.

And just the other night, suddenly, for no reason at all, out of nowhere, the strangest thought entered my head for a moment.

But then I promptly dismissed it again, as being too fantastic, too absurd.

I first met him on paper.

Jean was the one called my attention to the manuscript. Jean was my assistant on the magazine. Strange, I suppose, for that type publication to have an all-female staff. I've never run across another such instance before or since. It didn't deal with confessions or with the screen or with home-making; it dealt with murder mysteries purely and simply. And they were pure and they were simple, I assure you. Nothing else got in. Well, the backing was masculine, if capital can be said to have a gender; and they'd picked us to run it, so they must have liked the way we did it. We turned out a competent, craftsmanlike, he-man shocker and we signed it with first-initials, so the readers never knew the difference. "Editor, E. Aintree; Associate Editor, J. Medill." All my mail came addressed "Mr Aintree."

We had a hole left in the magazine. You work pretty close to deadline on a monthly, and that will happen now and then. One of our regulars had defaulted; gotten drunk, or gotten the grippe, or come through with a stinker that couldn't be used. I don't remember now any more. We didn't have enough of a backlog to help us out; we were too young yet. (That's an accumulation of stories already purchased and held in reserve for just such an emergency.)

"What about the slush-pile?" I asked. That's the stuff that goes back.

It varies all the way from abominable up to just plain not-so-good. That was poor Jean's department, first readings. She used to have to drink lots of black coffee with her lunch, to make her head feel better.

"There are a couple of shorts," she said, "but they're pretty bad. We'd have to use two."

"If we've got to use a bad one," I said, "I'd rather use just one long bad one than two short bad ones. See if you can't dig up something at ten thousand words."

She came into my office again in about an hour. "I've found something," she announced triumphantly. She made a face expressive of cynical appreciation. "Park Avenue," she said.

"What do you mean?" I glanced at the return address on the cover. " 'Dwight Billings, 657 Park Avenue, New York City.' " This was before the postal zones had come in.

Her eyebrows continued satirically arched. "We're getting contributions from the Four Hundred now."

"It runs all the way to 125th Street and beyond." I reminded her. "He may have rented a room in someone's apartment. Most likely receives his mail care of the doorman."

"Do they rent rooms on Park Avenue?" she wanted to know. Not sincerely; she seldom asked her questions sincerely. She already had the greater part of the answers, as a rule. She asked to see whether you had, that was the impression.

I read it. It was encased in dream-format, if you know what I mean. And that was taboo in our shop.

I'd read worse. But very infrequently.

"It's a first try," I let her know.

"Think we can take a chance on it?" she asked.

"We'll have to. We go to the printer tomorrow. If we lop off the dream-casing and run it straight, it might get by. A good retreading job ought to fix it up. Have Ann see if she can get him on the phone for me."

She returned breathlessly in a moment. "He's listed," she announced. She acted surprised, as though she'd expected at least the address – if not name and address both – to be feigned. "But we can't reach him. And it's quarter to five now."

I slapped the manuscript rather short-temperedly into my briefcase. "I'll have to take it home with me myself tonight, and try to hop it up."

"That," she said sweetly, "is what you get for being an editor."

It was on its way to the printer's by nine next morning; the hole had been filled up.

At nine-thirty the switchboard rang in.

"There's a Mr Billings here about a story –"

"Ask him to wait a minute," I said tersely. I was still a little resentful of the time I'd given up the night before; my own time.

The minute became twenty. Not intentionally, but there was office routine, and he'd come in so damned early.

Finally I picked up the phone. "Ask Mr Billings to come in." I lit a cigarette and leaned back in the chair.

He knocked subduedly. "Come in." I tilted my head and waited.

He was tall and he was thirty; brown eyes and lightish hair.

He looked at me, and then he looked around the room inquiringly. "Wrong office, I guess," he grinned. "I'm looking for Mr Aintree."

I was used to that. I got it all the time.

"Sit down," I said. "It's Miss Aintree, and I'm she."

He sat down. He looked well sitting; not too far forward, not too far back. Not too straight, not too sunken.

I thought of my hair. I'd never thought of it before, here in the office. I wished I'd had it dressed once a fortnight or so, like Jean; not just run a comb through loosely and be done for the day.

"Is this your first story, Mr Billings?"

He smiled deprecatingly. "I haven't fooled you, have I?"

I explained about the dream-format. " – so we took it out."

"But," he said incredulously, "that sounds as if you intended to –"

"Oh, didn't I tell you? We tried to reach you yesterday afternoon. You see, we're using it."

I watched closely. Just the right reaction; not too cocksure, not lackadaisical either. Modestly appreciative. Couldn't he do anything wrong? He should do something wrong. This wasn't good for me.

I rang for Jean. "I'd like you to meet the other half of the staff, now that you're under way with us."

He'd have to meet her sooner or later, so it was better right now. She only had on a pique shirtwaist and black skirt today, and she'd come in with an overnight cold.

"This is *Mrs* Medill, my associate." I deliberately emphasized the married title. "Mr Billings is our newest contributor, Jean."

"Welcome to our family."

The cold wasn't noticeable enough and the pique blouse looked too pert and chipper, I thought.

"I've been thinking about your story all night," she said.

"You've been thinking about it, but I've been working on it," I said caustically.

The three of us laughed.

Jean had a cigarette with us. We mulled over titles, finally decided on one. He'd been in with me for forty-five minutes, the longest interview I'd ever given since I'd been in the business.

He got up to go finally. He shook our hands.

"You'll come back at us again with another now, won't you?" I said. "We're wide open, you know."

"Yes," Jean concurred demurely, her eyes resting on me innocently for a moment, "we're wide open and our sales-resistance is practically nil."

"Thanks," he beamed. "You've both been perfectly swell." He closed the door after him. A moment later he reopened it and looked in again. "I have an idea. Why don't you both come up and have dinner with me at my place? I'm batching it, but I have some one up there who'll look after us."

"I have a miserable thing called a husband," Jean said. "He doesn't make any noise, he's very well-trained, but the poor creature depends on me to be fed."

"Bring him along!" he said. "Only too glad. Shall we say Tuesday, then?"

"Tuesday's fine."

"Tuesday at seven. Just the four of us. Goodbye, Miss Aintree."

"Oh, make it Lizzie," I said with a touch of bravado. That was another thing that had to be out and over with, too, so the sooner the better. All the "Beths" and "Elspeths" when I was seventeen and eighteen hadn't been able to improve on it. "Goodbye, Dwight."

He closed the door, and I could hear his step going away down the corridor outside. He had a fine, firm tread; clean-cut, without any slurring.

She stood there looking at me with her brows raised.

"Why are your brows up?" I asked, finally.

"Are they up?"

"Well, they don't grow that way."

"I've never seen you so patient with a writer before," she mused, gathering up her papers to take back with her.

Yes, he *was* here as a writer, wasn't he?

Jean and her husband, the Cipher, stopped by for me Tuesday in a cab, and the three of us went on together. The Cipher was singularly uncommunicative, on any and all subjects, after five o'clock in the afternoon. He was resting from business, she and I supposed. "He *has* a voice," she had once assured me. "I called for him one day, and I heard it through the office door."

On the present occasion he said, " 'Lo, Lizzie," in a taciturn growl as I joined them, and that, I knew, was all we were likely to get out of him for the next hour to come, so it had to do. But Jean had settled for it, and Jean was smarter when it came to men than I could ever hope to be.

657 was one of the tall monoliths that run along Park Avenue like a picket fence from Forty-fifth to Ninety-sixth; but a picket fence that doesn't do its job. It doesn't seem to keep anyone out; everyone gets in.

We stepped out of the elevator into a foyer, and there was only a single door facing us. Meaning there was but one apartment to a floor, in this building. The little waiting-place was made as attractive as if it were part of the apartment itself. The carpeting was Oriental, there was a heavily-framed mirror on the wall, a carved table below that, and a Louis XVI armchair with grape satin back-and-seat upholstery. A small rock-crystal chandelier was suspended overhead.

"Is this one of your writers, Lizzie?" Jean inquired quizzically.

"Not on our rates," I said drily. And unnecessarily.

"Why does he bother fiddling around with writing?" the Cipher shrugged.

We both gave him a cold look. Meant to be taken as haughty reproof.

A colored man opened the door. None of the faithful old family-retainer type. A streamlined version. His accent was pure university. "If you'll allow me, sir." He took the Cipher's hat. "If you ladies would care –" He indicated a feminine guest-room to one side of the entrance gallery.

Jean and I went in and left our wraps in there.

She unlidded a cut-crystal powder receptacle, being Jean, and sniffed at it. "Coty's, unless I'm slipping. Vibrant for brunettes, and –" She unlidded a second one on the opposite side," – Rachel for blonds. Evidently there are no redheads on his list."

I didn't answer.

We rejoined the Cipher and the butler in the central gallery. It ran on for a length of about three rooms, cutting a wide swath through the apartment, and then ended in a short flight of about four ascending steps. Beyond these was the living room. But it was lateral to the gallery, not frontal to it.

There was again a matter of steps, two this time, to be descended. You stopped, and turned to your left, and came down two steps onto the floor of the room. It was artfully constructed for dramatic entrances, that room.

Desultory notes of "None but the Lonely Heart" played with one hand alone stopped short. He raised his head at the bustle of our coming down the two steps, and I saw his eyes for a moment, fitted evenly into the crevice between the top of the instrument and its upraised lid. There was something sinister about the vignette. It was as if he were wearing a flesh-colored mask between eyebrows and cheekbones, and the rest of his face were ebony-black.

Then he stood up and came forward, one hand each for myself and Jean.

I got the left. "Nearest to the heart," I had to say to myself, to fool myself that I'd got the best of the bargain.

His man brought in a frost-rimmed shaker and poured bacardis and offered them to us.

"This is Luthe," he said.

Luthe dipped his head slightly, with the same dignified reticence he'd shown at the door.

I wondered what Billing did. I wondered how to find out, without asking him. And Jean rushed in. It was a great convenience having her along, I couldn't help reflecting.

"Well, what do you do?" she queried. "I mean, outside of writing for Lizzie, now that you are writing for Lizzie?"

"Nothing," he said bluntly. "Simply – nothing."

"Now, there's a man after my own heart!" she blurted out. "Let me shake hands with you." And proceeded vigorously to do so.

The Cipher made his hourly utterance at this point. "I admire you," he stated emphatically. "You carry out what you feel like doing."

"Do you always carry out the things you feel like doing?" Jean suggested mischievously. "I'd hate to be the lady in front of you at the theatre wearing that tall, obliterating hat."

After dinner, with a great show of importance, he took me to see the room he did his work in. We went by ourselves. I don't know why; leaving Jean and Cipher behind. I didn't mind that.

He keyed open the door, as though revealing a site of very great intrinsic worth. "I don't even let Luthe in here when I'm at it," he said. "I'm sort of self-conscious about it, I guess."

"You'll get over that," I assured him. "Some of them can work in the middle of the street at high noon."

He showed me the typewriter. It had been left open with an insert at mid-page.

"I sit there and look at it and nothing happens. I hit the side of the machine, I hit the side of my head –"

I'm afraid I wasn't as interested in him professionally as I should have been. I bent down close as if to look, but my eyes went past the roller toward the girl's photograph standing farther back on the desk.

It said: "To my Dwight," down in a lower corner, "from his loving wife, Bernette." But he'd said he was batching it.

Divorced then.

I hummed a little, under my breath. Humming is a sign of contentment.

And then he called, in about a week, and invited us to dine with him a second time, starting the whole thing over.

We went. We were sitting there in his living room, just the four of us, about ten o'clock. And suddenly drama had come fuming in around us, like flash-flood.

Luthe appeared, went over to him, bent down and said something not meant for our ears.

I saw Dwight look up at him, in complete disbelief.

"No," he mouthed in astonishment. I caught the word. Then he pointed to the floor. "*Here*?"

Luthe nodded. "Right outside."

"*With* him?" I caught those two words too.

"All right," he said finally, and gave his hand an abrupt little twist of permission. "All right. She knows I'd never –"

I got it then.

She has somebody else. But not only that:

She's come right here with the somebody else!

Luthe showed up at the gallery-opening, announced formally: "Mr and Mrs Stone."

That told me the rest of it. She'd remarried, and the somebody else who'd come with her was her second husband.

I felt his wrist shaking a little, but it was safely out of sight behind the turn of my shoulder. For support purely, you understand; to sustain him against the settee-back. Nothing personal. I didn't have to be told.

I turned my head. She'd come out onto the entrance-apron, two steps above the rest of us. She, and a husband tailing her. But what it amounted to was: *she'd* come out onto the entrance-apron. He might just as well not have been there.

She was familiar with the stage-management of this particular entry-way, knew just how to get the most out of it. Knew just how long to stand motionless, and then resume progress down into the room. Knew how to kill him. Or, since she'd already done that pretty successfully, perhaps I'd better say, know how to give him the shot of adrenalin that would bring him back to life again, so that she could kill him all over again. To be in love with her as he was, I couldn't help thinking, must be a continuous succession of death-throes. Without any final release, I could feel that hidden wrist behind me bounce a little, from a quickened pulse.

She stood there like a mannequin at a fashion-display, modeling a mink coat. Even the price-tag was there in full view, if you had keen enough eyes, and mine were. Inscribed "To the highest bidder, any-time, anywhere."

She had a lot of advantages over the picture I'd seen on his desk. She was in color; skin like the underpetals of newly-opened June rosebuds, blue eyes, golden-blond hair. And the picture, for its part, had one advantage over her, in my estimate: it couldn't breathe.

She had on that mink she was modelling, literally. Three-quarters length, flaring, swagger. She was holding it open at just the right place, with one hand. Under it she had on an evening gown of white brocaded satin. The V-incision at the bodice went too low. But evidently not for her; after all she had to make the most of everything she had. She had a double string of pearls close around her neck, and a diamond clip at the tip of each ear.

They have the worst taste in women, all of them. Who is to explain their taste in women?

She came forward, down the steps and into the room. Perfume came with her, and the fact that she had hip-sockets. The bodice-incision deepened, too, if anything.

I kept protesting inwardly, but there must be something more than just what I can see. There *must* be something more. To make him down a glass of brandy straight to keep from moaning with pain. To make his pulse rivet the way it is against the back of this settee. As though he had a woodpecker hidden in it.

I kept waiting for it to come out, and it didn't. It wasn't there. It was all there at first glance, and beyond that there was nothing more. And most of it, at that, was the mink, the pearls, the diamonds, and the incision.

She was advancing upon us. Her two hands went out toward him, not just one. A diamond bracelet around one wrist shifted back a little toward the elbow, as they did so.

He rose from the settee-arm, and his mask was that of the host who has been so engrossed in present company that he is taken completely by surprise by a new arrival. But his mask wasn't on very tight; you could see the livid white strain it was resting upon.

"Billy!" she crowed. And her two hands caught hold of his two, and spread his arms out wide, then drew them close together, then spread them wide again. In a sort of horizontal handshake.

So she called him Billy. That would be about right for her too. Probably "Billy-Boy" when there were less than three total strangers present at any one time.

"Well, Bernette!" he said in a deep, slow voice that came through the mask.

One pair of hands separated, then the other pair. His were the ones dropped away first, so the impulse must have come from him.

The nonentity who had come in with her was only now reaching us; he'd crossed the room more slowly.

He was a good deal younger than either one of them; particularly than Dwight. Twenty-three perhaps, or five. He had a mane of black hair, a little too oleaginous for my taste, carefully brushed upward and back. It smelled a little of cheap tonic when he got too near you.

Her hand slipped possessively back, and landed on his shoulder, and drew him forward the added final pace or two that he hadn't had the social courage to navigate unaided.

"I want you to meet my very new husband. Just breaking in." Then she said. "You two should know each other." And she motioned imperiously. "Go on, shake hands. Don't be bashful. Dwight Billings, Harry Stone. *My* Dwight. *My* Harry."

They looked at each other.

Dwight's crisp intelligent eyes bored into him like awls; you could almost see the look spiraling around and around and around as it penetrated into the sawdust. You could almost see the sawdust come spilling out.

It's not the substitution itself, I thought; it's the insult of *such* a substitution.

The wait was just long enough to have a special meaning; you could make of it what you willed. Finally Dwight shook his hand vigorously. "You're a very lucky – young fellow, young fellow."

I wondered what word he would have liked to use in place of "young fellow."

"I feel like I know you already," the new husband said sheepishly. "I've heard a lot about you."

"That's very kind of Bernette," Dwight said crisply.

I wondered where she'd got him. He had the dark, slicked-back good looks that would hit her type between the eyes. I cut him off below the neck, to try and visualize what would go with the face. And all I kept getting was a starched soda-jerk's jacket. The little white cap would show up, cocked over one eye. I couldn't keep it off. A devil with the three o'clock high-school shift.

Then again, why differentiate? They went well together. They belonged together.

The line of distinction didn't run between him and her, it ran between her and Dwight. And part of her, at that, belonged on one side of the line, and part belonged on the other. The mink coat and the pearls and the diamond clips belonged on Dwight's side of the line; and she herself belonged on the other side of it. She wasn't even an integrated personality. The husband, with all his cheapness and callowness, was at least that.

Dwight introduced the rest of us. Introduced us, after I already knew her better than he ever had or ever would, with a pitiless clarity that he would never have.

Jean might have aroused her antagonistic interest. I could see that, but the married title deflected it as quickly as the introduction was made. Then when it came to myself, one quick comprehensive look from head to foot, and she couldn't explain to herself what possible interest he could have in me, what anyone who looked like I did was doing there at all.

"Oh, *a business* friend," she said.

"No, a friend," he corrected firmly. And my heart applauded. That's my boy. If you don't love me, at least don't cut me off altogether.

"Drinks for Mr and Mrs —" he said over our heads to Luthe. He couldn't get the name yet. Or didn't want to.

"Stone," the husband supplied embarrassedly, instead of letting the embarrassment fall on Dwight, where it rightfully belonged.

She at least was perfectly self-possessed, knew her way around in this house. "My usual, Luthe. That hasn't changed. And how are you, anyway?"

Luthe bowed and said coldly that he was all right, but she hadn't waited to hear, the back of her head was to him once more.

Their drinks were brought, and there was a slow maneuvering for position. Not physical position, mental. She lounged back upon the settee as though she owned it, and the whole place with it; as she must have sat there so very many times before. Tasted her drink. Nodded patronizingly to Luthe: "As good as ever."

Dwight, for his part, singled out the new husband, stalked him, so to speak, until he had him backed against a wall. You could see the process step by step. And then finally, "By the way, what line are you in, Stone?"

The husband floundered badly. "Well, right now – I'm not –"

She stepped into the breach quickly, leaving Jean hanging on mid-word. "Harry's just looking around right now. I want him to take his time." Then she added quickly, just a shade too quickly, "Oh, by the way, remind me; there's something I want to speak to you about before I leave, Billy." And then went back to Jean again.

That told me why she'd dragged him up here with her like this. Not to flaunt him; she had no thought of profitless cruelty. The goose that had laid its golden yolks for one might lay them for two as well. Why discard it entirely?

Dwight was in torment, and when anyone's in pain too much to be borne, they strike back blindly.

"Where'd you go for your honeymoon, Bernette?"

She took a second, as though this required courage. She was right, it did. "We took a run up to Lake Arrow."

He turned to the husband. "That's where *we* went. How'd you like it?" Then back to her again. "How *is* the old lodge? Is Emil still there?"

She took a second. "Emil's still there," she said reticently.

"Did you remember me to him?"

She took two seconds, this time. "No," she said reluctantly, mostly into the empty upper part of her glass, as though he were in there. "He didn't ask about you."

He shook his head and clicked with mock ruefulness. "Forgetful, isn't he? Has he done anything about changing that Godawful wallpaper in the corner bedroom yet?" He explained to me with magnificent impartiality: "He was always going to. It was yellow, and looked as though somebody had thrown up at two-second intervals all over it." He turned and flicked the punchline at her. "Remember, Bernette?"

It was magnificent punishment.

I watched them at the end, when they were about to go. Watched Dwight and her, I mean, not her husband and self. When the good-byes had been said and the expressions of pleasure at meetings had been spoken all around – and not meant anywhere. They reversed the order of their entry into the room. The husband left first, and passed from sight down the gallery like a well-rehearsed actor who clears the stage for a key-speech he knows is to be made at this point. While she lingered behind a moment in studied dilatoriness, picking up her twinkling little pouch from where she had left it, pausing an instant to see if her face was right in a mirror on the way.

Then all at once, as if at random afterthought: "Could I see you for a minute, Billy?"

They went over to the side of the room together, and their voices faded from sound, it became pantomime. You had to read between the attitudes.

I didn't miss a gesture, an expression of their faces, a flicker of their eyes. I got everything but the words. I didn't need the words.

She glanced, as she spoke, toward the vacant gallery-opening, just once and briefly.

Talking about the husband.

She took a button of Dwight's jacket with her fingers, twined it a little.

Ingratiation. Asking him something, some favor.

She stopped speaking. The burden of the dialogue shifted to him.

He shook his head almost imperceptibly. But definitely. Refusal. His hand had strayed towards his back pocket. Then it left it again. The billfold pocket.

Money for the husband.

The dialogue was now dead. Both had stopped speaking. There was nothing more to be said.

She stood there at a complete loss. It was something that had never happened to her with him, before. She didn't know how to go ahead. She didn't know how to get herself out of it.

He moved finally, and touched her guidingly at the same time, and that broke the transfixion.

"Well – goodnight, Billy," she said lamely. She was still out of breath – mentally – from the rebuff.

He came and leaned over me.

"I've been neglecting you," he said solicitously.

I had him all to myself for a moment, at least the outside of him.

Not for long, just between the acts. It wasn't over yet. Suddenly she'd reappeared at the lower end of the room, was standing there.

He turned his head.

"Billy, talk to Luthe, will you? What's the matter with him, has he had a drink or something? I can't get him to give me my coat." And her whole form shook slightly with appreciative risibility.

He called Luthe. Luthe appeared almost instantly, holding the mink lining-forward in both arms. Like someone who has been waiting in the wings the whole time and takes just a single step forward to appear and play his part.

"Luthe," Dwight said amiably. "Is that Mrs Stone's coat you're holding?" And before she could interject, "Of course it is!", which it was obvious she was about to do, he added: "Read the label in the pocket-lining and see what it says."

Luthe dutifully peered down into the folds of satin and read "Mrs Bernette Billings."

There was a pause, while we all got it, including herself. Then suddenly Luthe had stepped from sight again, coat and all. While she still stood there, blankly and still coatless, not knowing what to do. Dwight stepped over to a desk, lowered the slab, and hastily inked something on a card. "Bernette," he said, "I want to give you something." And then he went to her with it and handed it to her. "Take this with you."

It was an ordinary visiting- or name-card. She held it bracketed by two corners and scanned it diagonally, puzzled.

"What's this for?"

"I'll call him and make an appointment for you," he said quietly. "Do me a favor, go in and talk to him. The whole thing'll be over in no time."

She still didn't get it.

"Why should I go in and see your lawyer?" she blurted out. "What have I got to see him about?"

I got it myself, then. An annulment.

Anger began to smolder in her eyes.

Her fingers made two or three quick motions and pieces of cardboard sputtered from them.

"Think it over," he urged, a second too late.

"I just did," she blazed. "Is Luthe going to give me my coat?"

"It'll be here waiting for you – any time you say —"

Her voice was hoarse now, splintered. "You think you're going to show me up, is that it? No, I'll show *you* up!"

Her hands wrestled furiously at the back of her neck. The pearls sidled down the bodice-incision. She trapped them there with a raging slap, balled them up, flung them. They fell short of his face, they were probably too light, but they struck the bosom of his shirt with a click and rustle.

"Bernette, I have people here. They're not interested in our private discussions."

"You should have thought of that sooner." Her hands were at her ear-lobe now. "You want them to know you gave me things, don't you? You don't have to tell them! *I'll* tell them!" The ear-clips fell on the carpet at his feet, one considerably in advance of the other.

Hers was the hot rage, incapacitating itself. His was the cold kind, the more deadly of the two, in perfect command of itself, able to continue its barbed, indirect insults.

"You can't carry that out down to its ultimate –"

Only his face was chalky; otherwise he was motionless, voice low.

"I can't, hunh? You think these people being here is going to stop me, hunh? The hell with them! The hell with you, yourself! I'll show you! I'll show you what I think of you!"

She was beside herself with rage. There was a rending of satin, and suddenly the dress peeled off spirally, like a tattered paper wrapper coming off her. Then she kicked with one long silk-encased leg, and it fluttered further away.

She had a beautiful figure. That registered on my petrified mind, I recall. We sat there frozen.

"Keep your eyes down, ducky," I heard Jean warn the Cipher in a sardonic undertone. "I'll tell you when you can look up."

For a moment she posed there, quivering, a monotoned apparition all in flesh-tints, the undraped skin and the pale-pink silk of vestigial garments blending almost indistinguishably. Then she gave a choked cry of inexpressible aversion, and darted from sight.

He called out: "Luthe, that raincoat in the hall. Put it over her. Don't let her go out of here like that. It's chilly tonight."

A door slammed viciously somewhere far down the gallery.

Jean was the first one to speak, after the long somewhat numbed silence that had followed. And, probably unintentionally, her matter-of-fact minor-keyed remark struck me as the most hilariously malapropos thing I had ever heard. I wanted to burst out laughing at it.

She stirred and said with mincing politeness: "I really think we should be going now."

A six-week interval, then.

Nothing happened. No word. No sight. No sign.

Was he with her once more? Was he with somebody else entirely different? Or was he alone, with nobody at all?

I had it bad. Real bad.

I was reading proof when the desk-phone rang one afternoon.

"Mr Dwight Billings calling," Ann said.

He said: "I don't dare ask you and the Medills to come up here after what happened that last time."

"Dare," I said faintly. "Go on, dare."

"All right, would you?" he said. "Let's all have dinner together and –"

Jean came into the room about fifteen minutes later, to see if the proofs were ready.

"Dwight Billings just called," I said, trying to right an inverted comma with the wooden cone of the pencil.

She said the strangest thing. I should have resented it, but she said it so softly, so understandingly, that it never occurred to me until later that I should have resented it.

"I know," she said. "I can tell."

She uncoupled my phone and turned it the other way around, so that it wouldn't come up to my ear reversed the next time I lifted it. She stooped and picked up two or three stray proof-sheets that were lying on the floor under my desk. She dredged a sodden blue cigarette out of my ink-well, and removed my pen from the ashtray.

"Either that, or there's a high wind out there on Fifty-third Street today."

So back we went, the three of us, for another glimpse at this real-life peep-show that went on and on, with never an intermission, even though there was not always someone there to watch it.

He was alone. But my heart and my hopes clouded at the very first sight of him as we came in; they knew. He was too happy. His face was too bright and smooth; there was love hovering somewhere close by, even though it wasn't in sight at the moment. Its reflection was all over him. He was animated, he was engaging, he made himself pleasant to be with.

But as for the source of this felicity, the wellspring, you couldn't tell anything. If I hadn't known him as he'd been in the beginning, I might have thought that this was his nature. He was alone, just with Luther. We were only four at the table, one to each side of it, with candles and a hand-carved ship-model in the center of it.

Then when we left the table, I remember, we paired off unconventionally. I don't think it was a deliberate maneuver on anyone's part, it just happened that way. Certainly, I didn't scheme it; it was not the sort of partners I would have preferred. Nor did he. And the Cipher least of all. He never schemed anything. That left only Jean: I hadn't been watching her —

At any rate, the two men obliviously preceded us, deep in some weighty conversation; she and I followed after.

She stopped short midway down the gallery, well before we had emerged into view of the drawing-room, which the two men had already entered.

"I have premonitions of a run," she said. "I don't trust these sheers." But what she did was jog her elbow into my side, in a sort of wordless message or signal, as she turned aside and went in through the nearest doorway.

So I turned and followed her: that was what her nudge had summoned me to do.

The lights went on.

"But this is his bedroom," I protested, with an instinctive recoil at the threshold.

"Oh, is it?" she said with utter composure. She had already crossed to the other side of it, to a dressing-table. I saw her squeeze the bulb of an atomizer so that its trajectory passed beneath her nose. "Chanel Twenty-two," she deciphered. "Are THEY using that now?"

I couldn't have given her the answer; she wanted none, it hadn't been a question.

She went toward the full-length mirror in a closet-door. She went through the motions of validating her excuse for stepping in here; raised her skirt, cocked her leg askew towards the mirror, dropped her skirt again. Then she reached out and purposefully took hold of the faceted glass knob of the closet-door.

"Jean," I said with misgivings, "Don't do that."

I saw she was going to anyway.

"Just coats and trousers," I prayed unavailingly. "Just tweeds and – and things like that." I couldn't think of an alternate fabric, there wasn't time.

She swept it wide, the door, with malignant efficiency, and stood back with it so that I could see, and looked at me, not it, as she did so.

Satins and silks, glistening metallic tissues, flowered prints; and in the middle of all of them, like a queen amidst her ladies-in-waiting, that regal mink.

Then there was a blinding silvery flash as the electric light flooded across the mirror, and the door swept closed.

"Back," was all she said, brittly.

She put out the light as she shepherded me across the threshhold; I remember the room was dark as we left it behind.

She held her arm around me tight as we walked slowly down the remainder of the gallery. And twice, before we got to the end of the way, she pressed it convulsively, tighter still.

I needed it.

"Tune in the stadium concert, Luthe," he suggested at one point. "It must be time for it."

I wondered what he wanted that for.

Some very feverish dance-band drumming filtered out.

"If that's the stadium concert," Jean said, "they've certainly picked up bad habits."

"Luthe," he said good-naturedly, "what're you doing over there? I said the open-air concert, at the stadium."

"I can't seem to get it. What station is it on?"

"ABC, I think."

"I'm on ABC now. Doesn't seem to be it."

"Does it?" agreed Jean, pounding her ear and giving her head a shake to clear it, as a particularly virulent trombone-snarl assailed us.

"Call up the broadcasting station and find out," he suggested.

Luthe came back.

"No wonder. It's been called off on account of rain. Giving it tomorrow night instead."

"It's not raining down here," Jean said. She turned from the window. "It's bone-dry out. Do you even have special weather arrangements, for Park Avenue?" she queried.

"Look who we are," he answered her. A little distractedly, I thought as though he were thinking of something else. "What time is it now, Luthe?" he asked.

She arrived about an hour and a half later. Perhaps even two hours. I don't know; since I hadn't been expecting her, I wasn't clocking her exactly. If he was, he'd kept it to himself, you couldn't notice it. No more parenthetic requests for the time, after that first one.

There were several things to notice about her arrival. One of them was, she was not announced. She simply entered, as one does where one belongs. Suddenly, from nowhere, she had taken her stance there on the auction-block (as I called it after that first time). Then, after flamboyant pause and pose there, she was coming down the steps to join us.

He'd made a few improvements in her. Surface ones only; that was the only part of her he could reach, I suppose. Or maybe he needed more time.

She'd even acquired an accent. I mean an accent of good, cultivated English; and since it was false, on her it *was* an accent.

When she walked, she even managed to use the soles of her feet, and not her hips so much any more: I wondered if he'd used telephone directories on her head for that.

"You remember Lizzie, and Jean, and Paul," he said.

"Oh, yes, of coh-ess, how are you?" she leered affably. She was very much the lady of the manor, making us at home in her own domain. "Sorry I'm so late. I stayed on to the very end."

"Did you?" he said.

And I thought: Where? Then, No! It can't be! It would be too good to be true –

But she rushed on, as though speaking the very lines I would have given her myself. She wanted to make a good impression, avoid the cardinal social sin of falling mute, not having anything to say; all those unsure of themselves are mortally afraid of it. So the fact of saying something was more important than the content of what it was she said.

"Couldn't tear myself away. You should have come with me, Billy. It was heavenly. Simply heavenly." Business of rolling the eyes upward and taking a deep, soulful breath.

"What'd they play first?" he said tightly.

"Shostakovich," she said with an air of vainglory, as when one has newly mastered a difficult word and delights in showing one's prowess with it.

I saw the Cipher's lips tremble preliminary to speech. I saw the tip of Jean's foot find his and squeeze it out unmercifully. Speech never came.

You couldn't tell she'd said anything. His face was a little whiter than before, but it was a slow process, it took long moments to complete itself. Until finally he was pale, but the cause had long been left behind by that time, would not have been easy to trace any more.

She caught something, however. She was not dense.

"Didn't I pronounce it right?" she asked, darting him a look.

"Oh, perfectly," he said.

"But here," she protested. "Here it is right here, on the program." She'd brought the program with her. She insisted on showing it to him. She thrust it on him.

I thought, What a great man Sheakespeare is. He has a line to cover every situation, even from four hundred years back, 'Methinks the lady doth protest too much.'

He crumpled it without looking at it. But not violently, with a sort of slow indifference.

I wondered how many days ahead they printed them. I wondered how you went about getting hold of one in advance. Well, it wasn't totally impracticable; there were ways, probably.

I thought once more, What a great man Shakespeare is: 'Love will find a way.'

She was uneasy now.

She didn't like us. She was hampered by our being there; couldn't defend herself properly against whatever the threat was, although she didn't know what it was herself, as yet. She couldn't even make the attempt to find out, because of our continuing presence.

She sat for a moment with the drink he'd given her, made a knot with her neck-pearls about one finger, let it unravel again. Then she stood up, put her drink down over where they had originally came from.

"I have a headache," she said and touched two fingers to the side of her head. To show us, I suppose, that that was where it was – in her head.

"Shostakovich always gives me a headache too," Jean said sweetly to her husband.

She shot Jean a quick look of hostility, but there was nothing she could do about it. There was nothing to get your teeth into. It had been addressed privately to the Cipher, not anyone else. And it had been said almost inaudibly. Almost, but not quite. If she'd picked it up, that would have been claiming it for her own.

"If you'll excuse me now," she said.

She was asking him, though not the rest of us. She was a little bit afraid. She wanted to get out of this false situation. She didn't know what it was, but she wanted to extricate herself.

"Oh, sure, 'right ahead," he said casually. "You don't have to stand on ceremony with us, Bernette." He didn't even turn to look at her, went ahead dabbling in drinks.

I thought of the old Spanish saying, *Aquitiene Usted su casa*. My house is yours. And it probably was as little valid in the present circumstance as in the original flowery exaggeration.

"But you just came," the Cipher said. He was only trying to be cordial, the poor benighted soul. He hadn't stepped aside into that room with us.

Jean and I simply looked at one another. I could almost lip-read what she was about to say before it came out. "She hasn't far to go." I nearly died for a minute as I saw her lips give a preliminary flicker. Then she curbed herself. That would have been going too far. I breathed again.

She made her goodnights lamely, and yet with a sort of surly defiance. As if to say, I may have lost this skirmish, but I haven't even begun to fight yet. This was on ground of *your* choosing; wait'll he's without his allies, and must come looking for me on ground of my own choosing. We'll see whose flag runs down then.

She climbed the steps, she turned galleryward, she passed from view. In her clinging black dress, her head held high, her chin out. A little cigarette-smoke that had emanated from her on the way, lingered behind for a moment or two. Then that dissolved, too.

And that's all the trace you leave behind in this world, sometimes. A little cigarette-smoke, quickly blown away.

Presently another figure passed the gallery opening, coming from further back in the apartment, but going the same way she had.

Dwight turned his head.

"Going now, Luthe?"

"Yes, sir. Goodnight."

This time you could hear the outer door. Close not loudly, but quite definitely.

"Luthe goes home to Harlem one night a week, and this is his night for it. The rest of the time he stays down here with me."

We left soon afterward ourselves.

As we moved down the gallery in leisurely deliberation, I looked ahead. That room that Jean and I had been in before was lighted now, not dark as we had left it. The door was partly ajar, and the light coming from it lay on the floor in a pale crosswise bar or stripe.

Then as we neared it, some unseen agency pushed it unobtrusively closed, from the inside. I could see the yellow outshine narrow and snuff out, well before we had reached it.

There was no sound accompanying it, and it was easy to pretend we had not noticed it happen. Those of us that had.

We were kept waiting for the elevator for some time. Finally when it appeared, it was being run, strangely, by a gnarled elderly individual in fireman's overalls. There was no night-doorman on duty below when we got down there, either.

"What happened?" Jean asked curiously. "Where's all the brass?"

"Walked off," he said. "Wildcat strike. The management fired one of the fellows for impudence, and they all quit. Les'n'n hour ago. They ain't nobody at all to run the back elevator. I'm pratic'ly running this whole building single-handed, right now. You'll have to get your own taxi, folks. Can't leave this car."

She and I were left alone in the doorway for several minutes, while the Cipher went semaphoring up and down Park Avenue in quest of one. We made good use of the minutes.

"She stayed," I breathed desolately.

"But not for long," Jean assured me. "I don't give her twenty minutes. Five'll get you ten that if you came back an hour from now, you'd find him alone."

I wished afterward she hadn't said that; it may have been what first put the idea in my head, for all I know.

The same elderly pinch-hitter was still servicing the building single-handed. "They ain't nobody at all looking after the back elevator," he complained unasked.

I felt like saying, "You said that before," but I didn't.

He took me up without announcing me.

I got out and I knocked at Dwight's door. The car went down and left me alone there.

I looked at myself in the wall-mirror. I knocked again, more urgently, less tentatively. I tripped the Louis XVI gilt knocker, finally. That carried somewhat better, since it had a metal sounding-board, not a wood one.

His voice said, "Who is it?", too quickly for this last summons to have been the one that brought him; it must have been the first one after all, and he had been waiting there for it to repeat itself.

"Lizzie," I whispered sibilantly, as though there were someone else around to overhear.

The door opened, but very grudgingly. Little more than a crack at first. Then at sight of me, it widened to more normal width. But not full width of passage, for he stood there in the way; simply full width enough to allow unhampered conversation.

He was in a lounging robe. His shirt was collarless above it, and the collar-band was unfastened. It had a peculiar effect on me: not the robe nor the lack of collar, simply the undone collar-band; it made me feel like a wife.

He smiled hospitably. The smile was a little taut. "Well, good Lord! You're the last one I expected to –"

"Don't look so stunned. Am I that frightening?" I couldn't resist saying.

"Did I get you out of bed?" I said.

He kept smiling with unwavering docility. It was a sort of vacant smile. The smile with which you wait for someone to go away. The smile that you give at a door, when you are waiting to close it. Waiting to be allowed to close it, and held powerless by breeding. It had no real candlepower behind it, that smile. "No," he said. "I was just getting ready, by easy stages."

He felt for the satin-faced lapel of his robe, as if to remind himself he had it on. He felt for the loose knot of the braided cord that encircled it, as if to remind himself that it was fastened.

His face looked very pale, I thought; unnaturally so. I hadn't noticed it the first moment or two, but I gradually became aware of it now. I thought it must be the wretched foyer-light, and I hoped I didn't look as pale to him as he did to me. I take pallor easily from unsatisfactory lights. The thing to do was to get inside away from it.

"It's my compact," I said. "I left it up here. Only take me a minute. I'd feel naked without it."

"Where are the others?" he said. His eyes shifted wearily from my face to the elevator-panel rearward of me, then back to my face again.

"I dropped them off first," I said. "Only missed it after they'd left me. Then I came straight back here."

"It couldn't have been up here," he said. "I would have – I would have found it myself right after you left." He gestured helplessly with one hand, in a sort of rotary way. "It must have been in the taxi. Did you look in the taxi?"

The light was the most uncomplimentary thing I'd ever seen. It made him look quite ghastly.

"It wasn't in the taxi," I insisted. "I didn't use it in the taxi. Up here was the last place I used it." I waited for him to shift, but he didn't. "Won't you let me come in and look, a moment?"

He was equally insistent. We were both extremely cordial about it, but extremely insistent. "But it isn't up here, I tell you. It couldn't be, Lizzie, don't you see? If it was, I would have come across it by now myself?"

I smiled winningly. "But did you look for it? Did you know it was lost, until I told you so myself just now, here at the door? Then if you didn't look for it, how do you know it isn't there?"

"Well, I – I went over the place, I –" He decided not to say that, whatever it was to have been.

"But if you didn't know *what* it was that was lost, you couldn't have had your eyes out for it specifically," I kept on, sugaring my stubborness with a smile. "If you'd only let me step in for a moment and see for myself –"

I waited.

He waited, for my waiting to end.

I tried another tack. "Oh," I murmured deprecatingly, turning my head aside, as if to myself, as if in afterthought, "you're not alone. I'm sorry. I didn't mean to –"

It worked. I saw a livid flash, like the glancing reflection from a sun-blotted mirror, sweep across his face. Just for an instant. If it was fear, and it must have been of a kind, it was a new fear at this point; fear of being misunderstood, and no longer fear of my entering. He stepped back like magic, drawing the door with him.

"You're mistaken," he said tersely. "Come in."

And then as I did, and as he closed the door after me, and pressed it sealed with his palm in one or two places, he added, and still quite brittly. "Whatever gave you that idea?" And turned to look the question at me, as well as ask it.

"After all," I drawled reassuringly, "I'm not anyone's grandmother."

He was no longer smiling. This point was evidently of importance to him, for some peevish reason that escaped me. Sheer contradictoriness, perhaps. Certainly I'd never detected any trait of primness in him before. "I never was so alone in my life," he said somewhat crossly. "Even Luthe went uptown."

"I know," I reminded him. "He left while we were still here."

But I had been thinking mainly of somebody else, not Luthe.

We moved slowly down the gallery, I preceding him.

She'd gone, just as Jean had said she would. The door that I had seen slyly closing before, shutting off its own beam of light, was standing starkly open now, and the room was dark. It looked gloomy in there, unutterably depressing, at that hour of the night.

"I didn't leave it in there," I said. I wasn't supposed to have been in there.

"No, you didn't," he agreed, with considerable alacrity.

We turned and faced across the gallery to the other door, the closed one, to that "writing-room" of his.

"In here, maybe," I suggested.

I heard him draw some sort of a crucial breath.

"No," he said quite flatly. "You didn't."

"I may have, just the same." I reached out to take the knob.

"No," he said. Tautly, almost shrilly, as though I were getting on his nerves.

I glanced at him in mild surprise, at the use of such a sharp tone of voice for such a trifling matter. The look I caught on his face was even more surprising. For a moment, all his good looks were gone.

He was ugly in mood and ugly of face.

Then, with an effort, he banished the puckered grimace, let his expression smooth out again. Even tried on a thin smile for size, but it didn't fit very well and soon dropped off again.

I tried the door and it was locked.

"It's locked," I said, desisting.

"I always keep it that way," he said. "I write in there, and leave my copy lying around, and – well, I'm sensitive about it; I don't like Luthe nosing into it. I caught him once snickering –"

"But you said he'd gone home."

"Well, the habit persists."

"Well, won't you let me go in and look at least?" I coaxed. I thought: I still love him, even when his face is all ugly and puckery like that. How strange; I thought it was largely his looks that had me smitten, and now I see that it isn't.

"But you weren't in there, so how could it get in there?"

"I was. I was in there once earlier tonight. I don't know whether you knew it or not, but I strayed in there one time this evening."

He looked at me, and he looked at the door. "I'll see if I have the key," he said quite suddenly, and gave the skirt of his robe a lift and plunged his hand into his pocket. There was a great commotion of jangling. The pupils of his eyes slanted far over into their corners for an instant, toward me, then righted themselves.

I'd caught the little secretive flicker; I read it. That was a look of hidden annoyance with me, I told myself, expressed quicker than he could master it.

Why do I drive him like this, I wondered? To see how far I can go? To make him fully aware of my being here alone with him? I didn't know myself.

He took out a considerable palmful of them; five or six, I should say. They were all secured together on a little ring-holder. The majority, it could be seen at sight, were not doorkeys at all. They were keys of special usage: to a desk-drawer, perhaps; to a safety-box; to the ignition of a car.

And as he paid them over, making considerable noise with them, I saw an additional one fall soundlessly to the carpet, from between his robe and the mouth of his pocket. One that must have been held in there separate, apart from the rest. One that had come up accidentally, perhaps, without his meaning it to, when he had drawn the rest of them up.

It was long-shanked, a typical interior-doorkey, this one.

I saw that he hadn't noticed its fall, the noise he was making with the others covered it. For a moment I was going to pick it up and restore it to him. Then, instead, I shifted my foot, put it over it, and stood there making no other move.

He tried one unsuccessfully, withdrew it again. It was far too small to be taken by that particular lock.

He creased his forehead querulously. "I've misplaced it," he said. "I don't seem to have it here." He restored them under his robe, without exploring with his fingers to see if there were any additional ones lingering in there. I could tell; his hand came out too swiftly. As if this were a point he himself needed no reassurance upon, he already knew the answer.

"I may have dropped it into something around the place. I do that sometimes." He scratched his head, and glanced the other way, as if in aid to his memory.

I stooped swiftly, in that instant he left unguarded, and took up the key, and kept it to myself in my hand.

"Well," he said, as if in conclusion to the whole interview, "if I come across it, I'll see that you get it back."

We stood and looked at one another for a moment, he waiting for me to make the next move.

"He wants me to go," I said, as though speaking ruefully to a third person. "He can't wait until I do."

What could he say then? What could anyone have said, except in overt offense? And that, you see, was why I'd said it. Though it was true, my saying so forced him to deny it, obliged him to act in contradiction to it. Though he didn't want to, and I knew that he didn't want to, and he knew that I knew that he didn't want to.

"No," he said deprecatingly. "No, not at all." And then warmed gradually to his own insistence: picked up speed with it as he went along. "Come inside. Away from that door." (As though my departure from a fixed point was now what he wanted to obtain, and if he could obtain it only by having me all the way in, rather than by having me leave, then he'd have me all the way in.) He motioned me the way with his arm and he turned to accompany me. And kept up meanwhile the running fire of his invitation at a considerably accelerated tempo, until it ended up by being almost staccato. "Come inside and we'll have a drink together. Just you and I. Just the two of us alone. As a matter of fact I need company, this minute."

On the rebound, I thought. On the rebound; I may get him that way.

They say you do. Oh, what do I care how, if only I do.

I went down the steps, and he went down close beside me. His swinging arm grazed mine as we did so, and it did something to me. It was like sticking your elbow into an electrical outlet.

That drawing room of his had never looked vaster and more sombre. There was something almost funereal about it, as though there were a corpse embalmed somewhere nearby, and we were about to sit up and keep vigil over it. There was only one lamp lit, and it was the wrong one. It made great bat-wing shadows around the walls, from the upraised piano-lid and other immovables, and now added our own two long, willowly emanations.

He saw me look at it, and said "I'll fix that."

I let him turn on one more just to take some of the curse off the gruesomeness, but then when I saw him go for the wall-switch, that would have turned on a blaze overhead, I quickly interposed "Not too many." You can't have romance under a thousand-watt current.

I sat down on the sofa Jean had been on that night of the striptease.

He made our drinks for us, and then came over with them and then sat down in the next state.

"No, here," I said. "My eyesight isn't that good."

He grinned, and brought his drink over, and we sat half-turned toward one another like the arms of a parenthesis. A parenthesis that holds nothing in it but blank space.

I saw to it that it soon collapsed of its own emptiness, and one of the arms was tilted rakishly toward the other.

I tongued my drink.

"It was a pretty bad jolt," I admitted thoughtfully.

"What was?"

"You don't have to pretend with me."

"Oh," he said lamely.

"You're still pretending," I chided him. "You're pretending that you haven't thought of it; that I'm the one just now brought it back to your mind for the first time. When all along it hasn't left your mind, not for a single moment since."

He tried to drown his face in his drink, the way he pushed it down into it. "Please," he said, and made a grimace. "Not now. Do we have to – Don't let's talk about it now."

"Oh, it hurts that much," I said softly.

The parenthesis had become a double line, touching from top to bottom.

"Why don't you put iodine on it?" I suggested.

He made a ghastly shambles of a smile. "Is there any for such things?"

"Here's the bottle, right beside you," I offered. "*And there's no death's head on the label.*"

That symbol seemed to frighten him, or at least be highly unwelcome. He screwed up his eyes tight, and I saw him give his head a shake, as though to rid it of that particular thought.

"It stings for a minute, and then you heal," I purred. "You heal clean. No festering. And then you're well again; even the mark goes away. And you have a new love." I dropped my voice to a breath. "Won't you try – iodine?"

So close his face was to mine, so close; all he had to do –

Then he turned it a little; oh, a very, tactful little. The wrong way; so that the distance had widened a little. And he could breathe without mingling his breath with mine. Which seemed to be what he wanted.

"Don't you understand me, Dwight? I'm making love to you. And if I'm awkward about it, it's because women aren't very good at it. Can't you help me out a little?"

I saw the look on his face. Sick horror. I wish I hadn't, but I did. I never thought just a look on a face could hurt so.

"Would it be that bad? Would it be that intolerable, to be married to me?"

"Married?" His backbone gave a slight twitch, as though a pin overlooked in his shirt had just pricked him. I caught him do it, slight as it was. That was no compliment, either, any more than the look on his face before had been.

"You've just been proposed to, Dwight. That was a proposal, just then. The first I've ever made."

He tried, first, to carry it off with a sickly grin. The implication: You're just joking, and I'm supposed to know you are, but you make me a little uncomfortable just the same.

I wouldn't let him; I wouldn't accept the premise.

"You don't laugh when a lady proposes to you," I said gently. "You don't laugh at her. You meet her on her own ground; you give her that much at least."

"I'm not – cut out –" he floundered. "It would be about the dirtiest trick I could play – I couldn't do that to you –" And then finally, and more decidedly, like a snap-lock to the subject: "You'd be sorry."

"I want to be. Let me be. I'd rather be sorry – with you – than glad – with anyone else."

He looked down his nose now. He didn't say anything more. A sort of stubborn muteness had set in. That was his best defense; that was his only one. He probably knew it. Their instincts are just as valid as ours.

I had to do the talking. Someone had to. It would have been even worse to sit there in silence.

I took a sip of my drink. I sighed in feigned objectivity. "It's unfair, isn't it? A woman can refuse a man, and she doesn't have to feel any compunction. He's supposed to take it straight, and he does. But if a man refuses a woman, he has to try to spare her feelings at the same time."

He hadn't as a matter of fact made any such attempt until now; he did now, possibly, because I had recalled his duty to him.

"You're a swell gal, Lizzie – It's you I'm thinking of – You don't know what you're asking – You don't want *me*."

"You're getting your pronouns mixed," I said sadly.

All he could repeat was: "No. I mean it, you're a swell gal, Lizzie –"

"You're a swell gal, Lizzie," I echoed desolately, "but you don't ring the bell."

He made the mistake of putting his arm around my shoulder, in what was meant as a fraternal embrace, I suppose. He should have left his hands off me; it was hard enough without that.

I let my head go limp against him. I couldn't have kept it up straight if I'd tried. And I didn't try.

He tried to jerk his arm away, as he realized this new danger, but I caught it, from in front, with mine, and held it there, around my shoulders, like a precious sable someone's trying to take away from you.

He shuddered, and hit himself violently in the center of the forehead. As if there were some thought lodged in there that he couldn't bear the contemplation of. "Good Lord," I heard him groan. "Good Lord! Right here, in this apartment —"

"Is there something wrong with this apartment?" I asked innocently.

"Not with the apartment, with me," he murmured.

"I won't dispute you there," I said cattishly.

I let go of his arm, and stood up. I got ready to go. I'd been rejected. To have prolonged it would have veered over into buffoonery. I had no self-respect left, but at least I still had my external dignity left. The law of diminishing returns would only have set in from this point on.

"Is it my age?" I said, with my back toward him for a moment, doing something private to my hair.

"No," he said. "I never think of age in – in connection with you."

"I'll be forty in November," I said, unasked, now that there was nothing further to lose. "So you can see how lucky you were just now."

"No," he protested. "You can't be – Why, I always thought you were about twenty-eight, somewhere along there –"

"Thank you for that much, anyway," I said. "At least I've salvaged something out of the evening's wreckage."

I turned and looked at him, still sitting there. "Proposals don't agree with you," I let him know. "You look positively harassed."

I saw him wince a little, as though he agreed with me; not only looked it, but felt. He stood now, to do the polite thing as host.

"I'll get over it," I said, speaking out loud to keep my own courage up. "It doesn't kill you."

He blinked at that word, as though it grated a lot.

I was ready to go now. He came closer, to accelerate the process.

"Won't you kiss me goodnight?" I said.

He did it with his brakes on; used just one arm to support my back. Put his lips to mine, but with a time-valve to them. Took them away as soon as time was up. Mine tried to follow, and lost their way.

We straightened ourselves. "I'll see you out," he said.

"Never mind, don't rub it in."

He took me at my word, turned back to pour himself another drink. His hand was shaking, and if that's a sign of needing one, he needed one.

I went down the long gallery alone. My heart was blushing and my cheeks felt white.

I came even with that door, the door to his workroom, and remembered I was holding the key to it, that he'd dropped before when we were out here.

I stopped, and took it out, and put it in the keyhole.

Then I felt his eyes on me, and turned, and saw him standing watching me at the end of the gallery, where I'd just come from myself.

"Lizzie," he said. "Don't. It won't be in there." His voice was toneless, strangely quiet. But his face looked terrible. It wasn't just white, it was livid; it was the shining white of phosphorus gleaming in the dark.

He didn't offer to approach, his feet stayed where they were; but his hands, as if restlessly feeling the need to be occupied with something during the brief pause while we stood and confronted one another like that, strayed to the cord of his robe and, of their own accord, without his seeming to know what they were doing, fumbled there, until suddenly the knot had disheveled, fallen open. Then each one, holding a loose end of the cord, flicked and played with it, all unconsciously. The way the two ends danced and spun and snaked, suggested the tentative twitching of a cat's tail, when it is about to spring.

He was holding it taut across his back, and out at each side, in a sort of elongated bow-shape. It was just a posture, a stance, a vagary of nervous preoccupation, I suppose.

An odd one.

I flexed my wrist slightly, as if to complete the turning of the inserted key.

The cord tightened to almost a straight line, stopped moving.

For a moment, out of sheer perversity, I was going to open the door, simply to prolong my presence. He was not really interested in whether I opened the door or not; it just seemed that way. What he really was interested in was having me leave once and for all, so he'd be let alone. The opening of the door would have delayed that, so that was why he set such store upon my not doing so. My own common sense told me this.

His eyes met mine and mine met his, the length of the gallery.

The impulse to annoy him died.

Indifferently, I desisted. I dropped my hand slowly, and left the key in the lock, and let the door be.

His hands dropped too. That taut pull of the cord slackened, it softened to a dangling loop.

"It wouldn't have been in there," he breathed with a sort of exhausted heaviness, as though all his strength had gone into holding the cord as he had been just now.

"I know it wouldn't," I said. "It's been safely in my bag the whole time." I opened the bag, took it out, and showed it to him. "I knew it was in there even when I started back here to look for it." I went on to the outside door and opened it. "The trick didn't pay off, that's all."

"Good night, Dwight," I added.

"Good night, Lizzie," he echoed sepulchrally. I saw him reach out with one arm and support himself limply against the wall beside him, he was so tired of me by this time.

I closed the outside door.

They tell you wrong when they tell you infatuation dies a sudden death. Infatuation dies a lingering painful death. Even after all hope is gone the afterglow sometimes stubbornly clings on and on, kidding you, lighting the dark in which you are alone. Infatuation dies as slowly as a slower love; it comes on quicker, that is all.

Twice I went by there in a taxi, in the weeks following that night. And each stopped a moment at his door.

But then I didn't get out after all. Just sat there. Perhaps to see if I could sit there like that without getting out. Perhaps to see if I was strong enough.

I was. I just barely made it, both times, but I made it.

"Drive on," I said heroically. It was like leaving your right arm behind, jammed in a door; but I left it.

But the third time, ah, the third time. I was practically over it. I was cured. I made the discovery for myself sitting there in the taxi, taking my own blood-pressure, so to speak, holding my own pulse, listening to my own heart. I could drive away now without a wrench, without feeling that I'd left a part of me behind, caught in his door.

I lit a cigarette and thought with a sigh of relief: It's passed. It's finished. Now I've got something more to worry about. I'm immune now, this attack will last me for the rest of my life. That was my last siege of love. Now I can go on and just work and live and be placid.

"Y'getting out, lady, or what?" the driver asked fretfully.

"Yes," I said coolly, "I think I will. I want to say goodbye to someone in there."

And in perfect safety, in perfect calm, I paid him and got out and went inside to visit my recent, my last, love.

But they tell you wrong when they tell you infatuation dies a sudden death. It doesn't. I know.

I seemed to have picked an inappropriate time for my farewell visit. Or at least, a non-exclusive one.

There'd been somebody else with him. The apartment-door was already open, when I stepped off at his foyer, and he was standing there talking to some man in dilatory leavetaking.

The man was heavily-built and none too young. In the milder fifties, I should judge. His hair was silvering, his complexion was florid, and there were little skin-like red blood-vessels threading the whites of his eyes. He had a hard-looking face, but he was being excessively amiable at the moment that I came upon the two of them. Almost overdoing it, almost overly amiable, for it didn't blend well with the rest of his characteristics, gave the impression of being a seldom-used, almost rusty attribute he had to push down hard on the accelerator to get it working at all. And he was keeping his foot pressed down on it for all he was worth so that it couldn't get away from him.

"I hope I haven't troubled you, Mr Billings," he was apologizing just as the elevator panel opened.

"Not at all," Dwight protested indulgently. There was even something patronizing in his intonation. "I know how those things are. Don't think twice about it. Glad to –" And then they both turned at the slight rustle the panel made, and saw me, and so didn't finish the mutual gallantries they were engaged upon. Or rather, postponed them for a moment.

Dwight's face lit up at sight of me. I was welcome. There could be no doubt of it. Not like that other night.

He shook my hand cordially. "Well! Nice of you! Where've you been keeping yourself?" And that sort of thing. But made no move to introduce the departing caller to me.

And his manners were too quick-witted for that to have been an oversight. So what could I infer but that there was a differentiation of status between us that would have made a social introduction inappropriate. In other words, that one call was a personal one and the other was not, so the two were not to be linked.

"Go in, Lizzie. Take your things off. I'll be right with you."

I went in. My last impression of the man standing there with him was that he was slightly ill-at-ease under my parting scrutiny; call it embarrassed, call it sheepish, call it what you will. He turned his head aside a moment and took a deep draught of an expensive cigar he was holding between his knuckles. As if: Don't look at me so closely. I certainly wasn't staring, so it must have been his own self-consciousness.

I went down the gallery of lost love. The writing-room door was open now. I went past it without stopping, and down the steps to the drawing-room arena.

I took off my "things" as he'd put it, and primped at my hair, and moved idly around, waiting for him to join me.

I looked at things, as I moved. One does, waiting in a room.

He'd left them just as they were, to take his visitor to the door. Probably I hadn't been announced yet, at that moment. I must have been announced after they were both already at the door, and he hadn't come all the way back in here since leaving it the first time.

There were two glasses there. Both drained heartily, nothing but ice-sweat left in their bottoms; the interview must have been a cordial one.

There were two strips of Cellophane shorn from a couple of expensive cigars.

There was a single burned matchstick; one smoker had done that courteous service for both.

His checkbook-folder was lying on the corner of the table. He must have taken it out of his pocket at one time, and then forgotten to return it again. Or perhaps thought that could wait until afterward, it was of no moment.

I didn't go near it, nor touch it, nor examine it in any way. I just saw it lying there.

There was a new blotter lying near it. Almost spotless; it had only been used about once.

That I did pick up, idly; and look at. As if I were a student of Arabic or some other right-to-left scrawl. I looked at it thoughtfully.

He still didn't come in.

Finally I took it over to the mirror with me and fronted it to that, and looked into that.

Part of his signature came out. "– illings." It was the thing he'd written last, so the ink was still freshest when the blotter'd been put to it. Above it were a couple of less distinct tracings. " – career." And two large circles and two smaller ones. Like this: "OOoo."

I turned swiftly, as though that had shocked me (but it hadn't – why should it?) and pitched it back onto the table from where I stood. Then I fixed my hair a little more, in places where it didn't need it.

He came in, looking sanguine, looking zestful. I don't remember that he rubbed his hands together, but that was the impression his mood conveyed: of rubbing his hands together.

"Who was that man?" I said indifferently.

"You'll laugh," he said. And he set the example by doing so himself. "That's something for you. Something for your magazine." Then he waited, like a good raconteur always does. Then he gave me the punch-line. "He was a detective. A real, honest-to-goodness, life-sized detective. Badge and everything."

I stopped being indifferent, but I didn't get startled. Only politely incredulous, as a guest should be toward her host's surprise climaxes. "Here? What'd he want with you?"

"Asking if I could give him any information," he said cheerfully. Then in the same tone: "You've heard about Bernette, haven't you?"

I said I hadn't.

"I think you met her up here once."

I visioned a Fury in pink lingerie. Yes, I said, I seemed to recall.

"Well, she's disappeared. Hasn't been heard of in weeks."

"Why do they come to you about it?" I asked him.

"Oh," he said impatiently, "some tommyrot or other about her never having been seen again after – after the last time she left here. I dunno, something like that. Just routine. This's the third time this same fellow's been up here. I've been darn good-natured about it." Then he said, more optimistically, "He promised me just now, though, this is the last time; he won't come back any more."

He was fixing two drinks for us, in two fresh glasses. The first two had been shunted aside. The checkbook and the blotter had both vanished, and I'd been facing him in the mirror the whole time; so maybe I'd been mistaken, they hadn't been there in the first place.

"And then there was something about some clothes of hers," he went on off-handedly. "She left some of her things here with me –" He broke off to ask me: "Are you shocked, Lizzie?"

"No," I reassured him. "I knew she stopped here now and then."

"I was supposed to send them after her; she said something about letting me know where she could be reached –" He shrugged. "But I never heard from her again myself. They're still waiting in there –"

He finished swirling ice with a neat little tap of the glass mixer against the rim.

"Probably ran off with someone," he said contemptuously.

I nodded dispassionately.

"I know who put him up to it," he went on, with a slight tinge of resentment. I had to take it he meant the detective; he offered no explanation to cover the switch in pronouns. "That dirty little ex-second husband of hers."

"Oh, is he ex?" I said. That was another thing I hadn't known.

"Certainly. They were annulled almost as soon as they came back from their wedding-trip. I even helped her to do it myself, sent her to my lawyer –"

And paid for it, I knew he'd been about to add; but he didn't.

"I told this fellow tonight," he went on, still with that same tinge of vengefulness, "that they'd better look into his motives, while they were about it. He was only out to get money out of her –"

(And she was only out to get money out of you, I thought, but tactfully didn't say so.)

"Do you think something's happened to her?" I asked.

He didn't answer that directly. "She'll probably turn up someplace, they always do." Then he said grimly, "It won't be here. Now let's have one, you and I." And he came toward me with our drinks.

We sat down on the sofa with them. He didn't need any urging tonight.

We had another pair. Then a third. We let the third pair stand and cool off awhile.

I was the upright arm of the parenthesis tonight, I noticed presently; he was the toppled-over one.

I didn't move my head aside the way he had his; his lips just didn't affect me. It was like being kissed by – cardboard.

"I want you to marry me," he said. "I want – what you wanted that night. I want – someone like you."

(That's not good enough, I thought. You should want just me myself, and not someone like me. That leaves it too wide open. This is the rebound. You want the older woman now. Safety, security, tranquility; not so much fire. Something's shaken you, and you can't stand alone; so if there was a female statue in the room, you'd propose to that.)

"Too late," I said. "I've passed that point, as you arrive at it. You got it too late. Or I left it too soon."

He wilted, and his head went down. He had to go on alone. "I'm sorry," he breathed.

"I am too." And I was. But it couldn't be helped.

Suddenly I laughed. "Isn't love the damnedest thing?"

He laughed too, after a moment; ruefully. "A devil of a thing," he agreed.

And laughing together, we took our leave of one another, parted, never to meet in closeness again. Laughing is a good way to part. As good a way as any.

I read an item about it in the papers a few days afterward, quite by chance. The second husband had been picked up and taken in for questioning, in connection with her disappearance. Nothing more than that. There was no other name mentioned.

I read still another item about it in the papers, only a day or two following the first one. The second husband had been released again, for lack of evidence.

I never read anything further about it, not another word, from that day on.

The other night at a party I met my last love again. I don't mean my latest; by last, I mean my final one. And he was as taking and as debonair as ever, but not to me any more – a little older maybe; and we said the things you say, with two glasses in our hands to keep us company.

"Hello Lizzie; how've you been?"

"Hello, Dwight; where've you been keeping yourself lately?"

"I've been around. And you?"

"I've been around too."

And then when there wasn't anything more to say, we moved on. In opposite directions.

It isn't often that I see him any more. But whenever I do, I still think of her. I wonder what really did become of her.

And just the other night, suddenly, for no reason at all, out of nowhere, the strangest thought entered my head for a moment.

But then I promptly dismissed it again, just as quickly as it had occurred to me, as being too fantastic, too utterly improbable. The people you *know* never do things like that; the people you *read about* may, but never the people you *know*.

Do they?

For the Rest of Her Life

Their eyes met in Rome. On a street in Rome – the Via Piemonte. He was coming down it, coming along toward her, when she first saw him. She didn't know it but he was also coming into her life, into her destiny – bringing what was meant to be.

Every life is a mystery. And every story of every life is a mystery. But it is not what *happens* that is the mystery. It is whether it *has* to happen no matter what, whether it is ordered and ordained, fixed and fated, or whether it can be missed, avoided, circumvented, passed by; *that* is the mystery.

If she had not come along the Via Piemonte that day, would it still have happened? If she had come along the Via Piemonte that day, but ten minutes later than she did, would it *still* have happened? Therein lies the real mystery. And no one ever knows, and no one ever will.

As their eyes met, they held. For just a heartbeat.

He wasn't cheap. He wasn't sidewalk riffraff. His clothes were good clothes, and his air was a good air.

He was a personable-looking man. First your eye said: he's not young any more, he's not a boy any more. Then your eye said: but he's not old. There was something of youth hovering over and about him, and yet refusing to land in any one particular place. As though it were about to take off and leave him. Yet not quite that either. More as though it had never fully been there in the first place. In short, the impression it was was agelessness. Not young, not old, not callow, not mature – but ageless. Thirty-six looking fifty-six, or fifty-six looking thirty-six, but which it was you could not say.

Their eyes met – and held. For just a heartbeat.

Then they passed one another by, on the Via Piemonte, but without any turn of their heads to prolong the look.

"I wonder who that was," she thought.

What he thought couldn't be known – at least, not by her.

Three nights later they met again, at a party the friend she was staying with took her to.

He came over to her, and she said, "I've seen you before. I passed you on Monday on the Via Piemonte. At about four in the afternoon."

"I remember you too," he said. "I noticed you that day, going by."

I wonder why we remember each other like that, she mused; I've passed dozens, hundreds, of other people since, and he must have too. I don't remember any of *them*.

"I'm Mark Ramsey," he said.

"I'm Linda Harris."

An attachment grew up. What is an attachment? It is the most difficult of all the human interrelationships to explain, because it is the vaguest, the most impalpable. It has all the good points of love, and none of its drawbacks. No jealousy, no quarrels, no greed to possess, no fear of losing possession, no hatred (which is very much a part of love), no surge of passion and no hangover afterward. It never reaches the heights, and it never reaches the depths.

As a rule it comes on subtly. As theirs did. As a rule the two involved are not even aware of it at first. As they were not. As a rule it only becomes noticeable when it is interrupted in some way, or broken off by circumstances. As theirs was. In other words, its presence only becomes known in its absence. It is only missed after it stops. While it is still going on, little thought is given to it, because little thought needs to be.

It is pleasant to meet, it is pleasant to be together. To put your shopping packages down on a little wire-backed chair at a little table at a sidewalk café, and sit down and have a vermouth with someone who has been waiting there for you. And will be waiting there again tomorrow afternoon. Same time, same table, same sidwalk café. Or to watch Italian youth going through the gyrations of the latest dance craze in some inexpensive indigenous night-place – while you, who come from the country where the dance originated, only get up to do a sedate fox trot. It is even pleasant to part, because this simply means preparing the way for the next meeting.

One long continuous being-together, even in a love affair, might make the thing wilt. In an attachment it would surely kill the thing off altogether. But to meet, to part, then to meet again in a few days, keeps the thing going, encourages it to flower.

And yet it requires a certain amount of vanity, as love does; a desire to please, to look one's best, to elicit compliments. It inspires a certain amount of flirtation, for the two are of opposite sex. A wink of understanding over the rim of a raised glass, a low-voiced confidential aside about something and the smile of intimacy that answers it, a small impromptu gift – a necktie on the one part because of an accidental spill on the one he was wearing, or of a small bunch of flowers on the other part because of the color of the dress she has on.

So it goes.

And suddenly they part, and suddenly there's a void, and suddenly they discover they have had an attachment.

Rome passed into the past, and became New York.

Now, if they had never come together again, or only after a long time and in different circumstances, then the attachment would have faded and died. But if they suddenly do come together again – while the sharp sting of missing one another is still smarting – then the attachment will revive full force, full strength. But never again as merely an attachment. It has to go on from there, it has to build, to pick up speed. And sometimes it is so glad to be brought back again that it makes the mistake of thinking it is love.

She was thinking of him at the moment the phone rang. And that helped too, by its immediacy, by its telephonic answer to her wistful wish of remembrance. Memory is a mirage that fools the heart . . .

"You'll never guess what I'm holding in my hand, right while I'm talking to you . . .

"I picked it up only a moment ago, and just as I was standing and looking at it, the phone rang. Isn't that the strangest thing! . . .

"Do you remember the day we stopped in and you bought it . . .

"I have a little one-room apartment on East 70th Street. I'm by myself now, Dorothy stayed on in Rome . . ."

A couple of months later, they were married . . . .

They call this love, she said to herself. I know what it is now. I never thought I would know, but I do now.

But she failed to add: if you can step back and identify it, is it really there? Shouldn't you be unable to know what the whole thing's about? Just blindly clutch and hold and fear that it will get away. But unable to stop, to think, to give it any name.

Just two more people sharing a common human experience. Infinite in its complexity, tricky at times, but almost always successfully surmounted in one of two ways: either blandly content with the results as they are, or else vaguely discontent but chained by habit. Most women don't marry a man, they marry a habit. Even when a habit is good, it can become monotonous; most do. When it is bad in just the average degree it usually becomes no more than a nuisance and an irritant; and most do.

But when it is darkly, starkly evil in the deepest sense of the word, then it can truly become a hell on earth.

Theirs seemed to fall midway between the first two, for just a little while. Then it started veering over slowly toward the last. Very slowly, at the start, but very steadily . . .

They spent their honeymoon at a New Hampshire lakeshore resort. This lake had an Indian name which, though grantedly barbaric in sound to the average English-speaker, in her special case presented such an impassable block both in speech and in mental pre-speech imagery (for some obscure reason, Freudian perhaps, or else simply an instinctive retreat from something with distressful connotations) that she gave up trying to say it and it became simply "the lake." Then as time drew it backward, not into forgetfulness but into distance, it became "that lake."

Here the first of the things that happened, happened. The first of the things important enough to notice and to remember afterward, among a great many trifling but kindred ones that were not. Some so slight they were not more than gloating, zestful glints of eye or curt hurtful gestures. (Once he accidentally poured a spurt of scalding tea on the back of a waitress' wrist, by not waiting long enough for the waitress to withdraw her hand in setting the cup down, and by turning his head momentarily the other way. The waitress yelped, and he apologized, but he showed his teeth as he did so, and you don't show your teeth in remorse.)

One morning when she woke up, he had already dressed and gone out of the room. They had a beautifully situated front-view of rooms which overlooked the lake itself (the bridal suite, as a matter of fact), and when she went to the window she saw him out there on the white-painted little pier which jutted out into the water on knock-kneed piles. He'd put on a turtle-necked sweater instead of a coat and shirt, and that, over his spare figure, with the shoreward breeze alternately lifting and then flattening his hair, made him look younger than when he was close by. A ripple of the old attraction, of the old attachment, coursed through her and then was quickly gone. Just like the breeze out there. The little sidewalk café chairs of Rome with the braided-wire backs and the piles of parcels on them, where were they now? Gone forever; they couldn't enchant any more.

The lake water was dark blue, pebbly-surfaced by the insistent breeze that kept sweeping it like the strokes of invisible broomstraws, and mottled with gold flecks that were like floating freckles in the nine o'clock September sunshine.

There was a little boy in bathing trunks, tanned as a caramel, sitting on the side of the pier, dangling his legs above the water. She'd noticed him about in recent days. And there was his dog, a noisy, friendly, ungainly little mite, a Scotch terrier that was under everyone's feet all the time.

The boy was throwing a stick in, and the dog was splashing after it, retrieving it, and paddling back. Over and over, with that tirelessness and simplicity of interest peculiar to all small boys and their dogs. Off to one side a man was bringing up one of the motorboats that were for rent, for Mark to take out.

She could hear him in it for a while after that, making a long slashing ellipse around the lake, the din of its vibration alternately soaring and lulling as it passed from the far side to the near and then back to the far side again.

Then it cut off suddenly, and when she went back to look it was rocking there sheepishly engineless. The boy was weeping and the dog lay huddled dead on the lake rim, strangled by the boiling backwash of the boat that had dragged it – how many times? – around and around in its sweep of the lake. The dog's collar had become snagged some way in a line with a grappling hook attached, left carelessly loose over the side of the boat. (Or aimed and pitched over as the boat went slashing by?) The line trailed limp now, and the lifeless dog had been detached from it.

"If you'd only looked back," the boy's mother said ruefully to Mark. "He was a good swimmer, but I guess the strain was too much and his little heart gave out."

"He did look! He did! He did! I saw him!" the boy screamed agonized, peering accusingly from in back of her skirt.

"The spray was in the way," Mark refuted instantly. But she wondered why he said it so quickly. Shouldn't he have taken a moment's time to think about it first, and then say, "The spray must have been –" or "I guess maybe the spray –" But he said it as quickly as though he'd been ready to say it even before the need had arisen.

Everyone for some reason acted furtively ashamed, as if something unclean had happened. Everyone but the boy of course. There were no adult nuances to his pain.

The boy would eventually forget his dog.

But would she? Would she?

They left the lake – the farewells to Mark were a bit on the cool side, she noticed – and moved into a large rambling country house in the Berkshire region of Massachusetts, not far from Pittsfield, which he told her had been in his family for almost seventy-five years. They had a car, an Alfa-Romeo, which he had brought over from Italy, and, at least in all its outward aspects, they had a not too unpleasant life together. He was an art importer, and financially a highly successful one; he used to commute back and forth to Boston, where he had a gallery with a small-size apartment above it. As a rule he would stay over in the city, and then drive out Friday night and spend the week-end in the country with her.

(She always slept so well on Mondays, Tuesdays, and Wednesdays. Thursdays she always lay awake half the night reminding herself that the following night was Friday. She never stopped to analyze this; if she had, what would it have told her? What *could* it have, if she didn't realize it already?)

As far as the house was concerned, let it be said at once that it was not a depressing house in itself. People can take their moods from a house, but by the same token a house can take its mood from the people who live in it. If it became what it became, it was due to him – or rather, her reaction to him.

The interior of the house had crystallized into a very seldom evoked period, the pre-World War I era of rococo and gimcrack elegance. Either its last occupant before them (an unmarried older sister of his) had had a penchant for this out of some girlhood memory of a war-blighted romance and had deliberately tried to recreate it, or what was more likely, all renovations had stopped around that time and it had just stayed that way by default.

Linda discovered things she had heard about but never seen before. Claw legs on the bathtub, nacre in-and-out push buttons for the lights, a hanging stained-glass dome lamp over the dining-room table, a gramophone with a crank handle – she wondered if they'd first rolled back the rug and then danced the hesitation or the one-step to it? The whole house, inside and out, cried out to have women in the straight-up-and-down endlessly long tunics of 1913, with side-puffs of hair over their ears, in patent-leather shoes with beige suede tops up to the middle of the calf, suddenly step out of some of the rooms; and in front of the door, instead of his slender-bodied, bullet-fast Italian compact, perhaps a four-cornered Chalmers or Pierce-Arrow or Hupmobile shaking all over to the beat of its motor.

Sometimes she felt like an interloper, catching herself in some full-length mirror as she passed it, in her over-the-kneetop skirt and short free down-blown hair. Sometimes she felt as if she were under a magic spell, waiting to be disenchanted. But it wasn't a good kind of spell, and it didn't come wholly from the house or its furnishings . . .

One day at the home of some people Mark knew who lived in the area, where he had taken her on a New Year's Day drop-in visit, she met a young man named Garrett Hill. He was branch head for a company in Pittsfield.

It was as simple as that – they met. As simple as only beautiful things can be simple, as only life-changing things, turning-point things, can be simple.

Then she met him a second time, by accident. Then a third, by coincidence. A fourth, by chance . . . Or directed by unseen forces?

Then she started to see him on a regular basis, without meaning anything, certainly without meaning any harm. The first night he brought her home they chatted on the way in his car; and then at the door, as he held out his hand, she quickly put hers out of sight behind her back.

"Why are you afraid to shake my hand?"

"I thought you'd hurt me."

"How can anyone hurt you by just shaking your hand?"

When he tried to kiss her, she turned and fled into the house, as frightened as though he'd brandished a whip at her.

When he tried it again, on a later night, again she recoiled sharply – as if she were flinching from some sort of punishment.

He looked at her, and his eyes widened, both in sudden understanding and in disbelief. "You're afraid *physically*," he said, almost whispering. "I thought it was some wifely scruple the other night. But you're physically afraid of being kissed! As if there were pain attached to it."

Before she could stop herself or think twice she blurted out, "Well, there is, isn't there?"

He said, his voice deadly serious. "*What* kind of kissing have you been used to?"

She hung her head. And almost the whole story had been told.

His face was white as a sheet. He didn't say another word. But one man understands another well; all are born with that particular insight.

The next week she went into the town to do some small shopping – shopping she could have done as easily over the phone. Did she hope to run across him during the course of it? Is that why she attended to it in person? And after it was taken care of she stopped into a restaurant to sit down over a cup of coffee while waiting for her bus. He came into the place almost immediately afterward; he must have been sitting in his car outside watching for her.

He didn't ask to sit down; he simply leaned over with his knuckles resting on the table, across the way from her, and with a quick back glance toward the door by which he had just entered, took a book out from under his jacket and put it down in front of her, its title visible.

"I sent down to New York to get this for you," he said. "I'm trying to help you in the only way I know how."

She glanced down at it. The title was: *The Marquis de Sade. The Complete Writings.*

"Who was he?" she asked, looking up. She pronounced it with the long A, as if it were an English name. "Sayd."

"Sod," he instructed. "He was a Frenchman. Just read the book," was all he would say. "Just read the book."

He turned to leave her, and then he came back for a moment and added, "Don't let anyone else see –" Then he changed it to, "Don't let *him* see you with it. Put a piece of brown wrapping paper around it so the title won't be conspicuous. As soon as you've finished, bring it back; don't leave it lying around the house."

After he'd gone she kept staring at it. Just kept staring.

They met again three days later at the same little coffee shop off the main business street. It had become their regular meeting place by now. No fixed arrangement to it; he would go in and find her there, or she would go in and find him there.

"Was he the first one?" she asked when she returned the book.

"No, of course not. This is as old as man – this getting pleasure by giving pain. There are some of them born in every generation. Fortunately not too many. He simply was the first one to write it up and so when the world became more specialized and needed a separate tag for everything, they used his name. It became a word – sadism, meaning sexual pleasure got by causing pain, the sheer pleasure of being cruel."

She started shaking all over as if the place were drafty. "It is that." She had to whisper it, she was so heartsick with the discovery. "Oh, God, yes, it is that."

"You had to know the truth. That was the first thing. You had to know, you had to be told. It isn't just a vagary or a whim on his part. It isn't just a – well, a clumsiness or roughness in making love. This is a frightful thing, a deviation, an affliction, and – a terrible danger to you. You had to understand the truth first."

"Sometimes he takes his electric shaver –" She stared with frozen eyes at nowhere out before her. "He doesn't use the shaver itself, just the cord – connects it and –"

She backed her hand into her mouth, sealing it up.

Garrett did something she'd never seen a man do before. He lowered his head, all the way over. Not just onto his chest, but all the way down until his chin was resting on the tabletop. And his eyes, looking up at her, were smoldering red with anger. But literally red, the whites all suffused. Then something wet came along and quenched the burning in them.

"Now you know what you're up against," he said, straightening finally. "Now what do you want to do?"

"I don't know." She started to sob very gently, in pantomime, without a sound. He got up and stood beside her and held her head pressed against him. "I only know one thing," she said. "I want to see the stars at night again, and not just the blackness and the shadows. I want to wake up in the morning as if it was my right, and not have to say a prayer of thanks that I lived through the night. I want to be able to tell myself there won't be another night like the last one."

The fear Mark had put into her had seeped and oozed into all parts of her; she not only feared fear, she even feared rescue from fear.

"I don't want to make a move that's too sudden," she said in a smothered voice.

"I'll be standing by, when you want to and when you do."

And on that note they left each other. For one more time.

On Friday he was sitting there waiting for her at their regular table, smoking a cigarette. And another lay out in the ashtray, finished. And another. And another.

She came up behind him and touched him briefly but warmly on the shoulder, as if she were afraid to trust herself to speak.

He turned and greeted her animatedly. "Don't tell me you've been in there that long! I thought you hadn't come in yet. I've been sitting out here twenty minutes, watching the door for you."

Then when she sat down opposite him and he got a good look at her face, he quickly sobered.

"I couldn't help it. I broke down in there. I couldn't come out any sooner. I didn't want everyone in the place to see me, the way I was."

She was still shaking irrepressibly from the aftermath of long-continued sobs.

"Here, have one of these," he offered soothingly. "May make you feel better –" He held out his cigarettes toward her.

"No!" she protested sharply, when she looked down and saw what it was. She recoiled so violently that her whole chair bounced a little across the floor. He saw the back of her hand go to the upper part of her breast in an unconscious gesture of protection, of warding off.

His face turned white when he understood the implication. White with anger, with revulsion. "So that's it," he breathed softly. "My God, oh, my God."

They sat on for a long while after that, both looking down without saying anything. What was there to say? Two little cups of black coffee had arrived by now – just as an excuse for them to stay there.

Finally he raised his head, looked at her, and put words to what he'd been thinking. "You can't go back any more, not even once. You're out of the house and away from it now, so you've got to stay out. You can't go near it again, not even one more time. One more night may be one night too many. He'll kill you one of these nights – he will even if he doesn't mean to. What to him is just a thrill, an excitement, will take away your life. Think about that – you've *got* to think about that."

"I have already," she admitted. "Often."

"You don't want to go to the police?"

"I'm ashamed." She covered her eyes reluctantly with her hand for a moment. "I know I'm not the one who should be, he's the one. But I am nevertheless. I couldn't bear to tell it to an outsider, to put it on record, to file a complaint – it's so intimate. Like taking off all your clothes in public. I can hardly bring myself even to have you know about it. And I haven't told you everything – not everything."

He gave her a shake of the head, as though he knew.

"If I try to hide out in Pittsfield, he'll find me sooner or later – it's not that big a place – and come after me and force me to come back, and either way there'll be a scandal. And I don't want that. I couldn't stand that. The newspapers . . ."

All at once, before they quite knew how it had come about, or even realized that it had come about, they were deep in the final plans, the final strategy and staging that they had been drawing slowly nearer and nearer to all these months. Nearer to with every meeting, with every look and with every word. The plans for her liberation and her salvation.

He took her hands across the table.

"No, listen. This is the way, this is how. New York. It has to be New York; he won't be able to get you back; it's too big; he won't even be able to find you. The company's holding a business conference there on Tuesday, with each of the regional offices sending a representative the way they always do. I was slated to go, long before this came up. I was going to call you on Monday before I left. But what I'm going to do now is to leave ahead of time, tonight, and take you with me."

He raised one of her hands and patted it encouragingly.

"You wait for me here in the restaurant. I have to go back to the office, wind up a few things, then I'll come back and pick you up – shouldn't take me more than half an hour."

She looked around her uneasily. "I don't want to sit here alone. They're already giving me knowing looks each time they pass, the waitresses, as if they sense something's wrong."

"Let them, the hell with them," he said shortly, with the defiance of a man in the opening stages of love.

"Can't you call your office from here? Do it over the phone?"

"No, there are some papers that have to be signed – they're waiting for me on my desk."

"Then you run me back to the house and while you're doing what you have to at the office I'll pick up a few things; then you can stop by for me and we'll start out from there."

"Isn't that cutting it a little close?" he said doubtfully. "I don't want you to go back there." He pivoted his wrist watch closer to him. "What time does he usually come home on Fridays?"

"Never before ten at night."

He said the first critical thing he'd ever said to her. "Just like a girl. All for the sake of a hairbrush and a cuddly negligee you're willing to stick your head back into that house."

"It's more than just a hairbrush," she pointed out. "I have some money there. It's not his, it's mine. Even if this friend from my days in Rome – the one I've spoken to you about – even if she takes me in with her at the start, I'll need some money to tide me over until I can get a job and find a place of my own. And there are other things, like my birth certificate, that I may need later on; he'll never give them up willingly once I leave."

"All right," he gave in. "We'll do it your way."

Then just before they got up from the table, that had witnessed such a change in both their lives, they gave each other a last look. A last, and yet a first one. And they understood each other.

She didn't wait for him to say it, to ask it. There is no decorum in desperation, no coyness in a crisis. She knew it had been asked unsaid, anyway. "I want to rediscover the meaning of gentle love. I want to lie in your bed, in your arms. I want to be your wife."

He took hold of her left hand, raised the third finger, stripped off the wedding band and in its place firmly guided downward a massive fraternity ring that had been on his own hand until that very moment. Heavy, ungainly, much too large for her – and yet everything that love should be.

She put it to her lips and kissed it.

They were married, now.

The emptied ring rolled off the table and fell on the floor, and as they moved away his foot stepped on it, not on purpose, and distorted it into something warped, misshapen, no longer round, no longer true. Like what it had stood for.

He drove her back out to the house and dropped her off at the door, and they parted almost in silence, so complete was their understanding by now, just three muted words between them: "About thirty minutes."

It was dark now, and broodingly sluggish. Like something supine waiting to spring, with just the tip of its tail twitching. Leaves stood still on the trees. An evil green star glinted in the black sky like a hostile eye, like an evil spying eye.

His car had hummed off; she'd finished and brought down a small packed bag to the ground floor when the phone rang. It would be Garry, naturally, telling her he'd finished at the office and was about to leave.

"Hello –" she began, urgently and vitally and confidentially, the way you share a secret with just one person and this was the one.

Mark's voice was at the other end.

"You sound more chipper than you usually do when I call up to tell you I'm on the way home."

Her expectancy stopped. And everything else with it. She didn't know what to say. "Do I?" And then, "Oh, I see."

"Did you have a good day? You must have had a *very* good day."

She knew what he meant, she knew what he was implying.

"I – I – oh, I did nothing, really. I haven't been out of the house all day."

"That's strange," she heard him say. "I called you earlier – about an hour ago?" It was a question, a pitfall of a question. "You didn't come to the phone."

"I didn't hear it ring," she said hastily, too hastily. "I might have been out front for a few minutes. I remember I went out there to broom the gravel in the drivew –"

Too late she realized he hadn't called at all. But now he knew that she hadn't been in the house all day, that she'd been out somewhere during part of it.

"I'll be a little late." And then something that sounded like "That's what you want to hear, isn't it?"

"What?" she said quickly. "What?"

"I said I'll be a little late."

"What was it you said after that?"

"What was it you said after that?" he quoted studiedly, giving her back her own words.

She knew he wasn't going to repeat it, but by that very token she knew she'd heard it right the first time.

He *knows*, she told herself with a shudder of premonition as she got off the phone and finally away from him. (His voice could hold fast to you and enthrall you too; his very voice could torture you, as well as his wicked, cruel fingers.) He knows there's someone; he may not know who yet, but he knows there is someone.

A remark from one of the nightmare nights came back to her: "There's somebody else who wouldn't do this, isn't there? There's somebody else who wouldn't make you cry."

She should have told Garry about it long before this. Because now she had to get away from Mark at all cost, even more than she had had to ever before. Now there would be a terrible vindictiveness, a violent jealousy sparking the horrors where before there had sometimes been just an irrational impulse, sometimes dying as quickly as it was born. Turned aside by a tear or a prayer or a run around a chair.

And then another thing occurred to her, and it frightened her even more immediately, here and now. What assurance was there that he was where he'd said he was, still in the city waiting to start out for here? He might have been much closer, ready to jump out at her unexpectedly, hoping to throw her offguard and catch her away from the house with someone, or (as if she could have possibly been that sort of person) with that someone right here in the very house with her. He'd lied about calling the first time; why wouldn't he lie about where he was?

And now that she thought of it, there was a filling station with a public telephone less than five minutes drive from here, on the main thruway that came up from Boston. An eddy of fear swirled around her, like dust rising off the floor in some barren drafty place. She had to do one of two things immediately – there was no time to do both. Either call Garry at his office and warn him to hurry, that their time limit had shrunk. Or try to trace Mark's call and find out just how much margin of safety was still left to them.

She chose the latter course, which was the mistaken one to choose.

Long before she'd been able to identify the filling station exactly for the information operator to get its number, the whole thing had become academic. There was a slither and shuffle on the gravel outside and a car, someone's car, had come to a stop in front of the house.

Her first impulse, carried out immediately without thinking why, was to snap off all the room lights. Probably so she could see out without being seen from out there.

She sprang over to the window, and then stood there rigidly motionless, leaning a little to peer intently out. The car had stopped at an unlucky angle of perspective – unlucky for her. They had a trellis with tendrils of wisteria twining all over it like bunches of dangling grapes. It blanked out the mid-section of the car, its body shape, completely. The beams of the acetylene-bright headlights shone out past one side, but they told her nothing; they could have come from any car. The little glimmer of color on the driveway, at the other side, told her no more.

She heard the door crack open and clump closed. Someone's feet, obviously a man's, chopped up the wooden steps to the entrance veranda, and she saw a figure cross it, but it was too dark to make out who he was.

She had turned now to face the other way, and without knowing it her hand was holding the place where her heart was. This was Mark's house, he had the front-door key. Garry would have to ring. She waited to hear the doorbell clarinet out and tell her she was safe, she would be loved, she would live.

Instead there was a double click, back then forth, the knob twined around, and the door opened. A spurt of cool air told her it had opened.

Frightened back into childhood fears, she turned and scurried, like some little girl with pigtails flying out behind her, scurried back along the shadowed hall, around behind the stairs, and into a closet that lay back there, remote as any place in the house could be. She pushed herself as far to the back as she could, and crouched down, pulling hanging things in front of her to screen and to protect her, to make her invisible. Sweaters and mackintoshes and old forgotten coveralls. And she hid her head down between her knees – the way children do when a goblin or an ogre is after them, thinking that if they can't see it, that fact alone will make the terror go away.

The steps went up the stairs, on over her, up past her head. She could feel the shake if not hear the sound. Then she heard her name called out, but the voice was blurred by the many partitions and separations between – as if she were listening to it from underwater. Then the step came down again, and the man stood there at the foot of the stairs, uncertain. She tried to teach herself how to forget to breathe, but she learned badly.

There was a little *tick!* of a sound, and he'd given himself more light. Then each step started to sound clearer than the one before, as the distance to her thinned away. Her heart began to stutter and turn over, and say: Here he comes, here he comes. Light cracked into the closet around three sides of the door, and two arms reached in and started to make swimming motions among the hanging things, trying to find her.

Then they found her, one at each shoulder, and lifted her and drew her outside to him. (With surprising gentleness.) And pressed her to his breast. And her tears made a new pattern of little wet polka dots all over what had been Garry's solid-colored necktie until now.

All she could say was, "Hurry, hurry, get me out of here!"

"You must have left the door open in your hurry when you came back here. I tried it, found it unlocked, and just walked right in. When I looked back here, I saw that the sleeve of that old smock had got caught in the closet door and was sticking out. Almost like an arm, beckoning me on to show me where you were hiding. It was uncanny. Your guardian angel must love you very much, Linda."

But will he always, she wondered? Will he always?

He took her to the front door, detoured for a moment to pick up the bag, then led her outside and closed the door behind them for good and all.

"Just a minute," she said, and stopped, one foot on the ground, one still on the wooden front steps.

She opened her handbag and took out her key – the key to what had been her home and her marriage. She flung it back at the door, and it hit and fell, with a cheap shabby little *clop!* – like something of not much value.

Once they were in the car they just drove; they didn't say anything more for a long time.

All the old things had been said. All the new things to be said were still to come.

In her mind's eye she could see the sawtoothed towers of New York climbing slowly up above the horizon before her at the end of the long road. Shimmering there, iridescent, opalescent, rainbows of chrome and glass and hope. Like Jerusalem, like Mecca, or some other holy spot. Beckoning, offering heaven. And of all the things New York has meant to various people at various times – fame, success, fulfillment – it probably never meant as much before as it meant to her tonight: a place of refuge, a sanctuary, a place to be safe in.

"How long does the trip take?" she asked him wistful-eyed.

"I usually make it in less than four hours. Tonight I'll make it less than three."

I'll never stray out of New York again, she promised herself. Once I'm safely there, I'll never go out in the country again. I never want to see a tree again, except way down below me in Central Park from a window high up.

"Oh, get me there, Garry, get me there."

"I'll get you there," Garry promised, like any new bridegroom, and bent to kiss the hand she had placed over his on the wheel.

Two car headlights from the opposite direction hissed by them – like parallel tracer bullets going so fast they seemed to swirl around rather than undulate with the road's flaws.

She purposely waited a moment, then said in a curiously surreptitious voice, as though it shouldn't be mentioned too loudly, "Did you see that?"

All he answered, noncommitally, was, "Mmm."

"That was the Italian compact."

"You couldn't tell what it was," he said, trying to distract her from her fear. "Went by too fast."

"I know it too well. I recognized it."

Again she waited a moment, as though afraid to make the movement she was about to. Then she turned and looked back, staring hard and steadily into the funneling darkness behind them.

Two back lights had flattened out into a bar, an ingot. Suddenly this flashed to the other side of the road, then reversed. Then, like a ghastly scimitar chopping down all the tree trunks in sight, the headlights reappeared, round out into two spheres, gleaming, small – but coming back after them.

"I told you. It's turned and doubled back."

He was still trying to keep her from panic. "May have nothing to do with us. May not be the same car we saw go by just now."

"It is. Why would he make a complete about-turn like that in the middle of nowhere. There's no intersection or side road back there – we haven't passed one for miles."

She looked again.

"They keep coming. And they already look bigger than when they started back. I think they're gaining on us."

He said, with an unconcern that he didn't feel, "Then we'll have to put a stop to that."

They burst into greater velocity, with a surge like a forward billow of air.

She looked, and she looked again. Finally to keep from turning so constantly, she got up on the seat on the point of one knee and faced backward, her hair pouring forward all around her, jumping with an electricity that was really speed.

"Stay down," he warned. "You're liable to get thrown that way. We're up to 65 now." He gave her a quick tug for additional emphasis, and she subsided into the seat once more.

"How is it now?" he checked presently. The rear-view mirror couldn't reflect that far back.

"They haven't grown smaller, but they haven't grown larger."

"We've stabilized, then," he translated. "Dead heat."

Then after another while and another look, "Wait a minute!" she said suddenly on a note of breath-holding hope. Then, "no," she mourned quickly afterward. "For a minute I thought – but they're back again. It was only a dip in the road."

"They hang on like leeches, can't seem to shake them off," she complained in a fretful voice, as though talking to herself. "Why don't they go away? Why *don't* they?"

Another look, and he could sense the sudden stiffening of her body.

"They're getting bigger. I know I'm not mistaken."

He could see that too. They were finally peering into the rear-view mirror for the first time. They'd go offside, then they'd come back in again. In his irritation he took one hand off the wheel long enough to give the mirror a backhand slap that moved it out of focus altogether.

"Suppose I stop, get out and face him when he comes up, and we have it out here and now. What can he do? I'm younger, I can outslug him."

Her refusal to consent was an outright scream of protest. All her fears and all her aversion were in it.

"All right," he said. "Then we'll run him into the ground if we have to."

She covered her face with both hands – not at the speed they were making, but at the futility of it.

"They sure build good cars in Torino, damn them to hell!" he swore in angry frustration.

She uncovered and looked. The headlights were closer than before. She began to lose control of herself.

"Oh, this is like every nightmare I ever had when I was a little girl! When something was chasing me, and I couldn't get away from it. Only now there'll be no waking up in the nick of time."

"Stop that," he shouted at her. "Stop it. It only makes it worse, it doesn't help."

"I think I can feel his breath blowing down the back of my neck."

He looked at her briefly, but she could tell by the look on his face he hadn't been able to make out what she'd said.

Streaks of wet that were not tears were coursing down his face in uneven lengths. "My necktie," he called out to her suddenly, and raised his chin to show her what he meant. She reached over, careful not to place herself in front of him, and pulled the knot down until it was loose. Then she freed the buttonhole from the top button of his shirt.

A long curve in the road cut them off for a while, from those eyes, those unrelenting eyes behind them. Then the curve ended, and the eyes came back again. It was worse somehow, after they'd been gone like that, than when they remained steadily in sight the whole time.

"He holds on and holds on and *holds on* – like a mad dog with his teeth locked into you."

"He's a mad dog all right." All pretense of composure had long since left him. He was lividly angry at not being able to win the race, to shake the pursuer off. She was mortally frightened. The long-sustained tension of the speed duel, which seemed to have been going on for hours, compounded her fears, raised them at last to the pitch of hysteria.

Their car swerved erratically, the two outer wheels jogged briefly over marginal stones and roots that felt as if they were as big as boulders and logs. He flung his chest forward across the wheel as if it were something alive that he was desperately trying to hold down; then the car recovered, came back to the road, straightened out safely again with a catarrhal shudder of its rear axle.

"Don't," he warned her tautly in the short-lived lull before they picked up hissing momentum again. "Don't grab me like that again. It went right through the shoulder of my jacket. I can't manage the car, can't hold it, if you do that. I'll get you away. Don't worry, I'll get you away from him."

She threw her head back in despair, looking straight up overhead. "We seem to be standing still. The road has petrified. The trees aren't moving backwards any more. The stars don't either. Neither do the rocks along the side. Oh, faster, Garry, faster!"

"You're hallucinated. Your senses are being tricked by fear."

"Faster, Garry, faster!"

"85, 86. We're on two wheels most of the time – two are off the ground. I can't even breathe, my breath's being pulled out of me."

She started to beat her two clenched fists against her forehead in a tattoo of hypnotic inability to escape. "I don't care, Garry! Faster, faster! If I've got to die, let it be with you, not with him!"

"I'll get you away from him. If it kills me."

That was the last thing he said.

If it kills me.

And as though it had overheard, and snatched at the collateral offered it, that unpropitious sickly greenish star up there – surely Mark's star not theirs – at that very moment a huge tremendous thing came into view around a turn in the road. A skyscraper of a long-haul van, its multiple tiers beaded with red warning lights. But what good were they that high up, except to warn off planes?

It couldn't maneuver. It would have required a turntable. And they had no time or room.

There was a soft crunchy sound, like someone shearing the top off a soft-boiled egg with a knife. At just one quick slice. Then a brief straight-into-the face blizzard effect, but with tiny particles of glass instead of frozen flakes. Just a one-gust blizzard – and then over with. Then an immense whirl of light started to spin, like a huge Ferris wheel all lit up and going around and around, with parabolas of light streaking off in every direction and dimming. Like shooting stars, or the tails of comets.

Then the whole thing died down and went out, like a blazing amusement park sinking to earth. Or the spouts of illuminated fountains settling back into their basins. . . .

She could tell the side of her face was resting against the ground, because blades of grass were brushing against it with a feathery tickling feeling. And some inquisitive little insect kept flitting about just inside the rim of her ear. She tried to raise her hand to brush it away, but then forgot where it was and what it was.

But then forgot . . . .

When they picked her up at last, more out of this world than in it, all her senses gone except for reflex-actions, her lips were still quivering with the unspoken sounds of "Faster, Garry, faster! Take me away –"

Then the long nights, that were also days, in the hospital. And the long blanks, that were also nights. Needles, and angled glass rods to suck water through. Needles, and curious enamel wedges slid under your middle. Needles, and – needles and needles and needles. Like swarms of persistent mosquitoes with unbreakable drills. The way a pincushion feels, if it could feel. Or the target of a porcupine. Or a case of not just momentary but permanently endured static electricity after you scuff across a woolen rug and then put your finger on a light switch. Even food was a needle – a jab into a vein . . .

Then at last her head cleared, her eyes cleared, her mind and voice came back from where they'd been. Each day she became a little stronger, and each day became a little longer. Until they were back for good, good as ever before. Life came back into her lungs and heart. She could feel it there, the swift current of it. Moving again, eager again. Sun again, sky again, rain and pain and love and hope again. Life again – the beautiful thing called life.

Each day they propped her up in a chair for a little while. Close beside the bed, for each day for a little while longer.

Then at last she asked, after many starts that she could never finish, "Why doesn't Garry come to me? Doesn't he know I've been hurt?"

"Garry can't come to you," the nurse answered. And then, in the way that you whip off a bandage that has adhered to a wound fast, in order to make the pain that much shorter than it would be if you lingeringly edged it off a little at a time, then the nurse quickly told her, "Garry won't come to you anymore."

The black tears, so many of them, such a rain of them, blotted out the light and brought on the darkness . . .

Then the light was back again, and no more tears. Just – Garry won't come to you anymore.

Now the silent words were: Not so fast, Garry, not so fast; you've left me behind and I've lost my way.

Then in a little while she asked the nurse, "Why don't you ever let me get up from this chair? I'm better now, I eat well, the strength has come back to my arms, my hands, my fingers, my whole body feels strong. Shouldn't I be allowed to move around and exercise a little? To stand up and take a few steps?"

"The doctor will tell you about that," the nurse said evasively.

The doctor came in later and he told her about it. Bluntly, in the modern way, without subterfuges and without false hopes. The kind, the sensible, the straight-from-the-shoulder modern way.

"Now listen to me. The world is a beautiful world, and life is beautiful life. In this beautiful world everything is comparative; luck is comparative. You could have come out of it stone-blind from the shattered glass, with both your eyes gone. You could have come out of it minus an arm, crushed and having to be taken off. You could have come out of it with your face hideously scarred, wearing a repulsive mask for the rest of your life that would make people sicken and turn away. You could have come out of it dead, as – as someone else did. Who is to say you are lucky, who is to say you are not? You have come out of it beautiful of face. You have come out of it keen and sensitive of mind, a mind with all the precision and delicate adjustment of the works inside a fine Swiss watch. A mind that not only *thinks*, but *feels*. You have come out of it with a strong brave youthful heart that will carry you through for half a century yet, come what may."

"*But*"

She looked at him with eyes that didn't fear.

"You will never again take a single step for all the rest of your life. You are hopelessly, irreparably paralyzed from the waist down. Surgery, everything, has been tried. Accept this . . . Now you know – and so now be brave."

"I am. I will be," she said trustfully. "I'll learn a craft of some kind, that will occupy my days and earn me a living. Perhaps you can find a nursing home for me at the start until I get adjusted, and then maybe later I can find a little place all to myself and manage there on my own. There are such places, with ramps instead of stairs –"

He smiled deprecatingly at her oversight.

"All that won't be necessary. You're forgetting. There *is* someone who will look after you. Look after you well. You'll be in good capable hands. Your husband is coming to take you home with him today."

Her scream was like the death cry of a wounded animal. So strident, so unbelievable, that in the stillness of its aftermath could be heard the slithering and rustling of people looking out the other ward-room doors along the corridor, nurses and ambulatory patients, asking one another what that terrified cry had been and where it had come from.

"Two cc's of M, and hurry," the doctor instructed the nurse tautly. "It's just the reaction from what she's been through. This sometimes happens – going-home happiness becomes hysteria."

The wet kiss of alcohol on her arm. Then the needle again – the needle meant to be kind.

One of them patted her on the head and said, "You'll be all right now."

A tear came to the corner of her eyes, and just lay there, unable to retreat, unable to fall . . .

Myopically she watched them dress her and put her in her chair. Her mind remained awake, but everything was downgraded in intensity – the will to struggle had become reluctance, fear had become unease. She still knew there was cause to scream, but the distance had become too great, the message had too far to travel.

Through lazy, contracting pupils she looked over and saw Mark standing in the doorway, talking to the doctor, shaking the nurse's hand and leaving something behind in it for which she smiled her thanks. Then he went around in back of her wheel chair, with a phantom breath for a kiss to the top of her head, and started to sidle it toward the door that was being held open for the two of them. He tipped the front of the chair ever so slightly, careful to avoid the least jar or impact or roughness, as if determined that she reach her destination with him in impeccable condition, unmarked and unmarred.

And as she craned her neck and looked up overhead, and then around and into his face, backward, the unspoken message was so plain, in his shining eyes and in the grim grin he showed his teeth in, that though he didn't say it aloud, there was no need to; it reached from his mind into hers without sound or the need of sound just as surely as though he had said it aloud.

Now I've got you.

Now he had her – for the rest of her life.

LIST OF SOURCES

"Rear Window" originally published as "It Had to be Murder" in *Dime Detective*, Feb. 1942; first book appearance in *After-Dinner Story* by William Irish, 1944.

"I Won't Take a Minute" originally published as "Finger of Doom" in *Detective Fiction Weekly*, 22 June 1940; first appearance in *Great American Detective Stories*, edited by Anthony Boucher, 1945.

"Speak To Me of Death" originally published in *Argosy*, 27 Feb. 1937; later expanded into the novel, *Night Has A Thousand Eyes* by George Hopley, 1945. First book appearance in *The Fantastic Stories of Cornell Woolrich*, 1981.

"The Dancing Detective" originally published as "Dime A Dance" in *Black Mask*, Feb. 1938; first book appearance in *The Dancing Detective*, 1946.

"The Light in the Window" originally published in *Mystery Book Magazine*, April 1946; first book appearance in *The Dancing Detective*, 1946.

"The Corpse Next Door" originally published in *Detective Fiction Weekly*, 23 Jan. 1937; first book appearance in *Nightwebs*, 1971.

"You'll Never See Me Again" originally published in *Street and Smith's Detective Story*, Nov. 1939; first book appearance in the 10¢ Dell paperback series as by William Irish, 1950.

"The Screaming Laugh" originally published in *Clues Detective*, Nov. 1938; first appearance in *Nightwebs*, 1971.

"Dead On Her Feet" originally published in *Dime Detective*, Dec. 1935; first book appearance in *Nightwebs*, 1971.

"Waltz" originally published in *Double Detective*, Nov. 1937; first book appearance in *Angels of Darkness*, 1978.

"The Book That Squealed" originally published in *Detective Story*, Aug. 1939; first book appearance in *The Fourth Mystery Companion*, edited by A.L. Furman, 1946.

"Death Escapes the Eye" originally published in *The Shadow*, Apr. May 1947; first book appearance (in a revised version) in *Violence*, 1958.

"For the Rest of Her Life" originally published in *Ellery Queen's Mystery Magazine*, May 1968; first book appearance in *Ellery Queen's Murder Menu*, 1969.